Reunion in Death

Reunion in Death

Nora Roberts

writing as

J.D. Robb

PIATKUS

Visit the Piatkus website!

Piatkus publishes a wide range of bestselling fiction and
non-fiction, including books on health, mind body & spirit, sex,
self-help, cookery, biography and the paranormal.

If you want to:
- read descriptions of our popular titles
- buy our books over the Internet
- take advantage of our special offers
- enter our monthly competition
- learn more about your favourite Piatkus authors

VISIT OUR WEBSITE AT: www.piatkus.co.uk

Copyright © 2002 by Nora Roberts
Material excerpted from *Purity in Death* by Nora Roberts writing as
J.D. Robb copyright © 2002 by Nora Roberts

First published in the United States in 2002 by Berkley Publishing
Group, a division of Penguin Putnam Inc., New York.

This edition published in Great Britain in 2004 by
Piatkus Books Ltd of
5 Windmill Street, London W1T 2JA
email: info@piatkus.co.uk

The moral right of the author has been asserted

A catalogue record for this book is available from the British Library

ISBN 0 7499 0680 4

Printed and bound in Great Britain by
Mackays of Chatham Ltd, Chatham, Kent

There are some meannesses which are too mean
even for man – woman, lovely woman alone,
can venture to commit them.

W.M. THACKERAY, *A Shabby Genteel Story*

The surest poison is time.

EMERSON

Chapter 1

Murder was work. Death was a serious chore for the killer, the victim, for the survivors. And for those who stood for the dead. Some went about the job devotedly, others carelessly.

And for some, murder was a labor of love.

When he left his Park Avenue condo for his regular morning stroll, Walter C. Pettibone was blissfully unaware he was in his last hours of life. He was a robust sixty and a canny businessman who'd increased his family's already considerable fortune through flowers and sentiment.

He was wealthy, healthy, and just over a year before had acquired a young, blonde wife who had the sexual appetite of a Doberman in heat and the brains of a cabbage.

His world, in Walter C. Pettibone's opinion, was just exactly so.

He had work he loved, two children from his first marriage who would one day take over the business he'd taken over from his own father. He maintained a reasonably friendly relationship with his ex, a fine, sensible woman, and his son and daughter were pleasant, intelligent individuals who brought him pride and satisfaction.

He had a grandson who was the apple of his eye.

In the summer of 2059, World of Flowers was a major intergalactic enterprise with florists, horticulturists, offices, and greenhouses both on and off planet.

Walter loved flowers. And not just for their profit margin. He loved the scents of them, the colors, the textures, the beauty of both foliage and blossom and the simple miracle of their existence.

Every morning he would visit a handful of florists, to check the stock, the arrangements, and just to sniff and chat and spend time among the flowers and the people who loved them.

Twice a week, he was up before dawn to attend the gardener's market downtown. There he would wander and enjoy, order or critique.

It was a routine that rarely varied over the course of a half-century, and one he never tired of.

Today, after an hour or so among the blooms, he'd go into the corporate offices. He'd spend more time there than usual in order to give his wife the time and space to finish preparations for his surprise birthday party.

It made him chuckle to think of it.

The sweetheart couldn't keep a secret if she stapled her lips together. He'd known about the party for weeks, and was looking forward to the evening with the glee of a child.

Naturally he would act surprised and had practiced stunned expressions in his mirror only that morning.

So Walter went through his daily routine with a smile at the corners of his mouth—having no idea just how surprised he was going to be.

●　　●　　●

Eve doubted she'd ever felt better in her life. Rested, recharged, limber and loose, she prepared for her first day back on the job after a wonderfully undemanding two-week vacation where the peskiest task facing her had been whether to eat or sleep.

One week at the villa in Mexico, the second on a private island. And in both spots there had been no lack of opportunities for sun, sex, and snoozing.

Roarke had been right again. They'd needed the time together. Away. They'd both needed a period of healing. And if the way she felt this morning was any indication, they'd done the job.

She stood in front of her closet, frowning at the jungle of clothes she'd acquired since her marriage. She didn't think her confusion was due to the fact that she'd spent most of the last fourteen days naked or near to it. Unless she was very much mistaken, the man had managed to sneak more clothes in on her.

She yanked out a long blue gown in some material that managed to sizzle and sparkle at the same time. "Have I ever seen this before?"

"It's your closet." In the sitting area of their bedroom, Roarke scanned the stock reports on the wall screen while he enjoyed a second cup of coffee. But he glanced over. "If you're planning to wear that today, the criminal element in the city's going to be very impressed."

"There's more stuff in here than there was two weeks ago."

"Really? I wonder how that happened."

"You have to stop buying me clothes."

He reached over to stroke Galahad, but the cat turned his nose in the air. He'd been sulking since their return the night before. "Why?"

"Because it's embarrassing." She muttered it as she dived inside to find something reasonable to wear.

He only smiled at her, watching as she hunted up a

sleeveless top and trousers to slip over that long, lean body he never quite stopped craving.

She'd tanned herself to a pale gold, and the sun had teased out blonde streaks in her short brown hair. She dressed quickly, economically, with the air of a woman who never thought about fashion. Which was why, he supposed, he could never resist heaping fashion on her.

She'd rested during their time away, he thought. He'd seen, hour by hour, day by day, the clouds of fatigue and worry lift away from her. There was a light in her whiskey-colored eyes now, a healthy glow in her narrow, fine-boned face.

And when she strapped on her weapon harness, there was a set to her mouth—that wide and generous mouth—that told him Lieutenant Eve Dallas was back. And ready to kick some ass.

"What is it about an armed woman that arouses me?"

She shot him a look, reached in the closet for a light jacket. "Cut it out. I'm not going to be late my first day back because you've got some residual horniness."

Oh yes, he thought, rising. She was back. "Darling Eve." He managed, barely, not to wince. "Not that jacket."

"What?" She paused in the act of shoving her arm in a sleeve. "It's summer weight; it covers my weapon."

"It's wrong with those trousers." He stepped to her closet, reached in, and plucked out another jacket of the same weight and material as the khaki trousers. "This one is correct."

"I'm not planning on doing a video shoot." But she changed it because it was easier than arguing.

"Here." After another dip into her closet, he came out with a pair of half-boots in rich chestnut brown leather.

"Where'd those come from?"

"The closet fairy."

She frowned at the boots suspiciously, poked a finger

into the toes. "I don't need new boots. My old ones are all broken in."

"That's a polite term for what they are. Try these."

"Just gonna mess them up," she muttered, but sat on the arm of the sofa to pull them on. They slid onto her feet like butter. Which only made her eye him narrowly. He'd probably had them hand-tooled for her in one of his countless factories and they surely cost more than a New York murder cop made in two months. "How about that. The closet fairy seems to know my shoe size."

"An amazing fellow."

"I suppose it's useless to tell him that a cop doesn't need expensive boots that were probably sewn together by some little Italian nun when she's clocking field time or hoofing it or knocking on doors."

"He has a mind of his own." He skimmed a hand through her hair, tugged just enough to tip her face up to his. "And he adores you."

It still made her stomach flop—hearing him say it, seeing his face as he did. She often wondered why she didn't just drown in those eyes of his, in all that wild, wicked blue.

"You're so damn pretty." She hadn't meant to say it aloud, nearly jolted at the sound of her voice. And she watched his grin flash, fast as fire across a face that belonged in a painting or carved into stone with its strong, sharp bones and seductive poet's mouth.

Young Irish God, she supposed it would be titled. For weren't gods seductive and ruthless and cloaked in their own power?

"I have to go." She got quickly to her feet, and he stood his ground so their bodies bumped. "Roarke."

"Yes, it's back to reality for both of us. But . . ." His hands stroked down her sides, one long, possessive move that reminded her, all too clearly, just what those quick and clever fingers were capable of doing to her body. "I think we can take a moment for you to kiss me good-bye."

"You want me to kiss you good-bye?"

"I do, yes." There was a lilt of both amusement and Ireland in the tone that had her cocking her head.

"Sure." In a move as fast as his grin, she took handfuls of the black hair that nearly skimmed his shoulders, fisting, tugging, then crushing her mouth against his.

She felt his heart jump even as hers did. A leap of heat, of recognition, of unity. And on his sound of pleasure, she poured herself into the kiss, took them both fast and deep with a little war of tongues, a quick nip of teeth.

Then she jerked him back, stepped nimbly out of reach. "See you, ace," she called out as she strode from the room.

"Have a safe day, Lieutenant." He blew out a long sigh, then sat back on the couch. "Now," he said to the cat, "what will it cost me for the two of us to be friends again?"

At Cop Central, Eve hopped on a glide to Homicide. And took a deep breath. Nothing against the cliffside drama of western Mexico or the balmy breezes of tropical islands, but she'd missed the air here: the smell of sweat, bad coffee, harsh cleansers, and above all, the fierce energies that formed from the clash of cop and criminal.

Her time away had only honed her senses for it—the low roar of too many voices talking at once, the steady yet discordant beeps and buzzings of 'links and communicators, the rush of people all having something important to do somewhere.

She heard someone screaming obscenities so fast they tumbled together into one vicious stew of words that was music to her ears.

Motherfuckingassholecopbastards.

Welcome home, she thought happily.

The job had been her home, her life, her single defining purpose before Roarke. Now even with him, or maybe because she had him, it remained an essential part of who and what she was.

Once she'd been a victim—helpless, used, and broken. Now, she was a warrior.

She swung into the detectives' bull pen, ready to fight whatever battle lay ahead.

Detective Baxter glanced up from his work, let out a low whistle. "Whoa, Dallas. Hubba-hubba."

"What?" Baffled, she looked over her shoulder, then realized Baxter's leering grin was for her. "You're a sick man, Baxter. It's reassuring to note some things don't change."

"You're the one who's all slicked up." He pushed himself up, skirted around desks. "Nice," he added, rubbing her lapel between his thumb and finger. "You're a frigging fashion plate, Dallas. Put the rest of us to shame."

"It's a jacket," she muttered, mortified. "Cut it out."

"Got yourself tanned, too. Would that be a full-body job?"

She bared her teeth in a fierce smile. "Do I have to kick your ass?"

Enjoying himself, he wagged a finger. "And what's that on your ears?" As she reached up, confused, he blinked as if in surprise. "Why, I believe those are called earrings. And they're real pretty, too."

She'd forgotten she had them on. "Did crime suddenly stop dead while I was gone so that you have time to stand around here critiquing my wardrobe?"

"I'm just dazzled, Lieutenant. Absolutely dazzled by this fashion presentation. New boots?"

"Bite me." She swung away on the sound of his laughter.

"And she is *back*!" Baxter announced to the sound of applause.

Morons, she thought as she marched toward her office. The New York Police and Security Department was peopled by a bunch of morons.

Jesus, she'd missed them.

She walked into her office, then just stood, one step over the threshold, goggling.

Her desk was clear. More, it was *clean*. In fact, the whole place was clean. Like someone had come along and sucked out all the dust and grime and then shined up what was left behind. Suspicious, she ran a thumb down the wall. Yes, that was definitely fresh paint.

Eyes narrowed, she continued into the room. It was a small space with one stingy window, a banged-up—and now scrubbed—desk, and a couple of chairs with bad springs. The file cabinet, also sparkling, had been cleared off. A green plant that appeared to be thriving stood on top of it.

With a little yelp of distress, she leaped to the file cabinet, yanked open a drawer.

"I knew it, I knew it, I knew it! Bastard hit me again."

"Lieutenant?"

Snarling, Eve glanced back. Her aide stood in the doorway, as shipshape as the room in her starched summer blues.

"Goddamn sneaking candy thief found my cache."

Peabody pursed her lips. "You had candy in the file cabinet." She angled her head. "Under *M*?"

"*M* for Mine, damn it." Annoyed, Eve slammed the drawer shut. "I forgot to take it out before I left. What the hell happened in here, Peabody? I had to read the name on the door to be sure this was my office."

"Since you were gone it seemed like a good time to have it cleaned and painted. It'd gotten pretty dingy in here."

"I was used to it. Where's all my stuff?" she demanded. "I had some backlog, and some fives, and the ME's and a sweeper's reports on the Dunwood case should've come in while I was away."

"I took care of it. I did the fives and caught up with the backlog, and filed the reports." She offered a smile that danced laughter into her dark eyes. "I had some time on my hands."

"You did all the paperwork?"

"Yes, sir."

"And arranged to have my office overhauled?"

"I think there were multicelled organisms breeding in various corners. They're dead now."

Slowly Eve slipped her hands into her pockets, rocked back on her heels. "This wouldn't be your way of telling me that when I'm around I don't give you time to take care of daily business."

"Absolutely not. Welcome back, Dallas. And I have to say that, wow, you look really terrific. Snappy outfit."

Eve dropped into the chair at her desk. "What the hell do I usually look like?"

"Is that a rhetorical question?"

Eve studied Peabody's face—the square, sturdy looks topped with a dark bowl of hair. "I'm trying to think if I missed your smart mouth. No," she decided. "Not a bit."

"Aw, sure you did. Great tan. I guess you spent a lot of time soaking up the sun and stuff."

"I guess I did. Where'd you get yours?"

"My what?"

"The tan, Peabody. You go in for a flash?"

"No, I got it in Bimini."

"Bimini, like the island? What the hell were you doing in Bimini?"

"Well, you know, vacationing—same as you. Roarke

suggested that, since you were heading out, maybe I should take a week off, too, and—"

Eve shot up a hand. "Roarke suggested?"

"Yeah, he thought McNab and I could use a little downtime, so—"

Eve felt the muscle just under one eye start to twitch. It had a habit of doing that whenever she thought too hard about Peabody and the fashion dish from the Electronic Detective Division as an item.

In defense, she pressed two fingers against it. "You and McNab. In Bimini. Together."

"Well, you know, since we're trying this whole we're-a-couple thing on for size, it seemed like a good idea. And when Roarke said we could use one of his transpos and this place he has on Bimini, we jumped."

"His transpo. His place on Bimini." The muscle leaped against her fingers.

Eyes shining, Peabody forgot herself enough to lower a hip to the corner of the desk. "Man, Dallas, it was absolutely ult. It's like this little palace or something. It's got its own waterfall into the pool, and an all-terrain, and hydroskis. And the master suite has this gel-bed that's about the size of Saturn."

"I don't want to hear about the bed."

"And it's really private, even though it's right on the beach, so we just romped around naked as monkeys half the time."

"And I don't want to hear about naked romping."

Peabody tucked her tongue in her cheek. "Sometimes we were only half-naked. Anyway," she said before Eve screamed, "it was mag. And I wanted to get Roarke some kind of thank-you gift. But since he has everything, literally, I'm clueless. I thought maybe you could suggest something."

"Is this a cop shop or a social club?"

"Come on, Dallas. We're all caught up with work."

Peabody smiled hopefully. "I thought maybe I could give him one of the throws my mother makes. You know, she weaves, and she does really beautiful work. Would he like that?"

"Look, he won't expect a gift. It's not necessary."

"It was the best vacation I ever had, in my life. I want him to know how much I appreciated it. It meant a lot to me, Dallas, that he'd think of it."

"Yeah, he's always thinking." But she softened; she couldn't help it. "He'd get a real kick out of having something your mother made."

"Really? That's great then. I'll get in touch with her tonight."

"Now that we've had our little reunion here, Peabody, isn't there some work to be done?"

"Actually, we're clear."

"Then get me some cold files."

"Any ones in particular?"

"Dealer's choice. I've got to do something."

"I'm on it." She started out, paused. "You know one of the best things about going away? It's coming back."

Eve spent the morning picking through unsolved cases, looking for a thread that hadn't been snipped, an angle that hadn't been explored. The one that interested her the most was the matter of twenty-six-year-old Marsha Stibbs, who'd been found submerged in the bathtub by her husband, Boyd, when he'd returned from an out-of-town business trip.

On the surface, it had appeared to be one of those tragic and typical home accidents—until the ME's report had verified that Marsha hadn't drowned, but had been dead before that last bubble bath.

Since she'd gone into the tub with a fractured skull, she hadn't slid into the froth and fragrance under her own power.

The investigator had turned up evidence that indicated Marsha had been having an affair. A packet of love letters from someone who signed himself with the initial *C* had been hidden away in the victim's lingerie drawer. The letters were sexually explicit and full of pleas for her to divorce her husband and run away with her lover.

According to the report, the letters and their contents had shocked the husband and everyone interviewed who'd known the victim. The husband's alibi had been solid, as were all the background checks.

Boyd Stibbs, a regional rep for a sporting goods firm, was by all appearances Mr. All-American guy, making a slightly better than average income, married for six years to his college sweetie who'd gone on to become a buyer for a major department store. He liked to play flag football on Sundays, had no drinking, gambling, or illegals problem. There was no history of violence, and he had volunteered for Truth Testing, which he'd passed with flying colors.

They were childless, lived in a quiet West Side apartment building, socialized with a tight circle of friends, and up to the point of her death had shown all signs of having a happy, solid marriage.

The investigation had been thorough, careful, and complete. Yet the primary had never been able to find any trace of the alleged lover with the initial *C*.

Eve tagged Peabody on the interoffice 'link. "Saddle up, Peabody. Let's go knock on some doors." She tucked the file in her bag, snagged the jacket from the back of her chair, and headed out.

"I've never worked a cold case before."

"Don't think of it as cold," Eve told her. "Think of it as open."

"How long has this one been open?" Peabody asked.

"Going on six years."

"If the guy she was doing the extra-marital banging with hasn't shown in all this time, how do you rout him out now?"

"One step at a time, Peabody. Read the letters."

Peabody took them out of the field bag. Midway through the first note, she let out an *Ouch!* "These things are flammable," she said, blowing on her fingers.

"Keep going."

"Are you kidding?" Peabody wiggled her butt into the seat. "You couldn't stop me now. I'm getting an education." She continued to read, eyes widening now and then, throat working. "Jesus, I think I just had an orgasm."

"Thanks for sharing that piece of information. What else did you get from them?"

"A real admiration for Mr. C's imagination and stamina."

"Let me rephrase. What didn't you get from them?"

"Well, he never signs his name in full." Knowing she was missing something, Peabody stared down at the letters again. "No envelopes, so they could have been hand-delivered or mailed." She sighed. "I'm getting a *D* in this class. I don't know what you're seeing here that I'm not."

"What I'm not seeing is more to the point. No reference to how, when, or where they met. How they became lovers. No mention of where they boinked each other's brains out in various athletic positions. That makes me pause and reflect."

At sea, Peabody shook her head. "On?"

"On the possibility that there never was a Mr. C."

"But—"

"You have a woman," Eve interrupted, "married for several years, with a good, responsible job, a circle of friends she's kept for, again, several years. From all statements none of those friends had any inkling of an affair. Not in the way she behaved, spoke, lived. She had no

time missing from work. So when did said athletic boink-
ing take place?"

"The husband traveled fairly regularly."

"That's right, which opens the possibility for an affair
if one is so inclined. Yet our victim exhibited all indi-
cations of loyalty, responsibility, honesty. She went to
work, she came home. She went out in the company of
her husband or with groups of friends. There were no
unsubstantiated or questionable calls made to or from her
home, office, or portable 'links. Just how did she and Mr.
C. discuss their next tryst?"

"In person? Maybe he was someone at work."

"Maybe."

"But you don't think so. Okay, she appears to have
been committed to her marriage, but outsiders, even close
pals, don't really know what goes on inside someone
else's marriage. Sometimes the partner doesn't even
know."

"Absolutely true. The primary on this agrees with you
and had every reason to do so."

"But you don't." Peabody acknowledged. "You think
the husband set it up, made it look like she was cheating,
either set up the alibi and snuck home to kill her, or had
it done?"

"It's an option. That's why we're going to talk to
him."

Eve shot up a ramp to the second-level street parking,
muscled her vehicle between a sedan and a jet-bike. "He
works out of his home most days." She nodded toward
the apartment building. "Let's see if he's there."

He was home. A fit, attractive man wearing athletic
shorts and a T-shirt and holding a toddler on his hip. One
look at Eve's badge had a shadow moving into his eyes.
One that had the texture of grief.

"It's about Marsha? Has there been something new?"

He turned his face, briefly, into the white-blonde hair of the little girl he carried. "I'm sorry, come in. It's been so long since anyone's gotten in touch about what happened. If you want to sit down, I'd like to settle my daughter in the other room. I'd rather she didn't . . ."

This time it was his hand that moved to the girl's hair. Protectively. "Just give me a minute."

Eve waited until they'd left the room. "How old's the kid, Peabody?"

"About two, I'd say."

Eve nodded and moved into the living area. There were toys strewn about the floor and cheery furnishings.

She heard a high-pitched, childish giggle, and a firm demand. "Daddy! Play!"

"In a little while, Tracie. You play now, and when Mommy gets home maybe we'll go out to the park. But you have to be good while I talk to these ladies. Deal?"

"Swings?"

"You bet."

When he came back, he ran both hands through his own dark blond hair. "I didn't want her to hear us talk about Marsha, about what happened. Has there been a break? Have you finally found him?"

"I'm sorry, Mr. Stibbs. This is a routine followup."

"Then there's nothing? I'd hoped . . . I guess it's stupid after all this time to think you'd find him."

"You have no idea who your wife was having an affair with."

"She wasn't." He bit the words off, fury leaping onto his face and turning it hard. "I don't care what anyone says. She wasn't having an affair. I never believed . . . At first I did, I guess, when everything was crazy and I couldn't think straight. Marsha wasn't a liar, she wasn't a cheater. And she loved me."

He closed his eyes, seemed to draw himself in. "Can we sit down?"

He dropped into a chair. "I'm sorry I shouted at you. I can't stand people saying that about Marsha. I can't stand knowing people, friends, think it of her. She doesn't deserve that."

"There were letters found in her drawer."

"I don't care about the letters. She wouldn't have cheated on me. We had . . ."

He glanced back toward the child's room where the little girl was singing tunelessly. "Look, we had a good sex life. One of the reasons we married so young was that we couldn't keep our hands off each other, and Marsha believed strongly in marriage. I'll tell you what I think." He leaned forward. "I think someone was obsessed with her, fantasized or something. He must have sent her those letters. I'll never know why she didn't tell me. Maybe, I guess maybe, she didn't want to worry me. I think he came here when I was in Columbus, and he killed her because he couldn't have her."

He was registering high on the sincere meter, Eve thought. Such things could be feigned, but where was the point here? Why insist the victim was pure when painting her with adultery served the purpose? "If that was the case, Mr. Stibbs, you still have no idea who that person might be?"

"None. I've thought about it. For the first year afterward, I hardly thought about anything else. I wanted to believe he'd be found and punished, that there'd be some kind of payment for what he did. We were happy, Lieutenant. We didn't have a goddamn care in the world. And then, it was over." He pressed his lips together. "Just over."

"I'm sorry, Mr. Stibbs." Eve waited a beat. "That's a cute kid."

"Tracie?" He passed a hand over his face as if coming back to the present. "The light of my life."

"So you remarried."

"Almost three years ago." He let out a sigh, gave his shoulders a little shake. "Maureen's great. She and Marsha were friends. She's one of the ones who helped me through that first year. I don't know what I'd've done without her."

Even as he spoke, the front door opened. A pretty brunette with an armful of groceries kicked the door shut with her foot. "Hey, team! I'm home. You'll never guess what I . . ."

She trailed off when she saw Eve and Peabody. And as her gaze fastened on Peabody's uniform, Eve saw fear jolt over her face.

Chapter 2

Boyd must have seen it, too, as he got up and crossed to her quickly. "Nothing's wrong." He touched her arm, a light gesture of reassurance before he took the bags from her. "They're just here about Marsha. For a routine followup."

"Oh, well . . . Tracie?"

"In her room. She's—"

Even as he spoke, the child shot out like a little blonde bullet, launched herself at her mother's legs. "Mommy! We go swing!"

"We'll get out of your way as quickly as possible," Eve said. "Would you mind if we talked to you for a moment, Mrs. Stibbs?"

"I'm sorry, I don't know what I can . . . The groceries."

"Tracie and I'll put them away, won't we, partner?"

"I'd rather—"

"She doesn't think we know where anything goes." Boyd interrupted his wife with a wink for their daughter.

"We'll show her. Come on, cutie. Kitchen duty."

The little girl raced ahead of him, chattering in the strange foreign tongue of toddlers.

"I'm sorry to inconvenience you," Eve began. Her gaze, steady on Maureen's face, was cool, flat, and blank. "This won't take long. You were a friend of Marsha Stibbs?"

"Yes, of both her and Boyd. This is very upsetting for Boyd."

"Yes, I'm sure it is. How long had you known Mrs. Stibbs before her death?"

"A year, a little longer." She looked desperately toward the kitchen where there was rattling and laughter. "She's been gone almost six years now. We have to put it behind us."

"Six days, six years, someone still took her life. Were you close?"

"We were friends. Marsha was very outgoing."

"Did she ever confide in you that she was seeing someone else?"

Maureen opened her mouth, hesitated, then shook her head. "No. I don't know anything. I talked to the police when it happened, and told them everything I could. What happened was horrible, but there's no changing it. We've got a new life now. A good life, a quiet one. You coming here like this, it'll only make Boyd grieve again. I don't want my family upset. I'm sorry, but I'd like you to go now."

Outside in the hall, Peabody glanced back as Eve strode to the elevator. "She knows something."

"Oh yeah, she does."

"I figured you'd push her a little."

"Not on her turf." Eve stepped into the elevator. She was already calculating, already resetting the pieces of the puzzle. "Not with her kid there, and Stibbs. Marsha's waited this long, a little more time won't matter to her."

"You think he's clean though."

"I think . . ." Eve pulled the file and disc out of her bag, held it out. "You should work it."

"Sir?"

"Work the case, Peabody. Close the case."

Jaw dropping, Peabody stared. "Me? Like the primary? On a homicide?"

"You'll have to work it mostly on your own time, especially if we get something active. Read the file, study the reports and statements. Re-interview. You know the drill."

"You're giving me a case?"

"You got questions, you ask them. I'll consult if and when you need it. Copy me on all data and progress reports."

Peabody felt the adrenaline surge through her blood, and the nerves flood her belly. "Yes, sir. Thank you. I won't let you down."

"Don't let Marsha Stibbs down."

Peabody hugged the file to her breast like a beloved child. And kept it there all the way back to Central.

As they rode up from the garage, Peabody sent Eve a sidelong look. "Lieutenant?"

"Hmm."

"I wonder if maybe I could ask McNab to assist on the electronic data. The victim's 'links, apartment building's security discs, and so on."

Eve jammed her hands in her pockets. "It's your case."

"It's my case," Peabody repeated, in an awed whisper. She was still grinning, ear to ear, when they headed down the corridor to the bull pen.

"What the hell is that racket?" Eve's eyebrows drew together, her fingers danced instinctively over her weapon at the sound of shouts, whistles, and general mayhem rolling out of the Homicide Division.

She stepped in first, scanned the room. No one was at their desk or in their cube. At least a dozen duly authorized officers of the law were crowded into the center of the room, having what sounded suspiciously like a party.

Her nose twitched. She smelled bakery goods.

"What the hell's going on here!" She had to shout, and her voice still fell short of cutting through the din. "Pearson, Baxter, Delricky!" Since she accompanied this with a quick punch on Pearson's shoulder, a sharp elbow jab to Baxter's gut as she pushed through the crowd, she managed to snag some attention. "Are you all under the illusion that death's taken a fucking holiday? Where the hell'd you get that cupcake?"

Even as she jabbed a finger, Baxter stuffed what was left of it in his mouth. As a result, his explanation was incoherent. He merely grinned around the frosting and pointed.

She saw it now—cupcakes, cookies, and what appeared to have been a pie before a pack of wolves had descended on it. And she spotted two civilians in the middle of that pack. The tall, skinny man and the robust, pretty woman were both beaming smiles and pouring some sort of pale pink liquid out of an enormous jug.

"Stand down! Every one of you, stand down and go back about your business. This isn't a damn tea party."

Before she could push her way through to the civilians, she heard Peabody scream.

She whirled, weapon leaping into her hand, and was nearly plowed down as her aide streaked by and launched herself at the civilians.

The man caught her, and skinny or not managed to lift the sturdy Peabody right off her feet. The woman spun, her long blue skirts swirling as she threw out her arms and made an odd and effective Peabody sandwich.

"There's my girl. There's my DeeDee." The man's

face glowed with such obvious adoration, Eve's hand slid away from her weapon and dangled at her side.

"Daddy." With something between a sob and a giggle, Peabody buried her face against his neck.

"Chokes me up," Baxter murmured and snagged another cupcake. "Got here about fifteen minutes ago. Brought the good stuff with them. Man, these things are lethal," he added and chomped into another cupcake.

Eve drummed her fingers on her thigh. "What kind of pie was that?"

Baxter grinned. "Exceptional," he told her, and strolled back to his desk.

The woman loosened her death grip around Peabody's waist and turned. She was remarkably pretty, with the same dark hair as her daughter worn in a long waterfall down her back. Her blue skirt swept down to simple rope sandals. Her blouse was long and loose and the color of buttercups, and over it were at least a half-dozen chains and pendants.

Her face was softer than Peabody's, with lines of time fanning out from the corners of direct and gleaming brown eyes. She moved like a dancer when she crossed to Eve, both hands outstretched.

"You're Lieutenant Dallas. I'd have known you anywhere." She gripped both of Eve's hands in hers. "I'm Phoebe, Delia's mother."

Her hands were warm, a little rough at the palms, and studded with rings. Bracelets clanged and jangled on her wrists.

"It's nice to meet you, Ms. Peabody."

"Phoebe." She smiled, and still gripping Eve's hands drew her forward. "Sam, let the girl loose so you can meet Lieutenant Dallas."

He shifted, but kept his arm tight around Peabody's shoulders. "I'm so happy to meet you." He took Eve's hand, still cupped in his wife's. "I feel like I already have, with everything Peabody's told us about you. And Zeke. We'll never be able to thank you enough for what you did for our son."

A little uneasy with all that good will beaming out at her, Eve slipped her hand free. "How's he doing?"

"Very well. I'm sure he'd have sent his best if he'd known we were coming."

He smiled then, slow and easy. She could see the resemblance now, between him and Peabody's brother. The narrow, apostle's face, the eyes of dreamy gray. But there was something sharp in Sam Peabody's eyes, something that had Eve's neck prickling.

This man wasn't the puppy dog his son was.

"Give him mine when you talk to him. Peabody, take some personal time."

"Yes, sir. Thank you."

"That's very kind of you," Phoebe said. "I wonder if it's possible for us to have a little of your time. You must be busy," she went on before Eve could speak, "but I'd hoped we might have a meal together tonight. With you and your husband. We have gifts for you."

"You don't have to give us anything."

"The gifts aren't from obligation but from affection, and we hope you'll enjoy them. Delia's told us so much about you, and Roarke and your home. It must be a magnificent place. I hope Sam and I will have an opportunity to see it."

Eve could feel the box being built around her, see the lid slowly closing. And Phoebe only continued to smile serenely while Peabody suddenly took an avid interest in the ceiling.

"Sure. Ah. You could come for dinner."

"We'd love to. Would eight o'clock work?"

"Yeah, eight's fine. Peabody knows the way. Anyway, welcome to New York. I've got some . . . stuff," she finished lamely and eased back to escape.

"Lieutenant? Sir? Be right back," Peabody murmured to her parents and lit out after Eve. Before they'd gotten to her office door, the noise level in the bull pen rose again.

"They can't help it," Peabody said quickly. "My father really likes to bake, and he's always bringing food places."

"How the hell'd they get all that here on a plane?"

"Oh, they don't fly. They'd have come in their camper. Baking all the way," she added with a fluttery smile. "Aren't they great?"

"Yeah, but you've got to tell them not to bring cupcakes every time they come in to see you. We'll end up with a bunch of fat detectives in sugar comas."

"Snagged you one." Peabody brought out the cupcake she held behind her back. I'll just take a couple hours, Dallas, get them settled in."

"Take the rest of the day."

"Okay. Thanks. Really. Um . . ." She winced, then closed the office door. "There's this thing I should tell you. About my mother. She has the power."

"The power of what?"

"The power to make you do things you don't want to do, or don't think you want to do. And she'll get you to say stuff you don't mean to say. And you may even babble."

"I don't babble."

"You will," Peabody said mournfully. "I love her. She's amazing, but she's got this thing. She just looks at you and knows."

Frowning, Eve sat. "Is she a sensitive?"

"No. My father is, but he's really strict about not infringing on people's privacy. She's just . . . a mother. It's something to do with being a mother, but she's got this deal in spades. Man, Mom sees all, knows all, rules all. Half the time you don't even know she's doing it. Like you inviting them for dinner tonight, when you never invite people to dinner."

"I do, too."

"Uh-uh. Roarke does. You could've said you were busy, or hey, fine, let's meet at some restaurant or whatever, but she wanted to come to your house for dinner, so you asked her."

Eve had to stop herself from squirming in her chair. "I was being polite. I do know how."

"No, you were trapped in The Look." Peabody shook her head. "Even you are powerless against it. I just thought I should tell you."

"Scram, Peabody."

"Scramming, sir. Oh and um . . ." She hesitated at the door. "I had a sort of date with McNab tonight, so maybe he could come along to dinner. That way, you know, he could meet them without it being as weird as it would be otherwise."

Eve put her head in her hands. "Jesus."

"Thanks! I'll see you tonight."

Alone, Eve sulked. She scowled. Then she ate the cupcake.

"So they painted my office, and stole my candy. Again." At home, in the spacious living area with its glossy antiques and gleaming glass, Eve paced the priceless Oriental carpet. Roarke had only just arrived home, so she'd had no one to bitch to for the past hour.

As far as she was concerned, a bitching partner was one of the top perks of marriage.

"And Peabody finished up all the paperwork while I was gone, which meant I didn't even have that to do."

"She should be ashamed. Imagine, your aide doing paperwork behind your back."

"Watch the smart-ass remarks, pal, because you've got some explaining to do as well."

He just stretched out his legs, crossed his feet at the ankles. "Ah. So how did Peabody and McNab enjoy Bimini?"

"You're a real Lord Bountiful, aren't you? Sending them off to some island so they can run around naked and slide down waterfalls."

"I take that to mean they had a good time."

"Gel-beds," she muttered. "Naked monkeys."

"Excuse me?"

She shook her head. "You've got to stop interfering in this . . . thing they've got going."

"Maybe I will," he said, lazily. "When you stop seeing their relationship as some sort of bugaboo."

"Bugaboo? What the hell is that?" She scooped a frustrated hand through her hair. "I don't see their thing as a bugaboo because I don't even know what that means. Cops—"

"Deserve lives," he interrupted. "Like everyone else. Relax, Lieutenant. Our Peabody has a good head on her shoulders."

Blowing out a breath, Eve dropped into a chair. "Bugaboo." She snorted. "That's probably not even a word, and if it is, it's a really stupid word. I gave her a case today."

He reached over idly to toy with the fingers she'd been tapping restlessly against her knee. "You didn't mention you'd caught a case today."

"I didn't. I dug one out of the cold files. Six years back. Woman, pretty, young, upwardly mobile, married. Husband's out of town, comes back and finds her dead in the bathtub. Homicide poorly disguised as self-termination or accident. His alibi's solid, and he comes off clean as a whistle. Everyone interviewed says how they were the perfect couple, happy as clams."

"Do you ever wonder how we determine the happiness of the clam?"

"I'm going to give that some real thought later. Anyway, there are letters hidden in her underwear drawer. Really explicit sex letters from someone who signs his name *C*."

"Extramarital affair, lover's spat, murder?"

"The primary of record thought so."

"But you don't?"

"Nobody ever found the guy, nobody ever saw the guy, nobody she knew ever heard her speak of the guy. Or so they said. I went by to see the husband, met his new wife and kid. Little girl, couple years old."

"One could assume, justifiably, that after his period of mourning, he moved on, made a new life."

"One could assume," she replied.

"Not that I ever would, of course. Under similar circumstances, I'd wander aimlessly, a broken man, lost and without purpose."

She looked at him skeptically. "Is that so?"

"Naturally. Now you're supposed to say something along the lines of you having no life at all without me in it."

"Yeah, yeah." She laughed when he bit the fingers he'd been playing with. "So back to the real world. I think I know how it went down. A couple of good, hard pushes and it's closed instead of cold."

"But instead of pushing, you gave it to Peabody."

"She needs the experience. A little more time won't matter to Marsha Stibbs. If Peabody goes down the wrong channels, I'll steer her back."

"She must be thrilled."

"Christ, she's got stars in her eyes."

It made him smile. "What was the first case Feeney handed you?"

"Thomas Carter. Got into his sedan one fine morning, coded in, and the sucker blew up, sending pieces of him flying all over the West Side. Married, two kids, sold insurance. No side pieces, no enemies, no dangerous vices. No motive. Case stalled, went cold. Feeney dug it out, told me to work it."

"And?"

"Thomas Carter wasn't the target. Thomas K. Carter, second-rate illegals dealer with a gambling addiction was. Asshole hired hitman tapped the wrong guy." She glanced back to see Roarke still grinning at her. "And yeah, I remember how it felt to be handed the file and to close it."

"You're a good trainer, Eve, and a good friend."

"Friendship has nothing to do with it. If I didn't think she could handle working the case, I wouldn't have given it to her."

"That's the trainer part. The friendship part should be here shortly."

"Dinner. What the hell are we going to do with them when we're not eating?"

"It's called conversation. Socializing. Some people actually make a habit of doing both, on practically a daily basis."

"Yeah, well some people are screwy. You're probably going to like the Peabodys. Did I tell you that when I got back to Central, they were feeding the bull pen cupcakes and cookies? Pie."

"Pie? What kind of pie?"

"I don't know. By the time I got there all that was left of it was the dish—and I think somebody ate that. But the cupcakes were amazing. Anyway, Peabody came back in my office and said all this weird stuff about her mother."

He toyed with the ends of Eve's hair now, enjoying the streaky look of it. He'd have understood perfectly Boyd Stibbs's claim of not being able to keep his hands off his wife. "I thought they got along very well."

"Yeah, they seem to cruise. But she said how she

needed to warn me that her mother had these powers."

"Wiccan?"

"Uh-uh, and not the Free-Ager hoodoo stuff either, even though she says her father's a sensitive. She said that her mother can make you do things you don't necessarily want to do, or say things you'd as soon keep to yourself. According to Peabody, I only asked them to dinner tonight because I was trapped in The Look."

Intrigued, Roarke cocked his head. "Mind control?"

"Beats me, but she said it was just a mother thing, and her mother was particularly good at it. Or something. Didn't make any sense to me."

"Well, neither of us know much about mother things, do we? And as she's not our mother, I imagine we're perfectly safe from her maternal powers, whatever they may be."

"I'm not worried about it, just passing on the warning."

Summerset, Roarke's majordomo and the bane of Eve's existence, came to the doorway. He sniffed once, his bony face set in disapproving lines. "That Chippendale is a coffee table, Lieutenant, not a footstool."

"How do you walk with that stick up your ass?" She left her feet where they were, propped comfortably on the table. "Does it hurt, or does it give you a nice little rush?"

"Your dinner guests," he said, curling his lip, "have arrived."

"Thank you, Summerset." Roarke got to his feet. "We'll have the hors d'oeuvres in here." He held out a hand to Eve.

She waited, deliberately, until Summerset had stepped out again before swinging her feet to the floor.

"In the interest of good fellowship," Roarke began as they started toward the foyer, "could you not mention the stick in Summerset's ass for the rest of the evening?"

"Okay. If he rags on me I'll just pull it out and beat him over the head with it."

"That should be entertaining."

Summerset had already opened the door, and Sam Peabody had his hand clasped, pumping away in a friendly greeting. "Great to meet you. Thanks for having us. I'm Sam, and this is Phoebe. It's Summerset, isn't it? DeeDee's told us you take care of the house, and everything in it."

"That's correct. Mrs. Peabody," he said, nodding at Phoebe. Officer, Detective. Shall I take your things?"

"No, thank you." Phoebe held on to the box she carried. "The front gardens and landscaping are beautiful. And so unexpected in the middle of such an urban world."

"Yes, we're quite pleased with it."

"Hello again." Phoebe smiled at Eve as Summerset shut the front door. "And Roarke. You were right, Delia, he is quite spectacular."

"Mom." Peabody choked out the word as the flush flooded her face.

"Thank you." Roarke took Phoebe's hand, lifted it to his lips. "That's a compliment I can return. It's wonderful to meet you, Phoebe. Sam." He shifted, shook Sam's offered hand. "You created a delightful and charming daughter."

"We like her." Sam squeezed Peabody's shoulders.

"So do we. Please, come in. Be comfortable."

He's so good at it, Eve thought as Roarke settled everyone in the main parlor. Smooth as satin, polished as glass. Within moments, everyone had a drink in their hands and he was answering questions about various antiques and art pieces in the room.

Since he was dealing with the Peabodys, Eve turned her attention to McNab. The EDD whiz was decked out in what Eve imagined he considered his more conservative attire. His periwinkle shirt was tucked into a pair of loose, silky trousers of the same tone. His ankle boots were also periwinkle. A half-dozen tiny gold hoops paraded up his left earlobe.

He wore his long blond hair in a ponytail that was slicked back from his face. And his pretty face, Eve noted, was approximately the color of a boiled lobster.

"You forget the sunblock, McNab?"

"Just once." He rolled his green eyes. "You should see my ass."

"No." She took a deep gulp of wine. "I shouldn't."

"Just making conversation. I'm a little nervous. You know." He nodded toward Peabody's father. "It's really weird making small talk with him when we both know I'm the one banging his daughter. Plus, he's psychic, so I keep worrying if I think about banging her, he'll know I'm thinking about banging her. And that's way too weird."

"Don't think about it."

"Can't help it." McNab chuckled. "I'm a guy."

She scanned his outfit. "That's the rumor anyway."

"Excuse me." Phoebe touched Eve's arm. "Sam and I would like to give you and Roarke this gift." She offered Eve the box. "For your generosity and friendship to two of our children."

"Thanks." Gifts always made her feel awkward. Even after more than a year with Roarke and his habit of giving, she never knew quite how to handle it.

Perhaps it was because she'd gone most of her life without anyone caring enough to give.

She set the box down, tugged on the simple twine bow. She opened the lid, pushed through the wrapping. Nestled inside were two slender candlesticks fashioned from glossy stone in greens and purples that melted together.

"They're beautiful. Really."

"The stone's fluorite," Sam told her. "For cleansing the aura, peacefulness of mind, clarity of thought. We thought, as you both have demanding and difficult occupations, this stone would be most beneficial."

"They're lovely." Roarke lifted one. "Exquisite workmanship. Yours?"

Phoebe sent him a brilliant smile. "We made them together."

"Then they're doubly precious. Thank you. Do you sell your work?"

"Now and again," Sam said. "We prefer making them for gifts."

"I sell when selling's needed," Phoebe put in. "Sam's too soft-hearted. I'm more practical."

"I beg your pardon." Once again, Summerset stood in the doorway. "Dinner is served."

It was easier than Eve thought. They were nice people, interesting and entertaining. And their pride in Peabody was so obvious it was impossible not to warm up to them.

"We worried, of course," Phoebe said as they began with lobster bisque, "when Dee told us what she wanted to do with her life, and where. A dangerous occupation in a dangerous city." She smiled across the table at her daughter. "But we understood that this was her calling, and trusted she would do good work."

"She's a good cop," Eve said.

"What's a good cop?" At Eve's frown, Phoebe gestured. "I mean, what would be your particular definition of a good cop?"

"Someone who respects the badge and what it stands for, and doesn't stop until they make a difference."

"Yes." Phoebe nodded in approval. Her eyes, dark and direct, stayed on Eve's.

And as something in that quiet, knowing stare made Eve want to shift in her seat, she decided Phoebe would be an ace in Interview.

"Making a difference is why we're all here." Phoebe lifted her glass, gesturing with it before she sipped. "Some do it with prayer, others with art, with commerce. And some with the law. People often think Free-Agers don't believe in the law, the law of the land, so to speak. But we do. We believe in order and balance, and in the right of the individual to pursue life and happiness without harm from others. When you stand for the law, you stand for balance, and for those individuals who have been harmed."

"The taking of a life, something I'll never understand, makes a hole in the world." Sam laid a hand over his wife's. "Dee doesn't tell us much about her work, the details of it. But she's told us that you make a difference."

"It's my job."

"And we're embarrassing you," Phoebe said as she lifted her wineglass. "Why don't I change the subject and tell you what a beautiful home you have." She turned to Roarke. "I hope after dinner we can have a tour of it."

"Got six or eight months?" Eve muttered.

"Eve claims there are rooms we don't even know about," Roarke commented.

"But you do." Phoebe lifted her brows. "You'd know all of them."

"Excuse me." Summerset stepped in. "You have a call, Lieutenant, from Dispatch."

"Sorry." She pushed away from the table, strode out quickly.

She was back within minutes. One look at her face told Roarke he'd finish the evening's entertaining on his own.

"Peabody, with me. I'm sorry." She scanned faces, lingered on Roarke's. "We have to go."

"Lieutenant? You want me to tag along?"

She glanced back at McNab. "I could use you. Let's move. I'm sorry," she said again.

"Don't worry about it." Roarke got to his feet, skimmed his fingertips down her cheek. "Take care, Lieutenant."

"Right."

"Occupational hazard." Roarke sat again when he was alone with Phoebe and Sam.

"Someone's died," Sam said aloud.

"Yes, someone's died. And now," Roarke said, "they'll work to find the balance."

Chapter 3

Walter C. Pettibone, the birthday boy, had arrived home at precisely seven-thirty. One hundred and seventy-three friends and associates had shouted "Surprise!" in unison the minute he'd walked in the door.

But that hadn't killed him.

He'd beamed like a boy, playfully scolded his wife for fooling him, and had greeted his guests with warmth and pleasure. By eight, the party was in full swing, and Walter had indulged lavishly in the enormous and varied spread of food the caterers provided. He ate quail's eggs and caviar, smoked salmon and spinach rolls.

But that hadn't killed him either.

He'd danced with his wife, embraced his children, and dashed away a little tear at his son's sentimental birthday toast.

And had survived.

At eight-forty-five, with his arm snug around his wife's waist, he lifted yet another glass of champagne, called for his guests' attention, and launched into a short but heartfelt speech regarding the sum of a man's life and the riches therein when he was blessed with friends and family.

"To you," he said, in a voice thick with emotion, "my dear friends, my thanks for sharing this day with me. To my children, who make me proud—thank you for all the joy you've brought me. And to my beautiful wife, who makes every day a day I'm grateful to be alive."

There was a nice round of applause, then Walter tipped back his glass, drank deep.

And that's what killed him.

He choked, his eyes bugged. His wife let out a little shriek as he clawed at the collar of his shirt. His son slapped him enthusiastically on the back. Staggering, he pitched forward into the party guests, tipping several of them over like bowling pins before he hit the ground and starting having seizures.

One of the guests was a doctor, and pushed forward to lend aid. The emergency medical technicians were called, and though they responded within five minutes, Walter was already gone.

The shot of cyanide in his toasting flute had been an unexpected birthday gift.

Eve studied him, the slight blue tinge around the mouth, the shocked and staring eyes. Caught the faint and telling whiff of burnt almonds. They'd moved him onto a sofa and loosened his shirt in the initial attempt to revive him. No one had swept away the broken glass and china as of yet. The room smelled strongly of flowers, wine, chilled shrimp, and fresh death.

Walter C. Pettibone, she thought, who'd gone in and out of the world on the same day. A tidy circle, but one most human beings would prefer to avoid.

"I want to see the doctor who worked on him first," she told Peabody, then scanned the floor. "We'll need to have all this broken shit taken in, identify which container or containers were spiked. Nobody leaves. That's guests *and* staff. McNab, you can start taking names and addresses for followups. Keep the family separate for now."

"Looks like it would've been a hell of a party," McNab commented as he headed out.

"Lieutenant. Dr. Peter Vance." Peabody escorted in a man of medium build. He had short, sandy-colored hair and a short, sandy-colored beard. When his gaze shifted past her to Walter Pettibone's body, Eve saw both grief and anger harden his eyes.

"That was a good man." His voice was clipped and faintly British. "A good friend."

"Someone wasn't his friend," Eve pointed out. "You recognized that he'd been poisoned, instructed the MTs to notify the police."

"That's correct. The signs were textbook, and we lost him very quickly." He looked away from the body and back at Eve. "I want to believe it was a mistake, some horrible accident. But it wasn't. He'd just finished giving a rather schmaltzy little toast, so like him. He was standing with his arm around his wife, his son and daughter and their spouses beside him. He had a big grin on his face and tears in his eyes. We applauded, he drank, then he choked. Collapsed right here and began having seizures. It was over in minutes. There was nothing to be done."

"Where did he get the drink?"

"I couldn't say. The caterer's staff was passing around champagne. Other beverages could be had from the bars that were set up here and there. Most of us had been here since about seven. Bambi was frantic about all of the guests being in place when Walt arrived home."

"Bambi?"

"His wife." Vance replied. "Second wife. They've been married a year or so now. She's been planning this surprise party for weeks. I'm sure Walt knew all about it. She's not what you'd call a clever woman. But he pretended to be surprised."

"What time did he get here?"

"Seven-thirty, on the nose. We all yelled *surprise* per Bambi's instructions. Had a good laugh out of it, then went back to eating, drinking. There was some dancing. Walt made the rounds. His son made a toast." Vance sighed. "I wish I'd paid more attention. I'm sure Walt was drinking champagne."

"Did you see him drink at that time?"

"I think . . ." He shut his eyes as if to bring it all back. "It seems to me he did. I can't imagine him not drinking after a toast by his son. Walt doted on his children. I believe he had a fresh glass—it seems to me it was full— when he made his own little toast. But I can't say for certain whether he picked it off a tray or someone handed it to him."

"You were friends?"

Grief clouded his face again. "Good friends, yes."

"Any problems in his marriage?"

Vance shook his head. "He was blissful. Frankly, most of us who knew him were baffled when he married Bambi. He was married to Shelly for, what would it be? More than thirty years, I suppose. Their divorce was amicable enough, as divorces go. Then within six months he was involved with Bambi. Most of us thought it was just some midlife foolishness, but it stuck."

"Was his first wife here tonight?"

"No. They weren't quite that amicable."

"Anyone you know of who'd want him dead?"

"Absolutely no one." He lifted his hands in a helpless gesture. "I know saying he didn't have an enemy in the world is a cliché, Lieutenant Dallas, but that's exactly what I'd say about Walt. People liked him, and a great many people loved him. He was a sweet-natured man, a generous employer, a devoted father."

And a wealthy one, Eve thought after she'd released the doctor. A wealthy man who'd dumped wife number-one for a younger, sexier model. As people didn't bring cyanide as a party favor, someone had been there tonight for the express purpose of killing Pettibone.

Eve did the interview with the second wife in a sitting room off the woman's bedroom.

The room was dim, the heavy pink drapes drawn tight over the windows so that the single lamp with its striped shade provided a candy-colored light.

In it, Eve could see the room, all pink and white and frothy. Like the inside of a sugar-loaded pastry, she thought. There were mountains of pillows, armies of trinkets, and the heavy scent of too many roses in one space.

Amid the girlish splendor, Bambi Pettibone reclined on a pink satin chaise. Her hair was curled and braided and tinted in that same carnival pink to set off a baby-doll face. She wore pink as well, a shimmering ensemble that dipped low over one breast and left the other to be flirtily exposed but for a patch of sheer material shaped like a rose.

Her big blue eyes shimmered prettily with the tears that trickled in tiny, graceful drops down her smooth cheeks. The face spoke of youth and innocence, but the body told another story altogether.

She held a fluffy white ball in her lap.

"Mrs. Pettibone?"

She let out a gurgling sound and pushed her face into the white ball. When the ball let out a quick yip, Eve decided it was, possibly, some sort of dog.

"I'm Lieutenant Dallas, NYPSD. This is my aide, Officer Peabody. I'm very sorry for your loss."

"Boney's dead. My sweet Boney."

Boney and Bambi, Eve thought. What was *wrong* with

people? "I know this is a difficult time." Eve glanced around, decided she had no choice but to sit on something fluffy and pink. "But I need to ask you some questions."

"I just wanted to give him a birthday party. Everyone came. We were having such a good time. He never even got to open his presents."

She wailed the last of it, and the little puff ball on her lap produced a pink tongue and licked her face.

"Mrs. Pettibone . . . could I have your legal name for the record?"

"I'm Bambi."

"For real? Never mind. You were standing next to your husband when he collapsed."

"He was saying such nice things about everybody. He really liked the party." She sniffled, looked imploringly at Eve. "That's something, isn't it? He was happy when it happened."

"Did you give him the champagne for his toast, Mrs. Pettibone?"

"Boney loved champagne." There was a sentimental and soggy sigh. "It was his very, very favorite. We had caterers. I wanted everything just so. I told Mr. Markie to be sure his servers passed champagne the whole time. And canapés, too. I worked really hard to make it perfect for my sweet Boney. Then he got so sick, and it happened so fast. If I'd known he was sick, we wouldn't have had a party. But he was fine when he left this morning. He was just fine."

"Do you understand what happened to your husband?"

She hugged the puffball dog, buried her face in its fluff. "He got sick. Peter couldn't make him better."

"Mrs. Pettibone, we think it's most likely the champagne was responsible for your husband's death. Where did he get the glass of champagne he drank right before he collapsed?"

"From the girl, I guess." She sniffed, stared at Eve with a puzzled expression. "Why would champagne make him sick? It never did before."

"What girl?"

"What girl?" Bambi repeated, her face a baffled blank.

Patience, Eve reminded herself. "You said 'the girl' gave Mr. Pettibone the champagne for his toast."

"Oh, that girl. One of the servers." Bambi lifted a shoulder, nuzzled the little dog. "She brought Boney a new glass so he could make his toast."

"Did he take it off her tray?"

"No." She pursed her lips, sniffled softly. "No, I remember she handed it to him and wished him a happy birthday. She said, 'Happy birthday, Mr. Pettibone.' Very politely, too."

"Did you know her? Have you employed her before?"

"I use Mr. Markie, and he brings the servers. You can leave everything up to Mr. Markie. He's just mag."

"What did she look like?"

"Who?"

God, give me the strength not to bitch-slap this moron. "The server, Bambi. The server who gave Boney the glass of champagne for his toast."

"Oh. I don't know. Nobody really looks at servers, do they?" She said it with a fluttering confusion as Eve stared at her. "Tidy," she said after a moment. "Mr. Markie insists on his staff presenting a neat appearance."

"Was she old, young, tall, short?"

"I don't know. She looked like one of the servers, that's all. And they all look the same, really."

"Did your husband speak to her?"

"He said thank you. Boney's very polite, too."

"He didn't appear to recognize her? The server," Eve added quickly as Bambi's mouth began to purse on what surely would have been another "Who?"

"Why would he?"

No one, Eve decided, could pretend to be this level of idiot. It had to be sincere. "All right. Do you know anyone who'd wish your husband harm?"

"Everyone loved Boney. You just had to."

"Did you love Boney while he was married to his first wife?"

Her eyes went bigger, rounder. "We never, ever cheated. Boney didn't even kiss me until after he was divorced. He was a gentleman."

"How did you meet him?"

"I worked at one of his flower shops. The one on Madison. He used to come in sometimes and look at the stock, and talk to us. To me," she added with a trembling smile. "Then one day he came by just as I was getting off and offered to walk me home. He took my arm while we walked. He told me how he was getting a divorce and wondered if I'd have lunch with him sometime. I wondered if it was just a line—guys say stuff like that, you know, how they're leaving their wife, or how she doesn't make him happy, and all sorts of things just to get you to go to bed with them. I'm not stupid."

No, Eve thought, *you redefine the word.*

"But Boney wasn't like that. He never tried anything funny."

She sighed and began to rub her cheek against the dog's fur. "He was romantic. After he was divorced we dated and he took me to really nice places and never tried anything funny then either. Finally I had to try something funny because he was just so cute and cuddly and hand-some. And after that, he asked me to marry him."

"Did his first wife resent that?"

"Probably. Who wouldn't resent not having Boney for their own sweetie? But she was always very nice, and Boney never said anything bad about her."

"And his children."

"Well, I don't think they liked me at first. But Boney

said they'd come to love me because he did. And we never had a fight or anything."

"Big, happy family," Eve repeated after another ten minutes with Bambi. "Everyone likes everybody and Pettibone is the original nice guy."

"Wife's a dink," Peabody offered.

"The dink was still smart enough to hook a rich husband. Could be smart enough to put a little something extra in his birthday bubbly." But she paused a moment at the top of the stairs to let various options play out in her mind.

"Have to be really smart, and have nerves of iron to pull it off when she's standing right next to him in front of a room full of well-wishers and witnesses. We'll dig into her background a bit, see how much of that sugar plum bit is real and how much is an act. Anybody who lives in that much pink goes to the top of my short list."

"I thought it was kind of pretty, in an 'I love being a girl' sort of way."

"Sometimes you scare me, Peabody. Do a standard run on her to start. Bambi," she added as she started down. "People who name their kid Bambi must know she's going to grow up a dink. Now we get to play with Mr. Markie. Who comes up with this shit?"

"We've got him and the catering staff in the kitchen area."

"Good. Let's find out who gave Pettibone the champagne and wished him happy birthday."

As she started across the main floor to the kitchen, McNab jogged up behind her. "Dallas? ME's here. Concurs with the MTs and the doc on-scene about the appearance of poisoning. Can't call it officially until they get the stiff back to the body shop and run some dead tests."

"Thanks for that colorful report, Detective. Relay to

the ME that I want confirmation of cause of death ASAP. Go ahead and take a look at the incomings and outgoings on the house 'links for the last twenty-four hours, just in case someone got sloppy."

"I'm on it." He managed to give Peabody a quick pat on the ass before splitting off.

"Having your parents bunking with you should put the kabosh on playing grabass with McNab for the next little while."

"Oh, they're not staying at my place. Said it was too small and they didn't want to crowd me. Couldn't change their minds. They'll just stay in their camper. I told them they're really not supposed to. City ordinances and stuff, but they just patted me on the head."

"Get them into a hotel, Peabody, before some uniform cites them."

"I'll work on it soon as we get back."

They turned into the kitchen. It was big, done in blinding whites and sparkling silver. And at the moment, chaos reigned. Food in various stages of preparation was spread all over the counters. Dishes were stacked in towers, glassware in pyramids. Eve counted eight uniformed staff jammed into an eating nook and chattering away with the nervous energy crime scenes often brought out in witnesses.

An enormous urn of coffee was being put to use by both cops and servers. One of her own uniforms was helping himself to a tray of fancy finger food and another was already hitting the dessert cart.

It only took her presence to have the room falling into stillness, and silence.

"Officers, if you can manage to tear yourselves away from the all-you-can-eat buffet, take posts outside the doors of both kitchen exits. As cause of death has not yet been officially called, I'll remind you that you're stuffing evidence in your faces. If necessary, I'll have you both cut open so that evidence can be removed."

"There's nothing wrong with my food." A man stepped forward as the two uniforms rushed out. He was short, homely, with an olive complexion. His head was shaved and gleamed as smooth as an ice floe. He wore a white butcher's apron over a formal black suit.

"You'd be Markie?"

"Mr. Markie," he said with cold dignity. "I demand to know what's going on. No one will tell us anything, just that we're required to stay in here. If you're in charge—"

"I'm in charge. Lieutenant Dallas, and what's going on is Walter Pettibone's dead and I'm here to find out how and why."

"Well, Lieutenant Dallas, I can tell you that Mr. Pettibone didn't meet his demise through any of my dishes. I won't have any rumors regarding my food and my business bandied about. My reputation is unimpeachable."

"Cool your thrusters, Markie. No one's accusing you of anything." She held up a hand before he could speak and turned her attention to his staff. "Which one of you served Mr. Pettibone before his toast?"

"It wasn't any of us. We've been talking about it."

Eve studied the attractive Asian woman. "And you'd be?"

"Sing-Yu. I was in the living area when it happened. But I was at the far end passing champagne so the guests in that section had glasses for Mr. Pettibone's toast. And Charlie—" She tapped the shoulder of the lean black man beside her. "He was bringing in the crab puffs."

"I was working the terrace bar." Another server raised a hand. "Robert McLean. And Laurie was working the terrace guests. We didn't leave our station until we heard everyone shouting."

"I was in the kitchen." Another man spoke up. "I'm, um, Don Clump. You remember, Mr. Markie? We were in here together when we heard the commotion."

"That's correct." Markie nodded. "I'd just sent Charlie out with the crab puffs, and was instructing Don to begin a pass with the stuffed mushrooms. Gwen was just coming in with empties, and we heard shouting."

"I have a witness who states that a female member of your staff handed Mr. Pettibone a glass of champagne just before he began his toast."

Gazes shifted, dropped.

"It had to be Julie." Sing-Yu spoke up again. "I'm sorry, Mr. Markie, but she's the only one who could've done it, and she's the only one who's not here."

"Who's Julie and why isn't she here?" Eve demanded.

"I don't like my employees gossiping about one another," Markie began.

"This is a police investigation. Witness statements aren't gossip, and I expect you and your staff to cooperate. Who is Julie?" Eve asked, turning to Sing-Yu.

"She's absolutely right." Markie let out a long sigh, then moved over to pat Sing-Yu's shoulder. "I'm sorry, my dear, I'm not angry with you. Julie Dockport," he said to Eve. "She's been with my company for two months. As to where she is, I can't say. She must have slipped out in the confusion immediately following Mr. Pettibone's collapse. It took me a few moments to realize there was a problem and to get from the kitchen to the living area. I didn't see her. When the police arrived and told us to come in here, to remain in here, she didn't come."

"She wearing this getup?" Eve nodded toward the trim black pants and starched white shirts of the serving staff.

"Yes."

"Describe her."

"Medium build, I suppose, on the athletic side. Short red hair, attractive. About thirty, give or take a year one way or the other. I'd have to check my employment files to be exact on that."

"Peabody, take the staff to another area. Put a uniform on them, then go find Julie Dockport."

"Yes, sir."

When they filed out, Eve sat, gestured to Markie. "Now. Tell me what you know about this woman."

It wasn't much. She heard words like competent, reliable, cooperative.

"She applied for a position," Markie went on. "Her references checked out. She's been an excellent employee. I can only think she was upset and frightened about what happened here tonight and left."

They both glanced over as Peabody came back in. "I can't locate her on the premises, Lieutenant."

"Do a run, get her address. I want her picked up." She got to her feet. "You can go."

"My staff and I will pack up the food and supplies."

"No, you won't. This is a crime scene. It stays as is for now. We'll contact you when it's clear for you to clean house."

She took the son and daughter next. With their spouses they were huddled together at one end of the table in the formal dining room. Four pairs of eyes red and swollen with weeping turned to Eve.

The man who stood, bracing one hand on the table, was light complected with hair of a dull, dense blond worn short and straight. He had a soft chin and lips that all but disappeared when he pressed them together in a grim line.

"What's happening? Who are you? We need some answers."

"Wally." The woman beside him was also blonde, but

her hair was brighter and upswept. "You'll only make it worse."

"How can it be worse?" he demanded. "My father's dead."

"I'm Lieutenant Dallas. I'm very sorry for your loss, and apologize for the delay in speaking with you, Mr. Pettibone."

"Walter C. Pettibone IV," he told her. "My wife, Nadine." He turned his hand under the one the blonde had laid over his, gripped tight. "My sister, Sherilyn, and her husband, Noel Walker. Why are we being kept in here this way? We need to be with my father."

"That's not possible at the moment. There are things that need to be done to get you those answers you need. Sit down, Mr. Pettibone."

"What happened to my father?" It was Sherilyn who spoke. She was a petite brunette, and Eve thought she was probably remarkably pretty under most circumstances. Now her face was ravaged from weeping. "Could you just tell us, please?" She reached out, taking her brother's free hand, and her husband's, forming them into a unit. "What happened to Daddy?"

"The cause of death hasn't been confirmed."

"I heard the MTs." She took a long deep breath, and her voice strengthened. "I heard them say he was poisoned. That can't possibly be true."

"We'll know very soon. It would help if you'd tell me what each of you were doing, where you were in the room when Mr. Pettibone collapsed."

"We were right there, standing right beside him," Sherilyn began. "Everyone was standing there—"

"Sherry." Noel Walker brought their joined hands to his lips. It was a gesture Roarke often made, Eve noted. One of comfort, of love, of solidarity.

He turned his attention to Eve. His hair was dark like his wife's and waved around a strong, handsome face.

"Walt was making a toast. Sentimental and sweet. He was a sentimental and sweet man. Bambi was at his right side. Sherry was next to her and I was at her right. Wally was directly at his left, with Nadine beside him. When he finished his toast, he took a drink of champagne. We all did. Then he began to choke. I believe Wally slapped him on the back, the way you do. Bambi grabbed at him when he staggered. He pulled at his collar as if it was too tight, then fell forward."

He glanced at Wally as if for confirmation.

"He was gasping," Wally continued. "We turned him over on his back. Peter Vance, he's a doctor, pushed through the people who'd crowded around. And my father—he had some sort of seizure. Peter said to call the MTs. Nadine ran to do so."

"Was he able to speak to any of you?"

"He never said anything," Sherilyn answered. "He looked at me." Her voice cracked again. "He looked right at me just before he fell. Everyone was talking at once. It all happened so fast, there wasn't time to say anything."

"Where did he get the drink?"

"From a tray, I suppose," Wally said. "The caterers had been passing champagne since guests began to arrive at seven."

"No." Sherilyn shook her head slowly. "No, one of the servers handed it to him. She wasn't carrying a tray, just the one flute. She took his nearly empty glass and gave him a full one. She wished him happy birthday."

"That's right," her husband confirmed. "The little redhead. I noticed her. She had rather stunning green eyes. I paint," he explained. "Portraits primarily. I tend to notice faces and what makes them unique."

"What did she do after she gave him the drink?"

"She, ah, let me think. Walt called for everyone's attention. Most of the guests were in the living area at that time. Conversations quieted down while he began to speak. She stepped back. She was listening to him, just like the rest of us. Smiling, I think. Yes, I recall thinking she was very personable, and how she seemed to take an interest in what Walt was saying. I think I smiled at her when Walt finished his toast, but she was watching him. Then we all drank, and I didn't notice her once Walt began to choke."

"I think I saw her." Nadine lifted a hand to the long triple string of pearls she wore. "When I ran out to call for help, I saw her in the foyer."

"What was she doing?" Eve asked.

"I think, well, she must have been leaving. She was walking away, toward the door."

"None of you had seen her before tonight?" When they all looked at each other, a sort of baffled head-shaking, Eve went on, "Does the name Julie Dockport mean anything? Maybe your father mentioned it."

"I never heard him mention that name." Wally glanced around as the rest of his family shook their heads again.

"Do you know if he was concerned about anyone, or anything? A business deal, a personal problem."

"He was happy," Sherilyn said quietly. "He was a happy man."

"A happy man," Eve stated after she released the family, "loved by one and all doesn't get poisoned on his birthday. There's something under this pretty picture, Peabody."

"Yes, sir. The officers who went to Dockport's address report that she's not there. Her across-the-hall neighbor told them she moved out that morning. Claimed she was moving to Philly."

"I want sweepers over there, now. I want that place combed. They won't find anything, but I want it done."

"Sir?"

"Looks like we've got ourselves a pro."

Chapter 4

Though it was after one in the morning when she got home, Eve wasn't surprised to find Roarke in his office. It was rare for him to sleep more than five hours a night. Rarer still for him not to wait up until she was home.

The work fueled him, she knew. More than the obscene amounts of money he made every time he wheeled a deal, it was the deal itself—the planning, the strategizing, the negotiating, that engaged his interests and energies.

He bought because things were there to be bought. Though she often thought of the companies, the real estate, the factories, the hotels he acquired as his toys, she knew he was a man who took his toys very, very seriously.

He'd broadened her focus considerably since they'd been together. Travel, culture, society. Somehow he managed to carve out time for everything and more. The money was nothing to him, she thought, unless it was enjoyed.

The man who ruled a business empire with a scope beyond reason sat at a desk at one-fifteen in the morning with a brandy at his elbow, a fat, purring cat on his lap, and his sleeves rolled up while he worked at his computer like any lowly office drone.

And, she thought, he was enjoying it.

"Are you in the middle of something or are you playing?"

He glanced up. "A bit of both. Save data and file," he ordered the computer, then sat back. "The media's already got your homicide. I was sorry to hear about Walter Pettibone."

"You knew him?"

"Not well. But enough to appreciate his business sense and to know he was a pleasant sort of man."

"Yeah, everybody loved good old Walt."

"The media report said he'd collapsed at his home during a party to celebrate his sixtieth birthday; one we were invited to," he added. "But as I wasn't sure precisely when we'd be back or what mood we'd be in, I declined. Murder wasn't mentioned, just that the police were investigating."

"Media vultures wouldn't have the official ME's report yet. I just got it myself. It's homicide. Somebody slipped some cyanide in his drink. What do you know about the ex-wife?"

"Not a great deal. I believe they were married for a number of years, divorced without any scandal. He married some pretty young thing sometime after. There was some head shaking over that, but the gossip died down quickly enough. Walter wasn't the sort of man who made a target for gossip. Just not enough juice."

Eve sat, stretched out her legs. When she reached down to pet Galahad, the cat growled low in his throat. With a feline glare for Eve, he flicked his tail, leaped down, and stalked away.

"He's annoyed we didn't take him on vacation." Roarke smothered a grin as Eve scowled after the cat. "He and I have made up, but it appears he's still holding a grudge where you're concerned."

"Little prick."

"Name calling is no way to mend fences. Try fresh tuna. It works wonders."

"I'm not bribing a damn cat." She lifted her voice, certain the party in question was still within earshot. "He doesn't want me touching him, fine and dandy. He wants to be pissed off because . . ." She trailed off as she heard herself. "Jesus. Where was I? Pettibone. Juice. Well, he had enough juice for somebody to want him dead. And the way it's shaping up, to pay for a pro."

"A professional hit on Walter Pettibone?" Roarke lifted a brow. "That doesn't feel like a good fit."

"Woman gets a job at the caterers just about the time the current Mrs. Pettibone is planning the big surprise party. The same woman works the Pettibone affair, and brings the birthday boy the fatal glass of champagne. Hands it to him personally, wishes him happy birthday. Hangs back, but stays in the room while he makes his mushy toast, and drinks. When he's spazzing on the floor, she walks out of the apartment and poof! Vanishes."

She frowned a little as Roarke rose, poured her a glass of wine, then sat on the arm of her chair.

"Thanks. I had sweepers go over her place—a place she rented two days before she took the catering job, and one she moved out of this morning. One, according to her neighbors, she spent little time in. No prints, no trace evidence. Not a fucking stray hair. She sanitized it. I went by there myself. Little one-room place, low rent, low security. But she had police locks installed to keep the riff-raff out."

"Are you looking at—what is her name? Muffy? Twinkie?"

"Bambi. Comes off like she's got the mental capacity of broccoli, but we'll run her. She seems sincerely a dink, but she's now a really rich, widowed dink. Maybe the ex-wife bided her time," Eve mused. "Played nice while she worked things out. You're married to a guy thirty years, you've got a serious investment. Gonna irritate you when he trades you in."

"I'll keep that in mind."

"Me, I don't hire hits." She looked up at his mouth-watering face. "I'd give you the basic courtesy of killing you myself."

"Thank you, darling." He leaned over to kiss the top of her head. "It's comforting to know you'd take a personal interest in such a matter."

"I'll check out the first Mrs. Pettibone in the morning. If she did the hiring, she'd be my best link to this Julie Dockport."

"Interesting. A professional killer who selects the name of a prison as her surname."

She paused with the wineglass at her lips. "What?"

"Dockport Rehabilitation Center. I believe I had an acquaintance who spent some time in that particular facility," he replied as he toyed with the ends of her hair. "I think it's in Illinois, or perhaps Indiana. One of those Midwest places."

"Wait a minute, wait a minute." She pushed to her feet. "Dockport. Poison. Wait, wait." She pressed her fingers to her temples, drilled them for the data.

"Julie. No, not Julie. Julianna. Julianna Dunne. Eight, nine years back. Right after I got my gold shield. Poisoned her husband. Big charity fund-raiser at the Met. I worked the case. She was slippery, she was slick. She'd done it before. Twice before. Once in East Washington, again in Chicago. That's how we got her, the one in Chicago. I worked with the CPSD. She'd marry a rich guy, then she'd off him, take the money, and go reinvent herself for the next target."

"You sent her up?"

Distracted, she shook her head and continued to pace. "I was part of it. I couldn't break her in Interview, never got a confession out of her, but we got enough for an indictment, enough for a conviction. A lot of it weighed on the psych tests. She came up whacked. Seriously whacked. Hated men. And the jury didn't like her. She was too fucking smug, too cold. They added up three dead husbands and close to a half a billion dollars and gave her ten to twenty. It was the best we could do, and we got lucky at that."

"Three murders, and she gets ten to twenty?"

It was coming back, in a steady stream now. "East Washington couldn't pin her. What we had there went to pattern. Lawyers pleaded the other counts down and with mostly circumstantial, we had to swallow it. She got reduced for diminished capacity. Childhood trauma, blah blah. She used most of the first husband's money, the only scratch she could legally use, to wrangle that deal and pay for the trial and the appeals. Pissed her off. They held the trial in Chicago, and I was there for the verdict. I made sure I was there. Afterward, she asked to speak to me."

She leaned back on his desk, and though she looked at him Roarke knew she was ten years back, and looking at Julianna Dunne. "She said she knew I was the one responsible for her arrest, her conviction. The other cops . . . wait a minute," she muttered as she pushed back in time to hear Julianna's voice.

"The other cops were just men, and she'd never lost a battle to a man. She respected me, woman to woman, and understood I felt I was just doing my job. Then again, so was she. She was certain I'd come to see that eventually. We'd talk again, when I did."

"What did you respond?"

"That if it had been my call, she'd've gone down for all three murders and would never see the light of day again. That if I was responsible for putting her where she was going, good for me, but if I'd been the judge, she'd be serving three consecutive life terms. I hoped she'd come to see that eventually, because we had nothing to talk about."

"Clear, concise, and to the point, even with your shiny new gold badge."

"Yeah, I guess. She didn't like it, not one bit, but laughed and said she was sure the next time we got together I'd see things more clearly. And that was that. The caterer's going to transmit her employment records in the morning. I don't want to wait that long. Can you get into them, pull up her ID photo and data?"

"Who's the caterer?"

"Mr. Markie."

"Excellent choice." He rose and walked behind the desk.

"Can I use this other unit here?"

"Be my guest." He sat down and got to work.

While he did, Eve ordered up the data on Julianna Dunne. She skimmed the text that popped up on the wall screen, listened with half an ear to the background information as she studied the most recent ID photo.

At the time of the photo she'd still worn her hair long. Long and delicately blonde to go with her classic face and features. Wide blue eyes, thickly lashed, framed by slimly arched brown brows shades deeper than her hair. Her mouth was soft, a bit top heavy, her nose straight and perfect. Despite nearly a decade in prison, her skin looked smooth and creamy.

She looked, Eve realized, like one of those glamour girls in the old videos Roarke enjoyed so much.

RELEASED FROM DOCKPORT REHABILITATION CENTER, SEVENTEEN FEBRUARY, 2059. SERVED EIGHT YEARS, SEVEN MONTHS. SENTENCE REDUCED FOR GOOD BEHAVIOR. SUBJECT MET REHABILITATION REQUIREMENTS. FULFILLED MANDATORY SIXTY-DAY CHECKS, SIGNED OFF EIGHTEEN APRIL BY PAROLE OFFICER/REHABILITATION COUNSELOR OTTO SHULTZ, CHICAGO, WITH NO RESTRICTIONS. CURRENT RESIDENCE, 29 THIRD AVENUE, APARTMENT 605, NEW YORK CITY, NEW YORK.

"Not anymore," Eve commented.

"Your data, Lieutenant," Roarke said as he ordered it onto the next wall screen.

She studied Julianna's side-by-side images. "She cut her hair, went red, changed her eye color. Didn't bother with much else. That jibes with her old pattern. Logged her correct, if temporary address. Julianna dots her i's and crosses her t's. What does she have to do with Walter Pettibone?"

"Do you think she went pro?"

"She likes money," Eve mused. "It, I don't know, feeds some need. The same need killing men feeds. But it doesn't fit her old pattern. Point is, she's back, and she killed Pettibone. I have to update the all-points."

"Have you considered she came here, killed here, because of you?"

Eve blew out a breath. "Maybe. That would mean I made a hell of an impression on her all those years ago."

"You tend to—make an impression."

Since she couldn't think of a response, she pulled out her communicator and ordered the new all-points bulletin on Julianna Dunne.

"If she follows her old pattern, she's already out of the city. But we scooped her up once, we'll scoop her up again. I'll need to bring Feeney in on this. We were partners when Julianna went down."

"As I'm fond of him, I hope you don't intend to do that until morning."

"Yeah." She glanced at her wrist unit. "Nothing else to be done tonight."

"I don't know." He walked around the desk again, slid his arms around her. "I can think of one thing."

"You usually do."

"Why don't we go to bed, and I'll get you naked. Then we'll see if you think of it, too."

"I guess that's reasonable." She started out with him. "I didn't ask: Did the rest of the deal go okay with the Peabodys?"

"Mmm. Fine."

"Figured. You play with strangers better than I do. Listen, I hear they're going to stay in this camper thing they travel in, and that's not a good idea. I thought since you have hotels and stuff you could get them a deal on a room."

"That's not going to be necessary."

"Well yeah, because if they bunk in that thing on the street or in some lot, a beat cop's going to cite them, maybe pull them in. They won't flop at Peabody's because her place is pretty tight. You've got to have an empty hotel room or apartment somewhere they can use."

"I imagine I do, yes, but . . ." At the door to their bedroom, he pulled her inside, toward the bed. "Eve."

She began to get a bad feeling. "What?"

"Do you love me?"

A very bad feeling. "Maybe."

He lowered his mouth to hers, kissed her soft and deep. "Just say yes."

"I'm not saying yes until I know why you're asking the question."

"Perhaps I'm insecure, and needy, and want reassurance."

"My ass."

"Yes, I want your ass as well, but first there's the matter of your great and generous and unconditional love for me."

She let him release her weapon harness, noticed he put it well out of reach before turning back and loosening the buttons of her shirt. "Who said anything about unconditional? I don't remember signing that clause in the deal."

"What is it about your body that's a constant fascination to me?" He feathered his fingers lightly over her breasts. "It's all so firm and soft all at once."

"You're stalling. And you never stall." She grabbed his wrists before he could finish the job of distracting her. "You did something. What did you . . ." Realization struck, and her jaw dropped nearly to her toes. "Oh my God."

"I don't know how it happened, precisely. I really can't say how it came to be that Peabody's parents are even now tucked away in a guest room on the third floor. East wing."

"Here? They're going to stay here? You asked them to stay here? With us?"

"I'm not sure."

"What do you mean you're not sure? Did you ask them or not?"

"There's no point in getting into a snit." One must, he knew very well, switch to offense when defense was running thin. "You're the one who asked them to dinner, after all."

"To dinner," she hissed, as if they might hear her in the east wing. "A meal doesn't come with sleeping privileges. Roarke, they're Peabody's. What the hell are we going to do with them?"

"I don't know that either." Humor danced back in his eyes, and he sat and laughed. "I'm no easy mark. You know that. And I swear to you even now I'm not sure how she managed it, though manage it, she did. I'm showing them around after dinner as Phoebe wanted a bit of a tour. She's saying how nice it must be to have so many lovely rooms, and how comfortable and homey it all is despite all the size and space of it. And we're in the east wing, and she's wandering around one of the guest rooms and going to the window and saying what a wonderful view of the gardens. And look here, Sam, isn't this a beautiful view and so on. She misses her flowers, she tells me. And I say something about her being welcome to roam the garden here if she likes."

"How did you get from walking around the gardens to sleeping in the guest room?"

"She looked at me."

"And?"

"She looked at me," he repeated with a kind of baffled fascination, "and from there it's difficult to explain. She was saying how comforting it was to her and Sam to know their Delia had such good friends, generous souls and something of the like. And how much it meant to them to have this time to get to know those friends. Before I knew it I was arranging for their things to be fetched, and she was kissing me good night."

"Peabody said she has the power."

"I'm here to tell you, the woman has something. It's not that I mind. It's a big house, and I like both of them quite a lot. But, for Christ's sake, I usually know what I'm going to say before it comes spurting out of my mouth."

Amused now, she straddled him where he sat, hooked her arms behind his neck. "She put the whammy on you. I'm kind of sorry I missed it."

"There, you see? You do love me."

"Probably."

She was grinning when she let him roll her into bed.

In the morning, Eve did a thirty-minute workout in the gym, and finished it off with laps in the pool. When she had the time, it was a routine that invariably cleared her mind and got her blood moving. By the time she pushed off for the tenth lap, she'd outlined her next steps in the Pettibone case.

Tracking Julianna Dunne was priority, and that meant digging through the old files, taking a hard look at patterns, associates, routines, and habits. It meant, in all probability, a trip to Dockport, to interview any inmates or guards Julianna had formed a relationship with.

Though if memory served, Julianna was very skilled at keeping herself to herself.

Next priority was motive. Who'd wanted Pettibone dead? Who'd benefitted? His wife, his children. Possibly a business competitor.

A woman who looked like Bambi would have had other men in her life. That bore looking into. A former lover, jealousy. Or a long-term plan to hook the rich old guy, soak him, then eliminate him.

Then there was the ex-wife, who might have gained revenge and satisfaction in paying him back for dumping her.

Could be Pettibone wasn't the saint people were making him out to be. He might have known Julianna. He might have been one of her potential targets a decade ago, someone she'd seduced into an affair. Or she could have researched him while she was in prison, then played with him after her release.

That angle was high on her list, but it was too early to dismiss any possibility.

To know the killer, know the victim, she thought. This time she knew the killer, but to find the motive, she had to learn more about Pettibone. And reacquaint herself with Julianna Dunne.

At the end of twenty laps, feeling loose and limber, she slicked her hair back and stood in the shallows. As she started to hoist herself out, she caught a movement among the jungle of plants. Her head snapped up; her body braced.

"Well, if that's what the bad guys see before you arrest them, it's a wonder they don't fall to their knees begging for mercy."

Phoebe stepped forward, holding a towel. "I'm sorry," she added. "I know you didn't hear me come in. I got caught up watching you. You swim like a fish, in the best sense of the term."

Because she was also naked as a fish, Eve took the towel, quickly wrapped herself in it. "Thanks."

"Roarke said you'd be down here. I brought you some coffee." She took an oversized mug off the table. "And one of Sam's amazing croissants. I wanted to take a moment to thank you for your hospitality."

"No problem. You, ah, settle in okay?"

"It would be hard to do otherwise here. Do you have a minute, or are you in a rush?"

"Well, I—"

"The croissant's fresh." She held out the plate, close enough that the fragrance of it hypnotized. "Sam managed to charm Summerset into letting him use the kitchen."

"I can take a minute." Because putting on a robe would mean taking off the towel first, she sat as she was. And because Phoebe was watching her, she broke off a corner of the croissant.

"It's great." And immediately broke off another piece. "Seriously great."

"Sam's a brilliant cook. Eve—can I call you Eve? I know most don't."

Maybe it was that steady look, or the tone of voice or a combination of both, but Eve found herself wanting to squirm in her chair. "Sure, okay."

"I make you uncomfortable. I wish I didn't."

"No, you . . ." She did squirm. "I'm just not good with people."

"I don't think that's true. You've been good with Delia. Exceptionally good. And don't tell me it's just the job, because I know it's not." Phoebe picked up a mug of tea, watching Eve as she drank. "There's been a change in her this past year. She's grown, as a person. Dee always seemed to know what she wanted to do, to be, but since working for you she's found her place. She's more confident, sadder in some ways, I think because of the things she's seen and had to do. But stronger for them. Her letters and calls are full of you. I wonder if you know how much it means to her that you made her a part of who you are."

"Listen, Mrs. Peabody . . . Phoebe," she corrected. "I don't—I haven't—" She blew out a breath. "I'm going to say something about Peabody, and I don't want it getting back to her."

Phoebe's lips curved at the corners. "All right. What you tell me stays between us."

"She's got a good eye and a quick brain. Most cops do, or they don't last long. She remembers things, so you don't have to waste time going over the same ground with her. She knows what it means to serve and protect, what it really means. That makes a difference in what kind of cop you turn out to be. I went a long time working solo. I liked it that way. There wasn't anybody I wanted with me after my old partner transferred to EDD."

"Captain Feeney."

"Yeah, when Feeney got his bars and went into EDD, I worked alone. Then I come across Peabody, all spit and polish and sneaky sarcasm. I wasn't going to take on a uniform. I never intended to be anybody's trainer. But . . . she has a spark. I don't know how else to say it. You don't see that kind of thing every day on the job. She wanted Homicide, and I figure the dead need all the spark they can get. She'd have gotten there without me. I just gave her a boost."

"Thank you. I worry about her. She's a grown woman, but she's my little girl. She always will be. That's motherhood. But I'll worry less after what you've told me. I don't suppose you'd tell me what you think of Ian McNab."

Something like panic tickled Eve's throat. "He's a good cop."

Phoebe tipped back her head and laughed until the rich, rollicking sound of it filled the room. "How did I know you'd say that? Don't worry, Eve, I like him very much, more so since he's so goofily in love with my little girl."

"Goofy covers it," Eve muttered.

"Now, I know you need to get to work, but I have a gift for you."

"You gave us a gift already."

"That was from my man and me to you and your man. This is from me to you." She bent to pick up a box she'd set on the floor, then put it in Eve's lap. "Gifts shouldn't unnerve you. They're just tokens, of appreciation or affection. In this case both. I brought it with me before I was completely sure we'd come all the way to New York. Before I was completely sure I'd give it to you. I had to meet you first. Please, open it."

With no way out, Eve took off the lid. Inside was a statue of a woman, perhaps eight inches high, carved from some nearly transparent crystal. Her head was tipped back so that her hair rained down almost to her feet. Her eyes were closed, her mouth bowed up in a quiet smile. She held her arms out to her sides, palms up.

"She's the goddess," Phoebe explained. "Carved in alabaster. She represents the strength, courage, the wisdom, the compassion that is uniquely female."

"She's terrific." Holding it up, Eve watched the light streaming through the windows shimmer on the carved figure. "She looks old, in a good way," she added quickly and made Phoebe laugh again.

"Yes, she is old, in a good way. She was my great-great grandmother's. It's been passed down, from female to female until it came to me. And now you."

"She's beautiful. Really. But I can't take her. This is something you need to keep in your family."

Phoebe reached over, laid a hand over Eve's so that they both held the statue. "I am keeping it in my family."

Her office at Central was too small for a meeting where more than two people were involved. Her call in to book a conference room resulted in a short, bitter argument and no satisfaction.

With her options narrowed, she realigned and scheduled the briefing in her home office.

"Problem, Lieutenant?" Roarke asked as he stepped from his office into hers.

"No conference rooms available until fourteen hundred? That's just bullshit."

"So I heard you say, rather viciously, into the 'link. I've a meeting myself in midtown." He crossed to her, skimmed his fingertip along the shallow dent in her chin. "Anything I can do for you before I leave?"

"I'm set."

He laid his lips on hers, lingered over them. "I shouldn't be late." He stepped back, then spotted the statue on her desk. "What's this?"

"Phoebe gave it to me."

"Alabaster," he said as he lifted it. "She's lovely. A goddess of some sort. She suits you."

"Yeah, that's me. Goddess cop." She stared at the cool, serene face of the statue, remembered being trapped in the cool, serene face of Phoebe Peabody. "She had me saying stuff. I think it's the eyes. If you want to keep your thoughts to yourself, never look directly into her eyes."

He laughed and set the statue down again. "I imagine a number of people say exactly the same thing about you."

She'd have given that some thought, but she had work to do. She called up files, slotted data on various screens, then dived back into Julianna Dunne.

She was well into a second page of fresh notes when Peabody and McNab came in. "Raid the AutoChef now," she ordered without looking up. "I want you settled when Feeney gets here."

"You got a new lead?" Peabody asked.

"I'll brief everyone at one time. I need more coffee here."

"Yes, sir." As Peabody reached for Eve's empty cup, she saw the statue. "She gave you the goddess."

She looked up now, and to her terror, saw tears swim into Peabody's eyes. McNab must have seen them, too. He muttered, "Girl thing," and hightailed it into the adjoining kitchen.

"Listen, Peabody, about that—"

"And you put it on your desk."

"Yeah, well . . . I figure this is supposed to come to you, so—"

"No, sir." Her voice was thick as she lifted those drenched eyes to Eve's. And smiled. "She gave it to you, and that means she trusts you. She accepts. You're family. And you put it there, right there on your desk, and that means you accept. It's a real moment for me," she added and dug out a handkerchief. "I love you, Dallas."

"Oh jeez. If you try to kiss me, I'll deck you."

Peabody gave a watery laugh and blew her nose. "I wasn't sure you'd be speaking to me this morning. Dad called and said how they were staying here."

"Your mother put the whammy on Roarke. That takes some doing."

"Yeah, I had to figure. You're not pissed off?"

"Sam made croissants this morning. Your mother brought me one, with coffee."

The grin lit Peabody's face. "So it's okay then."

"Apparently." Eve picked up her cup, pursed her lips as she looked inside. "But it seems I don't have coffee at the moment. How could that be?"

"I'll correct that oversight immediately, Lieutenant." Peabody snatched the cup, then hesitated. "Um, Dallas? Blessings on you."

"What?"

"Sorry, I can't help it. Free-Ager training. It's just . . . Thanks. That's all. Thanks."

Chapter 5

"Julianna Dunne." Feeney gulped coffee, shook his head. He had the lived-in face of a basset hound, the droopy eyes of a camel. His coarse ginger-colored hair, wired through with silver, looked as if it had been hacked at by some maniac with hedge sheers. Which meant it had recently been trimmed.

He sat in Eve's office, his rather stubby legs stretched out. Since he was wearing one brown sock and one black, Eve concluded his wife hadn't managed to give him the once-over that morning.

A fashion plate he wasn't. But when it came to electronics, he ruled.

"Never expected to get another shot at that one."

"We've got no prints or DNA at either the crime scene or the apartment leased to Julie Dockport to verify. But the visual—" She gestured to the split screen ID photos— "gives me an eyeball verification. I ran a probability for form, and got a ninety-nine percent that Julie Dockport and Julianna Dunne are the same woman."

"If she just got out of a cage the first part of the year," McNab commented, "she works fast."

"She works," Eve said. "She's thirty-four. By the time she was twenty-five, she'd married three men, killed three men. That we know of. On the surface, it was for profit. She targeted wealthy guys—older, established men. Each of them had been married previously and divorced. Her shortest relationship was seven months, her longest, thirteen. Again, in each case she received a large inheritance at the spouse's demise."

"Nice work if you can get it," Peabody put in.

"She targeted each man, researched him, his background, his likes, dislikes, habits, and so on. Meticulously. We know this as we were able to locate a bank box in Chicago that contained her notes, photographs, and data on husband number two, Paul O'Hara. That's one of the bricks we used to close her up. We were never able to find similar boxes in New York or East Washington."

"Could she have had a partner?" Peabody asked. "Somebody who removed or destroyed evidence?"

"Unlikely. As far as any of the investigators were able to ascertain, she worked alone. Her psych profile corroborated that. Her basic pathology was pretty straightforward. Her mother divorced her father when Julianna was fifteen. Her step-father was also divorced, wealthy, older, a Texas yeehaw type who called the shots at home. She claimed he sexually molested her. The police psychiatrist was unable to determine whether or not Julianna's sexual relationship—which he did not deny—with her step-father was consensual or forced, though she leaned toward believing Julianna. In any case, as she was a minor it was abuse."

"And the main weight that kept her time down," Feeney added.

"So she's killing her step-father." Peabody glanced

back at the wall screen. "Again and again."

"Maybe."

And staring at the screen, Eve could see the child she herself had been, cowering in the corner of a cold, filthy room, mad from the pain of the last beating, the last rape. Covered in blood—his blood—with the knife she'd used to kill her father still slick and dripping in her eight-year-old hand.

Her stomach pitched, and she forced the image away.

"I never bought it." Eve kept her voice quiet, waiting for control to snap completely back into place. "She did the killing with calculation. Where was the rage, the terror, the despair? Whatever happened with her step-father, she used it. She's a stone cold killer. She was born that way, not made."

"I gotta go with Dallas on this one," Feeney agreed. "This one has ice for blood, and she's nobody's victim. She hunts."

"The APB hasn't turned up anything yet," Eve went on. "I don't figure it will. She'd have planned carefully, would already have a new name, new personality, new story. She won't change her looks much. She's too vain, and she likes the way she looks. She's girly. Likes clothes, hair, baubles, salons. She'll stick to better shops and restaurants. You won't find her at bargain basements, or in sex clubs or bars. She prefers major cities, on planet. We'll flash her picture on the media, and we could get lucky."

It would take some luck added to the cop work, Eve thought. Julianna made few mistakes. "Our problem is she blends. She's very skilled at it. People who notice her see an attractive woman, going about her business. If she makes friends, they're only temporary tools. No one gets close to her."

"If she's gone pro, you can bet your ass she'll be good

at it." Feeney puffed out his cheeks. "She could be any-fucking-where by now, Dallas."

"So we start looking. Every-fucking-where. You remember the primary in Chicago?"

"Yeah. Yeah, ah . . . Spindler."

"Right. And Block in East Washington. Can you contact them? See how far they'll reach out."

"Yeah. I've got some personal notes on her, too. I'll dig them out, add them to the mix."

"Profiler who did the work and the testing on Julianna's retired. I'm going to pass this onto Mira, ask her to consult with the profiler on record. McNab, right now you're a drone. I want you to take all data from all cases, index, cross-reference any and all similarities. Make me files. Family connections, known associates, financials. I want you to tag the prisoner liaison at Dockport and get the names of the inmates she worked with, the ones on her block. I want to know the people inside she spent any time with. I'm going to see what I can shake out of the first Mrs. Pettibone.

"Peabody, you're with me."

Eve got behind the wheel, and as Shelly Pettibone lived in Westchester, hit the in-dash map for the best route and directions. It was a pleasant surprise when the route actually popped onto the screen.

"Look at that! It worked."

"Technology is our friend, Lieutenant."

"Sure, when it's not screwing with us for its own sick enjoyment. This is only a couple miles from Commander Whitney's place. With my luck Mrs. Pettibone's the commander's wife's best pal."

Brooding over the possibility, she headed down the drive.

"Dad said he and Mom were going to head downtown today. Take in the Village and SoHo and stuff."

"Hmm? Oh yeah. Good."

"I'm going to take them out for dinner tonight, so they won't be in your hair."

"Uh-huh."

"Then I'm taking them to a sex joint, and me and McNab are going to perform various exotic sexual acts for them."

"Sounds good."

"I thought if you and Roarke wanted to come along, we could make it a nice little orgy. You know, a quartet."

"You think I don't hear you, but you're wrong." Eve squeezed into traffic.

"Oh. Oops."

Eve nipped through a light on yellow, snarled at the maxibus that lumbered into her lane. With a wrench of the wheel, she punched through a narrow break, slapped the accelerator, wrenched back, and cut the bus off as neatly as it had her.

The irritable blast of its horn brought her a nice little glow.

"So I guess between your parents and the fresh case, you haven't had much time to work on Stibbs."

"I did some. Maureen Stibbs, formerly Brighton, not only lived in the same building as the deceased, but on the same floor. As he does now, Boyd Stibbs often worked from home, while his first wife traveled to her place of employment during the work week. The former Ms. Brighton, while employed as a home design consultant, also worked out of her home office when not traveling to and from clients. This gives the currently married couple time and opportunity for hanky-panky."

"Hanky-panky. Is that a legal term?"

"Boyd Stibbs married Maureen Brighton two and a half years after Marsha Stibbs's tragic death. I figure that's a pretty long time if they were canoodling—"

"Another legal term. Peabody, I'm so impressed."

"—while Marsha was alive," Peabody continued. "But it would also be pretty smart. Still, if they were doing the horizontal rumba, that's a medical term, and wanted to make it a permanent deal, divorce was the easiest option. It's not like Marsha had a bunch of money Boyd would lose out on if he ditched her. I can't figure any motive for premeditation."

"And you're looking for premeditation because?"

"The letters. If we say that all the statements from friends, relatives, people she worked with, even her husband and her replacement are valid, we work the angle that there never was a lover. So somebody had to plant the letters. Somebody had to write them, and put them in her drawer. After the murder."

"Why after?"

"Because a woman knows what's in her underwear drawer. She goes into it for a pair of panties, she's going to find the letters." Peabody paused. "Is this like a test?"

"Just keep going. Play it out for me."

"Okay, somebody with access to her apartment, somebody who was there the night she died, put the letters in her drawer. And it seems to me that the choice of drawer is female. A guy isn't as likely to pick the lingerie department to hide something. We don't know when the letters were written because there were no envelopes, no date stamps. They all could've been written the night she was killed. And if they were, that might rule out premeditation and move into covering up an impulse. Crime of passion."

"So the theory is person or persons unknown killed Marsha Stibbs on impulse, then put her into the bathtub hoping to cover up murder as an accident. Concerned perhaps that wasn't enough, this person or persons then wrote letters from some nonexistent lover, planted them in the victim's underwear drawer so that it might then appear she was killed by said nonexistent lover during an argument."

"Okay, it sounds a little out-there."

"Then bring it in."

"I'm just nervous, because this really feels like a test." Peabody cleared her throat when Eve merely sent her a stony stare. "Some of the rest of the theory is just instinct. You look at the way the two of them reacted to us. Boyd seemed sad, a little shaky initially, but was glad we were there. It could've been an act, but with no time to prepare, it just feels real as does his insistence that Marsha didn't have a lover."

She paused, waiting for Eve's affirmation or rebuttal, and got nothing but silence. "Okay, on my own. His alibi's solid, and even if he knew or arranged the killing, it seems to me he'd have been nervous or annoyed that we'd walked into his nice new life and opened the possibility of exposing him. On the other hand, when she comes in, she's scared, she's angry, and she wants us out. Away from her nice new life with her dead pal's husband. Maybe that's a normal reaction, but it could just as easily be guilt and fear of exposure."

"Guilt because she was—what was it?—*canoodling* with said dead pal's husband *before* said pal was dead?"

"Maybe, but what if she wasn't?" Anxious, and just a little excited, Peabody shifted in her seat so she could see Eve's profile. "What if she just wanted to? What if she was in love with him, and here he is, just across the hall, day after day, happily married, seeing her as a friend of his wife's. She wants him for herself, but he's never going to look at her that way as long as Marsha's in the picture. It's Marsha's fault he doesn't love her. Marsha's fault she's not living that dream—nice home, great husband, maybe a couple of pretty kids down the line. Pisses her off, makes her unhappy. She's always got to be acting like the friend and neighbor and she just can't get the fantasy of what it could be like out of her head."

"What does she do?"

"She has a showdown with Marsha. Boyd's out of town, now's the time. She blasts Marsha for going off to work every day instead of staying home and taking care of her man. She doesn't deserve Boyd. If she was his wife, she'd be there to fix the meals, buy the groceries. She'd give him a child. She'd give him a *family*. They fight about it."

She wanted to see it, as she knew Eve could see such things. But the imagery was still indistinct. "Marsha probably tells her to get the hell out. To stay away from her husband. I bet she said she was going to tell Boyd everything. That neither of them would have anything to do with her again. That's too much for Maureen. She shoves Marsha, and Marsha falls, cracks her head. File said it was a fall against the corner of a reinforced glass table that killed her. She panics, tries to cover it up. Strips Marsha down, puts her in the bathtub. Maybe they'll think she slipped, hit her head on the tub and drowned.

"But then she starts to think again, and realizes that maybe they won't think it's an accident. More, this is an opportunity. Like a gift. She didn't mean to kill her, but it was done. She couldn't take it back. If Boyd and the police think Marsha'd had a lover on the side, it would solve everything. They'd go off looking for him as a suspect. Why should they ever look at her? So she writes the letters, plants them, then she goes home and waits for it to play out. I bet, after a while, she started to believe it really did happen the way she'd made it seem. It was the only way she could live with it, the only way she could sleep beside him night after night and not go crazy."

She blew out a breath, swallowed hard because her throat was dry. "That's the theory I'm working. Are you going to tell me it blows?"

"How'd you come to it?"

"I kept looking at the reports, the data, the photographs. I read the statements until my eyes hurt. Then I was lying in bed last night with all that running around inside my head. So I put it all like in this corner of my brain, and used the rest of it to try to think like you. Or how I thought you'd think. You know, how you walk onto a crime scene and you start visualizing, sort of like you're watching it all happen. And that was the way I watched it all happen. A little murky, but that's how I saw it."

She started to take another deep breath, then blinked. "You're smiling."

"You're going to want to get to her when he's not around. You'll want to question her when she's alone. With him and the kid, she's got defenses built up. She can tell herself she's protecting them. Get her into Interview. Make it formal. She won't want to, but the uniform will intimidate her into it. It's not likely she'll yell lawyer straight off, because she'll worry it'll make her look guilty. Let me know when you're ready to set it up, and I'll try to observe."

Peabody felt her heart beating again. "You think I'm right? You think she did it?"

"Oh yeah, she did it."

"You knew it. The minute she walked into the apartment, you knew."

"Doesn't matter what I knew or what I know. It's your case, so what matters is what you know and getting her to tell you."

"If you did the interview—"

"I'm not doing the interview, you are. Your case. Work out your approach, your tone, then bring her in and break her down."

Eve pulled into a driveway, and Peabody looked

around blankly. Somehow they'd gotten from city to suburb.

"Now put it away," Eve ordered. "Pettibone's front and center now."

She sat a moment, studying the rosy redbrick house. It was modest enough, even simple until you added the gardens. Floods, rivers, pools of flowers flowed out from the base of the house, streaming all the way to the sidewalk. There was no lawn to speak of, though there were tall clumps of some sort of ornamental grasses creatively worked in to the sea of color.

A stone walkway ribboned its way through to the base of a covered porch where flowering vines, thick with deep purple blooms, wound their way up round posts.

There were chairs with white cushions on the porch, glass-topped tables, and yet more flowers in pots that had artistically faded to verdigris. Obviously Shelly Pettibone liked to sit and contemplate her flowers.

Even as Eve thought it, a woman stepped out of the front door carrying a tray.

She was deeply tanned, her arms long and leanly muscled against the short sleeves of a baggy blue T-shirt. Her jeans were worn and cropped off at midcalf.

She set down the tray, watched Eve get out of the car. The mild breeze stirred her sun-streaked brown hair worn short and unstyled around the weathered, appealing face of a woman who lived a great deal of her life outdoors.

As Eve drew closer, she saw that the woman's eyes were brown and showed the ravages of weeping.

"Is there something I can do for you?"

"Mrs. Pettibone? Shelly Pettibone?"

"Yes." Her gaze shifted to Peabody. "This is about Walter."

"I'm Lieutenant Dallas." Eve offered her badge. "My aide, Officer Peabody. I'm sorry to disturb you at this difficult time."

"You need to ask me questions. I just got off the 'link with my daughter. I don't seem to be able to do anything to help her. I can't think of the right words. I don't think there are any. I'm sorry, sit down please. I was going to have some coffee. I'll just get more cups."

"You needn't bother."

"It gives me something to do, and just now I don't have nearly enough to do. I'll just be a minute. It's all right if we talk out here, isn't it? I'd like to be outside for a while."

"Sure, this is fine."

She went back in, left the door open.

"A guy dumps you for a younger model after thirty years or so," Eve began. "How do you feel about it when it kicks off?"

"Hard to say. I can't imagine living with anyone for three years much less thirty. You're the married one here. How would you feel?"

Eve opened her mouth to make some withering comment, then stopped. She'd hurt, she realized. She'd grieve. Whatever he'd done, she'd suffer for the loss.

Instead of answering, she stepped over, glanced in the door. "Nice place, if you go for this sort of thing."

"I've never seen anything like this yard. It's seriously mag, and it must take a ton of work. It looks natural, but it's really well-planned. She's got it all planted for maximum effect—seasonally, fragrance-wise, colors, and textures. I smell sweet peas." She took a deeper sniff of the air. "My grandmother always has sweet peas outside the bedroom window."

"Do you enjoy flowers, Officer?" Shelly stepped back out, cups in hands.

"Yes, ma'am. Your garden's beautiful."

"Thank you. It's what I do. Landscape design. I was studying horticulture and design when I met Walter. A million years ago," she said softly. "I can't quite believe he's gone. I can't believe I'll never see him again."

"Did you see him often?" Eve asked.

"Oh, every week or two. We weren't married any longer, but we had a great deal in common." She poured coffee with hands that wore no rings. "He'd often recommend me to clients, as I would him. Flowers were one of the bonds between us."

"Yet you were divorced, and he remarried."

"Yes. And yes, he was the one who wanted to end the marriage." She folded her legs under her, lifted her cup. "I was content, and contentment was enough for me. Walter needed more. He needed to be happy, to be excited and involved. We'd lost some essential spark along the way. With the kids grown and away from home, with it being back to the two of us . . . Well, we couldn't revive that spark. He needed it more than I did. Though it was difficult for him, he told me he wanted a change."

"You must have been angry."

"I was. Angry and hurt and baffled. No one likes to be discarded, even gently. And he was gentle. There isn't, wasn't a mean bone in his body."

Her eyes welled again, but she blinked the tears back, took a deep sip of coffee. "If I had insisted, if I had pushed him back into the corner our marriage had become for him, he would have stayed."

"But you didn't."

"I loved him." She smiled when she said it, heartbreakingly. "Was it his fault, my fault, that our love for each other had mellowed into something too comfortable, too bland to be interesting any longer? I won't say it wasn't hard to let him go, to face life on my own. We'd been married more than half my life. But to keep him with me out of obligation? I've too much pride for that, and too much respect for both of us."

"How did you feel when he married a woman younger than your daughter?"

"Amused." The first glint of humor crept over Shelly's face, and made it pretty and mischievous. "I know it's petty, it's small, but I think I was entitled to a moment or two of amusement. How could I be otherwise? She's a bit of foolish fluff, and frankly, I don't think they'd have stayed together. He was dazzled with her, and proud the way men are when they're able to hang something stupendously decorative on their arm."

"A lot of women would've felt embarrassed, angry."

"Yes, and how foolish is that to measure yourself against a silly ornament? My reaction was the opposite. In fact, his relationship with her went a long way to helping me resolve what had happened between us. If his happiness, even temporarily, depended on a beautiful set of breasts and a giggling young girl, well, he wasn't going to get that from me, was he?"

She sighed, set her cup down. "She did make him happy, and in her way loved him. You couldn't help but love Walt."

"So I've heard. Someone didn't love him, Mrs. Pettibone."

"I've thought about it." All humor fell away from her face. "Thought and thought. It makes no sense, Lieutenant. None at all. Bambi? God, what a name. She's foolish and flighty, but she's not evil. It takes evil to kill, doesn't it?"

"Sometimes it just takes a reason."

"If I thought, for one instant, that she had done this, I'd do everything I could to help you prove it. To see her pay for it. But, oh God, she's a harmless idiot who, if she manages to have two thoughts at once must hear them rattling together in that empty head of hers."

She couldn't, Eve thought, have said it better herself.

"And what reason could she have to do this?" Shelly demanded. "She had everything she could want. He was incredibly generous with her."

"He was a very rich man."

"Yes, and not one to horde his wealth. The divorce settlement was more than fair. I'd never have to work again if I didn't love my work. I know—because he told me—that he'd gifted Bambi with a substantial trust when they married. Our children were generously provided for and each has a large share of World of Flowers. The inheritance each of us, and yes, I'm also a beneficiary, will receive upon his death is considerable. But we *have* considerable already."

"What about business associates? Competitors?"

"I don't know anyone who'd wish Walt harm. As for business, killing him won't effect WOF. The company's well-established, well-organized, with both our children taking on more and more of the administration. Killing him makes no sense."

It had made sense to Julianna, Eve mused. The woman did nothing unless it made sense. "Since you've maintained a good relationship, why didn't you attend his party?"

"It just seemed awkward. He urged me to come, though not very hard. It was supposed to be a surprise, but of course he knew about it weeks ago. He was very excited. He always was like a little boy when it came to parties."

Eve reached into her bag, drew out Julianna Dunne's two photographs. "Do you know this woman?"

Shelly took both, held them side-by-side. "She's very pretty, in both looks. But, no, I've never seen her before. Who is she?"

"What were you doing the night of your husband's party?"

She drew a small breath, as if she'd known this was a blow she'd have to face. "I don't really have what you'd call an alibi as I was alone. I did work out in the garden until almost sunset, and one of the neighbors might have seen me. I stayed home that night. Friends had asked me to dinner at the club, The Westchester Country Club, but I didn't feel like going out. You might know them. Jack and Anna Whitney. He's a police commander in the city."

Eve felt her stomach sink. "Yes. I know the commander and his wife."

"Anna's been trying to fix me up since the divorce. She just can't understand how I can be happy without a man."

"And are you? Did you wonder that if your husband's relationship with his current wife failed, as you felt it would, he'd come back to you?"

"Yes. I thought of that, considered that. And the fact is I don't think he would have come back."

A butterfly, creamy white, flitted across the porch and fluttered down to flirt with the potted flowers. Watching it, Shelly sighed.

"And I know I wouldn't have had him if he did," she added. "I loved him, Lieutenant, and he'll always be a vital part of my life. Even now that's he's gone. This is a man I lived with, slept with, had and raised children with. We share a grandson we both adore. Memories no one else has, and those are precious. But we weren't in love with each other anymore. And I've come to like the life I'm making on my own. I enjoy the challenge, and the independence of it. And while that baffles Anna and some of my other friends, I'm not ready to give that independence up. I don't know that I ever will be. Walter was a good man, a very, very good man. But he wasn't my man anymore."

She handed the photographs back to Eve. "You didn't tell me who she was."

She would hear it, Eve thought, either through the media or her connection with Anna Whitney. "She's the woman who gave Walter Pettibone poisoned champagne. And our prime suspect."

"I liked her," Peabody said as they drove back to the city.

"So did I."

"I can't see her hiring a hit. She's too direct, and I don't know, sensible. And if the motive was payback for the divorce, why not target Bambi, too? Why should the replacement get to play grieving widow and roll around in an inheritance?"

Since Eve had come to the same conclusions herself, she nodded. "I'll see if Whitney can give me any different angle on the divorce and her attitude toward Pettibone. But at this point we bump her down the list."

"What's the next step?"

"If Julianna was a hired hitter, she'd be costly. We'll start on financials, see if anybody spent some serious money recently."

Julianna wasn't concerned about money. Her husbands, God rest them, had been very generous with the commodity. Long before she'd killed them, she'd opened secure, numbered accounts under various names in several discreet financial institutions.

She'd invested well, and even during her hideous time in prison, her money had made money for her.

She could have lived a long and indulgent life anywhere in the world or its satellites. But that life would never have been complete unless she could take the lives of others.

She really enjoyed killing. It was such interesting work.

The one benefit of incarceration had been the time, endless time, for her to consider how to continue that work once she was free again.

She didn't hate men. She abhorred them. Their minds, their bodies, their sweaty, groping hands. Most of all, she detested their simplicity. With men, it all came down to sex. However they dressed it up—romanticized, justified, dignified it—a man's primary goal was to stuff his cock inside you.

And they were too stupid to know that once they did, they gave you all the power.

She had no sympathy for women who claimed they'd been abused or raped or molested. If a woman was too stupid, too weak, to know how to seize a man's power and use it against him, she deserved whatever she got.

Julianna had never been stupid. And she'd learned quickly. Her mother had been nothing but a fool who'd been tossed away by one man and gone scrambling for another. And always at their beck and call, always biddable and malleable.

She'd never learned. Not even when Julianna had seduced her idiot second husband, had lured him to bed, and let him do all the disgusting things men lived to do to her fresh and supple fifteen-year-old body.

It had been so easy to make him want her, to draw him in so that he would sneak out of his wife's bed and into his wife's daughter. Panting for her like an eager puppy.

It had been so easy to use it against him. All she'd had to do was dangle sex, and he'd given her whatever she'd wanted. All she'd had to do was threaten exposure, and he'd given her more.

She'd walked away from that house at eighteen, with a great deal of money and without a backward glance. She'd never forget her mother's face when she'd told her just what had gone on under her nose for three long years.

It had been so viciously satisfying to see the shock,

the horror, the grief. To see the weight of it all crash down and crush.

Naturally, she'd said she'd been raped, forced, threatened. It always paid to protect yourself.

Maybe her mother had believed it, and maybe she hadn't. It didn't matter. What mattered was that in that moment Julianna had realized she had the power to destroy.

And it had made her.

Now, years later, she stood in the bedroom of the townhouse off Madison Avenue she'd purchased more than two years before. Under yet another name. Studying herself in the mirror, she decided she liked herself as a brunette. It was a sultry look, particularly with the gold dust tone she'd chosen for her skin.

She lit an herbal cigarette, turned sideways in the mirror. Ran a hand over her flat belly. She'd taken advantage of the health facilities in prison, had kept herself in shape.

In fact, she believed she was in better shape than she'd been before she'd gone in. Firmer, fitter, stronger. Perhaps she'd join a health club here, an exclusive one. It was an excellent way to meet men.

When she heard her name, she glanced toward the entertainment screen and the latest bulletin. Delighted, she watched her face, both as herself and as Julie Dockport flash on. Admittedly, she hadn't expected the police to identify her quite so quickly. Not that it worried her; not in the least.

No, they didn't worry her. They—or one of them— challenged her.

Detective Eve Dallas, now Lieutenant.

She'd come back for Dallas. To wage war.

There had been something about Eve Dallas, she thought now, something cold, something dark that had spoken to her.

Kindred spirits, she mused, and as the idea intrigued

her she'd found herself spending endless hours of her time in prison, studying that particular opponent.

She had time still. The police would be chasing their tails searching for a connection between her and Walter Pettibone. They'd find none because there was none to find.

That was the tone of her work now, other women's husbands. She didn't have to have sex with them. She just got to kill them.

Strolling out of the room, she walked toward her office to spend the next hour or two studying her research notes on her next victim.

She might have taken a forced sabbatical, but Julianna was back. And raring to go.

Chapter 6

Because stalling made her feel weak and stupid, Eve only managed to put off the trip to Commander Whitney's office until the middle of the day.

The only satisfaction in heading up was being able to ignore Channel 75's ace on-air reporter, Nadine Furst, as she requested an interview regarding the Pettibone-Dunne story.

That was something else she'd have to shuffle in, she thought as she caught a glide out of Homicide. Nadine's investigative skills were as sharp and savvy as her wardrobe. She'd be a handy tool.

As she was shown directly into Whitney's office without even a momentary wait, Eve had to figure he'd been expecting her.

He sat at his desk, a big-shouldered man with a worn, wide face. He had good, clear eyes, and she had reason to know his time off the streets hadn't softened him.

He sat back, giving her a little come-ahead signal with one finger. "Lieutenant. You've been busy."

"Sir?"

"You made a trip out to my neighborhood this morning, paid a visit to Shelly Pettibone." He folded those big hands, and his face was unreadable. "I just got an earful from my wife."

"Commander, it's standard procedure to question any and all connections to the victim."

"I don't believe I said otherwise." His voice was deep, rumbling, and as unreadable as his face. "What was your impression of Shelly Pettibone?"

"That she's a sensible, steady, and straightforward woman."

"I'd have to say that's a perfect description, and I've known her about fifteen years. Do you have any reason to believe she had anything to do with her husband's death?"

"No, sir. There's no evidence leading me in that direction."

He nodded. "I'm glad to hear it. Lieutenant, are you afraid of my wife?"

"Yes, sir," Eve said without hesitation. "I am."

His lips trembled for an instant in what might have been a smothered smile. Then he nodded again. "You're in good company. Anna is a very strong-willed woman with very definite and particular opinions. I'm going to do what I can to keep her off your back on this, and as Shelly isn't on your short list, that seems very doable. But if it comes down to you or me, you're on your own."

"Understood."

"Just so we know where we stand. Let me give you some basic background here." He gestured to a chair. "My family has been very friendly with the Pettibones for a number of years. In fact, one of my sons dated Sherilyn when they were teenagers. It was a bitter disappointment to my wife that the relationship didn't end in marriage, but she got over it."

There was a framed holograph of his wife on his desk. In a subtle move, Whitney tapped it until it faced toward the wall instead of toward him. "Anna and Shelly are very good friends, and I believe Anna took it harder than Shelly did when Walter left. In fact, Anna refused to see or speak to Walt, which is why we, and our children were not at the party. We were invited, but one doesn't butt heads with Anna over social issues."

"I don't think less of you for it, Commander."

His brows arched and for another instant there was a flash of humor in his eyes. "Anna is bound and determined that Shelly marry again, or at the very least develop a serious romantic interest. Shelly hasn't cooperated. She is, as you said, sensible and steady. She's made a comfortable life for herself and maintained, to Anna's bafflement, a cordial relationship with Walt. As for Walt himself, I was fond of him."

The humor died away. "Very fond of him. He wasn't a man to make enemies. Even Anna couldn't dislike him. His children adored him, and as I know them nearly as well as I know my own, I'll say that though you'll have to follow through on them investigatively, you'll find they had no part in his murder."

"I've found no evidence nor motive that leads in their direction, Commander. Nor toward their spouses."

"But you have found Julianna Dunne."

"Yes, sir."

He pushed away from his desk, rose. "There are times, Dallas, the system fails. It failed by not keeping that individual in a cage. Now a good man is dead because the system failed."

"No system is foolproof, but knowing that doesn't make it easier when you lose a friend."

He acknowledged this offer of condolence with a nod. "Why did she kill him?"

Because he stood, Eve rose. "Her pattern had been to

target a man of some wealth and prestige, develop a relationship with him that led to marriage, legally attaching
herself in order to gain all or a portion of that wealth
upon his death. In the three cases we know of, the target
was no less than twenty-five years her senior, and she
became his second wife. While Pettibone fits the general
type of her favored target, no evidence has come to light
that he knew her personally. She was not a legal heir to
his estate, and therefore couldn't profit from his death by
her usual means."

Eve took the discs of her reports out of her pocket,
set them on his desk. "The most logical motive remains
financial gain. I'm pursuing the possibility Dunne was
hired out. We've made a first-level pass on the financials
of the family and closest business associates. I've found
nothing to indicate any large withdrawals, or consistent
smaller ones that would meet the fee for a professional
hit. I need to go deeper, and have requested authorization
for a second level."

"She'd be good at it," Whitney commented.

"Yes, sir, she would."

"Her pattern's also been to move, to re-establish herself in another location after she has the money in hand."

"She's already broken pattern. But if she's left New
York, it would be for another major city. And one, in my
opinion, she's familiar with. She's still getting her legs
under her, and would prefer the familiar. I've asked Feeney to keep in touch with the police in Chicago and East
Washington. I've also asked Dr. Mira to consult. I want
her to study the reports and testing results on Dunne."

"You don't intend to tag the original profiler?"

"No, sir. In my opinion the previous profiler and
shrink were too soft on her, and I'd prefer Mira's take.
Dunne knows how to play people. Also, her mother and
step-father are still alive. She may attempt contact there
at some point. In addition, McNab has compiled a list of

people she may have formed a relationship with while in Dockport. I think a trip there might provide some insight."

"When do you plan to leave?"

"I'd hoped to go tomorrow, sir. I thought to request that Feeney come with me in this case. We both dealt personally with Dunne, and while Peabody could use the experience, her plate's full. Her parents are in town, and I recently gave her a cold case to investigate."

His brow furrowed. "A homicide? Is she ready for that?"

"Yes, sir, she's ready. She's on the right track, and I believe she can close it."

"Keep me apprised on all counts. I'll be out of the office most of tomorrow afternoon. Saying good-bye to a friend."

It felt strange to be able to clock off at end of shift and head home on time. It was stranger still to walk in the front door and not have Summerset lurking in the foyer ready with some pithy remark or observation. She actually found herself standing there for a minute or two, waiting for him, before she caught herself.

Oddly embarrassed, she started upstairs, almost certain he'd be there, sort of lying in wait. But she made it all the way to the bedroom without a sign of him. Or the cat.

It didn't, she realized, feel quite like home.

Until she heard the shower running, and voices murmuring from the adjoining bath. She stepped in and saw Roarke's long, lanky form through the wavy glass of the shower wall.

It was enough to make a woman want to lick her lips.

The voices came from a screen recessed in the shower tiles, and seemed to be some sort of financial report. The man's mind was full of numbers half the time, she thought, and decided to shift it to another occupation.

She stripped where she stood, moved quietly into the criss-crossing sprays behind him, slid her hands around his waist. And down.

His body braced, a quick ripple of muscle and animal instinct.

"Darling." His voice purred out. "My wife could come home any minute."

"Screw her."

He laughed. "Happy to," he said, and turning had her pressed against the wet tiles.

"Raise water temp to one-oh-one degrees."

"Too hot," he muttered against her mouth as the spray heated, steamed.

"I want it hot." In a quick move, she reversed their positions, clamped her teeth over his jaw. "I want you hot."

She was already wet, and she was randy. Her hands and mouth busy on him, taking him over in a kind of cheerful aggression. He no longer heard the brisk, clipped voice on-screen that detailed the latest stock reports, the market projections. Only the hiss of spray and the beat of his own blood.

He could want her, every minute of every day. Was certain he would go on wanting her after he was dead and gone. She was the pulse, the reason, the breath.

When he caught her dripping hair in his hand, yanked her head up so his mouth could fuse to hers, it was like feeding a hunger that was never, ever quite sated.

She felt it from him, the edge of that violent appetite he so often masked in elegance and style and patience. When she tasted it, it made her crave the primitive, made her lust for the danger of letting the animal inside them both spring loose to feed.

With him she could be tender, where there had never

been tenderness. And with him she could be brutal, without fear.

"Now. Now, now, *now*! Inside me."

He gripped her hips, fingers sliding over slick, wet skin until they dug in. Her breath caught when he shoved her back against the tiles, then released on a cry when he rammed himself into her.

Her body plunged through the first vicious orgasm, then raced for more.

Her eyes locked with his. She could see herself there, swimming in, drowning in that vivid blue. Trusting his strength, she wrapped her legs around his waist to take more of him.

Steam billowed, thin mists. Water streamed, hot rain. He drove himself hard and deep, watching, always watching that shocked pleasure radiate over her face. He could see her rising to peak again, the way her eyes blurred, the gilded brown of them deepening an instant before they went blind, an instant before her body gathered, then shuddered.

She clamped around him, a hot, wet fist, and nearly dragged him over with her.

"Take more." His voice was ragged, his lungs burning. "Take more, and more, until you come screaming for me."

She could hear the sharp, rhythmic slap of flesh against flesh, of flesh against tile, and could taste when his mouth crushed down on hers again the outrageous need in him. And as he thrust into her, as pleasure and pain and madness merged into one searing mass inside her, she heard herself scream.

Limp as rags, still tangled together, they slid down to the floor of the shower.

"Christ Jesus," he managed.

"Let's just stay here for an hour or two. We probably

won't drown." Her head dropped onto his shoulder like a stone.

"We might, as I think we're lying on the drains." But he made no effort to move.

She turned her head so the spray beat down on her face. "But it feels good."

He cupped her breast. "God knows."

"Where the hell is everybody?"

"I think we're right here." Her nipples were still hard, still hot, and inspired him to roll over enough to taste.

She blinked water out of her eyes. "You've got to be kidding."

"I don't believe I will be if you give me a few minutes here. Less if the water wasn't so bloody hot."

"Turn the temp down and face my wrath." She put her hands on either side of his face, lifted his head. Grinned. "We'd better get the hell out of here. The water level's rising."

Once they managed to pull themselves up, she headed for the drying tube. Roarke grabbed a towel.

"Really, where is everybody?"

"Last I checked, Phoebe was having a fine time playing in the greenhouse. Sam and Summerset had their heads together in the kitchen over some recipe. They've bonded like glue over herbs and sauces and whatever. I'm told they're going out with Peabody for the evening, so you don't have to worry about entertaining them."

She stepped out of the tube, took the robe he offered, then watched him hook a towel loosely at his hips. "Feeney and I are flying to Chicago tomorrow, taking a shot at Dockport. And no," she said before he could speak, "we're not taking one of your fancy transpos. We'll use the shuttle, like regular people."

"Up to you. Any new leads?"

"Nothing that's firming up for us yet." She followed him into the bedroom, hunted up a pair of jeans. "Found out that Pettibone's first wife and the commander's wife are tight. Makes it a little tricky, even though she's not high on my list. I've got to do a second-level search on the financials of the main players."

He glanced up as he hooked fresh trousers, met her scowl. "I didn't say a thing."

"I can hear you thinking, pal, and no. I've got authorization for second level, and that's as deep as I'm going right now. I don't need you using your unregistered equipment or dipping any deeper. We're moving along well enough playing this by the book."

"Do you ever ask yourself who wrote that book?"

"The long arm of the law. If you've got any free time, I wouldn't mind your take on the financials. You see numbers differently than I do."

"Lieutenant, I always have time for you."

He gave her two hours, even settled for eating pizza in her office as they studied the financial affairs of Pettibone's family and the top execs and accounts in his business. Deposits, withdrawals, transfers, bills, and bonuses.

"Nothing sends up any flags for me," Roarke said at length. "You've got a couple of business associates who could use better advice on their portfolios, and that account in Tribeca should be doing a bit more per annum, so I wouldn't be surprised if a bit is going in someone's pocket here and there. Nothing major, but if it were mine, we'd be plugging the holes."

"How much do you think is being skimmed?"

"Eight, nine thousand maybe, and that's only this year. Petty ante. Not enough to kill for."

"People kill for pocket change, Roarke."

"Not enough, I should say, to hire a professional. You might want to chat with the manager there, but I'd say you'd be doing it more for form. He hasn't enough to afford a pro's fee, barely enough for an amateur, and he hasn't shifted any real money out of his personals, or the flower shop to manage it. He'll have a minor gambling problem, or a fancy piece on the side."

"A fancy piece."

He glanced over. "Well now, side pieces tend to be fancy as a rule, don't they? Still, I'd opt for the gambling as I don't see any purchases that indicate he's got a woman. No hotel bills or out-of-the-way restaurant charges for dinner for two, no out-of-town trips where a man might sneak off with a woman not his wife."

"Seems to me you know an awful lot about how a man keeps that fancy sidepiece."

"Does it really? I'd say no more than your average man, and of course in a purely intellectual, even academic sense."

She picked up another slice of pizza. "Isn't it a good thing I agree with you, all around?"

"It's a great relief to me."

"I'll have a talk with the guy with sticky fingers." She rose, eating pizza as she paced. "It should be about money. It's the logical motive. But it doesn't *feel* like it's about money. Why does she come back to New York and target a man she's never met?"

"Maybe she had met him, or at least was planning to before she was interrupted nearly ten years ago."

"He was married ten years ago," Eve began, then paused to let it all sink in. "But maybe he was restless about the marriage even then. Maybe there are signs of that kind of dissatisfaction that a wife, a family, close friends don't see. But an outsider, one who looks for discord might spot it. He could have been on her list as a possible, someone she was researching with the idea of luring him away from his wife and into a relationship, then marriage. He'd have been a real challenge to her because he's basically a very decent, very honest man. Could she corrupt him?"

Considering, Eve turned back. "That would have appealed to her. We never pinned down how long she kept each of her targets in her sights. She may very well have been keeping Pettibone for a future mark, then she's caught, tried, imprisoned. While she's out of the picture, he divorces his wife, ends up with a fresh new wife. Maybe she killed him just because she never got the chance to play out her hand before."

"If that theory holds, you'd have no link."

"No, but I'd have a fucking motive. If she's not killing for money, then she's already got money, because she needs the lavish life. And maybe she killed just because she missed the rush. She had the money from the East Washington victim, but she hasn't touched it. I checked on that. So she's got other income and it's been sitting waiting for a decade. I find it, I find her."

"If I were stashing money away for a rainy day, it would be in numbered accounts, various institutions, various locations." He washed down pizza with some excellent cabernet Sauvignon. "Both in and out of the country, both on and off planet. Not too much in any one pot," he added when Eve frowned at him. "In that way, if you can't easily or safely get to that particular pot, there's always another."

"It wouldn't just be money. She liked stocks, bonds, that kind of thing. If you earmarked goodly chunks for the market, you couldn't just sit back and let it ride for almost a decade. Could you?"

"Not if you had a brain cell still working. You'd need to keep an eye on things, shift funds, sell, buy, and so on. Or have someone you trusted to handle it."

"She didn't trust anyone. That tells me she found a way from prison to deal with it personally. That means transmissions, to and from, and they're supposed to be monitored."

"A bribe in the right hand would take care of that.

Conservative investments, blue chip and so on, and she wouldn't need much time to supervise her accounts. A few hours a week at most."

"Feeney and I will have to find the hand she greased."

"Do you plan to come home again in this century?" He angled his head. "Looking for a prison guard or inmate who'd be open to bribes shouldn't take more than twenty, thirty years to pin down."

"Have a little faith." She licked pizza sauce from her thumb. "I'll be home by dinnertime."

"Two nights running? I'm going to mark my calendar." When she only continued to frown, he shook his head. "What?"

"Nothing. I was just thinking." She wandered back, pushed at another slice of pizza, decided against it.

Because he knew his woman, Roarke said nothing and waited her out.

"When I was interviewing Shelly Pettibone today, she was talking about her marriage. It came off like she still had a lot of feelings for him, even though he dumped her and married someone half her age, and with big tits. But it was more as if she were talking about a brother than a husband at this point. She said . . . Anyway, do you think the passion, the sex, the way it is with us is just going to mellow out and fade off after a while?"

"Bite your tongue."

"I mean, people don't end up on the floor of the shower all the time. And when that sort of thing stops happening, will you have anything left that keeps you together? Needing to be together, or do you end up being two people living in the same house?"

"Come here."

"I don't need reassurances, Roarke." And she was already wishing she'd kept her mouth shut. "It just struck me, that's all. It was sort of sad, but understandable."

"Come here anyway." He reached out a hand for hers,

and when she took it, drew her into his lap. "I can't imagine not wanting you so that it puts an ache inside me. Seeing you, smelling you, touching you so every-thing in me needs. But, if when we're a hundred and twenty and that's more memory than reality, I'll still need you, Eve, a thousand ways."

"Okay." She brushed the hair away from his face.

"Wait. Do you remember when first I saw you. In the winter, with death between us?"

"Yeah, I remember."

"I didn't make you for a cop. That disturbed me for some time later as I prided myself for spotting a cop at half a mile in the dark. But when I turned and looked at you, I didn't see cop. I saw a woman. I saw *the* woman, though I hadn't figured that out. I only knew that I looked, and I saw, and everything shifted. Nothing would be the same for me after that instant."

She remembered how he had turned, looked back over the sea of mourners at a funeral, how his eyes had locked with hers as if they'd been the only ones there. And the power of that look had shaken her to her toes.

"You bothered me," she murmured.

"I meant to. I looked, darling Eve, and saw the woman I would love, and trust, and need as I'd never expected to love or trust or need another living soul. The only woman I wanted to be with, to live with, to sleep and wake with. And *a ghra*, to grow old with."

"How do you do it?" She lowered her forehead to his. "How do you always manage to say what I need to hear?"

"There are people who live out their lives together, and not just from habit or convenience or a fear of change. But from love. Maybe love has cycles. We haven't been in it long enough to know, have we? But I know one thing utterly. I'll love you till I die."

"I know." Tears brushed her cheek. "I know it because it's the same for me. I felt sorry for that woman today because she'd lost that. She'd lost it, and didn't even know where or when. God." She had to take two long breaths because her throat was tight. "I was thinking about it later, thinking about what she'd said, how she'd said it. It just seemed to me that things were too easy between them, too smooth."

"Well then." He gave her a quick, hard squeeze. "Easy and smooth? Those are marital problems we'll never have to worry about."

Chapter 7

With slack jaws and shuffling feet, hundreds of commuters loaded on shuttles. Or were loaded on, Eve thought, like cargo and corpses, by the red uniformed drones and droids of Manhattan Commuter Transport Service.

The terminal was a hive of noise, a great cacophony of sound that had an insectile hum as an undertone. Over it, the incomprehensible voices of flight announcers buzzed, babies wailed, pocket-links pinged.

She wondered whose idea it was to design places like this with soaring ceilings and white walls so those who had the misfortune to use the services were like ants trapped inside a drum.

She smelled bad coffee, sweat, overpowering colognes, and what she assumed was a diaper in desperate need of changing.

"Like old times," Feeney said after they'd managed to muscle their way on and snag two of the seats designed for the narrow asses of twelve-year-old anorexics. "Guess it's been awhile since you used a public shuttle."

"I thought I missed it." She did her best to pull her face back from the parade of crotches and butts that pressed in to make the forced shuffle down the crammed aisle. "How wrong can you get?"

"Not so bad. Be there inside a half hour if they don't screw something up." He jiggled the sugared almonds in the bag he pulled out of his pocket. "We'd've shaved time off that with one of Roarke's transpos."

She dipped into the bag, munched, considered. "You figure I'm stupid for not using his stuff?"

"Nah. You're just you, kid. And being smothered in here helps keep us in touch with the common man."

When the third briefcase cracked her in the shin, and a guy corkscrewed himself into the seat beside her, plastering her against Feeney so they had less personal space than a pair of Siamese twins, Eve decided keeping in touch with the common man was overrated.

They took off with the kind of mechanical shudder that always pitched her stomach to her knees. She kept her teeth gritted and her eyes shut until landing. Passengers vomited off the shuttle, scattered. Eve and Feeney joined the herd heading for the east-bound train.

"Wasn't so bad," he commented.

"Not if you like to start your day with carnival rides. This dumps us out about a half block from the facility. Warden's name is Miller. We'll have to dance with him first."

"You want to go down the list together, or split off?"

"I'm thinking we split off, save time, but let's get the lay of the land first. Guess we need to play politics, stop in on the Chicago cops."

"Could be Julianna's backtracking from her past. If she is, Chicago'd be her next stop."

Eve opted to stand on the train, and grabbed a hook. "Yeah. I can't get inside her head. What's her purpose this time around? There's a logic to what she does. It's screwed-up, but it's a logic. I'm wondering if she came back to New York because that's where things went to hell for her. She's got something to prove, to us, Feeney. If that's it, then the targets are secondary. It's about beating us, beating the system, this time out." She shook her head. "Anyway you play it, she's already got her next mark."

Dockport resembled a small, self-contained, and tidy city with guard towers, bars, and shock-walls. She doubted the residents fully appreciated the well-maintained roads, the patches of green, or the suburban architecture. Not when an overwhelming urge for a stroll outside the boundaries would result in a sensor alert and a zapping shock that would knock you back a good ten feet on your ass.

Droid dogs patrolled the perimeter. The woman's recreation yard was vast and equipped with basketball court, running track, and scrubbed-down picnic tables painted a cheerful blue.

The walls around it were twelve-feet high and three-feet thick.

Inside, the floors were as clean and sparkling as a grandmother's kitchen. Walkways were wide and roomy. Areas were sectioned off with doors of riot glass designed to withstand the blast of homemade boomers or a laser shot.

Guards wore dark blue, other staff street clothes topped with chef-white coats. Inmates wore neon-orange jumpsuits emblazoned on the back with the black block initials DRC.

They were run through security at the main entrance, politely tagged with both ID shield and bracelets, and requested to surrender any and all weapons.

Miller, dapper and distinguished despite the silly coat,

was all smiles as he greeted them. He gripped Eve's then Feeney's hand in both of his, spewing welcomes like the owner of some fashionable resort.

"We appreciate you taking the time to see us, Warden Miller," Eve began.

"Supervisor." He gave a quick, hearty chuckle. "We no longer use antiquated terms such as warden. Dockport Rehabilitation Center is a completely modern facility. We were built just twenty-five years ago, and began accepting residents in '34. Here at the Women's Center of DRC, we house a maximum of fifteen hundred, and maintain a staff of six hundred and thirty full-time, fifty-eight part-time, and twenty outside consultants. We're fully self-contained with health facilities, banking, shops, and dining facilities. We do hope you'll join us for lunch in the staff eatery. Overnight accommodations for visitors and consultants, physical therapy and exercise, mental and emotional fitness centers, training facilities that offer classes in a variety of career choices and skills geared toward resocialization are all available on the premises. The Men's Center is similarly equipped."

They passed through an office area where people went busily about their business, clipping along the corridors, manning desks, answering 'links. A number of them wore the bright orange jumpsuits.

"Prisoners are allowed in this area?" Eve asked.

"Residents," Miller corrected mildly, "are allowed— encouraged—to apply for suitable jobs after they've completed half their rehabilitation training. It aids in their adjustment to the outside world when they leave us, so they may re-enter society with self-esteem and a meaningful purpose."

"Uh-huh. Well, one of your former residents has re-entered society with a meaningful purpose. She likes killing men. We need to talk about Julianna Dunne, Supervisor Miller."

"Yes." He pressed his palms together like a preacher about to call the congregation to prayer. "I was very distressed to learn you believe she's involved in a homicide."

"I don't believe she's involved. I know she's a murderer. Just as she was when she came here."

He paused. "I beg your pardon, Lieutenant, but from your tone I get the impression you don't believe in the basic tenets of rehabilitation."

"I believe in crime and punishment, and that some learn from it. Learn it well enough to change how they live in the real world. I also believe that there are some who can't change, or just don't want to."

Through the glass door at Miller's back, she watched two inmates make a quick, slick exchange of envelopes. Credits for illegals was Eve's guess.

"They like what they do," she added, "and can't wait for the chance to get back to it. Julianna likes what she does."

"She was a model resident," he said stiffly.

"I bet. And I bet she applied for a job position when half her time was up. Where'd she work?"

He drew air through his nose. Most of the warm bonhomie chilled under insult and disapproval. "She was employed at the Visitor's Coordination Center."

"Access to computers?" Feeney asked.

"Of course. Our units are secured and passcoded. Residents are not permitted unsupervised transmissions. Her immediate superior, Georgia Foster, gave Julianna the highest evaluations."

Eve and Feeney exchanged looks. "You want to point me in the direction of that center," Feeney said. "I'll speak with Ms. Foster."

"And I'd like interviews with the inmates on this list." Eve drew it out of her pocket. "Sorry, residents," she corrected, but not without a sneer in her voice.

"Of course. I'll arrange it." Miller's nose had gone up in the air, and Eve doubted the invitation for lunch was still on the table.

"See that pass?" Feeney muttered when Miller turned his back to speak into his in-house communicator.

"Yep."

"Wanna tell this asshole?"

"Nope. Residents' business ventures and recreational activities are his problem. And if I have to listen to him lecture much longer, I may go hit up that con for a little Zoner myself."

Eve took the interviews one at a time in a conference area outfitted with six chairs, a cheerfully patterned sofa, a small entertainment screen, and a sturdy table manufactured from recycled paper products.

There were bland paintings of flower arrangements on the walls and a sign on the inside of the door that reminded residents and their guests to behave in a courteous manner.

Eve supposed she was the guest portion of that statement.

There was no two-way mirror, but she spotted the four scan-cams snugged into corners. The door leading in was glass, privacy screen optional. She left it off.

The guard, a big-shouldered, pie-faced woman who looked like she had enough sense and experience not to think of the inmates as residents, brought Maria Sanchez in first.

Sanchez was a tough little Latin mix with a mop of curly black hair skinned back into a tail. There was a little tattoo of a lightning bolt worked into the jagged scar at the right side of her mouth.

She sauntered in, jauntily swinging her hips, then dropped into a chair and drummed her fingers on the table. Eve spotted sensor bracelets on both her wrists and ankles.

Miller might have been a moron, but even he wasn't stupid enough, it seemed, to take chances with a hard case like Sanchez. At Eve's nod, the guard retreated to the other side of the door.

"Got smoke?" Sanchez asked in a raspy, musical voice.

"No."

"Shit. You drag me off my morning rec time and you don't got smoke?"

"I'm real sorry to bust up your daily tennis game, Sanchez."

"Shit. Me, I play round ball." She eased back, craned her neck to look under the table. "You got a lot of leg, but I'd still whip your ass on the court."

"We'll have to find time for a pickup game one of these fine days, but right now I'm here about Julianna Dunne. You had the cage beside hers the last three years."

"We don't call them cages 'round here." She sent Eve a sneer. "They call 'em personal areas. Fucking personal areas. Miller, he's an asshole."

Eve wasn't sure what it said that she and Sanchez had that basic point of agreement. "What did you and Dunne talk about when you were in your respective personal areas?"

"I don't give nothing to cops. Oh wait, yeah, I give one thing to cops." She held up her middle finger.

"Bet they've got a salon in this country club. You could use a manicure. You and Dunne make any girl talk?"

"I got nothing to say to her, she got nothing to say to me. Bitch thought she was better than anybody."

"You don't like her, neither do I. We can start from there."

"Like her better than I do cops. Buzz is she offed some rich old bastard over in New York. What do I care about that?"

"She's out, you're not. Isn't that enough?"

Sanchez examined her nails as if she were indeed contemplating that manicure. "No skin off my ass where she is, but I bet yours is burning."

"I guess you think Julianna's pretty smart."

Sanchez snorted through her nose. "She thinks she is."

"Too smart for a cop to figure—then again, I'm one of the cops who put her in here."

A little smirk tipped up the right corner of Sanchez's mouth. "Didn't keep her in."

"That's not my job." Eve leaned back. "You're going to be in another ten to fifteen, given your fondness for jabbing sharp implements into sensitive area's of other people's anatomy."

"Don't do nothing to no motherfucker they don't try to do to me. Woman's got to defend herself out in the bad, bad world."

"Maybe, but you won't breathe the air in that bad, bad world for at least a dime more considering your in-house record won't earn you the crown for Miss Congeniality or cop you toward an early for good behavior release."

"What the fuck I care? Place like this, you can do a dime standing on your head scratching your butt."

"You get conjugals in here, Sanchez?"

Her eyes sharpened. "Sure. Part of the rehabilitation gig. Gotta keep the machine in tune, right?"

"But you're a violent tendency. VT's just get to hump droids. Could be I can wrangle you an lc. A genuine warm body for a night of romance. In exchange."

"You fucking with me?"

"No, but I'll get you a pro who will if you give me something I can use. Who'd she talk to, who did she use. What do you know?"

"I want a big guy, good-looking, who can keep his dick up till I get off."

"Tell me something I want to hear, and I'll get you the conjugal, the rest is up to you. Julianna Dunne."

It was a choice between real sex and screwing a cop. Sanchez went for real sex. "Bitch. Texas gringo beauty fucking queen. Kept to herself much as she could. Treated the guards like they were Sunday school teachers. Yes, ma'am, thank you, ma'am. Made you wanna puke. They lapped it up, gave her extra privileges. She got coin in. Greased palms, paid some of the lesbos to lay off her. Free time she spent in the library or the gym. She had Loopy for her bitch—not a sex thing, more like a puppy."

"And Loopy would be?"

"Lois Loop, funky junkie, doing twenty for icing her old man. Had the cage other side of the bitch. Heard them talking sometimes." Sanchez shrugged. "She'd promise to set Loopy up somewhere cozy when she got sprung, said how she had a lot of money and a nice place to live. Texas, maybe."

"She planned to go back to Texas?"

"She said she'd have business in Dallas. Unfinished business."

Eve let that simmer in her brain, and sent for Lois Loop.

She wouldn't have needed Sanchez's ID. The woman had the bleached out skin, colorless hair, and pink rabbit eyes of the funk addict. The mind mister had the side effect of eradicating pigment. Detox could turn the user around, but it didn't put the color back.

One glance at her pinprick pupils told Eve detox wasn't doing much good either.

"Have a seat, Loopy."

"Do I know you? I don't know you."

"Have a seat anyway."

She started toward the table, her movements a mechanical jerk. Wherever she was getting her fix, Eve thought, she hadn't had one recently.

"You jonesing, Loopy? How long since you scored?"

Loopy licked her white lips. "I get my daily synthetic. Part of detox. It's the law."

"Yeah, right." Eve leaned in. "Did Julianna give you coin, so you could score the real funk inside?"

"Julianna's my friend. Do you know Julianna?"

"Yeah, we go way back."

"She went back in the world."

"That's right. She staying in touch?"

"When you see her, you tell her they must be stealing her letters, 'cause I didn't get any and she promised. We're allowed to get letters."

"Where are the letters coming from?"

"She's going to write and tell me where she is, and when I go back in the world, I'll go there, too." Her muscles jerked as she talked, as if they weren't connected to flesh and bone. But she smiled serenely.

"Tell me where she went and I'll find her for you. I'll let her know about the letters."

"She'd maybe go here, she'd maybe go there. It's a big secret."

"You ever been to New York before?"

The wasted eyes widened. "She told you?"

"Like I said, we go back. But New York's a big place. It'll be hard to find her if I don't have an address."

"She has a house, all her own. Somewhere. And she's maybe gonna do some traveling. She's going to come visit me when she comes back to Chicago."

"When's she coming back?"

"Sometime. We going shopping. New York, Chicago, New L.A." She sang the cities, like a child singing a nursery tune. "Dallas and Denver. Ride 'em cowboy."

"Did she talk about the people she was going to see?

Old friends, new ones? Did she say the names, Loopy?"

"Should old acquaintance be forgot. We had a party for New Year's. There was cake. Do you know the bone man?"

"I might."

"She read me all kinds of stuff about the bone man. He lives in a big palace in the city. He has green thumbs and flowers grow out of them. She's going to visit him."

Pettibone, Eve thought. First hit. "Who else is she going to visit?"

"Oh, the sheep man and the cowboy and the Dallas dude. She has people to see, places to go."

"When she read you about the bone man, where were you?"

"It's a secret," she whispered.

"You can tell me. Julianna would want you to so I can find her and tell her about the letters."

"And the funk," Loopy said in a whisper. "She's gonna get me the funk."

"I'll tell her, but you have to tell me first."

"Okay. She had the little computer in her cage. The one that fits in your hand. She could do her work on it. She always had lots of work to do."

"I bet she did."

"Did she send you to see me? Did she send you with funk? She always got me the funk, but I'm almost out."

"I'll see what I can do for you."

Eve looked at her—the spastic muscle jerks, the ghostly skin. Rehabilitation, she thought. Mother of God.

By the time she met up with Feeney again, Eve was steaming. Every interview had added to the picture of Julianna Dunne, multiple murderer, waltzing her way through the system, stacking up privileges and favors, and conning, bribing, sweet-talking guards, staff, and other prisoners into doing whatever she needed or wanted to be done.

"Like they were goddamn servants," Eve exploded. "And this was her goddamn castle. She couldn't leave it, but she made certain what she wanted got in to her. A fucking PPC, Feeney. Christ knows what she sent or received on it."

"Had the office drone who worked over her buffaloed," he added. "I can guarantee she did plenty of authorized transmissions from the units in that complex. Free fricking rein."

"We get an impound warrant, can you track?"

"I already put in for one. Might be spitting in the wind, but we'll go through every one of them, see if she left a mark. Talked to her shrink—'scuze me—her *emotional well-being counselor*." His lips pursed on the term as if he were sucking a lemon ball. "Got an earful of early childhood trauma, acting out—nice pretty term for murder—flash points, ebbing, contrition, and Christ knows. All adds up to the head broad being convinced Dunne was successfully rehabilitated and ready to take her place as a productive member of society."

"Odds are we'll get the same song from her PO. We'll swing by and see him, check in with the locals, and get the hell out of Chicago." She blew out a breath. "Is something wrong with me, Feeney, that I look at this place and see a huge pile of bullshit being dumped on the taxpayers?"

"Must be the same thing that's wrong with me."

"But people can change, they can turn themselves around. Or be turned around. Prisons aren't just warehouses. Shouldn't be."

"They shouldn't be frigging resort hotels either. Let's get the hell out of here. Place gives me the creeps."

•　　•　　•

Parole Officer Otto Shultz was overweight, bucktoothed, and solved his male pattern baldness with a combover that started with a part at the tip of his left ear.

Eve imagined his civil servant salary was far from stellar, but wondered why he didn't earmark a portion of it for basic body maintenance.

He wasn't happy to see them, claimed to be very busy, murderously overworked, and tried to brush them off with promises of copies of all reports and evaluations on Julianna Dunne.

Eve would've been fine with that, if it hadn't been for the nerves she could all but smell pumping out of his pores.

"You helped pass her back out of the system, and the first thing she does is kill. I guess that's got you somewhat jittery, Otto."

"Look." He pulled out a handkerchief, mopped his pudgy face. "I followed the book. She passed all evals, followed the rules. I'm a PO, not a fortune-teller."

"I always figured most PO's have a really good bullshit barometer. How about you, Feeney?"

"Working with cons every day, hearing all the stories, the excuses, the crapola." Lips pursed, he nodded. "Yep, I gotta figure a PO with any experience is going smell out the bs."

"She aced all the tests," Otto began.

"Wouldn't be the first to know how to maneuver the techs and questions and machines. Where'd she bang you, Otto?" Eve asked pleasantly. "Here in the office, or did she get you to take her home with you?"

"You can't sit there and accuse me of having a sexual relationship with a client."

"Client, Christ. These politically correct terms are starting to piss me off. I'm not accusing you, Otto." Eve leaned forward. "I know you fucked her. I don't really give a damn, and I'm not interested in reporting that fact to your superiors. She's a piece of work and you'd have been child's play for her. You can be grateful she just wanted you to help push her through, and didn't want you dead."

"She passed the tests," he said and his voice shook. "She didn't make waves. Her slate was clean. I believed her. I'm not the only one who believed her, so don't dump this on me. We've got scum oozing through here every day, and the law says if they don't blow their parole obligations, we funnel them back into society. Julianna wasn't scum. She was . . . different."

"Yeah." Disgusted, Eve got to her feet. "She's different."

The first breath of fresh air of the day came in a crowded, dingy diner that smelled of badly fried food. The place was jammed with cops, and across the little table, Lieutenant Frank Boyle and Captain Robert Spindler chowed down on turkey sandwiches the size of Hawaii.

"Julianna." Spindler dabbed a condiment masquerading as mayo off his bottom lip. "Face of an angel, soul of a shark. Coldest, meanest bitch I ever met."

"You're forgetting my first wife," Boyle reminded him. "Hard to believe we're back here, the four of us, damn near ten years later." Boyle had a cheerful Irish face, until you looked in his eyes. They were hard and flat, and just a little scary.

Eve could see the signs of too much drinking, too much brooding in the red puffiness in his jowls, the souring droop of his mouth.

"We put out feelers," Spindler continued. "Fed the media, bumped up her old contacts. We've got nothing new on her." He'd kept his looks, militarily clean-cut, trim, authoritative. "We've got nothing on her, nothing to indicate she's blown our way. I went to her parole hearing," he continued. "Made a personal pitch that she

be denied. Brought case files, documentation. Got nowhere. She sat there, like a perfect lady, eyes downcast,
hands folded, the faintest glimmer of tears. If I didn't
know her like I know her, I might've bought the act
myself."

"You know anything about a funky junkie inside?
Lois Loop?"

"Doesn't ring," Spindler said.

"She was Julianna's gofer, sounding board, slave.
Whatever. She was starting to jones when I interviewed
her. I got some info, but she may have more. Maybe you
can work her again. She told me Julianna was going to
New York to see the bone man. Pettibone. And there was
a sheep man. Can you think of anyone who fits her standard target who has sheep in his name?"

Both Boyle and Spindler shook their heads. "But we'll
run it through," Spindler promised. "See what pops."

"Also a cowboy and the Dallas dude."

"Sounds like she's thinking of heading down to Texas
and paying a call on her step-father." Boyle took another
enormous bite of his sandwich. "Unless you're the Dallas, and she's looking at your dude."

Eve ignored the clutching in her stomach. "Yeah,
that's occurred. We'll notify Dallas PSD. I can take care
of my own dude. New L.A. and Denver were other cities
this Loopy remembered. I'm betting if her mind was
clearer, she'd remember more."

"I'll take a pass at her." Boyle glanced at Spindler. "If
that suits you . . . Captain."

"Likes to remind me I got the bars. Not much more
we can do for you. Frankly, I'd like to see you take her
down in New York. I'd miss the party, but fuck if I want
her dropped back in Dockport."

She was back in New York by five, and opted to head
home instead of swinging into Central. She'd work there
and reassure herself of Roarke's safety.

He didn't fit target profile, she reminded herself. He was too young, had no ex-wife. But he also had a wife who'd played a large part in bringing Julianna down.

She was nearly home when she made an impulsive detour and headed to Dr. Mira's.

She parked in a loading zone a half block down, flipped on her on duty light, then jogged to the dignified old brownstone. There were soft pink and white flowers in pale blue pots cheering up the entrance. A woman one door up led out an enormous dog with long golden hair decorated with red bows. It sent Eve a friendly woof, then pranced away with its owner as if they were off to a parade.

On the other side, a trio of boys burst outside, whooping like maniacs. Each carried a fluorescent airboard and zipped away down the sidewalk like rockets off a launch pad.

A man in a business suit with a palm-link stuck to his ear had to dodge clear, but rather than shouting or shaking a fist after them, he only chuckled, kept talking as he turned toward the door of another townhouse.

One more side of New York, Eve thought. The friendly, upper class neighborhood. In all probability people actually knew each other's name on this block. Got together now and then for cocktails, herded kids or grandchildren down to the park in groups, and stopped to chat on doorsteps.

It was exactly the sort of milieu that suited Dr. Charlotte Mira.

Eve turned to the door, rang the bell. Then immediately changed her mind. She had no business busting in on Mira's home time. She'd actually stepped back, thinking retreat, when the door opened.

She recognized Mira's husband though they'd rarely had personal contact. He was tall and gangly, a kind of comfortable scarecrow in a baggy cardigan and wrinkled slacks. His hair was pewter, a wild, interesting mop tangled around a long face that was somehow both scholarly and innocent.

He carried a pipe, and his sweater was misbuttoned.

He smiled, his eyes, the color of winter grass, puzzled. "Hello. How are you?"

"Ah. Fine. I'm sorry, Mr. Mira, I shouldn't be disturbing you at home. I was just—"

"You're Eve." His face cleared, warmed. "It takes me a minute. Recognized your voice. Come in, come in."

"Actually, I should—"

But he reached out, gripped her hand, and pulled her in the door. "Didn't realize you were coming by. Can't keep track. Charlie!" He shouted toward the steps. "Your Eve's here."

The protest died in Eve's throat at the idea of the elegant Mira being called Charlie.

"Come sit down. I think I was fixing drinks. Mind wanders. Drives Charlie crazy. Ha-ha."

"I'm interrupting. I'll just see Dr. Mira tomorrow."

"Yes, there's the wine. I was sure I brought it in. I'm sorry, help me out. Are we having dinner?"

He was still holding her hand, and she could find no polite way to tug free. And he was smiling at her with such amiable confusion and humor, she fell just a little bit in love.

"No, you weren't expecting me at all."

"Then what a nice surprise."

Chapter 8

Before she could respond, Mira rushed in and Eve experienced yet another shock at seeing the consistently elegant Mira in an oversized white T-shirt and black skinpants. Her feet were bare, the nails painted a pretty candy pink.

"Dennis? Who did you say . . . Why, Eve."

"I'm sorry. I shouldn't be here. I was on my way home, and I . . . I apologize for disturbing you at home. I'll just, ah, contact your office in the morning."

It was rare, Mira thought, to see Eve flustered. "We're not the least disturbed. Are we having wine, Dennis?"

"Are we?" He looked baffled again, then stared down at the bottle in his hand. "Oh. Yes, we are. I'll get another glass."

"No, please. Don't bother. I shouldn't be here. I should go."

"Don't be silly." Mira smiled at her. "Sit down. If you're on duty, we can offer you something soft rather than wine."

"No, I'm off, but—"

"Good." She crossed the room, pausing to rebutton her husband's cardigan with such simple intimacy that it made Eve feel more like an intruder than if they'd exchanged a wet, sloppy kiss. Mira chose another glass herself from a display cabinet, then simply laid a hand on Eve's shoulder to nudge her into a chair.

So Eve found herself sitting in Mira's pretty, colorful living room accepting a glass of wine.

"How was your vacation?" Mira began.

"Good. It was good."

"You look rested."

"Yeah, well, I played slug half the time."

"You needed it. Both you and Roarke. He's well, I trust."

"Yes." Eve shifted in her chair. "He's okay." And she meant to keep him that way.

Mira sipped wine, inclined her head toward her husband. "I often discuss aspects of cases with Dennis, but if you'd prefer we can talk upstairs in my office."

"No, I don't want to muck up your home time. I've got no right bringing a case into your living room. Anyway, you haven't had time to read through the data."

"But I have."

"What do you—" Eve cut herself off. "Then I'll call your office in the morning and make an appointment."

"Relax, Eve. We'll talk now. You wouldn't have come by this way if it wasn't important. And I'm pleased you felt comfortable enough, even momentarily, to do so. There was a time, not so long ago, you wouldn't have considered it."

"I've always respected your abilities, Dr. Mira."

"Respect and comfort are different matters. You're here about Julianna Dunne."

"Evil," Dennis Mira said to no one in particular, "comes in all forms, and often alluring ones." He turned suddenly clear, suddenly intense eyes on Eve. "Do you believe in evil?"

"Yes."

"Good. You can't stop it if you don't believe in it."

"Dennis is skilled at fining down a point to its most elemental level. It's helpful to me."

Mira sipped her wine again, then set it aside on a little round table before she continued. "Julianna Dunne was thoroughly tested, evaluated, examined before and during her trial. The opinion of the experts called in for these purposes was that the subject had suffered the trauma of sexual abuse by a family member, which had damaged her both mentally and emotionally. In this diminished capacity, she, as an adult, sought out other men who represented her abuser. She then punished this representative as she had been unable to punish the man who had harmed her."

She paused to tuck her pretty, shapely legs under her. "With the cold calculation of the murders and her profit from them, the defense was unable to negotiate a term in a mental health center, nor could they convince a jury that the subject was innocent, completely innocent, due to this diminished capacity. They were, however, able to keep their client out of a life sentence."

"I'd prefer your take on her to the initial profiler."

"Then here it is. In my opinion, given the data, the experts were incorrect in their evaluations and conclusions. Julianna Dunne wasn't operating under diminished capacity, not in any legal sense. She played the game perfectly," Mira continued. "Her answers were exactly right, as were her reactions, her gestures, her tone. And that was her mistake, one those who worked with her overlooked. That sort of perfection has to be calculated. She's a liar, but she's an excellent one."

"She was never raped as a teenager." Eve leaned forward. "She's not haunted, or hunted. There's no pain, no fear, no rage inside her."

Mira reached out, closed her hand over Eve's briefly. She knew they couldn't speak of Eve's childhood with Dennis in the room. "My opinion is, and I would have to test her personally to be certain, that the sexual relationship was consensual. To Julianna, sex is a weapon. Man is the enemy. It's unlikely she enjoys the sexual experience. It's a job, a means to an end. And the man's enjoyment of it, of her body, a matter of both pride and disgust."

"Why didn't she turn to women, sexually?"

"She has more respect for them, as a species. And again, sex isn't an interest. She doesn't look for pleasure there. Her pleasure comes from causing pain, humiliation, from conquering and gathering the spoils."

"If I may." Dennis spread his hands, catching Eve's attention. He'd been so quiet and still, she'd all but forgotten him. "Men aren't opponents," he said. "They're victims. She needs victims in order to thrive."

"She sets out to attract them," Eve agreed. "The way you would some sort of prey. She becomes what attracts them, sliding into a personality like you might a new suit. An older man, one who has grown tired or dissatisfied or just bored with his wife, his family, his sex life is the perfect target. More easily attracted to beauty, more easily duped."

"A man of a certain age is bound to be flattered by the romantic attentions of a younger and beautiful woman. Each gender has its weak points."

"She practiced on her step-father. She did the seducing there," Eve stated. "Sharpening her skills. He didn't testify at her trial. Prosecution couldn't take the chance of calling him, letting the jury see him. But the defense should have trotted him out. Look here, this man forced himself on this poor, innocent young girl. She was helpless, trapped. He was her father, she should have been safe with him. Instead he took her innocence, left her damaged. If anyone's responsible for the deaths, he is."

"She couldn't afford to let them call him in, under oath," Mira said. "And there she'd have dug in her heels. You'll want to talk to him yourself."

"He's in Texas. In Dallas."

"Yes, I know." Mira eyes spoke a million words. "I saw the data. Can you go?"

Not *will* you, Eve thought. *Can* you. "I don't know. I don't know," she repeated.

Mira reached out, touched her husband's hand. "Dennis" was all she said, and he unfolded the gangly length of him and got to his feet.

"If you ladies will excuse me, I've got something or other to do. You were right about her, Charlie." He leaned over to touch his lips to the top of Mira's head, then stroked a long, narrow hand over the sweep of her glossy brown hair. "But then, you always are. Nice seeing you, Eve. Don't be a stranger."

"You didn't have to send him away," Eve said when he wandered out of the room. "This isn't about me."

"Look at me. Look at me, Eve." Mira set down her glass, gripped one of Eve's hands in both of hers. "If you're not ready to go back to Dallas, send for him. Have him come here."

"I've got no cause and no authority to bring Jake Parker to New York."

"Then do the interview via 'link or holographics."

"You know it has to be done face-to-face if I'm going to push him to tell me what happened, how it happened, what she did, who she was. He's not going to want to go there. There's also a possibility from data I gathered today that he may be a target. I have to go, and I don't know if I can handle it."

"I'll go with you."

For a moment Eve could only stare, and as she stared her vision blurred. She had to stand up, turn away. "Jesus."

"I can help you, Eve. I want to. For a long time you wouldn't let me get close; you resented me. But that's changed."

"I didn't resent you. You scared the shit out of me. People who scare me piss me off."

"I'm glad I don't scare you anymore."

"Sometimes you do." She swiped the back of her hand under her nose, then turned back. "I'm not ready, or not willing to take all that was into what's now. It comes in pieces, and the pieces are getting bigger. I don't know what's going to happen to me when the picture's all there. But when I'm ready, I'll come to you. Okay?"

"Yes."

"Anyway." She had to take a couple of steadying breaths. "Like I said, this isn't about me. Feeney and I went to Dockport today."

She sat again, filled Mira in on the rest of the details.

"You think she may target Roarke. I wish I could tell you your instincts are wrong."

A fist jammed in Eve's throat, another clenched in her gut. "Why would she? He doesn't fit her target profile."

"Because he's yours. What Dennis said about men not being her opponents is accurate. But women are opponents, companions, tools, competitors. Her feelings toward them would have been enhanced and refined over her time in a women's correctional facility. Of the primary officers who brought about her arrest, you were the only female. The only one she asked to speak with personally. You bested her, and that impressed her. She wanted your respect and you refused to give it. It's logical that given the opportunity, she'd want a rematch, not just because you stopped her, but because you dismissed her. It answers why New York."

"And why she's still here. I know she's still here. She's cut out a step in her past procedure. She doesn't bother with the affair, the marriage. She won't try to seduce him. But if she is sighting Roarke, she'll be working out a way to get to him."

She pushed out of the chair again, jammed her hands in her pockets and paced. "Damn it, you know what's going to happen now. I'm going to go home, tell Roarke, demand he increase security and add police protection. He'll balk, tell me he can protect himself. Blah, blah, blah. Then we'll have a fight." She sighed. "Well, we haven't had a fight in a while. I guess we're due."

"If you're afraid for him, let him see it."

"I know he can take care of himself. But it doesn't stop me from worrying about him."

"I imagine he has the same conflict about you, every time you walk out of the house with that weapon strapped to your side. Whether or not you fight about it, you'll find a way to work through it together. That's marriage."

"A lot of marriage is a pain in the ass."

"Oh, it certainly is."

"You fixed his buttons," Eve murmured.

"What?"

Surprised she'd spoken aloud, Eve stopped and very nearly flushed. "Nothing."

"Buttons? What—Oh! Dennis's sweater." Mira pressed a hand to her heart and laughed. "Yes, I suppose I did. He never pays attention to his clothes or to mine, for that matter. It still annoys me when I have a new outfit, look particularly good, and he doesn't see it."

"I like him."

"So do I."

"I'll let you two get back to . . . things. Tell him thanks for the wine. I appreciate you taking the time like this."

"You're always welcome here." She rose to walk Eve out.

"Dr. Mira?"

"Yes?"

"What did your husband mean, that you were right about me?"

"He could have meant any number of things, but under those circumstances, I believe he meant I was right when I described you as brilliant, complicated, and valiant. Now I've embarrassed you." Gently, Mira touched her lips to Eve's cheek. "Go home and fight with Roarke."

She didn't want to fight. She just wanted him to fall into line for a change. Since the chances of that were nil, she outlined a couple of approaches on the drive home.

But when she walked into the house, there was a party going on.

She heard music, laughter, voices, and immediately felt her temples throb at the prospect of having to deal with people. Even the sound of her well-loved friend Mavis's wild giggles didn't stop the headache from coming on.

She imagined herself sneaking upstairs like a thief and hiding in a dark room with a locked door.

Valiant, my ass, she thought.

She took one cautious step toward the stairs when Summerset slithered into the foyer and caught her.

"Lieutenant. You have guests."

"What, am I deaf?"

"Perhaps your hearing is defective as you were going in the opposite direction from the gathering in the parlor."

"Maybe I was just going upstairs to change or something." Because she knew it was weak, because he simply stood with that saber-thin sneer on his cadaverous face, she hunched her shoulders. "Oh, bite me," she muttered and headed into the parlor.

"There she is!" Mavis spun across the room, a little whirlwind with bunches of purple flowers arranged in strategic points over her body. Her hair was moonbeam silver tonight, with more flowers bursting out of it. She gave Eve an enthusiastic hug, then bounced on silver shoes with four-inch flower stalk heels.

"Leonardo and I were heading down to the Down and Dirty for some action, and swung by to see if you and Roarke were up for it. And look who we found." She spun around to grin at Phoebe and Sam. "I tagged Peabody, and she and McNab are going to meet us at the D and D. Roarke said maybe you wouldn't get home in time, but here you are."

"Here I am. I've got work, Mavis."

"Hey, take a couple hours to rock." She pulled Eve into the room. "Start with my zinger. Leonardo, baby doll, where'd I put my zinger?"

At six and a half feet, the golden skinned love of Mavis's life was nothing like a baby doll. He was barechested but for a red satin X across his pecs that seemed to be holding up the fluid, shimmering pants that flowed from his waist to the toes of his red, crisscrossing sandals. Ruby studs forming a chevron at the corner of his left eye winked as he grinned and passed Mavis her glass.

"Good to see you, Dallas." He bent down, gave her one of his shy, butterfly kisses. "I'll get you a fresh zinger if you want."

"I'll pass, but thanks." She shot Roarke a grateful look when he turned down the volume of the music. "Sorry I'm later than I planned," she told him. "I had a stop to make on the way home."

"No problem." He came to her and under the guise of a welcome-home kiss, murmured, "Do you want me to get rid of them?"

She nearly said yes, but it seemed petty and mean. "No. We can take an hour at the D and D if you're up for it."

He tipped up her chin. "You have something on your mind."

"It'll keep."

"And a headache as well."

"It'll pass." And there was the possibility, however remote, that a few hours with friends might put him in the mood to cooperate.

"So are we on?" Mavis demanded as she swung by with her zinger.

"Sure. Just give me a minute to go up and take care of some things."

"Frigid! Roarke?" Mavis tugged on his sleeve as Eve started out. "Can we take the limo? It'd be so totally mag for all of us to pile in and ride down to the D and D in style."

As the Down and Dirty was a strip joint with as much class as a rabid squirrel, Eve figured they'd be making one hell of a splash arriving in a mile-long limo, with uniformed driver. She had to be grateful the thing was built like an armored tank.

She stripped off her weapon harness, strapped on an ankle holster, checked her smaller, off-duty clutch piece to be certain it was fully charged. For grooming purposes, she dragged her fingers through her hair and considered the job done.

She strode back out of the bedroom, then came up short when she saw Sam standing in the hall. "I didn't want to disturb you," he began. "But you have a headache. I felt it," he explained before she could speak. "I can help you with it."

"It's okay. It's nothing."

"I hate to see anything in pain." His expression was soft with compassion. "It'll only take a minute."

"I don't like doing chemicals."

Now he smiled. "I don't blame you. I'm a sensitive." He stepped toward her. "With a touch of the empath. It's here, isn't it?" He skimmed a fingertip down the center of her forehead, but didn't touch her. "And behind your eyes. It'll only get worse if you go out to a noisy club without tending it. I won't hurt you."

His voice was soothing and compelling. Even as she shook her head, he continued to speak, and drew her gently in.

"It's just a matter of touch, of concentration. Close your eyes, try to relax. Think of something else. You went to Chicago today."

"Yeah." Her lids drooped closed as he brushed that fingertip over her brow. "To interview people at the prison."

"All that violent and conflicting energy. No wonder you have a headache."

His fingertips fluttered against her closed lids. Warmth. His voice murmured. Comfort. No man had ever offered her both of those things, but for Roarke. She let herself drift; it was almost impossible not to. And the thought passed through her head, the wonder of what it would be like to have a man, a father, give kindness instead of pain.

Sam drew the ache out, into his fingertips, his fingers, into his palm. It throbbed there, dully, pulsed like an echo in his forehead, before he let it spread and dissipate.

As it faded, it felt another, sharper pain. Deeper, it cut fast and violent into his center. With it, he had a flash. And saw into her mind, her thoughts, her memory, before he broke the link and blocked.

"Wow." She swayed a little from the sudden lack of support, though she hadn't been aware of leaning. She was aware that the headache was gone, and in its place a sensation of calm well-being. "Better than any damn blocker," she began as she opened her eyes.

He was staring at her, his face drained of color, full of shock and sorrow. "I'm sorry. I'm so sorry."

"What? What's wrong? Does that deal make you sick?" She reached out to take his arm, but he gripped her hand. And now his were cold as winter.

"Eve, I never intended—such a strong mind. I should've realized. I was focused on relieving the pain. It's necessary to lower the block, very briefly, but I do light healing as a matter of course, and never intrude. I never meant to."

She stiffened. "What do you mean, intrude?"

"I didn't look, I promise you. It's against everything I believe to look into another person without express invitation. But you opened, and the image was there before I could block it. From your childhood." He saw from her face she understood him. "I'm so very sorry."

"You looked in my head?"

"No. But I saw. And seeing, however unintentional, is still a betrayal of trust."

She felt stripped and raw. Stepped back from him. "That's private."

"Yes, very private. I don't know what I can do to make this up to you, but—"

"You forget what you saw," she snapped. "And you don't talk about it. Ever. To anyone."

"You have my word I won't speak of it. Eve, if you want Phoebe and me to go—"

"I don't give a damn what you do. Just stay out of my head. Stay the hell out of my head." She strode away, had to force herself not to run. Instead she fought to compose herself before she went back down, into the parlor.

She couldn't think of anything she wanted more now than an hour at the D and D where she could smother out her own thoughts in horrible music played at a level to damage eardrums, to drink bad booze until misery was sunken and drowned.

Duty won out, and she only got half-drunk, which took some work in the single hour she'd allowed herself. She'd avoided Sam, sitting as far away from him as possible on the wild and noisy ride downtown, then making sure she was at the opposite end of the table from him during the stint at the club.

He'd made it easy for her, and kept his distance.

Even when Mavis had insisted everybody dance with everybody else, they'd bypassed each other. But neither that nor the burn of bad brew had improved her mood.

And the mood hadn't been lost on Roarke. He waited until they were home, alone, as the rest of the party had remained downtown. "Are you going to tell me what's wrong?"

"Got a lot on my mind."

"You often do, but it doesn't encourage you to drink with the express purpose of getting piss-faced."

"I'm not piss-faced. I stopped halfway." But her balance wasn't quite what it had been, and she stumbled on the bottom step going upstairs. "Mostly halfway. What's the matter, you've seen me half-drunk before."

"Not when you have work yet, and not when you're upset." He took her arm to steady her.

"Back off. I don't need more people poking at my fucking psyche."

He recognized the combative tone in her voice. He didn't mind a fight. He'd get to the bottom of things quicker that way. "Since you're my wife, I believe I have a legal right to poke at your psyche, among other things."

"Don't say *my wife* in that smug-ass tone. You know I hate that."

"I do, yes, and I so enjoy it. What went on between you and Sam before we left?"

"Get outta my face. I got work."

"I'm not in your face as yet. What went on?" he repeated, spacing each word carefully just before he pushed her up against the wall. "And now, Lieutenant, I'm in your face."

"We had a quickie on the bedroom floor. So what?"

"Fast sex doesn't usually make a man look so unhappy. And I happen to know it doesn't make you vile-tempered. But we can check that theory if you like." He hooked a hand in the waistband of her trousers, yanked, and popped the button.

She pivoted, but her reflexes were off. The elbow jab missed, and she ended up flat against the wall again. "I don't want to be touched right now. I don't want anyone's hands on me. Do you get it?"

He framed her face with them. "What happened?"

"He did some sort of mojo with the headache." She spat it out. "And while he was in there, he got a look at me. When I was a kid. He saw."

"Ah, Eve." He drew her in, kept drawing her in even when she struggled.

"Get off me. Damn it. Damn you."

"I'll get them a hotel room. I'll get them out tonight."

"It doesn't matter if you get them a room on the fucking moon. He *knows*." Somehow she'd stopped pushing him away and was holding on. "It doesn't matter that he didn't do it on purpose. It doesn't matter that he's sorry." Feeling more sick than drunk now, she dropped her head on Roarke's shoulder. "He knows, and nothing changes that."

"Why does it shame you? You were a child. An innocent child. How many innocents have you stood for?" He eased her face up so their eyes met. "And how many more before you're done? Yet there's still a part of you that steps back from yourself, and those who would feel for the child you were."

"It's my private business."

"Do you worry he won't honor that?"

"No." She let out a weary sigh. "No. He gave his word. Guy like that saws his tongue off with a rusty knife before he breaks his word. But he knows, and when he looks at me—"

"He'll see his daughter's friend. An amazing woman. He'll see what you too often forget to see when you look in the mirror. Courage."

She eased away now. "Lot of people making noises about how brave I am today."

"Well then, why don't you be brave enough to tell me the rest of it. You already had trouble on your mind when you walked in the door this evening."

"Yeah, I did. We need to talk, but I have to go throw up first."

"As long as we have our priorities straight. Come on then." He slipped an arm around her. "I'll hold your head."

She sicked up the worst of the booze, downed without much protest, the mixture Roarke pushed on her when she was finished. She took a blistering shower, dressed in loose pants and a muscle shirt, and felt human again by the time they regrouped in her office. She added one final cure, black coffee, then filled him in on her visit to Dockport.

"You're thinking by Dallas dude, she means me."

"It's a strong possibility, one I passed by Mira on the way home. She agrees with me. I'm the only woman who had a part in taking her down, and that makes me her competition. No, more like her opposition. She comes back to my turf, kills here, and shows me she's back and ready to rumble. But she takes you out, she beats me. Whatever happens in the battles before or after, she wins the war."

"A reasonable theory, and an interesting one." He swirled brandy. Unlike the rest of the group, he hadn't touched a drink at the D and D. "I wonder how she expects to get through my security, to get close enough to me to cause me any harm."

"Roarke—"

He smiled, leaned in as she had. "Eve."

"Cut it out. Look, I know you've got ace security, the best money can buy. I know your instincts are better yet. But she's smart, she's thorough, and she's very, very good at what she does."

"So are you. Which," he continued, "would add another edge for her. How to kill me when I'm so completely, even intimately protected."

"You'll add to your security," she said briskly. "We'll work out the logistics of that, get some input from Feeney. I'll put cops on you, mix some in with your people at your midtown office. I'll need to know your schedule, down to the last detail so I can have men planted wherever you have meetings set up. If you're going out of the city, using any transpo, it needs to be scanned and swept first—coming and going."

He sat back, sipped his brandy. "We both know I'm not going around with cops on my heels."

"You'd prefer protective custody and me keeping you locked in this house?"

He angled his head. "You know my lawyers will tear any attempt at that into tiny shreds, so let's save both of us the time and trouble."

"You hard-headed son of a bitch. I'll chew your lawyers up and spit them back out on your thousand-dollar shoes."

"You can try."

She sprang to her feet. "I pick up that 'link, I'm getting authorization to lock you up, at a location I see fit, and slap a goddamn bracelet on your wrist until I'm sure your ass is safe."

He got to his feet as well. "Then I pick up the 'link, make my call, and have a restraining order trumping your bloody authorization before it's printed. I won't be caged, Eve, not by you or anyone. And I won't hide or run, so put your considerable temper and energies into tracking your woman, and I'll see to my own ass very well."

"It's not just your ass anymore. It belongs to me, too. Goddamn it, I love you."

"And I love you right back." As his temper ebbed, he laid his hands on her shoulders. "Eve, I'll have a care. I promise you."

She shrugged his hands off, paced away. "I knew you wouldn't do it my way."

"Do you think I'd be where I am if every time there's a threat I bolt into some safe house? I face what comes at me. I deal with it. I deal with it a bit different than I once did."

"I know. I know you're more savvy about security than anyone, but will you let Feeney look things over?"

"I've no problem with that."

"I'm asking for you to give me your schedule, where you'll be, when and with who. I won't throw cops at you." She turned back now. "You'd make them and ditch them anyway. But I'd feel better if I knew."

"I'll copy you."

"Okay. I'm going to have to go to Dallas." She said it very fast, as if the words might burn her tongue. "I'm going to need to talk to the step-father. I'm not sure when I can manage it, but within the next two days. She'll be moving in on someone else before much longer. He could be a target, too. You know, Texas, cowboys. Maybe that's the sheep angle, too. They've got sheep in Texas, I think. I—"

He'd come to her while she'd rambled, and cut her

off by gently taking her arms. "I'll go with you. You won't do this without me."

"I don't think I could." She relaxed deliberately, muscle by muscle. "I'm okay. I've got work."

Chapter 9

Eve spent hours doing probabilities, running scans on names that linked to *sheep* and *cowboy*.

While the computer worked, she read over the Pettibone file, hoping she'd missed something, anything that indicated a more direct link between the killer and her victim.

All she found was a nice, middle-aged man, well-loved by his family, well-liked by his friends, who'd run a successful business in a straightforward, honest manner.

Nor could she link anyone else. There was no evidence that either of the victim's wives or his children or the spouses of his children knew or had known Julianna Dunne, and no motive she could find that leaned toward any of them arranging a murder.

The two wives might have been totally different types, but they had one patch of common ground. An obvious affection for Walter C. Pettibone.

As far as the data, the evidence, and the probability scans indicated, Julianna had picked Pettibone out of a hat. And that canny capriciousness meant the next target could be one of millions.

She left the computer sorting names when she went to bed, and was up at six A.M. going over it all again.

"You'll wear yourself out again, Lieutenant."

She looked over to where Roarke stood, already dressed, already perfect. She'd yet to so much as brush her teeth.

"No, I'm fine. I got a solid five. I'm working with sheep." She gestured toward the wall screen. "You got any clue how many names have something to do with stupid sheep?"

"Other than the variations that include the syllable sheep itself? Lamb, Shepherd, Ram, Mutton, Ewes—"

"Shut up."

He grinned and came into her office, offered her one of the mugs of coffee he held. "And, of course, countless variations on those and others."

"And it doesn't have to be a name. Could be a job, the way he looks. Christ, I got this angle from a jonesing funky junkie named Loopy."

"Still there's a logic to it. The bone man, the sheep man. I'd say you're on the right track."

"Big fricking track. Even cutting it to multiple married males from fifty to seventy-five, her usual target area, I've got tens of thousands just in the metropolitan area. I can cut that back again by financial worth, but it's still too many to cover."

"What's your plan?"

"Cutting it down again by following the theory that Pettibone was considered eight to ten years back. If her next mark was in the running back then, I look at men who were successfully established in the city ten years ago. Then I hope to hell Julianna's not in a hurry."

She ordered the computer to start a new listing using

that criteria, then took a casual sip of coffee. "What've you got going today?"

He took a disc out of his pocket. "My schedule for the next five days. You'll be updated on any changes to it."

"Thanks." She took it, then looked up at him. "Thanks," she repeated. "Roarke, I shouldn't have taken it all out on you last night. But you're so damn handy."

"It's all right. The next time you get drunk and surly, I'll just slap you around."

"I guess that's fair." She eased back when he leaned in. "I haven't cleaned up yet. I was going to catch a quick workout while the lists are compiling."

"A workout sounds perfect."

"You're already dressed," she said when he took her hand and started for the elevator.

"The brilliant thing about clothes is you can put them on and take them off as often as you like." He turned, tugged up her sweatshirt when they were in the elevator. "See?"

"We've got house guests wandering all over the place," she reminded him.

"So, we'll lock the door." His clever hands trailed up and closed over her breasts. "And have a quick, private workout."

"Good thinking."

While Eve was finishing off a very satisfying exercise program with a swim, Henry Mouton strode across the polished marble floors of Mouton, Carlston, and Fitch, attorneys at law.

He was sixty-two, film-star handsome athletically trim, and one of the premier corporate attorneys on the East Coast.

He walked with purpose. Lived with purpose. In the thirty-odd years he'd been a lawyer, he had arrived at his office at precisely seven o'clock, five days a week. That routine hadn't altered when he'd established his own firm twenty-three years ago.

Self-made men, Henry liked to say, were works in progress. And work was the key word.

He loved his, loved climbing the slippery, tangled vine of the law.

He approached his life the same way he approached his work. With dedication and routine. He maintained his health, his body, and his mind with habitual exercise, a good diet, and exposure to culture. He vacationed twice yearly, for precisely two weeks in each locale. In February, he selected a warm weather clime, and in August earmarked an interesting location where museums, galleries, and theater would be offered in abundance.

The third weekend of every month, he stayed at his shore home in the Hamptons.

Some said he was rigid, including his two ex-wives, but Henry thought of himself as organized. As his current wife was nearly as detail- and routine-oriented as he was himself, Henry's world was in perfect order.

The main floor of Mouton, Carlston, and Fitch was as grand as a cathedral, and at seven A.M. quiet as a grave.

He walked straight to his corner office, with its eagle-perch view of uptown Manhattan. His desk was a perfect rectangular island topped only by his data and communication center, his sterling pen set, a fresh blotter bordered in burgundy leather, and a silver-framed photo of his wife, the third image to grace that same frame in the past twenty-four years.

He set his briefcase on the blotter, opened it, and removed his memo book and the disc files he'd taken home with him the night before.

While commuter trams streamed the sky at his back, Henry closed the briefcase, set it on the shelf beside his desk for easy access.

A faint sound had him glancing up, and frowning in puzzlement at the neatly dressed brunette in his doorway.

"And who might you be?"

"I beg your pardon, Mr. Mouton. I'm Janet Drake, the new temp. I heard you come in. I didn't realize anyone would be in this early."

Julianna folded her hands at her waist and offered a shy smile. "I didn't mean to disturb you."

"You're in early yourself, Miss Drake."

"Yes, sir. It's my first day. I wanted to familiarize myself with the office and organize my cube. I hope that's all right."

"Initiative is appreciated around here." Attractive, Henry thought, well-spoken, eager. "Would you be hoping for a permanent slot here, Miss Drake?"

She worked up a faint flush. "I'd be thrilled to be offered a permanent position with your firm, sir. If my work warrants it."

He nodded. "Carry on, then."

"Yes, sir." She stepped back, stopped. "Could I bring you a cup of coffee? I just programmed fresh."

He let out a grunt as he slid a file disc into his desk unit. "Light, no sugar. Thank you."

In her practical pumps, Julianna clipped back to the staff break room. There was plenty of time. Her careful research told her that the head of the firm arrived in the offices at least thirty minutes, often a full hour before anyone else. But there was always a chance some eager-beaver law clerk or drone, some maintenance droid could come in and interrupt things.

She preferred getting the job done and moving on while the day was young. She was sure Henry himself would applaud the efficiency.

The idea tickled her so much she chuckled as she poisoned his coffee.

"Could've worked out this way nine years ago,

Henry," she murmured as she stirred in the cyanide. "But you didn't draw the short straw." She patted her short, dark hair. "Sort of a pity, really. I think you'd have enjoyed being married to me. For the short-term."

She carried the thick, practical mug back into his office. His computer was already blathering about some legal precedent. Outside the glass wall a traffic copter whisked by as the morning commute heated up. Julianna set the coffee by his elbow, stepped back.

"Is there anything else I can do for you, Mr. Mouton?"

Obviously lost in thought, he picked up the coffee, sipped absently while he stared out at the traffic, listened to his notes.

"No, I've everything I need, Miss . . ."

"Drake," she said pleasantly, her gaze ice-cold as she watched him sip again. "Janet Drake."

"Yes, well, good luck on your first day, Miss Drake. Just leave the door open when you go out."

"Yes, sir."

She stepped outside the office, and waited. She heard him begin to choke, that shocked, desperate attempt to draw air. Her face held a terrible beauty when she stepped back in to watch him die.

She liked to watch, when the opportunity presented itself.

His face was beet red, his eyes bulging. He'd knocked what was left of the coffee on the floor as he thrashed, and the brown seeped in to stain the stone gray carpet.

He stared at her, the pain and fear alive in the room as he died.

"Go down the wrong pipe?" she said cheerfully, and strolled over as he fell to the floor. "There's been a little change in routine today, Henry." She angled her head, her expression fascinated as his body convulsed. "You get to die."

It was, Julianna thought, the most incredible sensation

to witness death come, and know it marched in at the direction of your own hand.

It was a wonder to her more people didn't try it.

When it was finished, she blew him a sassy kiss, and sauntering out, closed the door behind her. A pity it was too early for the shops to be open, she thought as she picked up her handbag and strolled to the elevator. She felt like a nice splurge.

Crouched over the body of Henry Mouton, Eve felt anger, frustration, and guilt. None of those emotions would help, so she did her best to clamp down on them.

"This is her work," Eve stated. "How the hell does she just walk in, through building security, and get this guy to drink poisoned coffee? Blending. She blends. Who do I need to be, and that's who I'll be. She had to know he'd be here, alone. This wasn't a lucky shot. And I'm off chasing fucking sheep."

"Lieutenant. *Mouton* is sheep in French." Peabody held out her PPC. "I looked it up."

"Great, fine. Loopy comes through. A lot of good it did *him*." Annoyed with herself, she straightened up. "Have him tagged and bagged and turned over to the ME. I need building security discs, the witness who found him, ah . . . office manager. Data on next-of-kin."

"Yes, sir. Dallas?" Peabody hesitated, then spoke her mind. "You couldn't have stopped this."

"Sure I could have. Turn the right key in the right lock. But I didn't, so we go from here."

When Peabody moved out, Eve took out her notebook and began to plug in data.

"Excuse me. Lieutenant Dallas?"

She glanced back, saw the smartly dressed woman with jet-black hair in perfectly styled waves. "I have to ask you to keep clear of this room."

"Yes, I understand. They told me you were in charge.

I'm Olivia Fitch, one of Henry's partners. And his second wife." When her gaze wandered to the body, her lips trembled. But she pressed them together, and her voice stayed steady. "I was hoping you could tell me . . . something. Anything."

"Is there somewhere we can talk, Ms. Fitch?"

"Yes, of course. My office? I want to be able to tell the staff something," she began as she led the way. "And I need, for myself, to be able to think about this in some rational way."

She opened the door to another corner office. It was similar in size to Mouton's, faced east instead of north, and had a bit more flair and less spartan regimentation.

"This is a difficult time for you."

"Yes, very." Rather than move to the desk or the sitting area, Olivia walked to the wall of windows. "Henry and I were divorced four, no five years ago. He's remarried and this will be a devastating blow for Ashley. His death would have been difficult enough, but murder. I've never known anyone who's been murdered." She turned back. "It shakes me down to the bone."

"Do you know anyone who'd wish Mr. Mouton harm?"

"We're lawyers," Olivia returned with a shrug. "Who doesn't wish us harm? But no, I honestly can't think of anyone who'd do this to Henry. He's an irritating man, impossible to live with in my viewpoint. He's—he was so linear, so absolutely fixated on maintaining his routines, so absolutely set in his ways. You might want to kick him in the ass occasionally, but you wouldn't want to kill him for it."

"Not many people who'd been married would remain business partners."

"Another one of Henry's annoying traits." Tears shimmered, but she held them back. "He was a logical bastard. Why should we have an upheaval in the firm because the marriage was over? Worked together fine before, didn't we? In this case, we were in agreement. The fact is we made better business partners than lovers. I don't know if we were friends. I should probably be asking for my own lawyer by now." She sighed. "I can't work up the energy for it."

"Why would he have been here before office hours?"

"Henry sat down at his desk every blessed morning at seven A.M. Rain, shine, flood, or famine. Whatever else could be said about him, his work ethic was golden. He cared about this firm, about his work, about the law."

Now her voice caught and she pressed a hand to her mouth. "Damn it. Damn it, damn it."

"Do you want something? A glass of water?"

"No. I'm not a crier." She bore down, visibly. "And I also care about the law. I want whoever did this caught and punished. So ask your questions. I can promise you you'll have full cooperation from everyone in this firm or I'll skin them."

"Appreciated." Eve paused, turned when Peabody stepped in.

"Can I speak to you a minute, Lieutenant?"

"If you'll hold here, Ms. Fitch." She shifted to just outside the office door. "What have you got?"

"Julianna Dunne's fingerprints in the break room. She was here, and she didn't bother to seal up. I've got the discs from security. They're labeled."

"Good. Find me the office manager and send her in here when I'm done with Fitch."

She stepped back inside. "Ms. Fitch, do you know a woman named Julianna Dunne?"

"Dunne? That name sounds familiar." Her brow furrowed, then arched in surprise. "The Walter Pettibone murder—and the others. I saw the media reports and bulletins. Do you think she . . . but why? How could she just . . ." She did sit now, heavily.

"Have you seen a woman matching her description in or around these offices?"

"No." Olivia pressed her hands to her face. "I can't get my head around this."

"She was here, in your break room. I assume your cleaning service wipes down that area every night."

"Yes, yes. We have a very good, very thorough service."

"If that's the case, she was here this morning. Can I use this?" she asked, gesturing to the computer.

"Yes. Go ahead."

Eve plugged in the lobby disc. "Do you know what time the cleaning service does this area?"

"They're scheduled to do this floor between twelve and two A.M."

Eve programmed the disc to begin its run at two A.M. She zipped through, pausing periodically when someone entered or exited the lobby. Traffic was light, running to weary office drones who'd put in a late shift, maintenance people, and a change of lobby personnel. At oh-six-forty-five, an attractive brunette in a smart business suit strode in and walked straight to the reception desk.

Eve froze the frame, enhanced. "Do you recognize this woman?"

Olivia turned back, studied the image. "No. I don't recall seeing her before. There are a number of offices and companies in this building. I don't see how—"

"Look closer. Just the face. Forget the hair."

There was a flicker of impatience, but Olivia did as she was asked. "I know everyone on this level, and she's not . . . Wait. My God. That's Dunne, isn't it? I didn't recognize her at first glance."

"Yeah, most people wouldn't."

By noon she had a conference room booked and her team assembled.

"Here's how it went," she began. "Julianna forges a firm ID—child's play—and passes it off to the security guard. Same guard was on duty the day before—six to noon shift—and she signed in as Janet Drake, clerical temp for Mouton, Carlston, and Fitch at eight-forty-three on that date. Made a point in giving him a big, flirty smile and making some small talk so he'd remember her when she came in this morning. Walks in early," Eve continued, gesturing to the disc running on-screen. "Bops right on up to the main floor of the firm. We've got her until she walks into the offices. Eight minutes later, we have Mouton following the same route. For the next twenty minutes, we deduce."

She paused the run. "Statements from staff and associates confirm that Mouton habitually entered his office at oh-seven hundred. He was a creature of routine, and no doubt Julianna researched his habits. The most likely scenario is she introduced herself as a temp, claimed to be eager to start work, flattered him in the area most important to him—his firm, his work, his work ethic. She offers to bring him coffee, goes to the break room, orders a cup, poisons it. She'd have stayed to make sure he drank it, make sure he died. She likes to see the job through. At seven-eighteen, she exits the offices."

Eve ordered the run to continue, zipped it up. "She's got a glow about her now," she commented. "She really gets off on this. Exits by a second-floor fire door so she doesn't have to bother with the guard. She could catch the glide to street level and be home for brunch."

"She's changed her pattern," Feeney put in. "She's stayed in New York, she's greasing guys not previously known to her. But some habits die hard. She's still going for the same type of target, still modifying her appearance without any permanent changes."

"She's dug in here." Eve reached for coffee as a matter of habit more than need. "Mira's opinion is I'm part of the appeal—the only woman she's ever really combated with. She needs to be better than I am, and the way to do that is to kill on my turf while I chase my tail."

"Good." McNab caught her attention. "Then it'll hurt more when you rear back and bite out her throat."

"Sucking up, Detective?"

"Yes, sir." He flashed a grin as bright as his trio of earrings. "But hey, what is, is. She's not better than you."

"Right now I've got two dead men who aren't likely to agree with you. We need to keep on those units impounded from Dockport. She's got a place here."

Somewhere, Eve thought. Classy uptown digs, trendy downtown.

"Swank apartment or house, in the city. She either bought it while she was in the cage, or arranged for it to be maintained during that period." She gulped more coffee, waited for the kick. "There have to be transmissions. She's smart enough to have used her smuggled PPC for that, but she might have gotten sloppy. She researched targets. There has to be data."

"We're cleaning out the excess," Feeney assured her. "If it's there, we'll find it."

"Find it fast. There are disc copies of Mira's report for all of you. You'll read her opinion, and I concur with it, that Julianna's story regarding her step-father sexually abusing her is inaccurate. I need to interview him, push out the truth. The more we know about her, the quicker we hunt her down. In addition, it's possible he's a future target. I'll be going to Texas as soon as it can be arranged."

"Am I with you, sir?" Peabody asked.

"No, I need you here." Can't take you to Dallas. Can't risk it. Can't stand it. "Keep running the poison. She's getting it from somewhere." She was careful to keep her voice professional as she continued. "You'll also read in Mira's report that regardless of the low probability percentage on the computer scans, she believes Roarke is also a potential target."

"Fucking A."

Though it arrowed straight to her heart, she ignored McNab's outburst. "While he doesn't fit her standard profile, and the accumulated data, which gives this target a negligible computer probability, he suits her needs to war with me. Being aware of the identity of a potential target will help us close in. I have Roarke's schedule for the next five days, and there are copies of that as well in your packets. He's refused direct police protection, but has agreed to basic precautions."

Her mind flashed back to Mouton's body, sprawled on his office floor. Before Roarke's face could superimpose over the image, she shut it down. "His security is superior, but as primary . . ."

She let out an oath, short, vicious, pushed her fisted hands in her pockets. "Feeney, I'd like you to go over security at his offices, at home, in his vehicles."

"He tagged me an hour ago. I'm meeting him this afternoon."

"Thanks. Okay. That's all we've got, so let's make it work. I'll be in my office."

"She's shook," McNab whispered to Peabody when Eve headed out. "And she doesn't shake easy."

"I'm going to go talk to her." She bolted out of the room, scanned the corridor, and just caught sight of Eve moving down on a glide. She had to run, then elbow a few people aside, but she caught up just as Eve stepped off.

"Dallas. Hold on just a minute."

"I don't have time for chatter, Peabody. If I'm going to clean things up so I can take this travel time, I've got to move."

"She won't get to him. She won't even get close." She touched Eve's arm, then took hold of it to stop Eve's forward progress. "Maybe if it was just one of you she could get lucky and do some damage. But she's going up against both of you. There's no way. Just no way in the known universe."

The frustration and fear bottled up in Eve's throat spewed out in a low, harsh tone. "All she has to do is tip something in a cup of coffee, a glass of wine, a fucking glass of water."

"No, that's not all." *More than shook*, Peabody thought. *Scared to the bone.* "You know it's not. She has to get through his radar and yours. Look, I don't know the facts about where he came from, how he got here, but I can deduce. It's not just that he knows how to handle himself, which he does. It's that he's dangerous. It's one of the things that makes him so goddamn sexy."

Eve turned, stared blindly at a vending machine. "He's not even worried, particularly."

"That doesn't mean he won't be careful, that he won't be smart."

"No, it doesn't. I know it doesn't." To give her hands something to do, she dug out a credit, plugged it in, and ordered a candy bar.

I'M SORRY, THAT ITEM IS CURRENTLY OUT OF STOCK. WOULD YOU CARE TO MAKE ANOTHER SELECTION?

"Don't kick it!" Peabody said hurriedly even as Eve reared back. "You'll lose your vending privileges again. Try this one. It's really good." Before her lieutenant could do any damage, Peabody chose another item.

YOU HAVE SELECTED A GOOEY-CRUNCH BAR, THE YUMMY-TUMMY TREAT WITH THREE LAYERS OF CHOCOLATE SUBSTITUTE, A COOKIE CRUNCH, AND A CREAMY NONDAIRY FILLING.

Eve snatched it out, moving away while the machine detailed the ingredients along with fat grams and caloric contents.

"Can I ask you something about the Stibbs's case?" Peabody asked, jogging to keep up.

"Walk and talk."

"I've been studying the file and I'm about ready to bring her in for an interview, but I thought maybe I should surveil her when I can manage it, for a day or two. Get her rhythm, you know. And I wondered if I should let her make me or not."

With some effort, Eve adjusted her line of thought. "Stay in uniform, let her make you. It'll keep her off-balance."

"And I'm going to try to talk to a couple of the people who gave statements about the homicide, people who knew all three subjects. It won't hurt if she hears about it?"

"Goes to keeping her shaky, wondering what's up. She'll be primed when you bring her in."

"I want to wait until you're back from Texas before I bring her in. In case I screw up."

"Wait until I'm back, but you're not going to screw up. I don't work with screwups," she added, and made Peabody smile as they parted ways in the bull pen.

In her office, Eve took a moment to steady herself, bit off a chunk of the candy bar and decided it was pretty much a yummy-tummy treat. With Roarke's schedule in her head, she put in a call to his midtown offices.

"I know you've got a meeting in five," she began when he came on. "Christ knows how you stand meeting all those people every day of your life."

"I'm just a people person, Lieutenant. An amiable soul."

"Yeah, right. How much hassle is it going to be for you to ditch all those meetings tomorrow?"

"What's the point of being master of all you survey if you can't ditch meetings when it suits you? What do you need?"

"I want to leave for Dallas in the morning. First thing."

"All right, I'll take care of it."

"I don't know how long it'll take, but we should be able to get it done and get back all in the same day. An overnight at the most."

"Whatever it takes. Eve, you're not alone anymore."

She nodded, and though it felt foolish, touched her fingers to his face on the screen. "Neither are you."

Chapter 10

PROBABILITY ROARKE IS NEXT TARGET IS FIFTY-
ONE-POINT-FIVE EIGHT PERCENT. . . .

Eve stood, staring out her skinny office window.

The fifty-fifty chance given in the computer's soulless tones didn't comfort her.

"Where will she come at him?"

INSUFFICIENT DATA FOR PROBABILITY. . . .

"I wasn't asking you," she grumbled and pinched her fingers to the bridge of her nose. "Think," she ordered herself. "Think, think. What's in her head?"

More impact, Eve decided, if Julianna went for Roarke when his cop was close. At home then, or at a public or private social event they'd both attend. She called his schedule back on-screen and studied it. Again.

She didn't know how any one person managed that

many meetings, deals, conversations, and contacts in one day and stayed sane. But that was Roarke.

All those people, she thought, that he brushed against in any given day. Business associates, staff, employees, waiters, assistants, and assistants to assistants. However brilliant his security, there was always a crack to slither through.

But he was aware of that, she reminded herself, on the most elemental level. The way a tiger would be aware of both predator and prey in his own jungle.

And if she allowed herself to worry into fear over him, she'd miss something.

She sat again, cleared her mind.

In the first wave of Julianna Dunne's killings, she had assumed the role of society princess. A young, glamorous butterfly who'd flitted among the abundant blooms of the wealthy. As one of them, Eve mused.

Her new pattern was efficient employee. Smart, Eve conceded. People rarely took full notice of those who served them. She would stick with that, Eve thought. Almost certainly stick with that level. Server, clerk, domestic.

Whoever the next target, she would likely find her way into his business or his home through his company.

Preferred method, poison. Old-fashioned poison, Eve added. Why? You didn't get your hands dirty that way, and most usually had the opportunity to watch it work. See the shock, confusion, pain. The victim understood a blaster or a blade when it came for him. But poison was subtle, even elegant. And it confused.

But you didn't bop into your local 24/7 and pick up a bottle of cyanide. It was time to track down the source.

Before she did, there was a little business to clear up. She put in a call to Charles Monroe.

The handsome licensed companion picked up on his pocket-link. Eve could hear the murmuring of voices, the

quiet clink of china and crystal of a classy restaurant as
his face filled the screen.

"Lieutenant Sugar." He beamed. "What a nice surprise."

"You got company?"

"Not quite yet. Client's late, she usually is. What can
I do for my favorite avenger of the law?"

"Have you got any professional pals or associates in
the Chicago area?"

"Dallas, when one is in the oldest profession, one has
pals and associates everywhere."

"Yeah. Well, I need one who's willing to go to Dockport Rehabilitation Center, do a conjugal for an inmate,
for the standard police scale."

His face, his tone, went all business. She saw him
move, glance down, and knew he'd taken out an e-book.
"Male or female companion?"

"Female inmate seeks attractive man with staying
power for conjugal episode."

"Time frame?"

"Within the next couple of weeks would be good.
Sooner the better. The budget will spring for a two-hour
call, no frills, and basic transpo."

"Since I doubt the police are overly concerned with
this woman's sexual health, I assume this is payment for
information or cooperation in some ongoing investigation."

"Assume whatever." Her face, her tone, mirrored his
now. "I need the contact. Can you reach out to an asso-
ciate in that area? One who can handle himself. She's
just after a solid bounce, but she has a violent tendency
and I don't want to put anybody green in this situation."

"I could, but why don't I just take care of it for you?
I'm certainly not green, and I owe you enough favors to
cover this."

"You don't owe me anything."

"I owe you Louise," he corrected, and everything in his face brightened on her name. "Give me the information I'll need, and I'll work it into my schedule. On the house for you, Lieutenant Sugar."

She hesitated. It felt weird to book him for sex. To think of his developing romance with the dedicated Dr. Louise Dimatto while she arranged to send him off for a conjugal with Maria Sanchez.

This friendship gig was almost as complicated and boggy as the marriage gig.

It was his job, Eve reminded herself. And if it didn't bother Louise, why should it bother her?

"You'll get scale. I want to keep this on the books. Maria Sanchez," she began, and gave him the information he'd need. "I appreciate this, Charles."

"No, you're embarrassed, and that's very sweet of you. Give my love to Peabody, and I'll give your best to Louise. My lunch and bounce client's just walked in. If there's nothing else, I'd as soon not be talking to a cop when she gets to the table. These are the things that can mar the delicate balance of a romantic afternoon."

His lips curved when he said it, and made Eve shake her head. "Let me know when you've nailed down the date and time and if you get any hassles with the arrangements at Dockport. Warden there's an asshole."

"I'll keep that in mind. Later, Lieutenant Sugar."

When he ended transmission, she made the next call on her list. Directing it, purposefully, to Nadine Furst's voice mail, Eve left a terse message.

"You got a one-on-one, my office, sixteen hundred. Sharp. No live feed. If you're late, I'll have something better to do."

She pushed away from the desk, strode out, and swung by Peabody's cube. "With me" was all she said.

•   •   •

"I'm getting nowhere trying to track a supplier for the cyanide through standard sources." Peabody hustled into the elevator behind Eve. "Even considering the number of legal sources for that kind of controlled substance, it's necessary to show authorization with prints. Prints are run through a stringent search and scan. Dunne's are on file, and would have popped."

"Illegal sources?"

"I've run cyanide poisonings through IRCCA. Stuff's more popular than you might think, but most got their supply through a legal source. The dude in East D.C. where Dunne previously shopped was the major on-planet player, and he's dead. The others on record are mostly small-time, and the majority of them are *doing* time—primarily illegals distribution, with poisons as a sideline. Research indicates poisons aren't very cost effective, narrow profit margin, and are generally not a specialty."

"Possible she found a way through to a legal source but let's try the other route." Eve strode to her vehicle, paused. "A lot of talk and jive in prison, and she might have followed up on a contact there. Plus, she had her finger on the world through computer access. Plenty of time to search and research. Her source might not be in New York, but people know people who know people. We're going underground."

Peabody, a stalwart soldier, paled. "Oh boy."

Beneath New York was another world, a seamy city of the lost and the vicious. Some went under to toy with that keen edge, the way a child might play with a sharpened knife, just to see how it would slice. Others enjoyed the elemental meanness, the stink of violence that permeated the air as thickly as the stench of garbage and shit.

And some simply got lost there.

Eve left her jacket in the car. She wanted her weapon in full view. Her clutch piece was strapped to her ankle, and she'd shoved a combat knife into her boot.

"Here." She tossed Peabody a small shock bat. "Know how to use it?"

She had to gulp once, but nodded. "Yes, sir."

"Hook it to your belt, keep it in plain sight. You kept up with your hand-to-hand?"

"Yeah." She blew out a breath. "I can handle myself."

"That's right." Eve not only wanted her to say it, she wanted her to believe it. "And when you step down there, you remember you're one bad bitch cop, and you drink blood for breakfast."

"I'm one bad bitch cop, and I drink blood for breakfast. Yuck."

"Let's go."

They headed down filthy steps and veered off from the subway entrance into the rat hole of a tunnel that led to the underground. Lights glowed dull red and dirty blue in a kind of snarling carnival of sex, games, and entertainment suited for the cold and the cruel.

Eve caught the stink of vomit and glanced over to see a man down on his hands and knees, puking horribly.

"You okay?"

He didn't look up. "Fuck you."

Feeling other eyes on her, she squeezed into the passageway behind him, then gave him a solid shove with her boot that sent him facedown in his own vomit. "Oh no," she said pleasantly, "fuck you."

Her knife was out of her boot with its honed point at his filthy throat before he could curse her again. "I'm a cop, asshole, but don't think I won't slice your useless throat ear-to-ear just for the fun of it. Where can I find Mook today?"

His eyes were fire-red, his breath amazing. "I don't know no mother-fucking Mook."

She risked all manner of vermin, fisted a hand in his stringy hair, and yanked his head back. "Everybody knows mother-fucking Mook. You want to die here, or live to puke another day?"

"I don't keep tabs on the cocksucker." His lips peeled back as the point of the knife pressed against his jugular. "Maybe VR Hell, fuck do I know?"

"Good. Go right on back to what you were doing." She released him with just enough force to send him sliding into the muck again, then made a show of slapping the jagged-edged knife back in her boot for the benefit of the onlookers lurking in the shadows.

"Anybody here wants trouble, I'm happy to oblige." She lifted her voice just enough to have it echo, to have it punch through the mean flood of viper rock pumping out of doorways. "Otherwise my business is with Mook, who's been described by this fine example of humanity as a mother-fucking cocksucker."

There was a slight movement, shadow in shadow, to her left. She laid her hand on her weapon, and the movement stilled. "Anybody hassles me or my uniform, we start busting asses, and we aren't particularly delicate about how many of those busted asses end up in the city morgue, are we, Officer?"

"No, sir, Lieutenant." Peabody prayed her voice wouldn't crack and embarrass both of them. "In fact, we're hoping to win the pool on morgue count this week."

"What's that up to, anyway?"

"Two hundred and thirty-five dollars. And sixty cents."

"Not too shabby." Eve cocked a hip, but her eyes were keen as a blade. "Could use it. When we're finished kicking the shit out of anybody who gives us grief," Eve added pleasantly. "There'll be a squad down here shaking down what's left. Which will really irritate me as I'd have to share the pool with them. Mook," she said again, and waited ten humming seconds.

"VR Hell," someone said in the dark. "Dancing with the S&M machines. Asshole."

Eve merely nodded, deciding to attribute the asshole comment to Mook rather than herself. "And where do I find VR Hell in this delightful and intriguing paradise many of you call home?"

There was another movement, and she whirled, braced, felt Peabody go on full alert beside her. At first she took him for a boy, then saw he was a dwarf. He was crooking his finger.

"Back-to-back," Eve ordered, and they started down one of the dripping tunnels, facing out, guarding each other's backs.

The dwarf moved fast, skittering along in the steaming, stinking tunnels like a cockroach on shoes that flapped against the damp stone floor. He zipped past the bars, the clubs, the joints and dives, twisting and turning through the labyrinth of the underworld.

"Morgue pool was a nice touch," Eve said under her breath.

"Thanks." Peabody resisted swiping at the sweat dripping down her face. "I live to improvise."

From somewhere deeper in the dank, Eve heard a woman scream in pain or passion. She saw a huge man crumpled on the ground sucking on a filthy brown bottle of home-brew. Against the wall beside him a man and woman copulated in an ugly parody of lovemaking.

She smelled sex and piss, and worse.

The tunnel widened, opened into an area jammed with video, VR, and hologram dens.

VR Hell was black. Its walls, its windows, its doors all coated with the same unrelieved, and somehow greasy black. Across it, in letters she assumed were supposed to reflect the devil's fire, was its name. A poorly painted

image of Satan, complete with horns and tail and pitch-
fork, danced over the flames.

"Mook's in there." The dwarf spoke for the first time
in a voice like a bass drum constructed from sandpaper.
"Digs on the Madam Electra machine. Bondage shit. Sick
fucker. Got fifty?"

Eve dug for credits. "Got twenty. Blow."

He showed his grayed, pointy teeth. The twenty disappeared, then so did he.

"You meet such interesting people down here," Peabody said shakily.

"Stay close," Eve ordered. "Anybody moves in, bang
'em."

"You don't have to tell me twice." With her hand
gripped tight on her bat, Peabody followed Eve into Hell.

The noise was awesome: screams, sirens, grunts, and
groans from dozens of clashing machines and patrons.
The lighting was an ugly red that shimmered and swayed.
It flashed her back to a freezing room in Dallas, made
her stomach pitch before she controlled it.

She heard the ragged breathing, the hissed words of
violent sex. She'd heard those in that room, too, before
the end. Heard them in too many rooms to count where
the walls were thin as tissue and brutality was only a
whisper away.

The sound of flesh striking flesh. Gleeful punishment.
Stop it! Goddamn you, Rick, stop! You're hurting me!

Whose voice was that? Eve wondered as she stared
around blindly. Her mother's? One of the whores he'd
used when he wasn't using his daughter?

"Dallas? Lieutenant?"

The uneasy tremble in Peabody's voice snapped her
back. This wasn't the time to lose her focus. It wasn't
the time to remember.

"Stay close," Eve repeated, and began to thread
through the machines.

Most were too intent on the game, on the world they'd created to notice her. But others still had instincts sharp enough to make a cop. Though plenty of those people were armed, nothing was aimed in their direction, for the moment.

She passed a tube titled Whips and Chains where a woman, thin as a stick, wearing VR goggles, screamed in ecstasy. Sweat poured down her body like oil, over the tight leather loincloth, beaded on the restraints that locked her arms and legs to the console of her machine.

"Looks like we're in the right section. There's Mook."

He, too, was locked in a tube. Stripped down to a black leather cock sheath and studded dog collar, his impressively muscled body jerked, his throat worked with gasps. His hair was candlelight gold, shoulder-blade length, and damp with sweat.

His back was crisscrossed with lash marks, proving that he didn't always settle for virtual punishment.

Though it wasn't quite proper procedure, Eve used her master to unlock the tube. His body was arched, his lips peeled back in a grimace of erotic pain. Eve hit the main switch and left him trembling on the brink.

"What the fuck." His body sagged, muscles quivering. "Mistress, please. I beg you."

"That's Lieutenant Mistress to you, creep." Eve whipped off his goggles. "Hi, Mook. Remember me?"

"This is a privacy booth."

"No kidding? And here I was looking forward to a fun group session. Well, next time. Now, let's you and me go somewhere quiet and talk."

"I don't have to talk to you. I got rights. Damn it, I was about to get off here."

With someone else, she might have given him a quick little jab. But Mook, well, he'd just enjoy it. "I take you in, nobody's going to hurt you for the next thirty-six hours. You don't want to go that long without pain, do you, Mook? Let's talk, then you can get back to Madam Electra and her—what is it?—six million tortures."

He leaned in, straining against the restraints. "Make me."

"Want me to rough you up, Mook?" She kept her voice low, in a purr. "Force you?" And when excitement filled his face, she shrugged. "Nope, not in the mood. But I will give your dominatrix here a quick blast. I don't guess they're real quick on repair and replacement of equipment in this joint."

"Don't!" His voice squeaked in protest. Moving fast now, he nudged the toe release so that the restraints popped open. "Why do you want to mess me up this way?"

"Just part of my daily entertainment. Let's get us another privacy booth, Mook, one without the toys."

She stepped back, and when he followed she saw his gaze land on Peabody's bat. He made a lunge. Peabody flipped it out of her belt, zapped him dead center of the chest. His body jerked, danced, then shivered.

"Thank you."

"Don't encourage him, Peabody." Taking Mook's arm firmly in hand, she strode to the nearest private-table booth. As it was occupied by a couple of chemi-heads in the middle of an illegals deal, she kicked the tube, flashed her badge. Jerked her thumb.

They slithered out and away like smoke.

"This is cozy." She settled in. "Watch the door, Peabody, and we'll keep this quick and private. Who's in the poison business these days, Mook?"

"I'm not your weasel."

"A fact that has always brought me joy and cheer. As does the fact I can put you in solitary lockup for those thirty-six hours during which time your life will not be the living hell you know and love. The Reverend Munch is dead as Hitler, Mook, and so are all his merry men, but for you."

"I testified," he reminded her. "I gave the Feds all the info."

"Yeah, you did. Seemed like mass suicide was just a little over the top even for someone with your particular appetites. But you never told them who provided that curare and cyanide cocktail the reverend mixed up with the lemonade for his congregation."

"I was low on the feeding chain. I told them what I knew."

"And the feebies were satisfied. But you know what? I'm not. Give me a name, and I walk out of your sick and pitiful life. Hold out on me, and I'll be coming down here, or whatever cesspool you try to frequent, every fucking day. Every day, interrupting your S&M games until orgasms are just a fond and distant memory for you. Every time you try to get off, jack off, whack off, I'll be there spoiling the fun. Come on, Mook, it's been what . . . better than ten years since the cult offed itself. What do you care?"

"I was sucked in. I was brainwashed—"

"Yeah, yeah, blah, blah. Who brought in the poison?"

"I don't know who he was. They just called him the doctor. Only saw him once. Skinny guy. Old."

"Race?"

"White-bread, through and through. I figure he drank the shit, too."

"Did he?"

"Look." Mook looked around, and though they were in the tube, lowered his voice. "Most people, they don't remember what went down back there; they don't know about it. People find out I was in the Church of Hereafter, they get all weirded out."

She glanced around as well, taking in the screams, the writhing bodies. "Oh yeah, I can see how people acting weird would be a major concern for you. Spill."

"What's it worth?"

Eve pulled out twenty credits, slapped it on the nail-head-sized table.

"Shit, Dallas, that don't buy me an hour VR time. Give me a frigging break."

"Take it. Or leave it and we'll stop being so friendly and go into Central. You won't see Madam Electra and her many exquisite tortures for thirty-six, minimum."

He looked sad, sitting there in his studded dog collar. "Why you gotta be such a bitch?"

"Mook, I ask myself that very question every morning. Never have come up with a satisfactory answer."

He scooped up the twenty, tucked it into his cock sheath. "Want you to remember I helped you out."

"Mook, how could I ever forget you?"

"Right." He looked around, through the smoky glass of the booth. Licked his lips. "Okay, right. Nothing coming down on me about this shit, right?"

"Not a thing."

"Well, see . . . I was going to tell the Feebs everything, total cooperation."

"Get to it, Mook. I have a life to get back to."

"I'm telling you. I was cooperating, and I was gonna name all the names. But I saw him outside, behind the barricades at the church when they started hauling bodies out. Man, that was some scene, right. You were there."

"Yeah, I was there.

"So . . . He looked at me."

Earnest now and just a little jazzed, he leaned in. "Scary guy, all pale and spooky. And me, I don't want to go out with no slurp of some poison. I could tell he knew I went in with the cops instead of following through on the promise. So I had to cover myself, didn't I? I just left him out of it. What's the big deal?"

"So, he's alive?"

"He was then." Mook shrugged his massive shoulders. "I never saw him again, and that was fine by me. I didn't know him," Mook insisted. "Swear on my dick."

"And that is a solemn oath."

"Yeah, it is." Pleased she understood, he nodded rapidly. "Only thing I ever heard was talk about how he used to be a real doctor, but they kicked him outta the club. And that he was fucking rich and fucking crazy."

"Give me a name."

"I didn't know him. That's solid, Dallas. Slave level wasn't allowed to speak to anyone over the rank of soldier."

"Need more."

"I don't got more. He was some old, crazy dude. Look liked a goddamn corpse. Skinny, sick-looking guy, come around and whisper with Munch time to time. Stare right through you so you got bone chills. Guys called him Doctor Doom. That's all I know about it. Come on, that's all I know about it. I want to get back to my game."

"Yeah, go back to your game." But she clamped a hand on his wrist as he started to rise. "If I find out you know more and aren't telling me, I'll pick you up, pull you in, and plunk you down in a locked room full of soft pillows, pastels, and moldy-oldy music."

His face hardened. "You're a cold bitch, Dallas."

"Bet your ass."

"Reverend Munch and the Church of Hereafter cult." Peabody was so impressed she forgot to kiss the sidewalk when they reached street level again. "Were you in on that?"

"Peripheral. Way peripheral. That was a federal op, and local law was just background. Two hundred and fifty people self-terminating because one mad monster preached that death was the ultimate experience." She shook her head. "Maybe it is, but we're all going to get there eventually anyway. Why rush it?"

"They said—people said not everyone in the cult was willing to go through to the end. But the soldier level forced them to drink. And there were kids. Little kids."

"Yeah, there were kids." She'd still been in uniform then, not quite a year out of the Academy. And it was one of the images that lived in the back of her brain. Always would. "Kids, and infants whose mothers fed them that shit in a bottle. Munch had vids taken of the ceremony. Part of his legacy. First and last time I ever saw a Feebie shed a tear. Some of them sobbed like babies."

She shook her head again, pushed the memory away. "We need to start searching for doctors who lost their licenses to practice, going back ten to twenty years to start. Mook said he was old, so let's assume, going by Mook's criteria, this guy was at least sixty during Reverend Munch's reign. Keep the search centered on men, Caucasian, sixty-five to eighty for now. Nearly all of Munch's people were located in New York. So we'll stick with the state's medical board."

Eve glanced at her watch. "I've got a meeting back at Central. Look, let's try this. Head down to the Canal Street Clinic, see if Louise knows anybody who fits this guy's ID, or if not, if she'll nudge some of her medical sources for a name. She's got good contacts, and it could save time."

But Eve hesitated. "You okay dealing with Louise?"

"Sure. I like her. I think it's really nice about her and Charles."

"Whatever. Call in with whatever you get, then take an hour to surveil Maureen Stibbs."

"Really? Thanks, Lieutenant."

"You can take whatever time you can squeeze out

tomorrow on the Stibbs matter when I'm out, but current load is priority."

"Understood. Dallas, one thing, on a personal front. I just wondered if maybe my parents are getting on your nerves? It seemed like maybe you and my father were off each other the other night."

"No, they're fine. Everything's fine."

"Okay, but they're only going to be here a few more days. I'll keep them occupied as much as I can. I guess Dad was just sensing some of your stress over the case. He picks up on stuff like that, even when he's blocking. About the only thing that shakes him up is getting something from somebody without their permission. Anyway." She brightened up again. "I can catch the subway to the clinic. Maybe we'll get lucky with Louise."

"Yeah." It was time, Eve thought, they got lucky with something.

Eve marched toward her office five minutes before the scheduled interview with Nadine. It didn't surprise her in the least to find Nadine already there. The reporter's silky legs were crossed as she meticulously applied fresh lip dye and checked her camera-ready face in her compact mirror.

Her camera operator stood slouched in a corner munching on a candy bar.

"Where'd you get that candy?" Eve demanded and moved in so quickly the operator's eyes popped wide.

"V-v-v-vending. Just down the hall." She offered what remained of the candy like a shield. "You want a hit?"

Eve scowled at her just long enough to see sweat bead on her brow, and concluded that the camera wasn't her dastardly candy thief.

"No." Eve dropped down at her desk, stretched out her legs.

"I was hoping you'd be late," Nadine began. "Then I was going to lord it over you."

"One of these days someone out there's going to do his job and keep you in the media area instead of letting you back here when I'm not in my office."

Nadine only smirked, clicked her compact closed. "You don't really believe that, do you? Now if you've finished intimidating my camera and your usual bitching, what's this about?"

"Murder."

"With you, it always is. Pettibone and Mouton. Obviously connected. Before we start I can tell you there's nothing in my searches that connects them personally and professionally. I'm sure you already know that. I've got nothing that puts any of their family on the same page, no particular links between colleagues. Pettibone used his own, in-house lawyers for WOF."

Watching Eve, Nadine used her perfectly manicured fingers to click off points. "They may very well have known each other vaguely on some thin social level, but didn't run in the same circles. The current wives used different salons, different health clubs, and tended to shop at different boutiques." Nadine paused. "But I imagine you know that, too."

"We do manage to cover some ground here at Central."

"Which is why I'm wondering how I got a one-on-one with you without begging for it."

"You don't beg, you wheedle."

"Yes, and quite well. Why the offer, Dallas?"

"I want to stop her, and I'll use all available tools. The more media exposure on this one, the better chance someone might recognize her. She'll be working toward her next target. Now this is off the record, Nadine, and I won't answer any questions pertaining to it on record. There's a better than fifty-fifty chance Roarke's a target."

"Roarke? Jesus, Dallas. That doesn't play. He's not her type. Hell, he's every woman's type, but you know what I mean. He's too young, he's too married."

"Married to me," Eve said. "That may be enough for her."

Nadine sat back again, let it settle in. She valued friendship as much as she valued ratings. "Okay. What can I do?"

"The interview. Give the story as much play as you can manage. Keep it and her on everyone's mind. She counts on being able to blend in. I want to take that advantage away from her."

"You want to piss her off."

"If shc's pissed off, she'll make a mistake. She's got ice for blood, that's why she's good at what she does. It's time to heat it up."

"Okay." Nadine nodded and signalled her camera. "Let's start the fire."

Chapter 11

"Julianna Dunne is a failure of the system to identify an active threat and separate that threat from society." Eve's voice was calm and clear. The camera crept in until her face filled the screen. "It was a failure of the system to properly incarcerate and punish Julianna Dunne as suited her crimes against society."

"And yet—" The camera cut to Nadine. Earnest. Interested. "You're part of that system. You purport to believe in that system."

"I do believe in the system. I'm speaking to you as a representative of that system and stating that where we failed, we will correct. The search for Julianna Dunne continues in every possible direction, on every possible level. Whether or not she remains in New York, Julianna Dunne will be tracked down, she will be found, she will be taken into custody, and charged with the murders of Walter C. Pettibone and Henry Mouton."

"In what directions, on what levels is this investigation proceeding?"

"I can't discuss the investigative details of this matter except to say that we're pursuing all leads. We know who and what she is."

"What is she, Lieutenant?"

"Julianna Dunne is a killer. It's what she does, what she'll continue to do until she's stopped."

"As a representative of the people of New York—"

"I'm not a representative of the people of New York," Eve interrupted. "I'm sworn to protect and to serve the people of New York. And I will. I'll keep that oath and for the second time assist in separating Julianna Dunne from society. I will, personally, put her in a cage."

"Is that right?" In her bedroom Julianna brushed her newly gilded curls and pouted at Eve's image on-screen. "You cocky bitch. You got lucky once, that's all. You got lucky. This time out, you're not even close. I'm sitting here right under your nose, and you don't have a *clue*!"

Infuriated, she threw the brush across the room. "We'll see what you have to say when that man you married falls dead at your feet. We'll see if you're so goddamn cocky when he's gasping for his last breath. We'll see how you like *that*! You keep right on chasing the trail on those two sorry old men. They meant *nothing*. It's you and yours, this time, Dallas. I'm taking you and yours down. It's payback time."

She turned, comforting, soothing herself with her own reflection in the mirror. "But you're right about one thing, Dallas. Killing is what I do. And I do it very well."

Smart, Roarke thought as he, too, watched his wife's interview. Very smart. Keep saying her name, the whole of it, so it becomes printed on the minds of everyone who hears it. And Nadine had done her part, flashing Dunne's various images on-screen.

No one who would view the four-minute interview, which was being rebroadcast every ninety minutes, would forget Julianna Dunne.

And the name and image of Eve Dallas would be similarly imprinted on Julianna Dunne's mind.

She was trying to turn Dunne's focus onto her, Roarke concluded. To save another innocent. Even if that innocent was her own, far from pure husband.

He had his own ideas about that, ideas they would undoubtedly clash over. But before it came to that, they would deal with the city of Dallas, and the memories that lived there still.

A part of him was relieved she would go, that she would face this nightmare. It might not free her, but he could hope it would at least lighten the burden she carried with her every day of her life.

But another part wanted her to turn away from it all, as she had turned away from it for so many years. Bury it deep, and look ahead.

And he of all people knew that the past was always stalking your back like a great black dog. Ready to pounce and sink fangs into your throat just when you thought you were safe.

Whatever he'd done to bury the past, it was never quite enough. It lived with him, even here in this grand house with all its treasures and comfort and beauty, the stink of Dublin's slums lived with him. Easier perhaps, he mused, than the past lived with his wife. His before was more like a poor and somewhat regrettable family relation that sat stubbornly in a corner and would never leave.

He knew what it was like to be hungry and afraid, to feel fists pounding him. Fists from hands that should have tended him, embraced him as fathers were meant to embrace sons. But he'd escaped from that. Even as a child he'd had his means of escape. With friends, bad company, with enterprises that, while far from legal, were vastly entertaining. And profitable.

He'd stolen, he'd cheated, he'd schemed. And though he'd never taken a life without cause, he'd killed. He'd built a name, then a business, then an industry. Then a kind of world, he supposed.

He'd traveled and absorbed. He'd learned. And the boy who'd lived his life by wit and guile, by nimble fingers and quick feet became a man of wealth and power. A man who owned whatever he damn well wanted to own and had danced skillfully on the dark side of the law when it suited him.

He'd had women, and some he'd cared for a great deal. But he'd been alone. He hadn't known how much alone until Eve. She'd shown him his own heart. It might have taken her longer to see it for herself, but she'd shown it to him.

And the world he'd built, the man who'd lived in it, had changed forever.

In a matter of hours, they would go back and face her past, the horrors of it. Together.

From his console came a quick beeping indicating the security gate was open. He glanced at the panel, saw the identification for Eve's police vehicle.

Then he walked to the window to watch her come home.

Eve saw the two figures beneath the arching branches of one of the weeping trees as she rounded the first curve toward the house. Most of their bodies were sheltered by the ripe green leaves and fading blossoms.

She punched the accelerator, and her weapon was in her hand before she saw who they were, and what they were doing.

Peabody's parents stood under those fragrant limbs locked in a passionate embrace.

Embarrassed amusement had her shoving her weapon back in its harness, and averting her eyes as she continued down the drive. She parked at the base of the steps because it served two purposes. It was convenient, and Summerset hated it. But her hopes that everyone would pretend that they hadn't seen everyone else were dashed as Sam and Phoebe strolled toward her, holding hands.

Eve stuck hers in her pockets. "How's it going?"

"A gorgeous day."

Phoebe's lips curved, but her gaze was steady and direct and made the back of Eve's neck itch. Deliberately Eve focused on a point in the center of Phoebe's forehead.

Don't look in her eyes, she reminded herself. Don't make direct visual contact.

"Sam and I were taking advantage of it." Phoebe shook back her hair and it tinkled musically from the silver rings woven through it. "I saw your interview with Nadine Furst of Channel 75 on the entertainment screen before I came out. You looked very strong and determined."

"I am determined."

"And strong. Roarke tells us the two of you need to go out of town tomorrow."

"Yeah. It's case-related," Eve replied uneasily, avoiding looking at Sam.

"Is there anything we can do for you here while you're gone?"

"No, thanks. Not unless you run into Julianna Dunne and want to make a citizen's arrest."

"I think we'll leave that to you and Delia. I need to check on something in the greenhouse. Sam, talk Eve into finishing your walk with you."

Before either of them could speak, Phoebe was gliding off with a swish of flowing, flowered skirts.

"I'm sorry," Sam said immediately. "She knows

there's some kind of tension. I didn't say anything to her."

"Okay."

"It's not okay." For the first time since she'd known him, Eve heard temper in his voice, saw it on his face as he turned to her. "I'm making you uncomfortable and upset in your own home. You and Roarke opened that home to us, and I abused the privilege. I was about to work up to talking Phoebe into moving to a hotel for our last few days, but you drove up . . ."

He trailed into silence, and like Eve, stuck his hands in his pockets as if he didn't know what else to do with them.

They stood like that a moment, staring out at the lawn, at the color and the green. She was no sensitive, but Eve thought the misery pumping off the man would have dented a steel wall.

"Look, let's just put it away. It's a couple of days, and I'm not here half the time anyway."

"I have a code," he said quietly. "Part of it's Free-Ageism, part of it's simply the way I believe a life should be led. To cherish family, to do good work. To enjoy the time we're given in this lifetime, and to try as best as we're able to cause no harm. With the gift I was given comes another responsibility, another code. To respect, always, the privacy and the well-being of others. Never to use what I've been given for my own gain, my own amusement or curiosity, or to cause harm. That's what I did."

Eve let out a heavy sigh. He'd hit her exactly where she lived. "I understand codes. Living by them, living up to them. I also understand mistakes. I know you didn't do it on purpose, and you'd probably bite off your own tongue before you discussed this with anyone but me. But I barely know you, and it's hard having someone who's practically a stranger look at me and see that kind of . . . ugliness."

"Do you think I see ugliness when I look at you?" His hand came out of his pocket, started to reach for her, then retreated. "I don't. I saw the ugliness of a memory, the horror no child should know exists much less experience. I'm not a violent man, by nature or creed, but I wish I could . . ."

He trailed off, his face flushed with fury, the hand at his side balled into a fist that looked oddly capable.

"I wish I could do what any father should do." He steadied himself, opened his fist again. "But when I look at you I see strength and courage and purpose beyond anything I've ever known. I see my daughter's friend, a woman I trust with my child's life. I know you're going back there tomorrow. Roarke said you were going to Dallas. I'll pray for you."

She stared at him. "Does anyone manage to stay pissed-off at you?"

His smile was slow, tentative. "Phoebe manages it for short spaces of time."

"Then she's tougher than she looks. We'll put it away," she said, and held out a hand.

When she walked inside, she saw Summerset polishing the newel post while the cat sat like a furry Buddha on the bottom step. They both gave her a long, gimlet stare.

"Your bag is packed for your trip. Roarke indicated a single day's supply of clothing would be sufficient.

"I've told you, I pack for myself. I don't want you poking your bony fingers through my things." She stepped over the cat, who studiously ignored her, froze. Then her hand whipped out and latched on the end of Summerset's polishing rag. "That's my shirt."

"I beg to differ." He'd counted on her making the ID. "While this may, at one time very long ago, have masqueraded as an article of clothing, it is now a rag. One which had somehow found its way into your bureau and has been removed and put to its only possible use."

"Give me my goddamn shirt, you pruny, skinny-assed cockroach."

She tugged. He tugged back.

"You have a number of perfectly respectable shirts."

"I want *this* shirt."

"This is a rag." They yanked at opposite ends, and the cloth ripped handily down the middle. "Now," he said with satisfaction, "it's two rags."

Eve snarled, and balling what was left of an ancient NYPSD T-shirt in her fist, stomped up the stairs. "Stay out of my drawers, you pervert, or I'll bite your fingers off at the knuckles."

"There now," Summerset addressed to the cat. "Isn't it nice to know the Lieutenant will go off on this difficult trip in a good frame of mind?"

She stormed into the bedroom, heaved the ripped cloth just as Roarke stepped out of the elevator. It hit him right on the chin.

"Well then, it's lovely to see you, too."

"Look what that son of a bitch did to my shirt."

"Mmm." Roarke examined the tattered scrap of material. "Is that what this was?" Idly, he poked a finger through an old hole. "Pity. I heard you and Summerset exchanging your usual words of affection. At the top of your lungs."

"Why the hell did you tell him to pack for me?"

"I could say because you have enough to do, which is true. But let's be frank, darling Eve; you're a miserable packer and never take what you end up needing if left to yourself."

"I bet he sniffs my underwear."

Roarke's lips trembled. "Now that's quite the image you've put in my brain." He crossed to her, cupped her face in his hands. "You made it up with Sam. I saw you out the window."

"He was so busy beating himself up I had a hard time getting a shot in."

"Softie."

"Watch it, pal."

He bent down and kissed her scowling mouth. "It'll be our little secret. Believe me, no one watching you in that interview with Nadine would suspect you've a soft center in there. You looked formidable, Lieutenant. Diamond bright and just as hard. But she still won't come after you."

"I don't know what you mean."

"Aye, you do."

She shrugged, started to step back, but he simply tightened his grip. "It's worth a shot."

"You won't stand in front of me on this, or anything else."

"Don't tell me my job."

"Fair enough. Don't tell me mine. I've one question to ask you, then we'll let this matter go for a bit. I want the truth, Eve, and I'll see the truth in your eyes whatever the words are."

He would, she thought. He was better at sifting out lies than a Truth Testor. "Why don't you ask the damn question instead of putting me on the defensive and irritating me?"

"Are we going to Dallas tomorrow to get me out of Julianna's way?"

"No. That's not the reason, but it's a side benefit and buys me some time. It's not the reason. Ease back a little, will you?"

He let his hands stroke down her cheeks, her shoulders, her arms. Then he let her go.

"I could ask Feeney to go. He could handle the interview with Parker. I nearly did ask him. Either one of us could make the trip, and I started justifying asking him to do it by telling myself he might get more out of Parker. Man to man, that kind of thing. Which is bullshit, because when it's cop to witness gender better not have dick to do with it. You're the badge, and that's that. I was on the point of asking him to take it because I wanted to save myself."

"There's no shame in that, Eve, if you're not ready."

"*When* will I be ready?" It burst out of her, bitter and bright. "Tomorrow, a year from tomorrow? Never? If I let this interfere with standard investigative procedure, where does that leave me next time I ram into something that scares me on a personal level? I won't be a coward. So I'm going to do my job. That's number one. Number two, I get you out of the way for a day or two so I can think it through. The rest . . . I'll deal with it when I get there."

She buried herself in work. Peabody had come through with a reasonably workable list of disbarred doctors who fit the basic criteria, and maintained a residence in New York.

"What are you looking for here to link one of these hundred and twenty disgraced physicians with Julianna?"

"A possible connection to her original source," Eve told Roarke. "Personality type. I figure any doctor who'd supply Mad Munch with enough curare and cyanide to take out the entire Church of Hereafter wouldn't quibble about supplying a psychopathic man-killer with what she needed. Or would know someone who would."

She studied the data as Roarke stood behind her office chair, rubbing her shoulders in that absent and perfect way he had that zeroed in on the exact spot that needed attention.

"If he's not her source, he might know her source. If I crap out on her connection, but ID Doctor Doom, I pass him to the Feds as my good deed for the decade."

"Why don't they already have him?"

"They didn't punch the right button with Mook at the right time and he was the only one left. I always knew he had a little more in his gut, but they thought he'd spilled it all, and I didn't have any juice to push it back then. They roughed him up a little instead of threatening to take away his pain, and when he said he'd told them everything, they figured he had."

"That case was ten years back, wasn't it?" Roarke asked.

"Yeah, I was still in uniform. So?"

"Born a cop," he declared and kissed the top of her head.

"According to Mook the doctor didn't help himself to any lemonade that night. That tells me the religious angle didn't tickle his fancy. So maybe it was the self-termination—as long as it wasn't his own—that pulled him in. I've got three guys here who lost their licenses to practice because they helped patients along to Jesus without their consent."

"Playing God's a weighty business."

"Oscar Lovett, David P. Robinson and Eli Young, in alphabetical order. Those are my three best bets. I'll sic Feeney on them. They don't play out, we'll start working our way down."

Her desk 'link beeped and as she was still frowning at the screen Roarke answered.

"Hello, Roarke." Louise Dimatto smiled silkily. "I hope I'm not interrupting anything."

"Always a pleasure to hear from you. How are you, Louise?"

"If I got much better, I'd be illegal, on the personal front at least. Professionally, I'm overworked, which is just the way I like it. I'd hoped you and Dallas might be able to come by the shelter sometime soon. We've finished and opened three more rooms, and the recreation area's complete. *Dochas* is already making an impact on lives."

"We'll make sure we stop in when you're on duty."

"That'll be great. Is Dallas available? I have some information for her."

"Right here. Overworking. I'll see you soon, Louise. Best to Charles."

"I'm sure giving him mine. Dallas," she continued, briskly now when Eve came on-screen. "I think I might have something useful for you regarding my little assignment. I remembered hearing bits of scandal discussed in my family when I was a girl. Things I wasn't supposed to hear, of course. Regarding a doctor who'd interned with my uncle. Apparently his private behavior was unseemly, and covered up by the white wall for years. He enjoyed young women, very young women. Some of whom were also patients. The white wall wouldn't stand for him when it was discovered he'd begun to terminate patients without specific and clear-cut authorization."

"Got a name?"

"I didn't, but I called my cousin upstate. And that you owe me for, Dallas, as my cousin Mandy is a thoroughly annoying diva who proceeded to interrogate me about my love life, my social life, and lecture me on wasting my skills on the dregs of humanity at the clinic. Et cetera."

"The name, Louise. You can bitch later."

"Eli Young. He was a chief resident, internal medicine, at Kennedy Memorial before going into private practice." Louise paused, lifted her elegant eyebrows. "And I can see by your expression you already have the data on him. Why did I waste my time?"

"You didn't. You just saved me considerable effort. Appreciate it." Eve glanced toward Roarke, shifted in her head. "Ah, listen, I tapped Charles for a favor today, too, and I feel kind of weird about it."

"The conjugal at Dockport?"

"Oh, well, then . . . Guess he mentioned it."

"Yes, he told me." Louise let out a quick laugh. "Dallas, loosen up. By the way, Peabody looked wonderful. Love's in the air."

"Something's in the air," Eve grumbled when they ended transmission. "What are you grinning at?" she demanded of Roarke.

"That, despite it all, there are some areas of sex that embarrass you."

"I'm not embarrassed, I'm baffled. But it's none of my never mind."

"The whole point of love is that it has no reason. It just is."

She looked at him. "I guess I've got that one." She pushed away from the desk. "I'm going to go pay a visit to this Eli Young, see what I can shake out."

"I'll go with you. Don't start the civilian routine, Lieutenant. Let's just say I'd enjoy taking a drive with my wife. It's a pretty night. Besides." He draped an arm around her shoulders as they started out of the room. "If memory serves, the bad doctor's address is in one of my buildings. You won't have any hassles getting up to see him with me along, will you?"

It did have certain advantages. When the electronic security panel informed Eve that Doctor Young was not in, she held up a hand to hold Roarke back. And pressed her badge against the view screen.

"Not in, or not accepting visitors?"

I AM NOT AUTHORIZED TO PROVIDE YOU WITH THAT SPECIFIC INFORMATION. DUE TO THE NECESSITY OF PROTECTING THE PRIVACY OF OUR RESIDENTS, I CAN ONLY REPEAT THAT DR. YOUNG IS NOT AVAILABLE AT THIS TIME. YOU MAY CHOOSE

FROM THE FOLLOWING MENU TO LEAVE A MESSAGE
FOR DR. YOUNG OR ANOTHER RESIDENT. MY APOL-
OGIES, DALLAS, LIEUTENANT EVE, FOR NOT BEING
ABLE TO ASSIST YOU IN YOUR REQUEST.

"You must admit," Roarke commented, "it's very
good security, as well as polite."

"With a warrant stuffed up its electronic butt it might
not be so polite."

LOITERING ON THE PREMISES BY NONRESIDENTS OR
APPROVED AND AUTHORIZED GUESTS IS DISCOUR-
AGED. IF YOU DO NOT WISH TO REQUEST ANOTHER
RESIDENT OR LEAVE A MESSAGE, I MUST ASK YOU
TO VACATE THIS LOBBY. IN FORTY-FIVE SECONDS,
BUILDING SECURITY WILL BE INFORMED OF YOUR
FAILURE TO COOPERATE. MY APOLOGIES FOR THIS
INCONVENIENCE.

"Would now be a good time?" Roarke asked. "Lieutenant, you know how it excites me when you snarl at
me."

"Just get us past this thing, and stop looking so smug."

Roarke simply laid his hand on the palm plate, then
coded in.

GOOD EVENING, ROARKE. WELCOME. HOW MAY I
ASSIST YOU THIS EVENING?

"We'll be going up to the twenty-second floor. Release the elevators."

YES, SIR. ELEVATORS ARE RELEASED. PLEASE EN-
JOY YOUR VISIT AND THE REST OF YOUR EVENING.
PLEASE LET ME KNOW IF I CAN BE OF ANY FUR-
THER ASSISTANCE.

"Don't you get tired of everything and everyone sucking up to you?" Eve demanded.

"Why, no. Why should I?" He gestured her into the elevator as the mirrored doors opened soundlessly. "Twenty-second floor," he ordered. "Young could very well be out, you know."

"I'll see for myself. There's a reasonable chance he's Julianna's supplier or knows who is. I don't walk away until I talk to him."

She stepped off on twenty-two, turned down the hall to the second door on the right. She rang the bell, kept her badge up so it could be seen through the apartment's security screen.

DOCTOR YOUNG IS NOT IN RESIDENCE AND HAS AUTHORIZED NO GUESTS TO ENTER HIS HOME IN HIS ABSENCE. MAY I TAKE A MESSAGE?

The second computerized response had Eve agitated. Without comment, she turned around and buzzed the apartment across the hall.

It was opened by a woman wearing a red lounging robe, holding a cocktail glass filled with some pale blue liquid. An entertainment screen roared out of the room behind her. "Police? What's wrong?"

"Nothing's wrong, ma'am. I'm sorry to disturb you. Do you know where I can find Eli Young this evening?"

"Doctor Young?" She blinked, then looked over her shoulder. "Marty, the police are here. She wants to see Doctor Young."

"Across the hall." The voice boomed out, over the shouted on-screen argument.

"I know he lives across the hall," Eve said with straining patience. "He doesn't answer his door. Can you tell me when you last saw him?"

"Oh, several days ago, I suppose." She lifted the glass,

sipped. From the glow on her face, she'd been sipping steadily for some time. "Oh, wait a minute, he's gone out of town. Could be gone a couple weeks."

"Did he mention where he was going?"

"No. Actually he didn't tell me. His niece did."

"Niece," Eve repeated as her mind went on alert.

"Yes, she was coming out of his apartment the other day as I was coming in from shopping. A very nice young woman, too. She said that she'd just been visiting her uncle, and how pleased she was that he was going to travel back to visit her parents with her. In Ohio. Or Indiana. Or maybe it was Idaho." She slipped again. "A nice long visit, she said."

"What did she look like?"

"Oh, young and pretty. Brunette, short, very chic do."

Eve pulled out her PPC, called up Julianna's picture as Janet Drake. "Does she look familiar?"

The woman angled her head, then beamed. "Why yes! That's Dr. Young's niece. I was caught by surprise as I didn't realize he had any family at all."

"Thanks." Eve stuck the PPC back in her pocket. "Do you ever watch the news media, ma'am?"

"News? With Marty it's thrillers and sports, sports and thrillers. I'm lucky if I get the screen for ten minutes a day to watch the fashion report."

"You might want to take a look at it tonight. Thanks for your help."

Eve turned away from the woman's puzzled look, and switched on her recorder. "I have positive ID that prime suspect, Julianna Dunne had contact with Eli Young at this location. Subject Young does not answer, and there is suspicion of foul play. I have probable cause to enter this residence and determine the well-being of Young and/or his complicity with Julianna Dunne. With me is Roarke, owner of the building. He has agreed to this procedure, and will witness same."

"That should cover it," Roarke commented.

Eve stepped to the door, used her master to uncode the locks. "Recorder on," she said as she drew her weapon, a subtle warning in case Roarke had armed himself without her knowledge.

She pushed open the door to the dark.

But she didn't need the lights to smell death.

"Christ." She hissed it between her teeth as her mouth filled with the rank air. "We've got a bloater. Stay in the hall. There's nothing you can do. Lights on full," she ordered.

The lights flashed on, revealing a lavishly appointed living area, its privacy screens shut tight over a wall of windows. Young was on the sofa, and the fabric would never be the same.

He wore what might have been a robe, but as the gases inside him had expanded, and the bodily fluids leaked, it was hard to tell.

There was a bottle of brandy and a wineglass on the coffee table, and a snifter on the rug where his fingers, fat as sausages now, had dropped it.

"You'll want your field kit," Roarke said.

"Yeah."

"And here." He handed her a handkerchief so she could cover her mouth and nose. "Best I can do for now."

"Thanks." She used it, staying at the doorway until he could return with her sealant, recording the scene. She pulled her communicator out of her pocket, and called it in.

She'd had sex with him first. Perhaps they'd been lovers before, but Eve thought not. Julianna had simply used her most effective method to distract a man, and then had killed him with the very poison he'd procured for her.

It was logical, clean, cold. It was Julianna.

They would find her on the building's security discs.

Once at least before Pettibone's murder when she'd bought her initial supply. She'd been a redhead then, Eve mused.

Then once again, a brunette, coming back to tie off the loose end.

Very likely, they would find transmissions on the victim's 'link from her, to her. But she wouldn't be foolish enough to have taken them at home, or on a personal 'link. They would follow it up, of course, but find the chats were made on public 'links.

He'd been dead four days. Four very nasty days. She'd strolled in, fresh from one kill, and topped herself off with another.

The body was gone now, but the air would reek of its decomposition for quite some time. Even after crews came in to clean the air, it would be there, a thin, evil underlayer.

"Lieutenant." Peabody came up behind her. "I have the security discs."

Absently, Eve took them. "I'll have copies in the file. I'll take a look at them tonight, but I don't imagine there will be any surprises.

"She came up the day after she killed Pettibone. Sporting her new hairdo, feeling fine and frisky. He let her in. Maybe they could do more business. She told him about the kill. Who better to share it with than the man who'd sold her the weapon, a man who'd be dead before she left the apartment? It would've amused her to tell him. Then she seduced him."

She stepped toward the bedroom. The linens had been stripped away, sent to the lab, but her scope had found traces of semen. "Easy enough. *I'm so wired up, so energized. All those years in prison, those lonely years. I need someone to touch me. You're the only one I can be with, the only one who knows what I'm feeling right now.*"

"He should've known," Peabody murmured. "Of all people, he should've known."

"Her eyes would be shining, all those lies in them. He's old enough to be her grandfather, and there she is. Young and beautiful, with that tight, smooth body. He likes them young. Younger even than she, but she's here. She lets him do whatever he wants to her, take all the time he needs. It doesn't matter to her. He's already dead. Her mind's on the next, even as she groans and writhes and pretends to get off. Afterwards, she'll flatter him. It was wonderful. Amazing. She knows what to say, how to say it to make him feel like the fuck king of the world. She'd have researched him, too."

She turned back into the living area. "She knows he likes brandy. She poisoned the bottle while he was in the shower, or taking a piss. Doesn't take long. Doesn't matter if he drinks it now, or later, but she'd rather now so she can watch. Cozy up to him on the couch, tell him all about what and who she's doing next. Can she have some wine? Can she stay awhile? It's so good to have someone to talk to, to be with.

"He pours the wine, he pours the brandy. It's his wine, his brandy. He's not worried. She probably drinks first, while she chats, just bubbling over with energy and enthusiasm. He'd smile at her while he drinks, caught up in her, sated from the sex, wondering if he'll be able to get it up for a second round. When he feels the poison in him, it's too late. He's shocked, horrified. Not him. It can't be. But he'd see it on her face then. She'd let him see it. That cold pleasure. Tidy herself up, secure the apartment. Run into the neighbor and have a friendly conversation. *Uncle Eli's going out of town for several weeks, isn't that nice?*"

"And she walks away," Peabody finished.

"And she walks away. Seal it up, Peabody. I'll go in, file the report. Then I'm going home."

Chapter 12

If the appeal of the suburbs baffled steadfast urbanite Eve Dallas, the appeal of the great flat stretches of Texas was foreign as a moonscape. Texas had cities, great, sprawling, crowded cities.

So why did anyone actually choose to live on the pancake grass of the prairie where you could see for miles, where you were surrounded by an endless spread of space?

Even so, there were towns, of course, with buildings that blocked that uneasy view, and straight-arrow roads that spilled into pretzel-curved freeways leading to and from civilization.

She could certainly understand people driving *toward* those towns and cities and buildings. But she'd never comprehend what pushed them to drive out into the nothingness.

"What do they get from this?" she asked Roarke as they zoomed down one of those roads. "There's nothing here but grass and fences and four-legged animals. Really big four-legged animals," she added as they traveled past a herd of horses with cautious suspicion.

"Yippee-ky-yay."

She shifted that suspicious stare to Roarke only briefly. She preferred to keep close watch on the animals. Just in case.

"This guy's loaded," she went on, slightly mollified by the roaring clack of a helicopter that buzzed the near field. "He's got a thriving, successful business in Dallas. But he chooses to live out here. Voluntarily. There's something really sick about that."

With a laugh, Roarke picked up her hand, the one that kept inching up toward her weapon, and kissed it. "There are all kinds of people in the world."

"Yeah, and most of them are crazy. Jesus, are those *cows*? Cows shouldn't be that big, should they? It's unnatural."

"Just think steaks, darling."

"Uh-uh, that's just creepy. Are you sure this is the right way? This can't be right. There's nothing out here."

"May I point out the several houses we're passing along this route?"

"Yeah, but I think the cows must live in them." She had a flash of bovine activities inside the low-slung houses. Watching some screen, having cow parties, making cow love in four-poster beds. And shuddered. "God, that's creepy, too. I hate the country."

Roarke glanced down at the in-dash navigation screen. He'd worn jeans and a white T-shirt, and a pair of sleek, black sunshades. It was a casual look for him, even simple. But he still looked like city. Rich city, Eve mused.

"We should be there in a few minutes," he told her. "There's a bit of civilization up ahead."

"Where?" She risked taking her attention away from the cows, looked through the windshield and saw the spread of a town. Buildings, fuel stations, shops, restaurants, more houses. Her gut loosened a little. "Okay, that's good."

"But we're not going through there. We veer off here." So saying, he turned off the wide ribbon of road onto a narrow offshoot. One that, in Eve's opinion, brought them entirely too close for comfort to those strange, flat grassy fields.

"Those fences don't look all that strong."

"If there's a stampede, we'll outrun them."

She moistened her lips, swallowed. "I bet you think that's funny."

But she was somewhat mollified as there were other vehicles on the road. Other cars, trucks, long sleek trailers, and a few topless power Jeeps.

Buildings began to spring up. Not houses, Eve thought. Farm buildings or ranch buildings. Whatever. Barns and sheds and animal shelters. Stables, she supposed. Granaries or whatever they were. Silos, and what kind of word was that? It looked like a painting with all that grass, the crops, the bored-faced cattle, and the strong reds and whites of the outbuildings.

"What's that guy doing?" she demanded, inching up in the seat to stare beyond Roarke's profile.

"He appears to be riding a horse."

"Yeah, yeah, I can see that. But why?"

"I have no idea. Perhaps he wants to."

"See?" To punctuate it, she slapped Roarke's shoulder. "Sick. People are just sick." She let out a little breath of relief when she spotted the ranch house.

It was enormous, sprawling all over hell and back on one story. Portions of it were painted that same bright white and others looked to be fashioned from stones cobbled all together on a whim. There were sections built of glass, and she nearly shuddered at the idea of standing there looking out at field after field. And having what was in those fields looking in at her.

There were smaller fenced areas, and while there were horses in them, there was also considerable human activity. That relieved her, even if those humans were all wearing cowboy hats.

She saw a helipad and a number of vehicles, many of which she couldn't begin to identify. She had to assume they were used for some sort of rural labor.

They drove through enormous stone pillars topped by rearing horses.

"Okay, he knows we're coming, and he's not happy about it," she began. "He's bound to be hostile, defensive, and uncooperative. But he's also smart enough to know I can complicate his life, dredge up the past, and press the local cops to add some pressure. He doesn't want all this crap uncovered in his backyard. Doing this on his turf lets him feel more in control."

"And how long are you going to let him feel that way?"

"We'll see how it goes." She stepped out of the car and nearly lost her breath in the heat.

A baking heat, she realized, very unlike the steambath of a New York City summer. She smelled grass and what had to be manure. "What's that clacking sound?" she asked Roarke.

"I'm not altogether sure. I think it might be chickens."

"Christ almighty. Chickens. If you tell me to think omelettes, I'll have to hit you."

"Understood." He walked up the pathway beside her. He knew her well enough to be certain her preoccupation with the local scene helped to keep her mind off her fears and worries. She'd yet to say anything about heading into Dallas itself, or what she could or would do there.

The doors were ten feet wide and crowned by the bleached-out horns of some sort of animal. Roarke pondered it, and the type of personality that enjoyed decorating with dead animals, while Eve rang the bell.

Moments later, the image of the old American West yanked open the door.

He was weathered as leather, tall as a mountain, wide as a river. He wore boots with toes sharp as stilettos and crusted with dirt. His jeans were dark indigo and looked stiff enough to stand tall without him while his shirt was a faded red-and-white check. His hair was a dull silver, slicked back from a hard and ruddy face, mapped with lines, toughened in a scowl.

When he spoke, his voice rattled like loose gravel in a very deep bucket. "You the city cops?"

"Lieutenant Dallas." Eve offered her badge. "This is my field assistant—"

"I know you." He pointed a finger, thick as a soy dog on his ham of a hand, at Roarke. "Roarke. You're Roarke, and you're no cop."

"Praise be," Roarke acknowledged. "I happen to be married to one."

"Yeah." He nodded as he considered Eve. "Recognize you now, too. Big city New York cop." He looked like he might spit, but restrained himself. "Jake T. Parker, and I don't have to talk to you. Fact is, my lawyers advise against it."

"You're not now under any legal obligation to speak with me, Mr. Parker. But you can be put under that legal obligation, and I'm sure your lawyers advised you of that as well."

He hooked his wide thumbs in the belt loops of his jeans. His scarred belt creaked at the movement. "Take you some little while to pull that off, wouldn't it?"

"Yes, sir, it would. I wonder how many more people Julianna can kill before the lawyers wrangle that out? You care to speculate?"

"I've got nothing to do with her, haven't in more than a dozen years. I made my peace there, and I don't need some city-girl cop from New York coming here and throwing that dirt in my face."

"I'm not here to throw dirt, Mr. Parker. I'm not here to judge you. I'm here to learn anything that might help me stop Julianna from taking more lives. One of them might be yours."

"Shit. Pardon my French," he added. "That girl's nothing but a ghost to me, and I'm less than that to her."

Eve pulled stills out of her field bag. "This is Walter Pettibone. He was nothing to her, either. And Henry Mouton. They had families, Mr. Parker. They had lives. She destroyed all that."

He looked at the stills, looked away. "Never should've let her out of prison."

"You won't get an argument there from me. I helped put her in a cage once before. I'm asking you to help me do it again."

"I got a life of my own. It took me a long time to get it back so I could wake up in the morning and look at myself in the mirror."

He took a dirt-brown Stetson hat from a stand with pegs just inside the door, fit it on his head. Then he stepped out, shut the door at his back. "I don't want this in my house. I'm sorry not to be hospitable, but I don't want her in my house. We'll talk outside. I want to take a look at the stock anyhow."

As a concession against the white glare of the sun, Eve dug out shaded glasses. "Has she been in contact with you at all?"

"I haven't heard a peep from that girl since she walked out the day she turned eighteen. The day she told her mama what had been going on. The day she laughed in my face."

"Do you know if she's been in contact with her mother?"

"Couldn't say. Lost track of Kara when she left me.

Heard she'd taken a job off planet. Farming satellite. Far away from me, I'd say, as she could manage."

Eve nodded. She knew Kara Dunne Parker Rowan's location. She'd remarried four years earlier, and refused to speak to Eve regarding her daughter. Her daughter, she'd informed Eve during their brief transmission, was dead. Eve imagined Julianna had the same attitude toward the woman who'd birthed her.

"Did you rape Julianna, Mr. Parker?"

His face tightened, like old leather stretching over a frame. "If you mean did I force myself on her, I did not. I've done a lot of atoning for what I did, Lieutenant."

He paused at a paddock fence, propped one booted foot on a bottom rung, and stared out at his men and horses. "There was a time I put all the blame on her. Took me a long while before I could spread that out to myself and deal with it. She was fifteen, chronologically speaking anyways. Fifteen, and a man more than fifty has no right touching those kinda goods. A man married to a good woman, hell to any woman's got no right touching her daughter. No excuses."

"But you did touch her."

"I did." He straightened his massive shoulders as if taking on weight. "I'm gonna tell this my way, just saying up front I know what I did was as wrong as it gets, and I take the blame and responsibility for that."

"All right, Mr. Parker. Tell me your way."

"She'd slither around the house wearing next to nothing. Crawl in my lap and call me Daddy, but there wasn't anything daughterly in how she said it."

He set his teeth, looked away from Eve, and out over his land. "Her own daddy was a man hard on women, but he next to worshipped that girl, so her mama told me. Julianna could do no wrong and when she did, he blamed her mama. I loved that woman. I loved my wife," he said, stepping back, flicking his gaze to Eve's face before he began to walk again. "She was a good woman, churchgoing, quiet-natured, sturdy. If she had a blind spot, it was that girl. She has a way of blinding people."

"She behaved provocatively with you."

"Shit. Pardon my French. Fifteen years old, and she knew just how to wrap a man around her finger, get whatever she wanted. She stirred up something in me that shouldn't've been stirred up. I shouldn't have let it happen. I started thinking about her, looking at her in a way that damned me straight to hell. But I couldn't stop. Maybe didn't want to, not then. I know right from wrong, Lieutenant. I know damn well where the line is."

"And you crossed it."

"I did. One night when her mama's out at one of her women's meetings, she came into the study, slid on my lap. I ain't going into the details of it, except to say I didn't force her into a damn thing. She was as willing as they come. But I crossed that line, one a man can't ever step back over."

"You were intimate with her."

"I was. That night, and whenever I could manage it for nearly three years after. She made it easy to manage. She talked her mother into going off with friends on a weekend shopping spree. And I lay with my step-daughter in my marriage bed. I loved her, God is my witness, I loved her in a kind of insane way. I believed she felt the same."

He shook his head at his own foolishness. "Man old enough to know better. I gave her money. God only knows how much over those three years. Bought her cars, fancy clothes, whatever she asked for. I told myself we'd go away together. Soon as she was old enough, I'd leave her mama and we'd go off anywhere she wanted. I was a fool. I've learned to live with that. Harder was to learn to live with the sins I'd committed."

She imagined him sitting in the witness chair at Julianna's trial, speaking in just that no bullshit way. Things, Eve decided, would have gone differently if he had.

"After her arrest, during her trial, she claimed you had raped and abused her, and used that to bargain for a lesser sentence. You made no attempt to set the record straight, to defend yourself."

"No, I did not." He looked down at Eve from under the wide brim of his hat. "Have you ever done anything, Lieutenant, something that shames you so deep it puts fear in your throat and ice in your belly?"

She thought of Dallas, and what lurked there. "I know what it's like to be afraid, Mr. Parker."

"I was afraid of her. I was afraid of what I became with her. If I'd testified about how it was, I'd still have been a grown man who'd committed adultery with the minor child of his own wife. That's about the time I went into counseling, starting working at accepting my responsibility. Nothing I could do for the men she'd killed. And the fact was, it would've been her word against mine. If I hadn't been there at the time, I'd've believed hers."

"Did she demonstrate violent behavior during the time she lived with you?"

"Hell." He snorted out a laugh. "Had a temper like a whiplash, struck out fast and sharp, cut straight through. Then it was done. Easier to see now what I couldn't then. She's cold, right down through the bone. She hated me from the moment I starting seeing her mother. I see that now, too. Hated me in that icy way of hers because I was a man, because I was a man who could step in and have some say over her. So she twisted that around until she had all the say. Then she humiliated me because I was weak, humiliated her mother because she'd loved me. She strutted out that door and left us broken. Just the way she wanted us."

"You didn't stay broken," Eve pointed out. "You rebuilt your life. She'd know that. She's cleaning up old business, Mr. Parker. Odds are strong that you're part of that."

"You think she'll come after me?"

"Yes, I do. Sooner or later. You're going to want to alert your security. Thoroughly screen any new employees at your place of business, at your home. It would be wise for you to speak with the local authorities, as I will, so they'll know who and what to look for."

"That girl couldn't wait to kick the Texas dust off her heels." He looked down at the toes of his boots, shook his head. "Can't see her coming back here to try killing a man who meant less than that dust to her." He blew out a breath. "But I'm sixty-six years old, and that's old enough to know you don't sit scratching your butt waiting for a snake to crawl up your pant's leg. Been meaning to take me a little busman's holiday, go over to Europe and look at some studs. Might do it sooner than later now."

"I'd appreciate it if you'd let me know where you go and when."

He studied Eve again. "You're going to get her, aren't you, city girl?"

"Yes, sir. I am."

"I believe it. But I don't know if anything I've said here's a help to that, and I can't see her wasting time on me. I wasn't the first for her."

"How do you know?" Eve asked.

"She wasn't a virgin when she slid on my lap that night. At least that's one sin off my plate."

"Do you know who she'd been with before you?"

Parker shifted his feet. "Telling tales on myself, and telling them on somebody else—"

"This isn't gossip. This is a murder investigation."

"No point getting riled," he said mildly, and puffed

out his cheeks. "I suspect she'd been tumbling with Chuck Springer. I know her mama had some worries about that. But then as I recollect, he started seeing one of the Larson girls. Maybe it was the Rolley girl. They were kids," he added. "I didn't pay much mind to it. Then when I started up with Julianna, I didn't pay mind to much of anything but her."

"Do you know where I can find this Chuck Springer?"

"He's one of my wranglers. Look now, he's a married man, got a little boy and another on the way."

"Wrangler? Would that be a cowboy?"

Parker snorted out another laugh, adjusted the brim of his hat. "New York City," he said with a shake of his head. "What the hell else is a wrangler but a cowboy?"

"I'd like to speak with him."

Parker sighed. "Then let's go hunt him down." He circled the paddock, jerked a head in the direction of the horses prancing inside. "Got some fine stock there. You ride?"

"Not on anything with more legs than I have," Eve answered and made him hoot with laughter.

"You?" he asked Roarke.

"I have done."

That stopped Eve dead. "On a horse? You've ridden a *horse*?"

"And survived. Actually, it's exhilarating. You'd probably like it."

"I don't think so."

"Just gotta let 'em know who's boss," Parker told her.

"They're bigger, they're stronger. I'd say that makes them boss."

He chuckled, then let out a shout to one of the hands. "Where's Springer?"

"Out the east pasture."

"Nice ride out there," Parker said conversationally,

and tucked his tongue into his cheek. "Could set you up on a nice, gentle hack."

"I'm going to pretend you didn't just threaten a police officer."

"I like you, city girl." He jerked a thumb. "We'll take a Jeep."

It was probably an exhilarating ride. It certainly seemed to Eve that Roarke enjoyed it. But as far as she was concerned, they were bumping through dangerous terrain full of large bovines, cow shit, and whatever might lurk in the tall grass.

She saw another Jeep. On the flat plain it might have been half a mile away, and closer in, riding along a fence line, a trio of men on horseback. Parker veered toward them, giving his horn a little toot-toot. Cattle lumbered out of the way with a few annoyed moos.

"Need a word with you here, Chuck."

A lean, rawboned man in the ranch uniform of boots, jeans, checked shirt, and hat, gave some signal to his mount. They trotted up, and had Eve easing cautiously toward the far door of the Jeep.

"Boss." He nodded at Roarke, tapped the brim of his hat at Eve. "Ma'am."

"This lady here's Lieutenant Dallas, city cop from New York. She needs to talk to you."

"Me?" He had a long face, tanned nearly as deep and gold as a deer hide. It registered puzzled shock. "I ain't never been to New York City."

"You're not in any trouble, Mr. Springer, but you might be able to help me in an investigation." And how the hell was she supposed to interview him when he was all the way up there on that horse? "If I could have a few minutes of your time."

"Well." He shifted in the saddle. It creaked. "If the boss says."

He dismounted, with more creaking, yet with a fluidity

that made Eve think of water sliding down a sleek rock. He kept the reins in one hand as his mount lowered its head and began to crop grass.

"It's regarding Julianna Dunne," Eve began.

"I heard she got out of prison. They say she killed a man."

"Her counts up to three on this leg," Eve corrected. "You knew her when she lived in this area."

"Yep."

"Have you had any contact with her since she left?"

"Nope."

"You were friends with her when she lived here."

"Not 'xactly."

Eve waited a beat. Texas interview rhythm, she decided, was a whole lot different from New York's. "What exactly were you then, Mr. Springer?"

"I knew her. She was my daddy's boss's step-daughter. My boss, too. Haven't seen hide nor hair of her since she lit out. No reason I should. Boss, I got fence to ride."

"Chuck, Lieutenant Dallas is trying to do her job. Now if you're thinking I'm going to be peeved over something that went on between you and Julianna when you were a knot-headed teenager, put that aside. You know me well enough, know what happened with me well enough." He paused there as Chuck frowned down at his boots. "I figure you don't hold that against me. The same's gonna go. The lieutenant wants to know if you tumbled Julianna."

The man blushed. Eve watched, fascinated, as dull red crept under the deep gold tan. "Aw, Jake T., I can't talk about that sort of thing with a woman."

Eve pulled out her shield. "Talk to the badge."

"Mr. Parker," Roarke began. "I wonder if we might walk the field a bit. I've a cattle ranch in Montana and some interest in the process."

"Watch your step," Parker advised, and climbed out. "Chuck, you do what's right here."

Because she felt stupid sitting in the Jeep alone, Eve risked getting out. The horse immediately raised its head, butted her shoulder. She didn't punch it with the fist balled at her side, but it was very close.

"He's just seeing if you got anything more interesting to eat than grass on you." Chuck ran a hand down the horse's nose. "This one's always looking for a handout."

"Tell him I'm empty." Eve scooted to the side, put Chuck firmly between herself and the horse. When it whinnied, it sounded like laughter. "Tell me about Julianna, Chuck."

"Jeez. I was sixteen." He pushed his hat back on his head, took out a bandanna to mop sweat from his brow. "Boy's sixteen, he doesn't think with his brain. If you know what I mean."

"You had sex with her."

"She'd come out to the stables. Mucking out was part of my chores. She'd smell like glory and be wearing some tight shirt and tiny little shorts. God almighty, she was a looker. We started fooling around the way kids do. Then we started fooling around some more." He stared down at his boots again. "We'd sneak out of the house a lot that summer, make love in one of the stalls. I'd always put fresh hay in. Then she started coming up to the house, climbing in through my window. It was exciting at first, but, Jesus, my ma found out, she'd of skinned me alive. And, well damn it, I was sixteen, and there were all these other girls. Guy starts looking around. Julianna, she'd barely give me room to breathe, and it started making me itchy."

"You broke it off with her."

"Tried to once, and she tore into me like a hellcat." He looked up again. "Biting, scratching. Nobody pushed her aside, she said. Scared me, cause she looked half-crazy. Then she started crying and begging, and well, one thing led to another and we were at it again. And the next day, Julianna marches right into my house, into the kitchen, and tells my mother I've been poking at her. And if she doesn't send me away somewhere, she's going to her step-daddy and have my daddy fired."

He paused, then to Eve's surprise, smiled. "My ma, she never did take shit off anybody. Boss's daughter or not. Tells Julianna she's not to come into her home without an invitation ever again. And she won't tolerate some little tramp—called her that—standing in her kitchen threatening her family. Told her to scat, and if there'd been poking going on, that poking would damn well stop. Said she'd be speaking to Julianna's ma about it."

"Did she?"

"My ma says she's going to do something, she does it, so I gotta figure. Never told me what was said between them, but Julianna didn't come 'round the stables again that summer. Didn't see her around at all. But I got house arrest for a damn month myself and a lecture that burned my ears off."

"And after that summer?"

"I never really talked with her again. She came up to me once when I was out with a girl, said insulting things about a sensitive part of my anatomy. Said it in a quiet voice, real cold, with a smirk on her face. And once I found a dead skunk in my bed—had to figure it was her. And . . ."

"And?"

"Never told anybody." He shifted, set his jaw. "Night before my wedding, that would be six years ago last month, she called me. Said she wanted to give me her best wishes. But it was the way she said it, like she was, beg pardon, telling me to screw myself. And how she knew I'd be thinking of her on my wedding night, because she'd be thinking of me. How maybe she'd come see me sometime, and we'd talk about old times. I knew she was in prison. It shook me up a little, but I didn't see the point in telling anybody. I was getting married the next day."

"Has she contacted you since?"

"No, but this past Valentine's Day I got a package. There was a dead rat inside. Looked like it'd been poisoned. I didn't tell anybody about that either. Just got rid of it. Ma'am, I was sixteen. We just rolled in the hay for a couple months one summer. I got a wife, a son, a baby on the way. What the hell does she want to mess with me for after all this time?"

"He rejected her," Eve told Roarke when they were back in the car. "She went after a boy her own age, and he stopped wanting her before she stopped wanting him. Then his mother stood up to her. Two slaps. Intolerable."

"If she'd been a normal girl, that would have crushed her temporarily. Then she'd have moved on. Instead, she decided to seduce her step-father. Older men, like her father, were more easily controlled, more inclined to see her as flawless."

"It was more than seducing him. It was using the sex to crush him, and her mother. To punish and to profit. She hadn't worked up to killing yet, but it was only a matter of time. Why damage when you can utterly destroy? She got what she wanted from that, but still couldn't forget that rejection."

She couldn't remember what it felt like to be a fifteen-year-old girl. Small wonder, Eve thought. She'd never been a normal teenager. And neither, it seemed, had Julianna Dunne.

"Calls him on his wedding night," Eve went on. "She's careful what she says in case he reports it, but she says enough to know he'll be upset, shaken up, and that he won't be able to stop himself from thinking about her on his wedding night. Plant the seed."

"What are you going to do about him?"

"He's worried enough about his family to work with the locals. He's going to talk to Parker as well, and my impression is Parker will go the extra mile with ranch security. I'll talk to the cops down here, make sure they're doing their job. Then I'll do mine and find her."

"Then we're off for New York now?"

She stared out the window. "No." Then shut her eyes. "No, we'll go into Dallas."

Chapter 13

When the Dallas skyline swam into view through waves of heat, it triggered no memory inside her, but instead brought on a vague puzzlement. It had the towering buildings, the urban sprawl, the jammed spaces. But it was so different from New York.

Age, she realized, was part of it. All of this was young when compared to the east. Brasher somehow, but without the edge. Dallas was, after all, one of so many settlements that had grown into towns, then towns that had boomed into cities, long after New York, Boston, Philadelphia were established.

And the architecture lacked the fancy fuss found in the older buildings of the east that had survived the Urban Wars or been restored afterward. Here the towers were sleek and gleaming and for the most part unadorned.

Blimps and billboards announced rodeos, cattle drive tours, sales on cowboy boots and hats. And barbecue was king.

They might as well be driving on Venus.

"There's more sky," she said absently. "More sky here, almost too much of it."

Sun flashed blindingly off steel towers, walls of glass, the ringing people glides. She pushed her shaded glasses more securely on her nose.

"More roads," she said, and could hear the steadiness in her own voice. "Not as much air traffic."

"Do you want to go to the hotel?"

"No, I . . . maybe you could just drive around or something."

He laid a hand over hers, then took a downtown exit.

It seemed more closed in, with the blue plate of the sky like a lid over the buildings, pressing down on the streets jammed with too many cars driving too fast in too many directions.

She felt a wave of dizziness and fought it back.

"I don't know what I'm looking for." But it wasn't this abrupt sense of panic. "He never let me out of the goddamn room, and when I . . . after I got out, I was in shock. Besides it was more than twenty years ago. Cities change."

Her hand trembled lightly under his, and his own clamped on the wheel. He stopped at a light, turned to study her face. It was pale now. "Eve, look at me."

"I'm okay. I'm all right." But it took a great deal of courage to turn her head, meet his eyes. "I'm okay."

"We can drive to the hotel, and let this go for now. Forever, if that's what you want. We can drive straight to the airport and go back to New York. Or we can go to where they found you. You know where it was. It's in your file."

"Did you read my file?"

"Yes."

She started to pull her hand back, but his fingers

closed tight. "Did you do anything else? Run any searches?" She asked.

"No. I didn't, no, because you wouldn't want it. But it can be done that way if and when you do."

"I don't want it that way. I don't want that." Her stomach began to hitch. "The light's turned."

"Fuck the light."

"No, just drive." She took a deep breath as horns began to blast behind them. "Just drive for a minute. I need to settle down."

She slid down a bit in the seat and fought a vicious war with her own fears. "You wouldn't think less of me if I asked you to turn around and drive out of here?"

"Of course not."

"But I would. I'd think less of me. I need to ask you for something."

"Anything."

"Don't let me back out. Whatever I say later, I'm telling you now I have to see this through. Wherever it goes. If I don't, I'll hate myself. I know it's a lot to ask, but don't let me rabbit out."

"We'll see it through then."

He wove through traffic, turning onto roads that weren't so wide now, weren't so clean. The storefronts here, when they weren't boarded up, were dull with grime.

Then everything began to spruce up again, slowly, as if some industrious domestic droid had begun work at one end and was polishing its way down to the other.

Small, trendy shops and eateries, freshly rehabbed apartments and town homes. It spoke, clearly, of the gradual takeover of the disenfranchised area by the upwardly mobile young urbanite with money, energy, and time.

"This is wrong. It's not like this." Staring out the window, she saw the shamble of public housing, the broken glass, the screaming lights of yesterday's slum quarter superimposed over today's brisk renewal.

Roarke pulled into a parking garage, found a slot, cut the engine. "It might be better if we walked a bit."

Her legs were weak, but she got out of the car. "I walked then. I don't know how long. It was hot then, too. Hot like this."

"You'll walk with me now." He took her hand.

"It wasn't clean like this." She clung to his hand as they walked out of the garage, onto the sidewalk. "It was getting dark. People were shouting. There was music." She looked around, staring through the present into the past. "A strip club. I didn't know what it was, exactly, but there was music pouring out whenever someone opened the door. I looked inside, and I thought maybe I could go in because I could smell food. I was so hungry. But I could smell something else. Sex and booze. He'd smelled like that. So I ran away as fast as I could. Someone yelled after me."

Her head felt light, her stomach clutched with a sharp, drilling hunger that came from memory.

"Little girl. Hey, little girl. He called me that. I ran across the street, through the cars. People shouted, beeped horns. I think . . . I think I fell, but I got up again."

Roarke kept her hand in his as they crossed.

"I couldn't run very far because my arm hurt so much, and I was dizzy. Sick."

She was sick now. Oily waves pitched in her belly and rose into her throat. "Nobody paid attention to me. Two men." She stopped. "Two men here. Must've been an illegals deal gone bad. They started to fight. One fell and knocked me over. I think I passed out for a minute. I must have because when I woke up, one of them was lying on the sidewalk beside me. Bleeding, groaning. And I crawled away. Into here. In here."

She stood at the mouth of an alley, tidy as a church pew now with a sparkling recycler.

"I can't do this."

He wanted to scoop her up, carry her away. Anywhere but here. But she'd asked, and he'd promised to see her through it. "Yes, you can."

"I can't go in there."

"I'm going with you." He brought her icy hand to his lips. "I'm with you, Eve. I won't leave you."

"It got dark, and I was cold." She made herself take the first step into the alley, then the second. "Everything hurt again, and I just wanted to sleep. But the smell. Horrible smell from the garbage. The recycler was broken, and there was garbage all over the alley. Someone came in, so I had to hide. If he comes after me, if he finds me, he'll take me back to the room and do awful things to me. I hide in the dark, but it isn't him. It's somebody else, and they're pissing against the wall, then they go away."

She swayed a little, didn't feel Roarke's hand steady her. "I'm so tired. I'm so tired, I'm so hungry. I want to get up, to find another hiding place. One that doesn't smell so bad, that isn't so dark. It's awfully dark here. I don't know what's in the dark."

"Eve." It worried him that she was speaking as if it were all happening now, that her voice was going thin and shaky as if she were in pain. "You're not hurt now, or alone, or a child." He took her shoulders, squeezed them firmly. "You can remember without going back."

"Yeah, okay." But she was afraid. Her belly was slick with fear. She concentrated on his face, on the clean, clear blue of his eyes until she felt steady again. "I was afraid to be in the dark, afraid to be out of it. But . . ." She looked back to where she'd huddled. "I couldn't get up anyway because I was sick again. Then I don't remember anything until it was light."

She lifted one shaking hand to point. "Here. I was here. I remember. There were people standing over me when I woke up. Blue uniforms. Police. If you talk to the cops they'll put you in a hole with the snakes and the bugs that like to eat you. Roarke."

"Steady. I'm right here. Hold on to me."

She turned to him. Turned into him. "I couldn't get away from them. I couldn't even move. I didn't remember where I was, or who. They kept asking questions, but I didn't know the answers. They took me away, to the hospital. There was a different smell there, just as scary. And I couldn't get away. They wouldn't let me go. But they didn't put me in a hole with the snakes. That was a lie. Even when I couldn't tell them who I was they didn't try to hurt me."

"No." He stroked her hair as he thought how she'd found the courage to grab on to a badge and make it her own. "They wanted to help you."

She let out a shaky breath, rested her head on his shoulder. "I couldn't tell them what I didn't know. I wouldn't have told them if I'd known. They would have taken me back to that room, and that would've been worse than any pit. I did something terrible in that room. I couldn't remember, but it was bad, and I couldn't go back. I can't breathe in here anymore."

He slid an arm around her waist, led her out of the alley where she bent from the waist, braced her hands on her thighs and drew greedy breaths.

"Better now?"

She nodded. "Yeah. I'm okay. Just need a minute. Sorry—"

"Don't apologize to me for this." His voice snapped out, whipped by fury before he could bank it. "Don't. Just take your time.

"The room was in a hotel," she said. "Old. Riot bars on the lower windows, middle of the street. Across from it was a sex club. Live Sex. Red light." Her stomach clutched, threatened to pitch, but she bore down. "The room was high up. He always got a high room so I couldn't get out the window. Ninth floor. I counted the windows across the street. There was a lighted sign out front, with the letters running down. Something foreign, because I couldn't read it. I could read some, but I didn't know what it said. C, A . . . C, A, S, A. Casa, Casa Diablo."

She let out a short laugh, straightened. Her face was clammy, white as ivory, but set. "Devil House. That's what that means, isn't it? Isn't that fucking perfect? Can you find it?"

"If that's what you want, yes. I'll find it."

"Now. Before I lose my nerve."

He went back to the car first. He wanted to get her away from the alley, to give her time to gather her resources. While she sat, head back, eyes closed, he took out his PPC and began the search.

"You've put a lot into one day already, Eve."

"I want to finish it."

The year before he'd finally gone back to the alley where his father had met someone meaner, someone quick enough to jam a knife in his throat. And he remembered the fury, the pain, and the ultimate release he'd experienced standing there as a man, looking down, and knowing it was finished.

"It's still there." He told her and saw her flinch. "The name's changed, but it's still a hotel. It's called The Traveler's Inn now, and rates three stars. It's fucking three miles from here."

When she opened her eyes, looked at him, he shook his head. "I'm with you, but by Christ, Eve, it's punishing to know you walked all that way, hurt and hungry and lost."

"Is that why you went alone when you went back to

where you'd lived in Dublin? Because you didn't want
to share that punishment with me?"

He shoved the PPC back in his pocket. "Give me a
bit of room, would you, for wanting to tuck you up safe
when I can manage it."

"You're churned up." She swiped the back of her hand
over her damp face, didn't know if it was wet from sweat
or tears. "The Irish gets thicker when you're churned up."

"Bugger it."

"I feel better because you're churned up. Go figure."
She leaned over to touch her lips to his cheek. "Thanks."

"Happy to help. You're ready then?"

"Yeah."

Nothing looked particularly familiar. She thought they'd
come in at night. Maybe at night. On a bus. Maybe on a
bus.

What the hell did it matter?

The city itself wasn't a huge revelation to her. There
was no sudden epiphany with all questions answered. She
didn't know if she wanted all questions answered, only
that she needed to do this one thing.

Wanted to do this one thing, she corrected. But despite
the climate control that kept the interior of the car comfortably cool, a line of sweat dribbled down her back.

Roarke swung to the curb, held up a hand to hold off
the uniformed doorman who hustled over. "Take your
time," he told Eve. "Take whatever time you need."

The building was a simple block with a rippled tile
roof. But it was painted a pleasant stucco pink now, and
rather than the lurid sign, there was a shady portico and
a couple of big concrete tubs filled with a rainbow of
flowers.

"Are you sure this is right?" She felt his hand close
gently over hers. "Yeah, of course you're sure. It didn't
look like this."

"It was rehabbed in the late forties. From the looks of it, I'd say most of this area got the same treatment."

"It won't be the same inside either. This is probably a waste of time, and I should be talking to the locals about Dunne."

He said nothing, just waited her out.

"I'm so scared. I'm so fucking scared. I can't even work up any spit in my mouth. If this was the job, I'd just do it. You just go through the door."

"I'm going through the door with you." He kissed her hand again, because he needed it. "We've been through others. We can go through this one."

"Okay." She sucked in a breath. "Okay." And got out of the car.

She didn't know what Roarke said to the doorman, or how much money changed hands, but the car remained parked where it was.

There was a roaring in her head she knew was fear, adrenaline, and dread. It remained there, dimming her hearing so that it was like walking through water as they entered the lobby.

The floors were a sea of blues, and added to the sensation of passing through some thin liquid. There were pleasant seating areas arranged, and a bank of elevators with silver doors to one side, a long check-in counter on the other where two bright-faced young clerks worked.

There were white carnations in the buttonholes of their snappy red jackets, and a generous bowl of hard candy on the counter.

"He had funny eyes." She stared at the tidy check-in area and remembered the grubby rat hole where a single droid had worked. "One wandered everywhere and the other stared right at you. He smelled, like burning. *Fucking droid's blown some circuits*. That's what he said. *You just stay there, little girl. Stay there with the bags and keep your mouth shut if you know what's good for you.*

And he went up to the counter and got a room."

"What room?"

"Nine-one-one. Emergency. Better not call 911 or he'll beat the shit out of you. Oh God."

"Look at me. Eve, look at me."

She did, and saw so much in his face. Concern, fury, and hints of grief. "I can do it. I can do this." She took a step toward check-in, then his hand took hers again.

"Good afternoon." The female clerk spilled welcome all over them. "Will you be checking in today?"

"We need room 911," Roarke told her.

"And do you have a reservation?"

"Nine-one-one," Roarke repeated.

Her smile faltered a little, but she began to work with her screen. "That room is blocked for a guest arriving this evening. If you'd like another room with a kitchenette, perhaps—"

He felt Eve reach down, knew she was going for her badge. He gave her hand a warning squeeze. "It's 911 we need." He'd already measured her. Some you bribed, some you intimidated, some you flattered. And others you simply rolled over. "The name's Roarke, and my wife and I will be needing that particular room for a bit. If there's a problem with that, you should speak to your supervisor."

"Just one moment, sir." Her face wasn't so friendly now, and her voice had cooled to that "You're a troublemaker" tone. She slipped through a door behind the counter. It took only twenty seconds or so before a man came rushing out ahead of her.

"I apologize for the wait, Mr. Roarke. I'm afraid my clerk didn't understand. We weren't expecting—"

"We need the room. Room 911. I take it you understand?"

"Of course, of course." He tapped nervous fingers over the screen. "Whatever we can do for you. Welcome to

The Traveler's Inn. Angelina, get Mr. Roarke's keycode and guest packet. We have two restaurants," he continued. "Marc's for fine dining, and The Corral for casual. May I make any reservations for you?"

"That won't be necessary."

"The Sunset Lounge is open from eleven A.M. to two A.M., and our gift shop carries souvenirs, apparel, snacks, and various sundries" The words tumbled out of his lips and he looked slightly terrified. "May I ask how long you and your wife plan to stay with us?"

"Not long." Roarke handed over a debit card.

"Ah, yes, thank you. I'll just scan this. We'll be happy to assist you with any of your plans or needs while you're in Dallas. Transportation, sightseeing, theater."

"Just the room, please."

"Of course. Yes, indeed." He handed back the debit card, then offered the keycode and the guest packet. "Will you need assistance with your luggage?"

"No. See that we're not disturbed, won't you?"

"Of course. Yes. If you need anything, anything at all . . ." he called after them as they walked to the elevators.

"He's wondering if we're going up there for some quick sex," Eve said. "You don't own this place, do you?"

"I don't, no, but he's certainly wondering if I'm going to."

The elevator opened and yawned, Eve thought, like a big, greedy mouth. She stepped into it. "I could've used my badge, kept your name out of it."

"This was simple enough."

"I guess. Anyway, it took my mind off things, watching you work him. Another ten seconds of you, and he'd've babbled."

The elevator doors opened again. She stood where she was, staring out at the quiet hallway.

"It was dark," she managed. "I think it was dark, and he was pissed off. But there were so many places, I'm not sure if I'm mixing it up with somewhere else. I was only outside the room twice, once when we went in. Once when I went out. I'm sure of that. It was almost always that way."

"He can't lock you in anymore."

"No." She stiffened her spine and walked out into the hall. "It smelled like wet socks. That's what I thought. Like wet, dirty socks, and I was tired. Hungry. I hoped he'd go out, get us something to eat. But more, I hoped he'd just go out. It's that way." She gestured toward the left.

It was to the left, and five rooms down.

"I'm scared stupid. Don't let me run."

"You won't run. Eve." He turned her face to his, touched his mouth to hers. "You were always stronger than him. Always."

"Let's see if you're right. Open it."

You just go through the door, she told herself. *That's what you do.*

How many times had she done just that, knowing death waited on the other side hoping to take her? There was no one on the other side of this door but ghosts.

The roar in her head was nearly a scream when she stepped in.

It was tidy, clean, pleasantly appointed. Viewing discs were fanned out artistically on a low table beside an arrangement of fake flowers. The floor was carpeted in a pale beige.

Was there blood on the floor under it? she wondered. Was his blood still there?

The bed was covered in a spread exploding with what she thought might have been poppies. A work area had been built into a corner and held a small, practical communication center. The kitchenette was separated from the sleeping area by an eating counter. There was a bowl on it holding a display of nubby fruit.

Through the window she could see another building, but there was no sign, no flashing light, no wash of dirty red.

"Looks like they redecorated." The feeble attempt at humor echoed back at her. "We never stayed in places like this—as nice as this—that I remember. Nothing this clean and, well, tended, I guess, as this is now. Sometimes there were two rooms, so I had my own bed. But sometimes I slept on the floor. I slept on the floor."

Her gaze was pulled down, over. She could see herself there, if she let it happen, see herself huddled on the floor under a thin blanket.

"It's cold. Climate control's broken. It's so cold it hurts my bones. There's no hot water and I hate washing in the cold. But I have to get his smell off me. It's worse than being cold to smell him on me after he's . . ."

She hugged her arms now, and shuddered.

He watched it come into her, and it tore him to pieces. Lanced through his heart till he could all but feel the blood pouring out of it for her.

Her eyes widened and blurred, and her face went more than pale. It went transparent.

"I slept there. Tried to sleep there. There's a light through the window, flashing off and on. Red then black, red then black, but the red stays like a mist. He goes out a lot. Places to go, people to see. *Keep quiet as a mouse, little girl, or the snakes'll get you. Sometimes they swallow you whole, the snakes do, and you're still alive inside them. Screaming.*"

"Good Christ." He barely breathed the oath, had to jam his fists into his pockets for there was nothing and no one to fight, to punish for terrorizing the child that was now his wife.

"If someone's coming here, I have to stay in the bathroom. Children aren't to be seen or heard. When he brings women up, he does to them what he does to me. It's safe when he does it to them, and they don't cry or beg him to stop unless he starts hitting them. But I don't like to hear it."

She covered her ears with her hands. "He doesn't bring them back very much. Then it's not safe. Sometimes he's drunk, drunk enough. But not always. When he's not, he hurts me. He hurts me."

Unconsciously she pressed a hand between her legs and rocked. "If I can't hold it back, if I cry, if I scream, if I beg, he hurts me more. *This is what you're supposed to do. You better learn, little girl. Pretty soon you're gonna earn your goddamn keep. You remember what I told you.*"

She looked at Roarke, looked through him, then took a staggering step forward. She didn't see the poppies now, or the pretty flowers, the pale, clean rug.

"I'm so cold. I'm so hungry. Maybe he won't come back. But he always comes back. Something bad could happen to him so he couldn't come back. Then I could get warm. I'm so hungry."

She stepped toward the kitchenette. "Not supposed to touch anything. Not supposed to eat unless he says so. He forgot to feed me again. There's cheese. It's green, but if you cut that off, it's okay. Maybe he won't know if I have just a little. He'll hit me if he finds out, but he'll hit me anyway, and I'm so hungry. I forget I'm not supposed to eat because I want more. I want more. Oh God, God, he's coming."

The hand she'd fisted opened. She heard the knife hit the floor.

What are you doing, little girl?

"Have to think fast, make excuses, but it doesn't help. He knows, and he's not very drunk. He hits me in the face; I taste blood, but I don't cry. Maybe he'll stop. But he doesn't stop, and now it's his fists. He knocks me down." She crumpled to her knees. "And I can't stop myself from begging him. Stop, oh please, don't. Please, please, it hurts. He'll kill me if I fight, but I can't help it. It *hurts!* And I hurt him back."

She peers down at her hand, remembering using her nails to claw at his face, how he'd howled. She could hear it.

"My arm!" She clutched it. Heard, felt the dry snap of that young bone, and the hideous bright pain. "He's pushing into me, pushing in, panting on my face. Candy breath. Mints," she realized dimly. "Mints over whiskey. Horrible, horrible in my face. I see his face. They call him Rick, or Richie, and his face is bleeding where I scratched him. He can bleed, too. He can hurt, too."

She was weeping now, the tears pouring down her face. Watching her, knowing he had no choice but to watch her live the nightmare, Roarke broke inside.

"I have the knife in my hand. My hand closes over the knife I dropped on the floor. Then the knife's in him. It punches into him, a little popping sound. And now he screams, and he stops. The knife made him stop, so I push it into him again. Again. Again. He rolls away, but I don't stop. He stopped, but I don't stop. I can't stop. He's staring at me, and I *won't* stop. Blood, the blood's all over him. All over me. His blood's all over me."

"Eve." She was on her hands and knees, snarling like an animal. Roarke crouched in front of her, took her arms. She hissed at him, but he tightened his grip. And his hands trembled. "Stay here. Stay with me. Look at me."

She shook violently, fought for breath. "I'm all right. I can smell it." She broke, and shattered into his arms. "Oh God, can't you smell it?"

"We're going to leave now. I'm taking you away from this."

"No. Just hold on to me. Just hold on. I remember what it was like. Like not being human anymore. Like the animal that lives inside us had leaped out. Then I crawled away, over there."

She shivered still as she looked over at the corner, but she made herself see it, see herself, as it had been. "I watched him for a long time, waiting for him to get up and make me sorry. But he didn't. When it was light, I got up and washed his blood off me in the cold water. And I packed a bag. Imagine thinking of that? I hurt— my arm, where he'd raped me again—but it was buried under the shock. Still, I didn't use the elevator—had enough wit for that. Used the stairs. Crept down the stairs and went outside. I don't remember a lot of that, except it was bright out and my eyes stung. Lost the bag some- where and just walked. And walked."

She eased back. "He never called me by a name. Be- cause I didn't have one. I remember that now. They didn't bother to give me a name because I wasn't a child to them. I was a thing. I can't remember her, but I re- member him. I remember what he said the first time he touched me. What he told me to remember. That was what he kept me around for, and when I'd learned, that was how I'd earn my keep. He was going to whore me. Nothing like young pussy, he said, so I'd better learn to take it without the whining and crying. He had a fucking investment in me, and I was going to pay off. We were going to start here. Here in Dallas, because I was eight and that was old enough to start carrying my weight."

"It ended here." He brushed tears from her cheeks. "And what started, darling Eve, was you."

Chapter 14

He ignored her request to head straight to the central police station and drove to the hotel, one he did own, and where the owner's suite was prepared for them.

The fact that she was too tired to argue told her he was right, again. She needed time to pull herself together.

She went through the enormous parlor into the equally sumptuous master bedroom and left Roarke to deal with the bellman. She was already stripping when he came in.

"I need a shower. I need to . . . I need to get clean."

"You'll need some food when you're done. What would you like?"

"Wait on that, will you?" She was in sudden, desperate need for floods of hot water, for waves of clean, fragrant soap. "Let me think about it."

"I'll be just in the other room then."

He left her alone as much for himself as for her. The rage he'd managed to chain down was threatening to snap free. He wanted to use his fists on something. Pound them until his arms screamed for rest.

She'd shower, he thought, with water that was brutally hot, because once she'd been forced to wash in cold. He never wanted her to be cold again, to shiver as she had shivered in that room where the ghosts, the viciousness of them, had been so tangible he'd seen them himself.

Watching her relive that night, as she too often did in dreams, had ripped him in two. It had left him helpless, useless, and with a violence borne of fury he had nowhere to vent.

To have birthed and bred her, beaten and raped her all for selling her to other scum. What god made such creatures as that and set them to prey on innocents?

Riding on rage, he stripped off his shirt as he strode into the small workout area. He yanked the speed bag into place. And attacked it, bare-fisted.

With each punch his anger grew, spreading through him like a cancer. The bag was a face he didn't know. Her father's. Then his own father's. He battered at it with a concentrated rage that bloomed into hate. Pounded, pounded, as the black haze of that hate narrowed his vision. Pounded, pounded, as his knuckles went raw and bloomed with blood.

And still he couldn't kill it.

When the bag snapped off its tether, plowed into the wall, he looked around for something else to hammer.

And saw her standing in the doorway.

She'd wrapped herself in one of the white hotel robes. Her cheeks were nearly as pale.

"I should have thought how this would make you feel. And I didn't." His torso gleamed with sweat. His hands were bleeding. When he saw her there his heart shattered.

"I don't know what to do for you." His voice was thick with emotion, with the accent that took over when his defenses were most compromised. "What to say to you."

When she took a step toward him, he shook his head,

stepped back. "No, I can't touch you right now. I'm not myself. I might break you in half. I mean it." His voice whipped out when she took the next step.

She stopped. Because she understood it wasn't just her that might be broken. "It hurts you as much as me. I forget that."

"I want him dead, and he's dead already." He flexed his battered knuckles. "So, nothing to be done about it. Still, I want to beat my fists into his face; I want to rip the heart out of his chest before ever he laid hands on you. I'd give everything I own if I could. Instead, there's nothing."

"Roarke—"

"My father was there." His head snapped up, his gaze boring into hers. "Maybe in that very room. We know that now. I don't know as his various and filthy appetites ran to young girls, but if the timing had been just a bit different, you might have been sold to him." He nodded, reading her face. "I see that's occurred to you as well."

"It didn't happen. There's enough that did without adding to it. And don't say there's nothing. Most of my life I kept all this buried, kept it in the dark. I've remembered more in the past year than I could in all the years before. Because you were there, and I could face it. I don't know if I'll ever have it all. I don't know if I'll ever want to have it all. And after today, I know that it's never going away. It's there."

She clenched a hand between her breasts. "It's here, inside me, and it'll bite off pieces when it can. But I can take it because you're there. Because you know how it feels. You're the only one who really knows. And because you love me enough to feel it. When you look at me, and I see that, I can take anything."

She took the last step to him, slipped her arms around him, drew him close. "Be with me."

He buried his face in her hair. His arms came tight

around her, viced them together as the rage drained out of him. "Eve."

"Just be with me." She skimmed her lips over his cheek, found his mouth. Poured herself into him.

Everything inside him opened for her, opened to her so that she filled the dark corners. The violence that lived with them both shrank back.

Mouth against mouth, he lifted her, cradling her there for a moment. As he would something precious. Something rare. He carried her into the bedroom where the strong sun streamed through the glass.

They would love in the light. He laid her on the wide bed, centered her on soft fabric. He wanted to give her softness, comfort, and the beauty they'd both once starved for. He needed to give her the beauty of what this act was meant to be, a beauty so strong it could smother the ugliness some made of it.

The hands that had pounded with rage until they'd bled were gentle when they touched her.

It was she who drew him down, held him close. Who sighed when he sighed. They would comfort each other now.

Her lips met his, parted. The softest, sweetest of matings. Her hands stroked his back, along the hard ridge of muscle as his body fit to hers.

She loved the weight of him, the lines and planes of him, the scent and the taste of him. When his lips roamed to her throat, she angled her head to give them both more.

There was tenderness in long, lush kisses, in slow, sliding caresses. And warmth, shimmering over skin, then under it until bones melted.

He parted the robe, trailed lazy kisses down her flesh. Steeped in her, he traced fingertips over subtle curves, lingering when she sighed or she trembled. And watched with pleasure as color bloomed on her face.

"Darling Eve." His lips found hers again, rubbed gently. "So beautiful."

"I'm not beautiful."

She felt his lips curve against hers. "This isn't the time to argue with a man." He closed a hand lightly over her breast, easing back to watch her. "Small and firm here." He flicked a thumb over her nipple, heard her breath catch. "Those eyes of yours, like old gold. Fascinating how they see everything but what I do when I look at you."

He lowered his head to nibble at her mouth. "Soft lips. Irresistible. Stubborn chin, always ready to take a punch." He skimmed his tongue over the shallow dent. "I love that spot there, and this," he whispered, trailing his lips down to the underside of her jaw.

"My Eve, so long and lean." He ran his hand down the length of her. And when he cupped her, she was already hot, already wet. "Go up, darling. Slide over."

She was, helplessly, with a quiet moan that was both pleasure and surrender.

He made her feel beautiful. Made her feel clean. Made her feel whole. She reached for him now, rolling with him in a kind of dance without heat or hurry. The sun splashed over them as the air went thick with sighs and murmurs. She touched and tasted and gave as he did. Lost herself as he did.

When she rose to him, when he slid inside her, her vision blurred with tears.

"Don't." He pressed his cheek to hers. "Ah, don't."

"No." She framed his face, let the tears come. "It's so right. It's so perfect. Can't you see?" She lifted to him again. "Can't you feel?" She smiled even as the tears sparkled on her cheeks. "You've made me beautiful."

She held his face in her hands as they moved together, took that silky glide. When she felt him quiver, saw his eyes go to midnight, she knew it was he who surrendered.

After, they lay quiet, wrapped in each other. He waited for her arms to go limp, to slide away so he knew she slept. When they didn't, he brushed a kiss over her hair.

"If you won't sleep, you'll eat."

"I'm not tired. I need to finish the job down here."

"After you've eaten."

She might've argued, but she remembered how he'd looked, ramming his fists into the speed bag. "Something fast and easy then." She lifted his hand, examined the knuckles. "Nice job, by the way. You're going to have to take care of these."

"Been awhile since I bashed them up quite this much." He flexed his fingers. "Just scraped up though. Nothing's jammed."

"It would've been smarter to put gloves on."

"But not as cathartic, I'd think."

"Nope, there's nothing quite like beating something into pulp with your bare hands for relaxation." She shifted, straddled him. "We come from violent people. We've got that in us. The difference is we don't let it loose whenever we feel like it on whoever's handy. There's something in us that stops that, that makes us decent."

"Some of us are more decent than others."

"Answer me this. Have you ever hit a child?"

"Of course I haven't. Christ."

"Ever beat or raped a woman?"

He sat up so she was forced to wrap her legs around his waist. "I've thought about giving you a quick shot now and again." He balled his fist, tapped her chin gently with his bruised knuckles. "I know what you're saying, and you're right. We're not what they were. Whatever they did to us, they couldn't make us what they were."

"We made ourselves. Now, I guess, we make each other."

He smiled at her. "That was well said."

"They didn't give me a name." She let out a slow breath. "When I remembered that, back there, it hurt. It made me feel small and useless. But now I'm glad they didn't. They didn't put their label on me. And, Roarke, right now anyway I'm glad I came here. I'm glad I did this. But what I want to do is get the information to the locals and get out. I don't want to stay here longer than I have to. I want to go home tonight."

He leaned into her. "Then we'll go home."

They got back to New York early enough for her to be able to say she needed to go into Central and make it sound plausible. She didn't think Roarke bought it, but he let it slide.

Maybe he understood she needed the space, she needed the work. She needed the atmosphere that reminded her who and what she was at the core.

She bypassed Peabody's cube, slipped quietly into her office, and shut the door. Locked it, as she rarely did.

She sat at her desk and was absurdly comforted at the way the worn seat fit to the shape of her butt. A testament, she thought, to all the hours she'd sat there, doing the job—the thinking, paperwork, 'link-transmissions, data-formulating part of the job.

This was her place.

She got up and walked to the window. She knew just what she would see, which streets, which buildings, even the most usual pattern of traffic that formed at that time of the day.

The part of her that was still quaking, the part she'd used every ounce of will to hide from Roarke, calmed just a little more.

She was where she was meant to be, doing what she was meant to do.

Whatever had come before, all the horrors, the fears, all funnelled into the now, didn't they? Who could say if she would be here without them. Maybe, somehow, she was more willing to live for the victim because she'd been one.

However it worked, she had a job to do. She turned, walked back to her desk, and got to work.

She asked for and was granted a quick meeting with Mira. Slipping out as quietly as she'd slipped in, she left her office for Mira's.

"I thought you might be gone for the day."

Mira gestured to one of her cozy scoop-backed chairs. "Shortly. Tea?"

"Really, this isn't going to take long." But Mira was already programming her AutoChef. Eve resigned herself to sipping the liquid flowers Mira was so fond of.

"You'd rather coffee," Mira said with her back turned. "But you'll indulge me, which I appreciate. You can always pump in the caffeine later."

"How do you—I was just wondering how you keep it going on that herbal stuff."

"It's all what your system's used to, isn't it? I find this soothes my mind, and when my mind's soothed, I have more energy. Or believe I do, which is nearly the same thing." She came back, offered Eve one of the delicate cups.

"In other words, you bullshit yourself into thinking you're wired up, when you're not."

"That's one way to put it."

"That's sort of interesting. Anyway, I have more data on Julianna Dunne, and I wanted to get it to you right away. I don't think we have much time before she moves again. I interviewed her step-father—"

"You went to Dallas?"

"I just got back about an hour ago. I want to do this now," Eve said firmly enough to have Mira arching her brows. "Okay?"

"All right."

She relayed the contents of the interview, citing only the facts given, then moving on to her discussion with Chuck Springer.

"The first man she was with sexually—boy, that is— was someone her own age," Mira commented, "and working-class. And he was the first to reject her. The last, by all accounts, who was permitted the luxury of doing so. She hasn't forgotten it."

"Yet she didn't target types like Springer. She went after types like her step-father."

"Because she was sure she could control them. They built her confidence and her bank account. But she was punishing Springer every time she was with another man. Look at this, look what I can have. I don't need you. Along the way, Springer became less of a personal affront and more a symbol. Men are worthless, liars, cheats, weaklings, and driven by sex."

"And wouldn't it irritate her to know that on a core level, she's the one driven by it."

Mira lifted her brows, nodded in approval. "Yes, exactly. You understand her very well. Springer said that they'd had sex after he'd broken it off with her, after she'd physically attacked him. It only showed her sex was the key, and in her mind, man's fatal downfall. She stopped being angry, and got down to the business of using that weakness to satisfy herself."

"That plays for me. But I can't figure who'll she'll go for next. I ran probabilities on Parker, on Springer, and on Roarke. Parker and Springer are neck-in-neck, with Roarke more than twenty percentage points behind them. I trust your opinion more than a computer's."

"It won't be Springer. Not yet. She may toy with him a bit more, but I believe she'll save him. Like a cat plays with a mouse before the kill. Her stepfather? It's possible, but I'd think she'd wait on him as well. He was her first real victory, a kind of practice tool. She'll want to savor him yet."

Mira set her tea aside. "I think, despite the results of the probabilities, it'll be Roarke, or someone else entirely. She's not finished here yet, Eve. She's not finished with you."

"That's the way I worked it, too. I'm going to keep him covered, and that's going to piss him off. But he'll get over it. Okay, thanks. Sorry, to have held you up."

"Are you all right?"

"A little shaky, maybe, but mostly I'm all right. I got through it, and I remembered some stuff."

"Will you tell me?"

It was foolish to deny, to either of them, that she was here as much for personal reasons as professional ones. "I remembered what it felt like to kill him. I remembered that rush of primal hate and rage. I know that's in me, and I know I can control it. I know that killing him, for me, at that moment, was the only way to survive. I can live with that."

She got to her feet. "And if you're thinking you need to put me through Testing to be sure I'm solid, I won't agree to it. I won't do it."

Mira kept her hands folded in her lap, kept her body very still. "Do you think I'd put you through that? Knowing you, understanding the circumstances, that I would use this confidence and play by the book? I thought you and I had come further than that."

She heard the hurt, and the disappointment, and had to turn away from it. "Maybe I'm shakier than I thought. I'm sorry." She pressed the heels of her hands to her temples. "Goddamn it."

"Oh, Eve." Mira rose, but when she reached out, Eve stepped quickly aside.

"I just need to find some level ground. Focus on work, and put this . . . He was training me," she blurted out.

"Training me so he could sell me to other men." Slowly, she lowered her hands as she stared at Mira's face. "You knew."

"I suspected. It made a terrible kind of sense. He could have moved quicker, easier, cheaper without you. You served no real purpose for him. From what I know, what you've been able to tell me, he wasn't a standard pedophile. He had relationships with women as a rule. You were the only child he abused that we're aware of. And if children were what he wanted, he could have availed himself of them without the inconvenience of having one underfoot otherwise."

"He kept me locked up. That's how you train something—brainwash it. You keep it locked up, totally dependent on you. You convince it that it has no choice but to stay because whatever's out there is worse. You keep it hungry, uncomfortable, and afraid, mix that with small rewards. Punish harshly and swiftly for any infractions, and accustom it to whatever task it's meant to do. Bind it to you with fear, and it's yours."

"You were never his. With all that he did, for all those years, he never really reached you."

"He's never let go either," Eve said. "I have to live with that, too. So does Roarke. This messed him up, maybe more than it did me. We're okay, but . . . hell, it screws up your head."

"Would you like me to talk to him?"

"Yeah." The tension spiking into the base of her skull eased. "Yeah, that'd be good."

It wasn't really stalling to go back to her office, add Mira's comments to her file on Julianna Dunne. It gave her time to smooth out her mood, and to update and copy all updated files to her team and her commander.

When it was done and she heard the general scuffle outside her office that meant change of shift, she programmed one last cup of coffee and stood drinking it at her window.

Uptown traffic, she thought, was going to be a bitch.

In a small office across the jammed street and sky, Julianna Dunne sat at a secondhand metal desk. The door that read DAILY ENTERPRISES was locked. The office consisted of a boxy room and a closet-sized washroom. The furnishings were sparse and cheap. She saw no reason her alter ego of Justine Daily, under which the rental agreement was signed, should waste overhead.

She wouldn't be here long.

The rent was steeper than it should have been, and the toilet ran continually. The thin, scarred carpet smelled ripely of must.

But the view was priceless.

Through her binoculars she had a perfect view of Eve's office, and the lieutenant herself.

So sober, so serious, she mused. So dedicated and devoted, worshipping at the altar of law and order. And such a waste.

All those brains, that energy, that *purpose* tossed away on a badge. And on a man. Under different circumstances, they'd have made an amazing team. But as it was, Julianna thought with a sigh, they were making challenging adversaries.

Eight years, seven months had given Julianna abundant time to examine her mistakes, replay her moves. There was no doubt in her mind that she would have outwitted the cops, the male cops, and spent those eight years, seven months doing what she loved to do.

But a woman was a cagier beast. And the then-freshly promoted Detective Dallas had been cagey indeed. Relentlessly.

More, she hadn't had the common courtesy to acknowledge her opponent's victories and skills.

But things were different now. She herself had changed. She was physically stronger, mentally clearer. Prison tended to hone away the excesses. In the same amount of time she knew Eve had been honed as well. But there was one vital difference between them, one essential flaw in the cop.

She cared. About the victim, about her fellow officers, about the law. And most important, about her man.

It was that flaw, in what Julianna considered a near-perfect machine, that would destroy her.

But not quite yet. Julianna set the binoculars aside, checked her wrist unit. Right now there was time for a little fun.

Eve ran into Peabody just outside the bull pen.

"Lieutenant. I thought you were in Texas."

"I was. Got back earlier. You've got updates waiting. You're out of uniform, Officer," she added as she skimmed Peabody's black cocktail dress and mile-high heels.

"Yeah, I'm off-shift. Changed here. I was heading to your place, actually, to scoop up my parents. McNab's taking us out to a fancy dinner. Can't figure what's up with that. He doesn't like fancy, and I'm pretty sure he's scared of them. Not fancy dinners, my parents. Anything I should tell him about the case?"

"Morning's soon enough. Let's do a conference at my home office. Eight hundred."

"Sure. You, ah, heading home now?"

"No, thought I'd go to Africa for an hour and see the zebras."

"Ha-ha." Peabody trotted after her as best she could in the cocktail shoes. "Well, I was just wondering if maybe I could catch a ride, since we're going to the same place at the same time."

"You going to Africa, too?"

"Dallas."

"Yeah, yeah, sure." She had to elbow her way onto the crowded elevator and was cursed roundly.

"You look a little wiped out," Peabody commented as she took advantage of the distraction and squeezed in.

"I'm fine." She heard the bite of irritation in her own voice and made the effort to soften it. "I'm fine," she repeated. "Long day, that's all. You put any time in on Stibbs?"

"Yes, sir." The elevator stopped and a number of passengers popped off like corks out of the tight neck of a bottle. "I was hoping to talk to you about that. I'd like to bring her in for a formal interview tomorrow."

"You set for it?"

"I think so. Yes," she corrected. "I'm set for it. I talked to some of the former neighbors. The suspect didn't have a relationship going. She'd had one, but broke it off just a few weeks after she moved into the same building as the Stibbs. When one witness loosened up, she told me that she hadn't been surprised when Boyd Stibbs married Maureen. How Maureen moved in on him quick, fast, and in a hurry after his wife's death. Taking him meals, tidying up his apartment, that sort of thing. Basic good-neighbor stuff until you look under it."

The elevator stopped eight times, disgorging passengers, taking more on.

An Illegals detective, undercover as a sidewalk sleeper, shambled on wearing a full-length duster stained with what appeared to be various bodily fluids. The stench was awesome.

"Jesus, Rowinsky. Why don't you use a damn glide, or at least stand downwind?"

He grinned, showing off yellowed teeth. "Really works, doesn't it? It's cat piss, with a little dead fish juice. Plus, I haven't showered in a week, so the BO's tremendous."

"You've been under way too long, pal," Eve told him and breathed through her teeth until he shambled off again. She didn't risk a good gulp of air until they hit garage level.

"I hope none of it got on me," Peabody said as she clicked along behind Eve. "That kind of smell gets right into the fibers."

"That kind of smell gets right into the pores, then it breeds."

On that cheerful note, Eve slid into the car. She backed out, spun the wheel, and arrowed for the exit. And was forced to slam the brakes as a man disguised as a mountain lumbered in front of her car. His rag-shoes flapped as he stepped forward and sprayed her windshield with a filthy liquid he carried in a plastic bottle in the pocket of his grimy Yankees jacket.

"Perfect. Must be my day for sleepers." Disgusted, Eve slammed out of the car as the man wiped at her coated windshield with a dirty rag.

"This is an official city vehicle, moron. It's a cop car."

"Clean it up." He nodded slowly as he smeared muck on muck. "Five bucks. Clean it right up."

"Five bucks, my ass. Make tracks, and make them now."

"Clean it right up," he repeated in a sing-song voice as he swiped the glass. "Just like she said."

"What I said was beat it." Eve started toward him, and she caught a movement out of the corner of her eye.

Across the street, flame-bright in a red skin suit, her golden hair gleaming, was Julianna Dunne. She smiled, then waved cheerfully. "Got a mess on your hands there, Lieutenant—oh and belated congratulations on your promotion."

"Son of a bitch."

Her hand went to her weapon as she started to charge. And the mountain backhanded her. One side of her face exploded as she was lifted off her feet, then went numb before she hit the pavement. She felt wild pain in her ribs as the brick of a foot covered in rags kicked her into a rolling skid. Through the ringing of her ears, she heard Peabody's shouts, the mountain's furious chant, "Five bucks! Five bucks!"

She shook her head to clear it, then came up fast, leading with her shoulder directly into his crotch. He didn't even howl, just crumpled.

"Dallas! What the hell?"

"Dunne," she managed, yanked out her restraints as she fought to pull in air and fill her lungs again. "Across the street. Red skin suit, blonde hair." She panted against the pain that was eating through the numbness. The right side of her face was starting to scream. "Heading west on foot. Call it in," she demanded as she snapped the street sleeper's beefy wrist to the car door. "Get me backup."

She came off the ground like a sprinter off the mark—low and fast. She zigzagged through traffic, was nearly creamed by a Rapid Cab. The blasts of horns and shouted obscenities followed her to the opposite side.

She could see the flashing red, with nearly a full block lead, and ran like a demon.

Legs pumping, she dodged pedestrians, plowed through those who didn't have the sense to get out of the way of a woman holding a lethal weapon. A man in a pristine business suit, a pocket-link at his ear, shouted in shock as she barreled toward him. Panicked, he stumbled back into a glide-cart, scattering tubes of Pepsi and soy dogs, inciting the vocal fury of the vender.

Eve leaped over him, pivoted north. She'd gained a quarter block.

"Backup, goddamn it, where's my backup?" She yanked out her communicator on the run. Her side was aching like a rotted tooth. "Officer needs assistance. In foot pursuit of suspect, identified as Julianna Dunne, heading north on Seventh at Bleeker. All units, all units in the vicinity, respond."

She raced across the crosswalk, against the light, springing onto the hood of a sedan, then catapulting herself off. "In pursuit, damn it, of female suspect, blonde, thirty-four, five four, one hundred-fifteen, wearing red skin suit."

She jammed the communicator away. Cursed the crowds of people that made it impossible to risk using her weapon. She holstered it, and dug for more speed.

There was blood in her mouth, blood dribbling into her right eye. But she'd eaten up another five feet of Julianna's lead.

Fast, Eve thought as the adrenaline hummed in her head. *Got herself in shape, knows how to run.*

She could hear sirens scream in the distance, and bore down. She was only two body-lengths behind when Julianna flicked back a glance. And smirked.

It took her out from behind, a low body slam that sent her flying up like a rock in a catapult. She had enough time to think, *What the fuck?* before she fell with a bone-rattling crash. The back of her head smacked smartly into the pavement, and turned her world into spinning stars. Voices came and went like the tide of the sea.

She managed to roll over, retching, and gain her hands and knees.

"Did I do it? Did I?" The bright, excited voice drilled into her spinning brain. She blinked up and stared into the freckled faces of two young boys. Another blink and the faces sucked into each other and became one.

"It looked good, it looked real, right? Man, you *flew!*" Clutching a fluorescent green airboard, he danced in place. "I slammed into you, just like I was supposed to."

She made some sound, spat out blood, then pushed up to her knees.

"Lieutenant! Dallas! God almighty." Thoroughly winded, Peabody pushed through the crowd. "She take you out?"

"This little . . ." She couldn't think of a word. "I'm all right. Go! Go! She's heading north."

With one fearful look at her lieutenant, Peabody took off.

"You." Eve crooked a finger at the boy. "Come down here."

"Boy, that blood looks real. That's iced."

His face wavered and split again, so she snarled at both of him. "You little schmuck, you just assaulted a police officer in pursuit of a suspect."

He hunkered down and lowered his voice. "Are we still on camera?"

"Did you hear what I said?"

"Where do you learn to do stunts like that anyway? How come you don't get hurt when you fall?"

"I *am* hurt, you stupid little—" She bit off the rest, fought to keep her vision from going from wavey gray to solid black. He couldn't have been more than ten, and his cheerful face was beginning to show some fear and confusion.

"Like for real hurt, or on the vid hurt?"

"This isn't a video."

"But she said it was a vid. And when you came running after her, I should slam right into you on my board. I got fifty dollars. And I get fifty more if I did a good job."

Two uniforms pushed through the crowd, ordering people back. "You need medical attention, Lieutenant?"

"Did you get her?"

They looked at each other, then down at Eve. "Sorry, sir. We lost her. We've got foot and vehicular patrols doing a sweep. We may get her yet."

"No." Eve dropped her head onto her knees as a vicious wave of nausea churned in her belly. "You won't."

"Are you really a cop?" The kid tugged Eve gingerly on the sleeve. "Am I in trouble? Man, my mom's going to kill me."

"Get a statement from this kid, then take him home." The sea rushed in again, ebbed again, but she got shakily to her feet.

"Sir." Red-faced, sweaty, and panting like a dog, Peabody limped up. "I'm sorry. I never even caught sight of her. We've got a net out, but . . ."

"Yeah, she's blown."

"You better sit down." Peabody grabbed Eve's arm when she swayed. "I'll call the MTs."

"I don't want the frigging MTs."

"You're really banged up."

"I said I don't want them. Back off." She started to pull free, watched Peabody's worried face turn to triplets. "Ah, shit," she managed, and actually felt her own eyes roll back in her head before she passed out.

Chapter 15

The next thing she knew she was flat out on the sidewalk
and a couple of medical technicians were hulking over
her.

"I said no."

One ran a sensor wand over her face. "Didn't break
the jaw or cheekbone. Lucky. Looks like she was hit in
the face with a fistful of bricks."

"Get away from me."

They both ignored her, which concerned her a great
deal. When she tried to sit up, she was held down easily.

"Shoulder's sprained, ribs bruised. No cracks. Damn
lucky. Lost a lot of skin, too. Good solid brain rattle here.
What's your name?"

"Dallas, Lieutenant Eve, and if you touch me, I'll kill
you."

"Yep, knows who she is. How's the vision, Lieutenant?"

"I see you well enough, asshole."

"And she's maintained her young, girlish charm. Follow the light. Just your eyes, don't move your head."

"Dallas." Peabody eased down. "You're really hurt. You've got to let them work on you."

"You called them after I told you not to. I can bust you down to a scooper for this."

"I don't think you'd say that if you could see what you look like."

"Think again."

"The light, Lieutenant." The MT took her jaw to keep her head still. "Follow the light."

She cursed him first, then followed the light. "Now let me up."

"I let you up, you're going to fall down again. You've got a concussion, a jammed shoulder, bruised ribs, gashed hip, assorted contusions and lacerations in addition to a face that looks like you rammed it into the back end of a maxibus. We're transporting you to the hospital."

"No, you're not."

Peabody glanced up, let out a relieved breath. "I wouldn't bet on that," she commented and shifted aside as Roarke knelt down.

"What is this?" Annoyance made way for panic. "Peabody, you are cooked."

"Quiet," Roarke ordered with such casual confidence both MTs goggled at him as if he were a god. "How bad is she?" he demanded.

The run-through of injuries was a great deal more coherent and professional, ending with the recommendation that the victim be transported to the nearest hospital for treatment and evaluation.

"I'm not going."

"You are." He feathered his fingers over her battered face, and a sick anger settled in his gut. "She needs something for the pain."

"Roarke—"

"Do you think I can't see it?" he snapped out, then drew himself back and shifted tactics. "Be a brave little soldier, darling, and let the nice MTs do what they must. If you're very good, I'll buy you some ice cream."

"I'll kick your ass for this."

"I look forward to you being able to try."

She struggled, catching the glint of a pressure syringe. "I don't want that shit. It makes me stupid. I took a spill, that's all. Where's that kid? I'm going to stomp all over his little freckled nose."

Roarke leaned over until his face filled her vision. "You let a kid take you down?" He saw immediately that the question, the amused tone of it had done the job. She stopped struggling to glare at him.

"Listen, ace—damn it, damn it!" She bucked once when she felt the faint nip of the syringe.

"Relax and enjoy it," he suggested. He felt the tension spill out of the hand he held. "That's the way."

"Think you're so smart." Body and mind began to float. "But you're more pretty. So pretty. Give me a kiss. Love that mouth. Like to bite it."

He kissed her limp hand instead. "She won't give you any more trouble."

"Bet I flew ten feet. Whee." She rolled her head to the side as she was lifted onto a gurney. "Hey, Peabody! Outta uniform. You got no shoes."

"Ditched them on the run. You're going to be okay, Dallas."

"Fucking-A. But I'm not going to any lame hospital. No, sir. Going home now. Where's Roarke? We're going home now, okay?"

"Eventually."

"That's right," she said, decisively, then slid under before they'd loaded her into the ambulance.

•　•　•

"She's going to be really mad when she comes out of it," Peabody said as she paced the ER waiting room.

"Oh yes." Roarke tapped his fingers against the side of the coffee cup. He'd yet to drink. "You did exactly right, Peabody, by calling the MTs, and me."

"Maybe you wouldn't mind mentioning that when she's lunging for my throat later. I don't know how she got up to pursue in the first place. That guy, he was big as a gorilla, and he flattened her. Probably jammed her shoulder when she rammed it into his groin. There I am, fumbling for my off-duty in this stupid little purse, and she's already taken him down and cuffed him. I should've been faster."

"I'd say you were quick enough. How are the feet?"

She curled up her toes. She had stripped off her ruined hose in the ladies' room. "Nothing a soak and a rub won't fix. Too bad about the shoes though. They were new and totally mag. Even without them I couldn't keep up with Dallas. She's like lightning."

"Long legs," he replied and thought of the blood he'd seen staining her trousers as she'd lain on the sidewalk.

"Yeah, she'd've apprehended if it hadn't been for the kid with the airboard. You can't beat her. She's—" She broke off, jittery when the ER doctor swung out.

"You're the husband?" the doctor asked with a nod to Roarke.

"Yes. How is she?"

"Spitting mad—I think she has some very ominous plans for you. And if you happen to be Peabody, you're in on them."

"She's okay." Peabody let out a gush of air. "That's great."

"She took a hard blow to the head. She's concussed, but that appears to be the worst of it. We've treated her shoulder, but she should refrain from lifting with it or any other strenuous activities for a couple of days, min-

imum. Her hip's going to give her some trouble, as are
the ribs. But minimal blockers should relieve the discomfort there. We've patched up the cuts, cold-packed the
bruises, the worst of which are facial. I'd like to keep
her overnight for observation. In fact, I'd like to keep her
for forty-eight hours."

"I can surmise her opinion of that idea."

"Mmm. A head injury of this nature is nothing to be
trifled with. Her other injuries are serious enough to warrant an overnight. She needs to be observed and monitored."

"And will be, but at home. She's phobic about hos-
pitals. I can assure you she'll recover more quickly, and
easier on all concerned, at home. I've a doctor I can call
on to make sure of it. Louise Dimatto."

"The Angel of Canal Street." The doctor nodded. "I'll
sign her out, but I'm going to give you very specific
instructions for her observation and care, and I'd like a
followup from Dr. Dimatto."

"Agreed, and thank you."

"Treatment Room Three," she added as she walked
away.

When he walked back a few minutes later, Eve was
trying and failing to pull her boots on. "When I get these
on, I'm using them to kick your balls into your throat."

"Darling, this isn't the time to think about sex." He
walked to the examination table, lifted her chin with a
fingertip. Her right cheek was a nightmare of bruising in
colors already going sickly. Her right eye was swollen to
a reddened, puffy slit. Her mouth was raw.

"Lieutenant." He touched his lips to her forehead.
"You've been well and truly bashed."

"You let them give me drugs."

"I did."

"And haul me in here."

"Guilty." His fingers slipped around to the back of her

head, gently measured the lump. "Your head may be hard, but even it has its limits. And let's just say I lost mine when I saw you lying there, bruised and bleeding."

"Peabody's going to fry for tagging you over this."

"She is not." On that single statement his voice went firm with command. "She's been out there pacing her poor, sore feet off worrying over you. So you'll go easy on her."

"You telling me my job now?"

"No, just your heart. She thinks if she'd been faster, you might not be here."

"That's bullshit. I had the lead, but she stayed in pursuit, even in those idiot shoes."

"Exactly so. You wouldn't happen to know what size she wears, would you?"

"Huh?"

"Never mind, I'll take care of it. Ready to go home?"

She slid off the table, but didn't object to having his hand support her. "Where's my ice cream?"

"You didn't behave, so there'll be no treat for you."

"That's just mean."

She was furious when she learned he'd called Louise in, but when she weighed that against the possibility of Roarke enlisting Summerset as a field MT, it was easier to swallow.

Especially when Louise walked into the bedroom carrying an enormous bowl of double chocolate chunk ice cream.

"Give me that."

"You get it after I get your word you won't give me any trouble during the examination."

"I've already had an examination."

Saying nothing, Louise scooped up a spoonful and slipped it between her own lips.

"Okay, okay. Jeez. Hand over the ice cream, and nobody gets hurt."

Louise passed Eve the bowl, then sat on the side of the bed, propped her medical bag in her lap. She pursed her lips as she studied Eve's face. "Ouch," she said.

"That your medical opinion, Doc?"

"It's a start. From the look of it, I'd say you're lucky he didn't shatter your cheekbone."

"I just knew this was my lucky day. It's not so bad now," she added over a mouthful of chocolate. "Those cold packs sting like a bitch, but they work. Roarke's being pissy about this, and he's got me outnumbered. So if you'd just clear me so I could get up and do some work—"

"Sure." Louise gestured.

Suspicious but game, Eve swung her legs off the bed, even managed to stand on them. For about three seconds before her head exploded and began to spin. Louise caught the ice-cream bowl handily as Eve dropped back on the bed.

"Some doctor you are."

"Yes, I am, and efficient with it. That just saved both of us arguing time."

Prone, Eve pursed her sore lips. "I don't think I like you anymore."

"I don't know how I'm going to go on with my life knowing that. You'll stay put until I tell you otherwise." She pulled a palm unit out of her bag, called up the copy of Eve's chart. "You don't know how long you were unconscious?"

"How the hell should I know? I was unconscious."

"Good point. I'm going to run some scans, give you a second round of cold packs. I can give you something for the discomfort."

"I don't want chemicals. Deal's off if you pull out a syringe."

"That's fine. I'd rather not give you anything with the concussion. We'll use external blockers there to take the edge off that whopper of a headache you must have."

She went back into her bag, calling out a "Come in," at the knock on the bedroom door.

"Excuse me." Sam stepped just inside the threshold. "Roarke said I should come up as I might be of some help."

"Are you a medical?" Louise asked.

"No, not a medical. I'm Sam, Delia's father."

"We're okay here," Eve said carefully, and set the bowl aside. "She's doing whatever she's got to do."

"Yes, of course." He backed up awkwardly.

"A healer then?" Louise asked, studying him with interest.

"I'm a sensitive." His gaze was drawn to Eve's face again, and pity for the pain rose in him.

"Empathic?"

"A bit." He shifted his soft eyes to Louise, smiled. "Medicals rarely put any stock in sensitives or empaths."

"I like keeping my mind and options open. Louise Dimatto." She rose to step off the platform and offer a hand. "It's nice to meet you, Sam."

"Why don't you two go have a drink downstairs," Eve said dryly. "Get acquainted."

"Unfortunately"—Louise glanced back over her shoulder—"I can't say her rudeness is a result of her injuries. She was born that way. Obviously a genetic defect beyond the scope of medical science."

"If you can't be rude in your own bedroom, where can you?" Eve picked up the bowl again, sulked over it.

"If I could just have a private word with her?" Sam asked.

"Sure. I'll just step outside."

When they were alone, Sam walked up to the bed. "You're in considerable pain."

"I've had worse."

"Yes, I'm sure you have." He lowered himself to the side of the bed. "You don't want chemical blockers, and while I'm sure Dr. Dimatto can relieve some of the discomfort externally, I can do more. It won't happen again, Eve," he said before she could speak. "Because I'm prepared. I know you're not sure if you can trust that, but you can. I don't lie, and I wouldn't offer if I wasn't sure of your privacy."

She pushed at her ice cream with the spoon. No, he didn't lie. "Will what you can do get me on my feet faster?"

"It should, especially in conjunction with the medical."

"Okay. Let's just get it done. I've got work."

It was mortifying as neither the healer nor the medical had bothered to mention she'd have to strip down to the skin for the exam and treatment. They discussed her anatomy as if she were a science droid in a lab, so that she finally shut her eyes in defense. She jerked at the first touch of fingertips, at the spread of cool, then of warmth along the blade of her hip that had rudely met pavement, twice.

The palm of another hand pressed to her injured cheek, and she clenched her teeth. But the sting passed, and she was floating. Not like the ride on blockers that was like a giddy trip on a carousel, but like a weightless drift on a cloud.

She could hear them speaking, but their voices were insubstantial.

"She's gone under," Louise said quietly. "You're very good."

"Her hip's causing her a great deal of pain. Most people would be screaming."

"She's not most people, is she? If you'll work on that,

I'll deal with the head injury. I think we can get the swelling down a bit more."

"Will I be in the way?"

Roarke. At the sound of his voice, Eve struggled to surface.

"No, shh. Lie still," he told her. "I'm right here."

Because he was, she let go again.

When next she woke, it was dark. There was a terrible moment when she thought she'd gone blind. Even as she tried to sit up, she saw a shadow move and knew it was him. "What time is it?"

"Late." He sat on the side of the bed. "You're to rest. Lights on, ten percent."

The faint glow brought her a flood of relief. Enough that she didn't snap at him when he moved closer to examine her pupils. "What's the date?"

"Depends. Is it before or after midnight?"

"Clever girl."

"I know where I am and when I am. And that we've got an anniversary coming up in a couple days. And, Carlo, I've never loved you more."

"I feel exactly the same way, Miranda." He touched his lips to her forehead, a sneaky way of checking for fever. "If you're feeling better perhaps I can let the children come in. Carlo Junior, Robbie, Anna, and little Alice are anxious to see their mum."

"Trying to scare an invalid. You vicious bastard."

"Go back to sleep." He brought her hand to his face, rubbed it against his cheek.

"I will if you will. I'm not going to sleep with you prowling around and lurking over me."

"I'll have you know I was valiantly standing watch over my concussed beloved." He slipped in beside her, settled her head gently on his shoulder. "Pain?"

"A little achy maybe, nothing major. Hey, remember?

I got hit in the face right before our wedding, too. Now it's like a tradition."

"And so uniquely us. Quiet down now, and go to sleep."

She closed her eyes. "Roarke?"

"Hmm?"

"I almost had her."

The next time she awoke, the room was dim. She spent the first twenty seconds worrying that this time she was *going* blind, then realized he'd lowered the sun screens on all the windows, including the skylight above the bed.

Okay, so her mind wasn't real sharp yet. She lay still and took mental inventory of the aches and pains. Not so bad, considering, she decided, and when she cautiously sat up was pleased there was no violent throbbing or disorienting dizziness.

She inched over to the side of the bed, planted her feet on the floor. After a bracing breath, she rose. The room bobbled a bit, but steadied quickly. Her head felt like it was caught in a vice, but at least nobody was tightening the screws.

As she was naked still she frowned down at the Arena Ball–sized bruise on her ribs, the raw, scraped area on her hip. The bruising in both areas was a miserably faded gray and yellow, and that was a good sign. Well into the healing stage, she decided, then tested her shoulder.

Stiff, but not painful. She turned her head to examine the impressive bruise on that area as well.

Roarke stepped off the elevator. "You're not to get up without clearance."

"Who says?"

"Common sense, but when have you listened to that particular individual?"

"I want a shower."

"As soon as Louise looks you over. She'll be up in a minute. She's just having breakfast."

"I have a conference at eight hundred."

"Rescheduled for nine." He got a robe out of her closet. "Tentatively."

She snatched the robe and would have shot her arms through if her shoulder had cooperated. Instead she eased into it. But when she started to stalk past him, he shifted to block.

"Where are you going?"

"To pee," she snapped. "Is that allowed?"

"Even recommended." Amused, he wandered to the AutoChef while she marched into the adjoining bath. He counted off the seconds, and thought it might take her eight.

"Holy shit!"

"Seven," he murmured. She was moving faster than he'd expected. "You should have seen it a few hours ago." He walked in behind her and stood while she stared at her face in the mirror.

The same sickly combination of gray and yellow—with a tinge of green—which she'd found on her hip and ribs, flowered over the entire right side of her face. It was a mottled pattern, a bit heavier along the ridge of cheekbone and around the eye where her skin puffed out and sagged like a deflating balloon. Her hair sprung out in untidy spikes, matted from sweat and blood, she imagined.

Her bottom lip looked tender and when she poked a finger at it, she found it felt the same way.

"Man, he really slammed me."

"Must've had a hand like a jet train."

"He was a big guy," she remembered, turning her head a little to study her profile. It wasn't any better than the full-on view. "I *hate* getting punched in the face. People are always staring at you and making moronic comments:

Oh, run into a wall? Wow, gee, does it hurt?"

He had to laugh. "Only you would be more pissed off about that than the blow."

"He was goony. Didn't know what he was doing. Bitch set me up, then didn't have the balls to come at me herself."

"As you'd hoped."

Her eyes met his in the mirror. "When I take her down, she's going to pay for this." Eve tapped fingers lightly over her jaw. "And she won't look so fucking pretty when I toss her in a cage."

"Girl fight? Can I watch?"

"Pervert." She stepped away, into the shower, and ordered the jets on full at a blistering temperature.

Because he was concerned she might get dizzy and fall, and because he enjoyed it, Roarke eased a hip on the sink and watched her wavery silhouette behind the patterned glass.

He turned his head when Louise came in. "Your patient's up and about."

"So I see." Setting her bag on the counter, Louise walked around the enclosure. "How are you feeling this morning?"

Eve let out a yip, spun with her wet hair dripping. In defense, she crossed one arm over her breasts. "Jesus, come on."

"Let me point out that I'm a doctor, have already seen you naked, and am also a member of the species that has the same equipment as you. Are you in any pain?"

"No. I'm trying to take a shower here."

"Carry on then. Light-headedness?"

Eve hissed, then dunked her head under the pumping spray. "No."

"If you're dizzy at all, sit down. Just sit down wherever you are. It's better than falling. Range of motion in the shoulder?"

Eve demonstrated it by raising her arms and scrubbing shampoo into her hair.

"Hip?"

Eve wiggled her butt and made Louise laugh. "Glad to see you're feeling frisky."

"That wasn't frisky. I was mooning you, which is supposed to be insulting."

"But you have such a cute little butt."

"So I've always said," Roarke added.

"Jesus, are you still in here? Go away, everybody go away." She flipped back her hair, turned, and let out a thin scream when Peabody walked in.

"Hey! How're you feeling?"

"Naked. I'm feeling naked and very crowded."

"The face doesn't look half-bad." Peabody looked around. "She's in here, McNab, doing a lot better."

"He comes in here," Eve said ominously, "and somebody's going to die."

"Bathrooms—veritable death traps," Roarke added. "Why don't I just take Peabody and McNab, and Feeney," he added when he heard the EDD captain's voice join McNab's, "up to your office. Louise will stay until she's satisfied you're fit to return to duty."

"I'm fit to kick righteous ass if one more person sees my tits this morning."

She turned away again and tried to bury herself in water and steam.

"You're very lucky," Louise told her a bit later as she closed her medical bag. "You could easily have fractured your skull instead of bruising it. Even so, it's a small miracle you're back on your feet this morning. Sam's very gifted, and was a great deal of help."

"I owe him." Eve buttoned up a shirt. "Owe both of you."

"And here's my bill. There's a fund-raiser on Saturday

night to drum up money for three new med-vans. You've already been sent an invitation, which you, or I imagine Roarke, has accepted. But I know you often find a way to wiggle out of these things. This time, be there."

Eve said nothing. She'd have to pay Louise back another time, another way. Roarke wasn't going to any public functions until Julianna Dunne was locked in a cage.

Louise glanced at her wrist unit. "Gotta go. I told Charles I'd pick him up at the airport. He's coming back from Chicago this morning."

"Okay." Hesitating, Eve reached for her weapon harness. "Louise, it really doesn't bother you? What he does?"

"No, it doesn't bother me. I think I'm falling in love with him, and it's just lovely." Her face seemed to radiate happiness. "You know what it's like when there's just the two of you, and that rush inside you?"

"Yeah. Yeah, I guess I do."

"The rest? It's just details. Don't overdo it, Dallas. When you get tired, sit. When you feel shaky, lie down, and don't be a hero. Take something for the discomfort." She angled her head as she paused at the doorway. "A little makeup would cover most of that bruising."

"What's the point?"

Laughing, Louise headed out the door, and Eve for the elevator.

Chapter 16

Eve smelled coffee and baked goods the minute the elevator doors opened into her office. Both were being consumed with apparent enthusiasm by her team. Roarke seemed to be content with coffee.

"You've got a nine o'clock conference via 'link," she reminded him.

"My admin's handling it." He handed her his cup of coffee. "Updated schedule's on your desk. Have a muffin." He chose one, bursting with blueberries, from a tray.

"Whatever your schedule, you should get to it. I have my own."

"In which I have a vested interest. Push at me on this," he added, lowering his voice, "and I'll push back. I doubt you're sufficiently recovered to be much of a challenge."

"Don't make book on it. But if you want to waste your time sitting in on this briefing, I've got no problem with it."

"That's lucky for both of us." He strolled away to get himself another cup of coffee.

To stop herself from saying something nasty she might not be able to back up, she stuffed her mouth with the muffin, then sat on the edge of her desk. "I need to be brought up to speed on the guy who clocked me yesterday, and the airboard vid-kid."

"I took those." Feeney polished off a Danish then took out his memo book for reference. "Sidewalk sleeper's Emmett Farmer, licensed beggar. Trolls the sector around Central, hangs around intersections and does the windshield gag to pick up loose change. A lot of the uniforms know him, and reports are he's excitable but basically harmless."

He glanced up at Eve, pursed his lips as he eyeballed her face. "Don't guess you'd agree with the harmless part under the circumstances. His statement is the blonde gave him five dollars and told him he was supposed to wait for your vehicle, do the windshield, and you'd give him another five. She told him he had to keep you by the vehicle or he wouldn't get paid. Farmer tends to be really insistent about being paid."

"So she'd picked him specifically—smear the windshield so my vehicle's blinded and I can't pursue that way. Pit me against Gibraltar so she buys enough time to get a good lead on me."

Feeney nodded. "And if you get kicked around in the process, so much the better. Statement the airboard kid, Michael Yardley, gave you on-scene's what he's sticking to. Given his age, the fact he's never been in trouble, it holds. She claimed to be a vid producer, set the scene for him. Kid lapped it up. He's scared brainless he's going to go to jail for taking you down."

"A lot of flaws in the plan." Eve frowned as she drank her coffee. "Timing's off, just a little, either one of her stooges doesn't follow through, or doesn't follow through hard enough to immobilize me, she's the one eating pavement."

And oh, she thought as she rolled her achy shoulder, *what a glorious day that would have been.*

"But she took the risk," Eve continued. "That tells me the interview with Nadine got under her skin."

"She wanted to hurt you." Peabody could still see Farmer's slab of a hand flying out, striking, lifting Eve clear off her feet.

"Yeah, but more, she wanted to psych me out. Shake my confidence. It's personal."

Idly she picked up the alabaster statue Phoebe had given her, turned it in her hand. "Everything's personal with Julianna. She set me up, and she did it fast. So, how did she know when I was leaving Central? She couldn't afford to keep the sleeper and the kid hanging around long. They get bored, she loses them. Couldn't afford to stand around Cop Central herself, or some uniform might make her."

"Not that hard to find out your shift," McNab put in.

"No, but how often do any of us come and go on shift schedule? I didn't yesterday. So, she was watching me. She's been watching me, so she can get a pattern. Getting patterns is one of her best things."

She set the statue down again. "McNab, get me the buildings that face my office at Central. Get me a visual."

"Do you think she's been staking you out?" Peabody asked as McNab hopped up to comply.

"She stakes out her victims, learns all she can about them. Their routines, their habits. Where they go, what they do. Who they are." Eve glanced at Roarke. How much, she wondered, could Julianna Dunne find out about Roarke?

Only as much, she decided, as he allowed any of the public to know. And half of that was fiction.

"She'd see it as an advantage to keep my office under surveillance." Eve turned to the screen as the grid of streets began to come up.

"Like a game?" Peabody asked.

"No, this isn't a game, not to her. First time around it was business. Now, it's war. And so far, she's taken all the important battles." She picked up a laser pointer from her desk, ran its needle-point light over the screen. "These three buildings would give her the best access to my office window. We need a tenant list."

She caught the look that passed between Feeney and Roarke, then shot Feeney one of her own as Roarke slipped into his own office.

"He'll get it faster." Feeney lifted his coffee cup, but not quite in time to hide the grin.

She let it pass. "We'd be looking for a leased space, short-term. Month-by-month is probable. She wouldn't spend a lot of time there. She'd have surveillance equipment set up, feed it into another location where she could comfortably study and assess. But she was there yesterday, personally, because she'd decided to move on me."

Eve saw herself, standing at her office window, looking out. She put herself back there, behind that narrow glass, and studied the buildings and windows across the street.

"This one gets my vote." She ringed one of the buildings in light. "Or if there wasn't space available on one of these levels . . ." She ran a line through five stories. "This building. Those are her best angles. Hold on a minute."

She walked into Roarke's office where he sat at his desk while his equipment hummed with efficiency. "I've got a priority location," she told him. "I want you to list that one so I can run a probability."

"I'm running probabilities, on all three. Though I think that's your location."

She glanced at his screen where he had the same visual up, and the building she'd earmarked highlighted.

"Showoff."

"Come sit on my lap and say that. You'd be looking for short-term leases, I imagine, and would want the run to move from the latest rentals back. How am I doing?"

"You bucking to make that expert consultant, civilian gig permanent?"

"Wouldn't that be fun?" He patted his knee, but she ignored him. "Ah, well, so much for fringe benefits. Your probabilities are coming up. I did these by line of sight. Easy enough to punch her data from your files into the mix and whittle this down considerably."

"Just wait." She scanned the list of names that he ordered on-screen. "Bam! Daily Enterprises. Justine Daily, proprietor. That's our girl."

She wanted to move, fast and hard, but reined herself in. "We'll be sure first. Dump this data onto my unit, would you? Let's try to keep this investigation reasonably official."

"Of course. Lieutenant? I'll be going with you on this bust. Wait," he said as she opened her mouth. "However slim the chance you'll find her there, I'm going to be a part of it. She owes me."

"You can't get whacked out every time I get banged up on the job."

"Can't I?" The easy lilt had gone out of his voice, chilling it. "She's got a mind to come after us both, so I'm in this. I'll be there when you take her down. Whenever, wherever that might be."

"Just remember who's taking her down." She turned back into her office. "Feeney, we've got a Justine Daily in the primary building. Data's in my unit. Run a background on her, and her Daily Enterprises."

"Likes sticking with her own initials." He rose to take McNab's place at Eve's desk. "Those are the little foibles that screw bad guys to the wall."

"I'm going to be the foible that screws her." Eve went

to her 'link and requested the search-and-seize warrant, and the manpower to enforce it.

In under an hour, she was moving down the corridor toward the offices of Daily Enterprises. The stairways were blocked, the elevators shut down. All exits were covered.

And she knew in her gut they wouldn't find Julianna Dunne.

Still, she would see it through, and motioned her team into place with hand signals. She drew her weapon, then flipped out her master and prepared to bypass the locks.

Pulled back.

"Wait. She'd have thought of this. She'd have counted on this." She stared hard at the cheap door, the cheap locks, then crouched down for a closer study. "I need some microgoggles here. A boom scan."

"You figure she booby-trapped the door?" Feeney pursed his lips, crouched down with her. "She never worked with explosives before."

"You learn a lot of handy household hints in prison."

Feeney nodded. "Yeah, that you do."

"You see anything hinky?"

"Old locks. Feeble shit. Standard alarm from the looks of the panel. Want to call in the bomb sniffers?"

"Maybe. I'm trying to out-think her, but I don't want pieces of my team scattered all over this hallway." She glanced up. Roarke was moving in behind her.

"Why don't you let me have a look?" He already was, hunkering down and dancing those nimble fingers over the panel, the frame of the door. He drew his PPC out of his pocket, programmed in a task code, then interfaced it to the panel by a hair-thin cable.

"It's hot," he confirmed.

"Back. Pull back." Eve gestured to her team as she yanked out her communicator. "Clear civilians off this floor, and the ones directly above and below."

"That won't be necessary, Lieutenant, if you'll just give me a minute here." Roarke already had the panel open by the time she turned back.

"Get the hell away from there." She took two strides back to him, then stopped herself. She'd seen him defuse devices a great deal more destructive than a door blaster.

"There." He spoke calmly to Feeney as he worked with tiny silver tools. "You see it?"

"Yep, I do now. Not my field, but I've seen a few homemades in my time."

"Amateurish, but effective. She'd have done better to take more time, add in a couple of secondaries, or at least one failsafe. It's set to trip when the door's open. Very elementary. She'd have a bypass, of course, so she wouldn't ruin her manicure by blowing her fingers off."

His hands were rock steady. He paused only once, to shake his hair back away from his face. When he did, Eve saw the cold gleam of concentration on it.

"Not particularly powerful this. Wouldn't have killed anyone who'd been five or six feet back. That'll do it." He replaced his tools, stood again.

Eve didn't ask if he was sure. He was always sure. She gave the all-clear signal to her team, then indulged herself by leaving her master in her pocket. And kicking in the door.

She swept the door with her weapon, then gestured for Feeney to take the adjoining washroom.

There were a couple of ratty chairs, a dented desk. And a scent in the air that was both female and expensive. She'd left the communications center and a small, exotic arrangement of fresh flowers.

Eve stepped to the window, looked out, across, and into her own office. "She'd have needed equipment. You can't see enough from here with the naked eye. Good equipment she wasn't willing to leave behind. Start knocking on doors," she ordered without turning around. "Talk to the other tenants, see who knows what. Find the building manager, get him up here. All building security discs. Feeney run the 'link and data center."

"Sir." Peabody cleared her throat. "This was in the flowers."

She handed Eve a small envelope marked EVE DAL-LAS. Inside was a handwritten card and a data disc. The card read:

With best wishes for your speedy recovery,
—Julianna

"Bitch," Eve grumbled, turning the disc over in her hand. "Feeney, disperse the men. We won't be finding her here today. Peabody, call in the sweepers."

She turned the disc over again, then plugged it into the desk unit. "Run data," she ordered.

Julianna's face swam on-screen—a blue-eyed blonde now, and the closest to her own coloring and style than any of her looks since she'd started her latest murder spree.

"Good morning, Lieutenant." She spoke in the lazy, somewhat breathy Texas drawl Eve remembered. "I'm assuming that salutation is correct. I doubt you'd have managed to get this far last night—but I have such confidence in your abilities that I'm certain you'll be playing this before afternoon. Feeling better, I hope. And as you're playing this, you detected and defused my little welcome gift. It was really just an afterthought."

She angled her head and continued to smile. But it was the eyes Eve studied. Eyes that were like ice over a deep, empty pit.

"I have to tell you how nice it's been to see you again. I thought about you a great deal during my . . . rehabili-tation. I was so proud when I learned about your promotion to lieutenant. And Feeney's to captain, of course. But I never felt quite the same connection for him as I did for you. There was something there, wasn't there?"

She eased forward, face intent now. "Something deep and strange between us. A true bond. A recognition. If you believe in reincarnation, perhaps we were sisters in some other life. Or lovers. Do you ever wonder about such things? Probably not," she said with a little wave of the hand. "You're such a practical-minded woman. It's appealing, in its way. Does your new husband find that part of you appealing? Oh, belated best wishes, by the way. It's been nearly a year, hasn't it, since the joyful event. Well . . . time passes.

"It passes slowly in a cage." The drawl hardened like prairie dust under a baking sky. "I owe you for those years, Eve. You'd understand about payback. You never really understood what I did, why I did it, never respected that. But you understand about payback."

"Yeah," Eve said aloud, unconsciously brushing her fingers over her bruised cheek. "Damn right I do."

"I've watched you, sitting in your office hard at work, standing at the window looking out as if the weight and worry of the entire city is on your shoulders. Pacing that horrible little space of yours. You'd think a lieutenant would be afforded a better work area. You drink far too much coffee, by the way.

"I had equipment set up in here. You know that now. I thought it best not to leave that behind. My own practical streak. I have several hours of you on disc. You dress better these days. Careless still, but with a style you once lacked. Roarke's influence, I'm sure. It's good to be rich, isn't it? So much better than . . . not being. Has it corrupted you, I wonder, in some secret part of yourself? Come on, Eve honey." She laughed lightly. "You can tell me. After all, who'd understand better?"

Talking too much, Eve thought. *Been lonely, hasn't it,*

Julianna, with nobody to talk to who you feel is on the same level?

"I'm sure he's excellent in bed, if you find such things important." She settled back, made a movement that had Eve imagining her crossing her legs.

Getting cozy. A little girl-talk.

"I've always felt fucking's overrated and so demeaning to both parties. What is it, really, but a woman allowing herself to be plundered, penetrated. Invaded. And a man plunging away as if his life depended on it. And as we know, with the men I fuck, their lives do depend on it. For a short time, anyway. Killing is so much more exciting than sex. You've killed, so you know. Deep down, you know. I wish we had the time and opportunity to talk, really talk, but I don't think that's going to happen. You want to stop me, to put me back in a cage. Remember what you said to me? Remember what you said? You'd have left me there if it had been up to you. Left me to spend the rest of my life caged like an animal. Then you turned your back on me like I was nothing. You didn't get your way, did you? But I got mine. I *always* get mine. You'd better remember that. You'd better *respect* that."

Her voice had risen, her breath had quickened. Now she drew in a long stream of air, fluffed a hand over her hair as if composing herself. "I thought of you when I killed Pettibone and Mouton. I've been thinking of you for a very, very long time. How does that make you feel, to know they died because of you? Does that upset you, Eve? Does that make you angry?"

Julianna tipped her head back and laughed. "Payback's a bitch, and I haven't even started. I want what I've always wanted. To do what pleases me and to live very, very well. You took eight years, seven months, and eight days from me, Eve. I'm going to balance the scales. I can and I will, tossing the bodies of silly old men at your feet. So you know how simple it is for me, here's a tip. The Mile High Hotel, Denver. Suite 4020. The man's name is Spencer Campbell. I'll see you again soon. Very soon."

"Yeah, you will," Eve retorted as the screen went blank. "Peabody, get me that hotel on the 'link. I want head of security."

The suite had been reserved in the name of Juliet Darcy, who had checked in the night before, securing the room for two nights with cash.

"The victim is Spencer Campbell, of Campbell Investment Consultants. The top man." In the conference room at Central, Eve brought his image on-screen. "Age sixty-one, divorced, currently separated from wife two. He had an appointment scheduled for a personal consult with Juliet Darcy in her hotel suite. Breakfast meeting, eight hundred Denver time. About the same time I was kicking in the door here in New York. She's very fucking cocky these days. Campbell had been dead less than thirty minutes when security broke in. Julianna didn't bother to check out, just grabbed her overnight bag, set the DO NOT DISTURB light on the door, and waltzed out. Autopsy and lab reports will confirm that Campbell's coffee was poisoned."

"She goes all the way to Denver to off this guy." Feeney dragged a hand through his wiry hair. "What's the point?"

"To prove she can. He was nothing to her. Just an easily sacrificed pawn to show me she can keep racking them up, when and where she wants, while I scramble around trying to find her. She breaks pattern again, because she wants to show me she's unpredictable."

And, Eve thought, *she doesn't want me to sniff out that she's looking at Roarke.* For victims she'd stick with what she'd called silly old men. Killing them as decoys to disguise her ultimate goal.

They died because of you.

Eve blocked out the voice, and the guilt. Most of the guilt.

"She had potential targets selected before she went down, and may have continued to select and research from inside."

"Did some electronic surveillance and research on Pettibone and Mouton from the prison office units," Feeney confirmed. "We dug out bits and pieces of it. Nothing on this guy or any others at this point. Nothing on personal business—financials, real estate, travel inquiries."

"She used her personal for that." Supervisor Miller, she thought in disgust, would have a lot to answer for before she was done with him. "Most likely diddled on the office machines early on, but made sure she had a personal for data she couldn't risk having traced."

She took a pass around the room. "She's got grease, and plenty of it. My personal grease expert states that it's most likely she stashes it in various numbered accounts in various locations. We've got no line to tug to the money. Loopy claims Julianna told her she had her own place here in New York. She's stuck to that during Interview with the Chicago cops, but can't or won't expand. My guess is she doesn't know the location. Julianna might have passed the time chatting with her, but wouldn't give her anything traceable."

"We're running private residences through EDD." Feeney dug out a handful of nuts. "But with no time frame of purchase or lease, no area, no name or names to feed in, we're mostly jerking off there."

"She'll spend money on herself." Eve thought how polished and fit Julianna had looked in person, in the vid. "But she'd be smart enough to use cash. We run highend stores, salons, restaurants. But as this is goddamn

New York, needless shopping nirvana, we're jammed there, too."

She tried to clear her head. "We keep at that. Put some drones on the 'links to shops. Maybe we can hook that red skin suit she had on. We've got her height and weight from Dockport, translate that to size, push purchases of the suit in that size."

"She may have purchased that in Chicago, or anywhere," Peabody pointed out. "And red skin suits are legion."

"Yeah, so it's a long shot. We keep blasting away, every detail, we're going to hit something eventually. Meanwhile, we'll check all the public and private transpos in and out of Denver. We'll find what she used, and by the time we do, she's in the wind again. But we have data."

"She's taking more chances," Peabody said. "Telling you about Campbell when she couldn't be sure of the timing. If she'd left it alone, it would've been hours before he was found."

"Risk makes winning the war more satisfying. This is a grudge match, and it's no good unless the enemy bleeds. And she wants to shake me. She doesn't want to kill me, but she wants me to think that I'm a target. She wants me to live, with loss. She wants Roarke. And that's our advantage. She doesn't know I'm on that."

In midtown, Roarke ended one meeting and prepared for another. The morning's activities had put him a bit behind schedule. He'd have to put in extra time that evening, but would find a way to do it from home. He intended to stay as close to Eve as their respective work schedules allowed.

"Caro." He tagged his admin on his interoffice 'link. "Shift the Realto meeting to holographic, out of my home office. Seven-thirty, and we'll move the lunch with Finn and Bowler to the executive dining room here. See that Lieutenant Dallas is copied on these changes."

"Yes, sir. There's a Dr. Mira here to see you. You have ten minutes before your next meeting if you'd like me to bring her back. Or I'll schedule an appointment."

"No." He frowned, shuffled time in his head. "I'll see her now. If the Brinkstone reps arrive before I'm done, have them wait."

He clicked off, then rose to pace his office. Mira wasn't the type to drop in unannounced, nor to pay social calls in the middle of a work day. Which meant she had business she felt was important enough to add a burden to both their schedules.

Absently, he crossed to the AutoChef and programmed in the tea she preferred.

When Caro knocked, he opened the door himself, extended a hand to Mira. "It's nice to see you."

"I'm sure it's not." She squeezed his hand. "But thank you for making the time. I'm overwhelmed just from the walk from reception. Your glass breezeway is amazing."

"Gives competitors a chance to think about a long plunge before they reach here. Thank you, Caro." He drew Mira in as his admin closed the door quietly behind them.

"And this . . ." Mira glanced around the office with its lush furnishings, stunning art, sleek equipment. "It certainly suits you. It manages to be both sumptuous and efficient all at once. I know you're busy."

"Not too busy for you. It's tea, isn't it? Jasmine, most usually?"

"Yes." It didn't surprise her that he'd remember such a minor detail. He had a mind like a computer. She took the seat he offered on a deeply cushioned sofa, waited for him to sit beside her. "I don't want to waste your time with small talk."

"I appreciate it. Did Eve send you?"

"No, but she knows I intended to talk with you. I haven't seen her yet today, though I intend to do that as well. I know she was injured last evening."

"She's resilient. Not quite as much as she likes to think, but she springs back somehow or other. Bruised damn near top to toe. All but cracked her head open like an egg. Would have, if it wasn't made of rock."

"Which is one of the reasons you love her."

"True enough."

"And still you worry. Being married to a cop is an enormous commitment of restraint. She understands that, which is one of the reasons she tried to resist, or deny what she felt for you. One of them." Mira reached out to cover his hand. "And another reason was her father. She told me you've been to Dallas."

"Good. It's good she can talk with you about it."

"And you can't." She could feel the tension gather in him like a bruise. "Roarke, you've spoken frankly with me before. There aren't many who know the circumstances of this. There aren't many you can speak with."

"What do you want me to say? It isn't my nightmare, but hers."

"Of course it's yours. You love her."

"Yes, I love her, and I'll stand with her. I'll do whatever can be done—which is bloody little. I know talking to you from time to time can settle her mind. I'm grateful for that."

"She's concerned for you."

"She's no need to be." He could feel the anger rising into his throat, bit back on it. Felt it bleed. "Nor have you. But it was kind of you to take the time to come by."

She saw the cool dismissal on his face, a thin veil of it over the heat. She set her tea aside, smoothed the skirt of her pale blue suit. "All right. I'm sorry to have interrupted your day. I won't keep you any longer."

"Bloody hell!" He lunged to his feet. "What's the point in spilling my guts out here? What good will it do her?"

Mira sat where she was, picked up her tea again. "It might do you some."

"How?" He spun back around, frustrated fury alive on his face. "It changes nothing. Do you want to hear how I stood there and watched her suffer, watched her remember it, and feel it as if it were happening still? She was helpless and terrified and lost, and watching her, so am I. I go after what comes for me, and I make a habit of going after it first. And this . . ."

"This can't be gone after, not the way you mean." How difficult for him, she thought, this man who looks like, thinks like, a warrior to stand without a lance to protect what he values most.

"It can't be changed," she added, "it can't be stopped because it's already done. So it preys on you, just as it does on her."

"Sometimes she screams in the night." He sighed. "Sometimes she only whimpers, like a small animal might when it's afraid, or in pain. And sometimes she sleeps easy. I can't go inside her dreams and kill him for her."

Professional objectivity couldn't stand against the tidal wave of his emotion, or the flood of her own. Tears gathered in her throat as she spoke. "No, you can't, but you're there when she wakes. Do you understand what a difference you've made for her? How you've given her the courage to face her past? And the compassion to accept yours."

"I know, realistically, we are what we are because of what we were, and what we've made of that. I believe in fate, in destiny, and also in giving fate a good twist of the arm when it's not going your way." When she smiled at that, he felt his shoulders relax. "I know what's done is done, but it doesn't stop me from wishing I could go back and use these on him." He balled his fists, then spread his fingers out again.

"I'd say that was a very healthy attitude."

"Would you?"

"I hope so as I often feel the same myself. I love her, too."

He looked at her, that serene face, those eyes so filled with quiet understanding. "Yes, I see you do."

"And you."

He blinked once, slowly, as if translating some foreign tongue. With a soft laugh, she got to her feet.

"The pair of you always seem so baffled and suspicious when offered free affection. You're a good man, Roarke," she said and kissed his cheek.

"Not really."

"Yes, really. I hope you'll be comfortable coming to me, speaking with me if you ever feel the need. I'll let you get back to your meetings. I'm already late for one of my own."

He walked her to the door. "Does anyone manage to resist you?"

She winked. "Not for long."

Chapter 17

Hacking through red tape with the finesse and subtlety of a chainsaw, Eve tracked down the private shuttle Julianna hired for her trip to and from Denver. Diamond Express advertised itself as the fastest and most luxurious private charter company servicing the continental U.S.

A quick check showed her there was little truth in advertising as they were a solid third in the ratings, behind two of Roarke's companies.

Julianna wasn't bold enough to hire one of his, Eve mused as she navigated around shuttles, cargo vehicles, and trams winding around the Diamond Express hangars.

The headache was back, a hammer punch on the back of her skull where it had met pavement. She felt a desperate need for a nap, which told her she'd have to take a short break soon or end up flat on her face.

"What's the pilot's name again?"

"It's Mason Riggs." Peabody shifted, took another look at Eve's profile. "You feeling okay—don't get pissed off. It's just you're looking a little pale and shiny."

"What the hell does that mean? Shiny?" Eve parked, eased over to examine herself in the rearview mirror. Damn, she did look shiny. "It's summer, it's hot. People sweat. And no, I'm not feeling okay. Let's just do this."

"I'm driving back."

With one leg out of the car, Eve swiveled around. "What did you say?"

"I said," Peabody repeated, courageously laying her life on the line, "I'm driving back. You shouldn't be behind the wheel, and I promised Louise I'd make you take breaks when you got shaky."

Very slowly, Eve took off the sunshades she'd worn as a concession to the glare, the headache, and the appearance of her bruised face. The black eye only added an edge to the drilling stare. "*Make* me?"

Peabody swallowed, but stuck firm. "You don't scare me—hardly—because you're pale and shiny. So I'll take the wheel when we're done here. You can put the seat back and catch a nap. Sir."

"Do you think adding 'sir' on the end of that is going to save you from my considerable wrath?"

"Maybe, but I'm more confident I can outrun you in your current state of health." She held up two fingers. "How many do you see?"

"The two I'm going to rip off and stuff in your ears."

"Oddly, it reassures me to hear that, Lieutenant."

With a sigh, Eve pushed herself out of the car. The noise screaming out of the hangar lanced straight through her skull. Hoping to avoid going in and having her head fall off, she signalled to a woman wearing coveralls emblazoned with Diamond's logo.

"I'm looking for Pilot Riggs," Eve shouted. "Mason Riggs."

"That's his shuttle getting its weekly maintenance." The woman jerked a thumb toward the mouth of the hangar. "He's either in there guarding his baby or in the break room."

"Where's the break room?"

"Second door down on the left. Sorry, but the hangar and the break room are employees-only areas. You want I can page him for you."

Eve pulled out her badge. "I'll just page him with this. Okay?"

"Sure." The woman held up her gloved hands, palms out. "Wouldn't go in there without ear protectors. Against safety regs." She flipped up the top on a crate, brought out two clunky sets. "It's murder without them."

"Thanks." Eve fit them on and immediately felt relief from the shrieking noise.

She headed inside. The hangar held three shuttles at the moment, each covered with a swarm of mechanics who were either wielding complicated-looking tools or holding conversations in sign language.

She spotted two uniformed pilots, one male, one female, and crossed into the heart of the hangar. The noise was like a whooshing wave through the ear protectors, and there was a smell of fuel, of grease, and someone's spicy meatball sandwich.

The latter made her stomach sit up and beg. She had a weakness for meatballs.

She tapped the male pilot on the shoulder. He was vid-star handsome, with the caramel-colored skin of a mixed-race heritage smooth and tight over sharp bones.

"Riggs?" She mouthed it slowly, then offered her badge when he nodded. At his polite yet baffled look, she gestured toward the break room.

He didn't look pleased, but he crossed the hangar quickly, coded in at the door, then yanked it open. The minute he was inside he pulled tiny protectors out of his ears, tossed them in a container.

"That's my shuttle. I've got to put it through its safety tests in twenty minutes. I've got a run."

Eve pulled off her own protectors. She hadn't heard a word he'd said, but she got the point. He lifted his brow at the condition of her face.

"Run into a door, Lieutenant?"

"I was just waiting for that one."

"Looks painful. So. What's the problem?"

"You had a private shuttle run last night, to Denver, return this morning. Juliet Darcy."

"I can verify the trip, but I can't discuss clients. That's a privacy issue."

"You don't want to go all regulation on me here, Riggs, or you're not going to make your next run."

"Look, lady—"

"I'm not a lady, I'm a cop. And this is a police investigation. Your client went to Denver last night, ordered herself a nice late supper from room service, probably got a good night's sleep. This morning she killed a man named Spencer Campbell in her hotel room, took a cab back to the airport, hopped on your shuttle at which time you returned her to New York."

"She—she *killed* somebody? Ms. Darcy? You can't be serious."

"You want to see how serious I am? We can take this down to Central."

"But she . . . I want to sit down." He did so, dropping into a wide black chair. "I think you must have the wrong woman. Ms. Darcy was charming and refined. She was just in Denver overnight to attend a charity function."

Eve held out a hand. Peabody slapped a photo into it. "Is this the woman you know as Juliet Darcy?"

It was a still taken from the disc found in Daily Enterprises and one that matched the image sent by hotel security.

"Yes, that's . . . Jesus Christ." He took off his cap,

raked his fingers through his hair. "This shakes you up."

"I'm sure Spencer Campbell feels the same way." Eve took a seat. "Tell me about the trip."

Once he'd decided to cooperate, she couldn't have stopped him with a laser blast. He paged the flight attendant to fill in any blanks and as a result Eve was given a full account of the round trip.

"She was extremely polite." Riggs downed his second cup of coffee. "But friendly. I'd noted by the log that she'd insisted on being a solo. No other passengers coming or going. When she boarded, I thought she looked like someone famous. We get a lot of celebs, and minor celebs, who insist on solos but who don't want the trouble and expense of housing and maintaining a private transpo."

"I didn't think she was friendly." The attendant, Lydia, sipped bottled water. She was already dressed for her flight, perfectly groomed in a navy jumpsuit with a military touch of gold braid.

"What did you think she was?" Eve countered.

"A snob. Not that she wasn't pleasant, but it was a veneer. There was a tone, mistress to servant, when she spoke to me. We offer caviar and champagne along with a fruit and cheese plate to our premier level passengers. She was a little put out by the brand of champagne. She said we could never hope to overtake Platinum or Five-Star in the ratings if we didn't upgrade our service."

"Did she make or receive any transmissions during the flight?"

"No. She did some work on her personal, turned it over so I couldn't see the screen—like I cared—when I came back into the cabin to offer her coffee before landing. She called me by name every time she spoke to me. Lydia, this, Lydia that. The way people do when they want you to think they're warm and friendly but that comes off as insulting somehow."

"She seemed perfectly pleasant to me," Riggs cut in.

"You're a man." Lydia managed to make the comment soothing and withering. And Eve decided she must be aces at her job.

"How about the return this morning. What was her mood?"

"Really up. Happy, sunny, relaxed. I figured she got laid the night before."

"Lydia!"

"Oh, Mason, you know you thought the same. She took the full breakfast: eggs Benedict, croissant, marmalade, berries, coffee. Ate like an athlete, and washed it down with two mimosas. Selected the classical music, and kept her privacy light on. I had the screen on the morning media reports, but she ordered it off. A little snippy on that, too. I guess we know why now. That poor man."

"When she got off the shuttle, did she have ground transpo waiting?"

"She went into the terminal. Struck me funny at the time." Lydia shook her head. "Somebody snobby like that usually has a car waiting in the private transpo area. But she went inside."

And through the terminal, Eve thought, where she could go back out and catch any number of transportation options. Cab, bus, tram, private car, even the goddamn subway. And in effect, disappear.

"Thanks. If you remember anything else, contact me at Cop Central."

"I hope you get her." Lydia gave Eve a sympathetic look as she scanned her face. "Does that hurt?"

Outside again, Eve rubbed her aching neck. "We'll head back to Central, see what the Denver cops have sniffed out. Once it's verified it was Dunne, and we're multistate homicides, this is going to turn federal."

"We can't let them take this over."

"I wish I could say I'd hand it to them on a platter if they could scoop her up, but I'd be lying. I want her." She let out a long breath. "I'm counting on Denver being willing to stall on the identification for a few days."

Eve fished the sunshades out of her pocket, put them on. Immediately felt better. "Why don't you drive, Peabody? I want to catch a nap."

Lips twitching, Peabody slid behind the wheel. "Yeah, why don't I?"

"Is that smug I see on your face?"

"Damn." Peabody dabbed at her cheek. "I thought I'd got all that off."

"Swing by a deli on the way. I want a meatball sandwich." Eve kicked the seat back, shut her eyes, and dropped straight into sleep.

Meat was not the operative word in meatball sandwich. It consisted of a couple of hunks of tough bread softened up by an ocean of rusty red sauce and between which swam a trio of ball-like substances, which where, perhaps, some distant cousin to the meat family. To disguise this very loose connection, they were coated with a stringy cheese substitute and spiced so generously they set the average mouth on fire, and successfully cleared the sinuses.

They were both disgusting and delicious. The smell woke Eve out of a dead sleep.

"I got the jumbo and had them cut it in half." Peabody was already driving away from the deli in the steady, cautious manner that normally drove Eve insane. "Figured you for a tube of Pepsi this time of day."

"What? Yeah." Her mind was dull as chamber music. "Jeez. How long was I out?"

"About twenty, but you were at rock bottom. I kept

waiting for you to snore, but you sleep like a corpse. Got some color back though."

"It's the fumes from the meatballs." Eve broke open the tube, took a huge glug of Pepsi before taking mental inventory. The headache had backed off, and so had the vague other-worldly feeling that had been creeping up on her. "Where are you heading, Peabody, and what century will we be in when we get there at this snail's pace?"

"I'm simply obeying the city traffic laws while showing courtesy and respect for my fellow drivers. But I'm glad you're feeling better, and I figured since we're in midtown and it's a nice day, we could eat these outside at Rockefeller Plaza. Fuel up, sneer at the tourists, and grab some rays."

It didn't sound half-bad. "No shopping of any kind."

"The thought never crossed my mind. For more than a minute."

Peabody eased down the pedestrian walkway off Fiftieth, slid the front wheel onto the curb, parked, and flipped up the ON DUTY sign.

"What was that about obeying city traffic laws?"

"That's driving, this is parking. No point in being obsessive about it."

They got out, wound their way through the pack of tourists, lunchers, messengers, and the street thieves who loved them, and plopped down on a bench in the plaza with the ice rink at their backs.

Peabody divided the tower of napkins and handed Eve her half of the sandwich. And they got down to the serious business of eating.

Eve couldn't remember the last time she'd taken an actual lunch break, one where she'd had what passed for real food somewhere other than at her desk or in the car.

It was noisy and crowded, and the temperature was deciding whether it would settle for really warm or inch up all the way to hot. Sun lasered off the glass fronts of shops and a vender putting along on a mini glide-cart sang some soaring aria from an Italian opera.

"*La Traviata*." Peabody let out a gusty sigh. "I've been to the opera some with Charles. He really gets off on it. Mostly it's okay, but it sounds better out here. This is the best part of New York. Being able to sit out here and eat this really superior meatball sandwich on a summer afternoon and see all these different kinds of people while some guy hawks soy dogs and sings in Italian."

"Um" was the best Eve could manage with a full mouth as she managed to save her shirt from a wayward gush of sauce.

"Sometimes you forget to look around and notice and appreciate it. You know, the diversity and all. When I first moved here I did a lot of walking and gawking, but that wears off. How long have you been here? In the city?"

"I don't know." Frowning, Eve sucked in another bite. She'd bolted out of foster care, out of the system the second she'd been of legal age. And straight into the Academy, into another section of the system. "About twelve, thirteen years, I guess."

"Long time. You forget to notice stuff."

"Uh-huh." Eve kept eating, but her attention was on a clutch of tourists and the slick-looking airskater who dogged them. He made the snatch clean, dipping skilled fingers into two back pockets without breaking rhythm. The wallets vanished as he did a fancy turn and veered away.

Eve merely shot out her leg, catching his shins and sending him into a short but graceful swan dive. When he rolled, she pressed a booted foot to his throat. She munched on her sandwich until his vision cleared, then waved her badge in front of him and jerked a thumb at the uniformed Peabody.

"You know, ace, I can't figure if you're stupid or

cocky, lifting wallets with a couple of cops in the audi-
ence. Peabody, you want to confiscate the contents of this
moron's pockets?"

"Yes, sir." She hustled up, went through the half-
dozen pockets and slits in the baggy trousers, the three
in the loose shirt, and came up with ten wallets.

"The two you got out of the right knee slit belong to
them." She gestured toward the happily unaware tourists
who were taking holo-shots of each other. "Brown-haired
guy with sunshades, blonde guy with the Strikers ballcap.
Why don't you save them some shock and dismay and
return them before you call in a beat cop to deal with the
rest."

"Yes, sir. Lieutenant, I never saw the move."

Eve licked sauce off her fingers. "We all notice different kinds of stuff, Peabody."

As her aide rushed off, the street thief decided to try
his luck. But as he started to scramble up, Eve bore
down, closing off his windpipe for ten warning seconds.
"Ah, ah, ah." She wagged a finger at him and polished
off her tube of Pepsi.

"Cut me a break, why doncha?"

"What, like go and sin no more? I look like a priest
to you?"

"Goddamn cop."

"That's right." She heard the amazed tourists take
back their property with babbling thanks. "I'm a goddamn cop. Nice day, isn't it?"

"I'll drive back," Eve said when that little bit of lunch-
time business was finished. "I'd like to get to Central
before my retirement kicks in." She read her wrist unit.
"And you're going to have to get moving if you're going
to pick up Maureen Stibbs and bring her in for Interview."

"I thought I'd put that off a day or two."

Eve glanced over as she slid behind the wheel. "You said you were ready."

"I am. But, well . . . You're really busy right now, and not a hundred percent yet. I need you to observe in case I run into trouble. It can wait until you're up for it."

"I'm up for it today, so don't use me as an excuse."

Peabody's stomach jittered. "If you're sure."

"You're the one who has to be sure. If you are, tag Trueheart. Two uniforms are more intimidating than one on a pickup. Fill him in, and have him go with you, then have him stand post inside the door in the interview room. He should say as little as possible, and look grim. As much as Trueheart can look grim. Snag a black-and-white for transpo. Use my authorization."

"Should I drive or should he?"

"Let him. Tell him he should give her the occasional blank stare in the rearview. You do all the talking. Try to keep her from lawyering up too fast. You've just got a few questions, need to clear a few things up. You know she wants to cooperate as she was the victim's friend, and this procedure may bring her husband some closure. Blah, blah. Get her in, then start playing her."

"I just need one favor. If I start to lose her, if I start to go wrong, will you step in?"

"Peabody—"

"I'd just feel better about it, more confident, if I knew I had a net."

"Okay. You take a tumble, I'll catch you."

"Thanks." Peabody took out her communicator to signal Trueheart and fill him in on the assignment.

Eve went straight into a 'link conference with the primary in charge of the Denver homicide. Detective Green was seasoned and irritable.

Eve liked him immediately.

"Got a shit load of latents off the rooms. Coupla

housekeepers, maintenance guy who dinked with the entertainment system after a complaint from the last tenants. Last tenants ID'd as Joshua and Rena Hathaway out of Cincinnati. Had the rooms for three days, checking out the day our girl checked in. They're clean. Got the vic's—just in the living area on him—coffee table, knife and fork, cup and saucer, juice glass. And we got Julianna Dunne's every-fucking-where."

He paused, slurped some coffee. "Got her visually ID'd from hotel discs, from the bellman and lobby staff. We're running hair outta the bathroom traps for DNA, just to sew her up."

"Sewing her up isn't the problem. It's bagging her first. Have you contacted Federal yet?"

Green shifted, snorted, slurped. "Don't see there's any fucking hurry for the Feebs."

"You're playing my song. That's a lot of latents to sort through, Detective. Seems to me it might take some time to clear out all the excess and pinpoint Dunne."

"Might. And shit has a habit of getting misplaced around here. Could be misplaced forty-eight hours anyway. Could be seventy-two if we have, say, a little equipment problem. Especially if I were pursuing other leads."

"There's a lot of data on her through IRCCA, but I've got more. Stretch that time frame out some, and I'll send you everything, including my personal notes."

"It so happens I'm a slow reader. And you know how you want to make sure you got everything in a nice package with a bow before you go and bother those busy Feebies with pesky stuff like murders. When I get to the point I have to make that call, I'll contact you first and give you some lead time."

"Appreciate it."

"Campbell was one of the good ones. The genuine article. You bag her, Lieutenant, and you can count on

Denver to help you sew her up so she can't ooze her way out again."

When she'd completed transmitting the data to Green, Eve pushed away from her desk, walked to her window. She focused on the window in the building across the street.

Hours of disc time, Julianna had said. *So you watched me,* Eve mused, *but you didn't see. Not what you thought you saw. Sisters, my butt. The only bond between us is murder.*

Notching a hip on the narrow sill, she let her mind clear and empty as she watched the fretful air traffic. An ad blimp crept by hyping rental condos on the Jersey shore.

She'd gone to the Jersey shore once with Mavis for a very strange, very drunk weekend. Mavis had reminisced sentimentally about working the boardwalk one summer, scoping for marks, running cons. Just a couple of years before Eve had busted her for doing the same on Broadway.

That was a bond, Eve thought. If she had any sort of sister, it was Mavis.

Mavis changed her appearance more often than the average teenage boy changed his underwear. Julianna was doing the same now, but not for the fashion statement.

Or maybe that was part of it. It was that female exploration—one that had always baffled Eve—to re-invent oneself, to experiment with new looks. To attract someone? Maybe, maybe, she mused as she pushed away to pace. But there had to be more, something satisfying to self first. A person would look in the mirror and find themselves new, fresh, different.

When it came to fussing with hair and enhancements and treatments, Eve felt her personal space, and her control over self was violated. But it occurred to her that the opposite was true for most people. They *liked* having everything focused on themselves, on their appearance.

Julianna would have missed that in prison. Making use of the prison salon would hardly have satisfied her.

Would she risk giving herself that satisfaction here? Not in the city, Eve decided. She wouldn't be so foolish as to risk exposing herself to a beauty consultant in the same pool where she killed. Where her face was splashed all over the screen.

No, they were spinning wheels looking there.

People who worked on faces, on features and hair and bodies *noticed* faces and features and bodies. How many times had she heard Mavis and the terrifying consultant Trina chattering about this one or that one.

Eve didn't doubt Julianna was dealing with her own hair these days. Somehow most women appeared to know how, even though those who could afford it went to consultants. But she'd be yearning for a relaxing, indulgent day, even a weekend, of treatments.

And it would have to be top drawer.

Europe, Eve decided. She'd continue to check all the major salons and spa centers in the city, but her money was on Paris or Rome.

"Computer." She whipped back to her desk. "Run a global search on beauty salons, spas, and treatment centers. List top twenty. No, make that fifty. Worldwide."

WORKING . . .

"Secondary search. Top five transportation companies that have service between New York and Europe."

SECONDARY SEARCH ACKNOWLEDGED. WORKING . . .

"Okay, it's worth a shot." She checked at her wrist unit, swore. "When search is complete, save data on hard drive, copy and save same on disc."

ACKNOWLEDGED . . .

Satisfied with the new thread to tug, Eve made one quick 'link call then headed out to keep her promise to Peabody.

On the way, she juggled her mental notes. Poison, she thought as she nipped onto a glide. Both personal and aloof, traditionally more a female weapon than blades or bludgeons.

Kill without contact. That was important to Julianna. The sex had been a kind of necessary evil in the past.

Demeaning to both parties, she'd said, Eve remembered. Penetrating. Plunging.

No, she'd never use a blade, ramming it into flesh was too much like sex.

Another difference between us, Eve thought before she could stop herself. Then wiped her suddenly damp hands on her trousers.

You've killed. Julianna's voice echoed in her head. *You know.*

Not for pleasure, Eve reminded herself. *Not for profit.*

Yet she'd taken her first life at the age of eight. Even Julianna couldn't top that.

Feeling slightly ill, Eve rubbed her hands over her face.

"Interview C."

When she jumped, McNab grabbed her elbow. "Hey, sorry. Didn't mean to spook you. I hopped on behind you. Thought you heard me."

"I was thinking. What are you doing in this section?"

"I wanted to catch some of Peabody in action. I didn't

say anything to her in case it distracts her. But I thought I could slip into observation for ten or fifteen. Is that okay with you, Lieutenant?"

"Yeah, sure. McNab?"

"Sir?"

She started to speak, then shook her head. "Nothing."

They moved down a narrow corridor past a grim set of gray doors that led to a temporary holding tank and coded into Observation.

It was little more than another corridor, fronted by two-way glass. There were no chairs. The lighting was dim and dreary and it smelled of someone's obsessively pine aftershave or a pine-scented cleaner. Either way, it filled the air like a forest.

They could have opted for one of the trio of more comfortable screen rooms in this section where there were chairs, credit-operated Auto-Chef, and equipment that would allow them to hear and view the interview.

But Eve found the facilities there kept the observer too distant and detached. She preferred the glass.

"You want me to get you a chair or something?"

Distracted, she looked over at McNab. "What?"

"You know, a chair in case you get tired of standing."

"Golly, McNab, are we on a date?"

He jammed his hands into his pockets and sulked. "Boy, try to be considerate because somebody got her head cracked and her face pounded and see where it gets you."

She'd all but forgotten about the state of her face, and found herself annoyed at being reminded. "If I need a chair, I can get one myself. But thanks."

When the door opened on the other side of the glass, he brightened. "Here she comes. Go get 'em, baby."

"Officer Baby," Eve corrected and settled in to watch the show.

Chapter 18

She watched while Peabody settled Maureen Stibbs in a chair at the wobbly table, set the record, offered the interview subject a drink of water.

Brisk, professional, Eve thought with approval. Not too threatening. Not yet.

And there was Officer Troy Trueheart posted at the door looking young and All-American . . . and about as grim as a cocker spaniel puppy.

She could sense Peabody's nerves, see them in the quick glance she flicked toward the glass as she poured the water.

But the uniform was enough, Eve decided as Maureen's eyes darted between Peabody and Trueheart.

People usually saw what they expected to see.

"I still don't understand why I had to come all the way down here." Maureen took a tiny sip of water, like a butterfly at a blossom. "My husband and daughter will be expecting me home soon."

"This shouldn't take long. We appreciate your cooperation, Mrs. Stibbs. I'm sure your husband will appreciate your help in this matter. It must be difficult for both of you to have this case remain open."

Good, good, put it in her lap, Eve urged. Make her a part of it, bring up the husband every chance you get.

Eve shifted her weight, tucked her thumbs in her front pockets as Peabody took Maureen through the story and statement she'd given before, asked her to repeat or expand on certain details.

"In EDD we don't do a lot of interviews." McNab toyed restlessly with the nest of earrings on his left ear. "How's she doing?"

"Good, she's doing good. Getting her rhythm."

Inside, Peabody wasn't quite as confident, but she kept plugging.

"I've said all this before. Over and over." Maureen pushed the cup of water aside. "What good does it do to make us all live through it again? She's been gone for years."

"She doesn't say dead," Eve commented. "She doesn't say Marsha's name. She can't because it brings it too close to home. Peabody needs to press that button."

"Marsha's death must have shocked you very much at the time. You were close friends."

"Yes, yes, of course. Everyone was shocked and upset. But we've put it behind us."

"You and Marsha were close," Peabody said again. "Friends and neighbors. But you say she never mentioned being dissatisfied in her marriage, never spoke of a relationship with another man."

"Some things even friends and neighbors don't discuss."

"Holding in a secret like that would be hard, stressful."

"I don't know." Maureen pulled the water back toward her, drank. "I've never cheated on my husband."

"Your marriage is secure. Solid."

"Of course it is. Of course."

"You had a difficult obstacle to overcome."

Water spilled over the rim of the cup as Maureen's hand shook. "I'm sorry?"

"Marsha. She was an obstacle."

"I don't know what you mean. What are you saying?"

"A first wife in what was by all accounts a happy marriage. You agree, and have stated for the record in this investigation that Boyd Stibbs loved Marsha and you never observed any dissent or trouble between them."

"Yes, but—"

"And you and others have stated, on record, that Boyd and Marsha were devoted to each other, enjoyed each other's company, had many mutual interests, many mutual friends."

"Yes, but . . . That was before. Before anything happened."

"Would you state now, Mrs. Stibbs, that Boyd loved his first wife, Marsha Stibbs?"

"Yes." Her throat worked. "Yes."

"And to your personal knowledge, through your personal observations, Marsha Stibbs was committed to Boyd, and to her marriage?"

"She spent a lot of time on her work. She rarely bothered to prepare meals for him. He—he took care of the laundry more often than she did."

"I see." Peabody pursed her lips, nodded. "So you would say she neglected him, and their marriage."

"I didn't say that . . . I didn't mean that."

"Push," Eve ordered from Observation. "Push now."

"What did you mean, Mrs. Stibbs?"

"Just that she wasn't as perfect as everyone likes to think, to say. She could be very selfish."

"Did Boyd ever complain to you about this neglect?"

"No. Boyd never complains. He's much too good-natured."

"No one's that good-natured." Peabody used a smile now, big and wide, girl to girl. "Surely if he'd known or suspected his wife was seeing someone else, he'd have complained."

"No, no." Eve rocked up on her toes. "Don't circle back, don't give her space to think."

"What?" Alarmed, McNab grabbed Eve's arm. "What did she do wrong?"

"She should keep pressing on the victim, dig out the suspect's buried resentments, get her to voice them. And she needs to keep hitting her with the husband, so she can allude that maybe we're looking at him after all. The suspect's obsessed with Boyd Stibbs and the perfect world she's created around him. You've got to chip at the foundation of that, let her feel it crumbling. She's going off on the other man now, and that gives the suspect the chance to rebuild the fantasy, helps her believe there *was* another man."

"Is she losing it?"

Eve dragged a hand through her hair. "She lost some ground."

"Maybe you should go in."

"No. She can get it back."

They went well over McNab's fifteen minutes, but Eve didn't order him back to work. She watched Maureen's confidence rebuild and Peabody's falter. At one point, Peabody stared into the glass with such obvious panic, Eve had to imagine her own boots bolted to the floor so she couldn't stride in and take over.

"Got anything to write on?" Eve asked.

"You mean, like paper?" McNab asked. "I'm EDD. We don't use paper. That would just be wrong."

"Give me your e-book." She snatched it from him, coded in a few key phrases. "Go around and knock. Try to look like a cop for a change. Pass this to Trueheart, tell him to pass it to her, then you get out again. Got that?"

"You bet." He scanned the miniscreen as he hurried out.

Shatter her fantasies
Implicate husband
Make her talk about victim—by name
Obstacle angle was good, keep using it
Watch her hands. Plays with wedding ring when she's
nervous
Dallas

It made McNab grin, so he had to take a minute to set his face into serious lines before he knocked.

"From Dallas," he whispered, putting his mouth close to Trueheart's ear, and adding the little flourish of skimming a hard look over Maureen.

"I beg your pardon, Officer Peabody." Trueheart stepped to the table. "This data just came in."

He handed her the mini-unit, then stepped back to his post.

When Peabody read the note, she experienced a flood of relief, a geyser of new energy. Very carefully, she set the unit screen down on the table, folded her hands over it.

"What is that?" Maureen demanded. "What did he mean by data?"

"It's nothing to worry about," Peabody said in a tone that indicated there was a great deal to worry about. "Can you tell me, Mrs. Stibbs, when you and Mr. Stibbs began to see each other as more than friends?"

"What difference does that make?" Maureen looked down fearfully at the e-book. "If you're trying to intimate that there was anything going on before Boyd was free—"

"I'm trying to get a timeline, a picture before and after Marsha's murder. Women know when a man's interested in them. Was Boyd interested in you?"

"Boyd would never, *never* have betrayed his vows. Marriage isn't a convenience to him."

"The way it was with Marsha."

"She didn't fully appreciate him, but he would never have blamed her for it."

"But you did."

"That's not what I said. I simply meant that she wasn't as devoted to the marriage as it looked from the outside."

"And you, being a friend of both Boyd's and Marsha's were on the inside, and saw the flaws. Boyd was even deeper inside this relationship. The flaws must have been very apparent to him. Very distressing if he felt Marsha was careless about the marriage, about his happiness."

"She wouldn't see he was unhappy."

"But you did. You saw he was unhappy, consoled him when he talked to you about it."

"No. No. I never . . . he never. He—he's a very tolerant man. He never said a bad word about Marsha. Not ever. I have to get home."

"Was he tolerant enough to overlook infidelity? To do laundry, fix his own meals while his wife sneaks around having sex with another man? I didn't know there were still saints in the world. Does it ever worry you, Mrs. Stibbs, that you may be married to a man who arranged for his first wife's death?"

"Are you crazy? Boyd would never—he's incapable. You can't possibly believe he had anything to do with . . . with what happened. He wasn't even *there*."

"An out-of-town business trip's a smart alibi." Peabody eased back in her chair, nodded wisely. "Did you ever wonder if he'd suspected his wife was sleeping around? The letters were right there. The signs were all around him. He could have stewed about it for days, weeks, until he bubbled over. Until he paid someone to come in while he was gone, hit her over the head, and dump her body in the tub. Then he comes home and plays the grieving husband."

"I won't have you say that. I won't sit here and listen to you say such things." She pushed back from the table with enough force to knock over the water glass. "Boyd would never have hurt her. He'd never hurt anyone. He's a gentle man. A decent man."

"A decent man is capable of a great deal when he finds out the woman he loves is screwing another man in his bed."

"He wouldn't lay a hand on Marsha, or allow anyone else to."

"A moment of rage when he found the letters."

"How could he find them when they weren't there?"

She was wild-eyed and panting. Peabody felt a cool control settle over her.

"No, the letters weren't there, because you wrote them and you put them in her drawer after you killed her. You killed Marsha Stibbs because she was your obstacle to Boyd––a man you wanted and she didn't prize him enough to suit you. You wanted Marsha's husband and her life and her marriage, so you took them."

"No." Maureen pressed her hands to her cheeks, shook her head. "No. No."

"She didn't deserve him." Peabody had the hammer now and used it to coldly shatter Maureen with fast, hard strokes. "But you did. He needed you, someone like you to tend to him the way she wouldn't. She didn't love him, not the way you did."

"She didn't need him. She didn't need anyone."

"Did you confront her when Boyd was out of town? Did you tell her she wasn't good enough for him? He deserved better, didn't he? He deserved you."

"No. I don't want to be here anymore. I need to go home."

"Did she argue with you, or did she just laugh? Didn't take you seriously, and neither would Boyd until she was out of the picture. He wouldn't see you until she was out of the way. You had to kill her so you could really live. Isn't that right, Maureen?"

"It wasn't like that." Fat, fast tears poured down her cheeks. She held out both hands, clasped together as if in prayer. "You have to believe me."

"Tell me what it was like. Tell me what happened the night you went into Marsha's apartment."

"I didn't mean it. I didn't mean it." Sobbing now, she collapsed in the chair, laid her head on the table and covered it with her arms. "It was an accident. I didn't mean it. I've done everything right since. I've done everything to make it up to him. I love him. I've always loved him."

In observation, McNab grinned like a madman. "She did it! She broke her down. Closed a cold case. I gotta . . . jeez, I gotta go get her flowers or something." He started to dash out, turned. "Dallas, she did good."

"Yeah." Eve continued to look through the glass, look into the pity she saw stir in Peabody's eyes. "She did good."

By the time she sent Maureen Stibbs down to Booking, Peabody was drained. She felt as if her insides had been put through some huge mechanical wringer that squeezed all the juices out.

When she headed back toward the bull pen, her parents rose from a bench and walked to her.

"What are you guys doing here? We're not supposed to meet up until we have that fancy dinner we had to postpone last night."

"We're so proud of you." Her mother cupped her face, laid a soft, warm kiss on her forehead. "Very proud of you."

"Okay . . . why?"

"Eve called us in." She bent down, brushed her cheek over Peabody's. "She arranged for us to watch you work."

"My interview?" Peabody's mouth fell open. "You saw?"

"It was very difficult, what you did." Phoebe drew her close.

"It's the job."

"A very difficult job. And one you were meant to do." She eased her daughter back to study her face. "When we leave tomorrow, it'll be easier to say good-bye knowing that."

"Tomorrow, but—"

"It's time. We'll talk more tonight. You have work now."

Sam reached down, gave his daughter's hand a squeeze. "Officer Peabody." He grinned from ear to ear. "Go be a cop."

A little misty-eyed she watched them walk toward the down-glide. Then the sentiment dried up in amused shock as McNab bounded off the up-glide carrying an armload of white and yellow daisies.

"Where'd you get those?"

"Don't ask." He handed them to her, then broke their mutual agreement by hauling her in for a hard kiss in a public area. "She-Body, you rocked."

"I nearly blew it."

"Hey. You kicked ass, you did the job, you closed the case. End of story." He was so proud he could have burst the pink buttons on his purple shirt. "And you looked really sexy doing it. I was thinking we could play Interview later tonight." He winked at her.

"You were observing?"

"You think I'd miss it? It was a big fucking deal for you, so it was bfd for me, too."

She sighed, gave in, and buried her nose in flowers that were no doubt stolen. "Sometimes, McNab, you're really sweet."

"So, I'll give you a good taste of me later. Got to roll. I'm behind."

Carrying the flowers, she walked into the bull pen, and was flustered, delighted, embarrassed when several detectives called out congratulations. Flushing, she went into Eve's office. "Lieutenant?"

Eve held up a hand to hold her off and continued to study the results of the probability scan on spa centers. She and the computer agreed that Europe was the most likely destination given Julianna's profile, with Paris just nipping out the rest of the field.

"I don't know, I don't know. Major city, major media, major cops. Why not this place, what's it, Provence, or this other near the Swiss border in Italy?"

SUBJECT PREFERS URBAN ATMOSPHERE WITH CONVENIENT ACCESS TO THEATER, RESTAURANTS, AND SHOPPING. QUESTIONED OPTIONS ARE LOCATED IN THE COUNTRYSIDE, APPEALING TO THOSE WISHING A MORE BUCOLIC SETTING AND HAVING LITTLE OR NO DESIRE FOR OUTSIDE ACTIVITIES. L'INDULGENCE IS THE TOP-RATED TREATMENT CENTER IN PARIS, WITH FULL SALON, SPA, BODY SCULPTING, AND EMOTIONAL WELL-BEING FACILITIES. THEIR PRODUCTS ARE FORMULATED OF ALL-NATURAL INGREDIENTS AND CAN BE PURCHASED ONLY THROUGH THIS CENTER. SKIN AND BODY TREATMENTS ARE—

"If I'd wanted a PR quote, I'd've asked for one. How do you book?"

RESERVATIONS FOR DAY PACKAGES AND/OR HOTEL
SERVICES MUST BE MADE DIRECTLY WITH THE FA-
CILITY BY GUEST, GUEST REPRESENTATIVE, OR AU-
THORIZED TRAVEL AGENCY. IT IS RECOMMENDED
THAT REQUESTS FOR RESERVATIONS BE MADE AT
LEAST SIX WEEKS IN ADVANCE.

"Six weeks." Eve pondered, drummed her fingers.

"Are you going to Paris to a spa, Lieutenant?"

"Sure, if someone knocks me unconscious, puts me in
shackles, and drags my lifeless body in. But I'm thinking
this might be right up Julianna's alley. A girl needs a
break from killing to relax, be pampered, and make sure
her skin retains that youthful, dewy look."

She glanced up, gestured at the flowers. "So, McNab
came through. Where'd he steal them?"

"I don't know." Peabody sniffed them sentimentally.
"Anyway, it's the thought that counts. You let my parents
come in and observe. You don't like having civilians
observe an interview."

"I made an exception."

"They said they were proud of me."

"You're a good cop. Why shouldn't they be proud of
you?"

"It just means a lot to hear them say it. I want to thank
you for sending that note in, snapping me back on track.
I'd gone way off. I knew I was losing her and couldn't
figure where I'd gone off."

"You picked it back up, and you got it done. How do
you feel about it?"

"Good, I guess. I feel good about it." But she lowered
her arms, drooping the flowers toward the floor. "Jesus,
Dallas, I feel sorry for her. Her whole world's broken
into little pieces. It was an accident. She's being straight
about that. She worked herself up to confront Marsha,
told her how she felt about Boyd. They argued, it got

physical, and Marsha went down hard, hit her head. Hit it wrong. Then Maureen panics and tries to cover up."

"And they'll plead it down to Manslaughter. Manslaughter when it should be Murder Two."

"Lieutenant."

"Maybe she panicked, for a minute or two, she panicked and was sorry and shocked. But then what did she do? Does she call for help? On the slim chance Marsha Stibbs could be revived or saved, does she call for help? No, she seized an opportunity. She not only covers up the crime, but she goes just a few steps further. She plants false evidence that paints a dead woman with adultery, leaves that dead woman's husband, a man she herself claims to love, with the pain and doubt and misery of wondering if his wife could have lied to him, cheated on him, betrayed him. She casts a cloud over the life she stole so that everyone who knew Marsha Stibbs would look through that cloud and see a woman who was a cheat, so she can bide her time, pave the road, and eventually step into her place."

Eve shook her head. "Don't waste your pity on her. If you've got pity, give it to Marsha Stibbs, who had her life taken for no reason other than she had what someone else wanted."

"Yes, sir, I know you're right. I guess it just has to settle in."

"Peabody. You stood for Marsha Stibbs in that interview. You did a good job for her."

Peabody's face cleared, and so did her lingering doubts. "Thank you, Lieutenant."

"Go home, snazz yourself up for this fancy deal you've got going tonight."

"It's not end of shift."

"I'm springing you an hour early and you want to argue about it?"

"No, sir!" Peabody pulled a yellow daisy out of her bunch, offered it.

"You passing on stolen property, Officer?" Amused, Eve twirled it, then turned to her beeping interoffice 'link. "Hold on. Dallas."

"Lieutenant." Whitney's face filled the screen. "I want you and your team in my office. Fifteen minutes."

"Yes, sir. Sorry, Peabody." Eve pushed to her feet. "Want your flower back?"

Fifteen minutes didn't give Eve enough time to finish compiling and analyzing all the data to support her hunch on Julianna's personal holiday. Instead she worked out an oral pitch in her head to pursue that hunch on the way to Whitney's office.

The pitch stalled when she walked in and saw Roarke.

He sat in one of the chairs facing the commander's desk, apparently very much at home. Their gazes met, locked, and she knew instantly that whatever was going on she wasn't going to like it.

"Lieutenant." Whitney gave a quick come-ahead signal. "Officer Peabody, I'm told you closed a homicide case this afternoon, with a full confession in Interview."

"Yes, sir. The Marsha Stibbs matter."

"Good job."

"Thank you, Commander. Actually, Lieutenant Dallas—"

"Had complete confidence in Officer Peabody's ability to investigate and close this case," Eve interrupted. "That confidence was justified. Officer Peabody pursued this investigation primarily on her own time while continuing to serve as my aide and as part of the investigative team formed in the Julianna Dunne homicides. A commendation regarding this matter has been added to Officer Peabody's file."

"Well done," Whitney said while Peabody stood

speechless. "Come," he called out at the knock on his door. "Captain, Detective." He nodded at Feeney and McNab.

"Nice work." Feeney gave Peabody a wink and a little arm punch as he joined them. "Roarke." He dipped his hands in his pockets, gave his bag of nuts a little rattle. Something was up, he thought, and it was bound to be interesting.

"Julianna Dunne." Whitney began with the name, pausing on it as he scanned the faces of his officers. "She has committed three homicides in this city. A fourth in another—though Denver Police and Security is . . . reluctant to confirm that at this time." His lips curved, a sharp, knowing smile as he looked at Eve. "She is also responsible for seriously injuring an officer."

"Commander—"

He cut off Eve's protest with one narrowed stare. "It's fortunate you recover quickly, Lieutenant. However, these are the facts, facts that the media are actively broadcasting. Facts that this department must respond to. Two of the victims were prominent men, with prominent connections. The families of Walter Pettibone and Henry Mouton have contacted this office, and the office of Chief of Police Tibble, demanding justice. Demanding answers."

"They'll get justice, Commander. My team is actively, doggedly, pursuing all leads. An updated progress report will be in your hands by end of shift."

"Lieutenant." Whitney eased back in his chair. "Your investigation is stalled."

"The investigation is multipronged." Eve swallowed the outrage that burned into her throat. "And with respect, Commander, is not stalled but rather complex and layered. Justice isn't always served swiftly."

"She'd been kept where she belonged, there wouldn't be an investigation." Feeney's anger snapped out. "We put her away once, and now because a bunch of morons and bleeding hearts open the cage door, we've got to put her away again. That's a damn fact. It was Dallas who pinned her then, and maybe the media, this office, and the office of the damn chief should remember that."

When Eve put a hand on his arm, he shook her off. "Don't tell me to calm down," he shot out, though she hadn't said a word.

"I'm fully aware of the history in this matter." Whitney's voice stayed level. "And so is Chief Tibble. And the media, I can promise you, will be reminded of it. But it's today we have to deal with. Julianna Dunne remains at large, and that's a very big problem. She taunted you," he said to Eve. "And the opinion is she'll continue to do so. Would you agree, Lieutenant, that Dunne selected New York as her primary location as payback? That her work here is a personal attack on you?"

"I would agree, Commander, that the subject harbors a grudge, and while her work is satisfying in and of itself to her, by killing here she gains the added benefit of involving me in combat."

"She has no particular interest in or connection to the men she's killed. Which makes your investigation more problematic."

"It's unlikely we'll track and apprehend her by identifying her next target or targets." She felt a little warning beat at the base of her skull. "The investigation is better served by concentrating on the subject's pattern—personal pattern. How she lives, works, plays. She isn't a woman to deny herself the comforts and luxuries she's always believed she deserves and which were denied to her for nearly nine years in prison. I'm currently compiling and analyzing data in that area to support what I believe is a valid theory."

"I'd be interested in reviewing that data and hearing that theory, but in the meantime, let's just backtrack a minute." He steepled his hands, tapped the index fingers together. "The computer probabilities oppose the view held by Dr. Mira and the primary as to the identity of one of the potential targets. Who—after reviewing all data and reports—I believe is and has been the central target all along. This individual's willingness to cooperate could very well result in Dunne's early apprehension and a closure to this case."

The beat became a pounding. "Utilizing civilians—"

"Is often expedient," Whitney finished. "Particularly when the civilian is known to be . . . skilled in pertinent areas."

"Permission to speak with you privately, sir."

"Denied."

"Commander." Roarke spoke for the first time, in a soft tone, a direct contrast to the rising tension in the room. "If I may? She'll come at me sooner or later, Eve. We arrange to make it sooner, it gives us the advantage and may save another life."

"I object to using a civilian as bait." She looked directly at Whitney. "Whoever, whatever he might be. As primary of this investigation, I have the right to refuse employing tactics I feel generate unacceptable risk to my men, or to civilians."

"And as your commander, I have the right to overrule your refusal, to order you to employ those tactics or remove you as primary."

This time it was Feeney who grabbed Eve's arm. But Roarke was already getting to his feet. "Jack." His voice wasn't quite as soft now when he addressed Whitney. Deliberately, he stepped between him and Eve, turned so she had no choice but to look him in the face.

"You'll have control. She's had the upper hand till this. You'll draw her in where and how you choose. That's the first point. The second being I won't sit back and wait until she picks the time and place to have at me. I'm asking you for help, and offering you mine."

It was easy to see why he was so good at what he did. At winning whatever he wanted. Bending wills to his own with reason—at first anyway. Then by whatever method worked best.

But she wasn't a company to be absorbed, or a suit to be intimidated. "You're not asking or offering anything. And you're not giving me control, you're taking it."

"That would depend on how you look at it."

"I see just fine. Step back, Roarke, you're not in charge here yet."

Something flashed in his eyes, something deadly. It only served to add punch to a temper that was already fuming to peak. When she moved toward Roarke, Feeney grabbed her arm a second time, and Whitney came to his feet.

"Ease down, kid," Feeney muttered.

"Lieutenant Dallas." Whitney's voice cracked like a whip. "This office is not the place for your marital disagreements."

"You made it the place. This is an ambush, and one that circumvents my authority, that puts that authority on the block in front of my team."

Whitney opened his mouth, then closed it again in a tight line. "Point taken. Your team is dismissed."

"I'd prefer they remain at this point, sir. Completing this meeting privately now is a useless gesture."

"You're a hardass, Lieutenant, and you're skirting very close to the line."

"Yes, sir, I am. But you already crossed over it. I respect both your authority and your office, Commander."

He had to take a calming breath. "And you imply I show none for yours."

"That would depend . . ." She glared at Roarke. "On how you look at it."

"And if you were looking at this situation objectively rather than through what is arguably justified anger at the way this particular avenue was presented to you?"

"I strongly believe Julianna Dunne may be out of the country, or that she has plans to leave New York for a short period of time. If I'm allowed to pursue *that* avenue, I believe I can confirm her location, or planned destination in a few hours."

"And this belief is based on?"

"My instincts and my considerable understanding of the subject." *Pitch it now,* Eve ordered herself, *and pitch it hard.*

"She's a girl. She has a deep-seated need to indulge her femininity, in the most luxurious and exclusive manner available. She's been hard at work for some time now, planning and executing her agenda. She'll want a break. In the past, she took a short vacation between every hit. Resorts primarily, with top-flight treatment centers. It's pattern. She's moved on her victims in rapid succession this time out, and this after being incarcerated for a number of years. She'll need to renew herself, recharge, and her most likely method would be a spa facility where she can be pampered and can relax before she . . ."

She trailed off, then dug back in. ". . . before she moves on what I believe is and has been the central target. She'll want to groom, prepare, relax, before she comes at him. I've run a probability on this theory and got just over ninety percent. She doesn't change, Commander. At the core, she doesn't change."

"Assuming your theory is correct, there are countless facilities of this nature—numerous in this city alone."

"It wouldn't be here. She'd want to get away, that's indulgence, and she wouldn't risk having a consultant who might have seen her on the media, get up close and personal with her face. That's brains. It's most likely she'd go out of the country where the media attention on murders in New York City isn't as intense."

She watched his expression, saw him consider that. Agree with that. "I've already narrowed down the field, and intend to start checking with the most likely locations and working my way down the list."

"Then do so. However, that angle doesn't preclude preparing for another option. If you tag her, are successful in tracking and apprehension, then this is put to rest. If you don't, we'll have a trap in place. Settle yourself down, Lieutenant. And listen."

Whitney turned to Roarke, and nodded.

Chapter 19

"In three day's time," Roarke began, "there's a charity function, a dinner dance to raise funds for medical transports and equipment needed by the Canal Street Clinic. I believe Dr. Dimatto mentioned this to you, Lieutenant."

"I know about it."

"I accepted the invitation to attend some weeks ago, so that's public knowledge if anyone was wondering when I might be socializing at some public function in the city. The event is being held at one of the ballrooms at the Grand Regency Hotel. Happens that's one of mine."

"Shock," Eve said in a voice that dripped sarcasm like poisoned honey. "Amazement."

"It also happens that the ownership is held by one of my subsidiaries, and isn't so easily traced to me. Not that all appropriate business fees and taxes aren't promptly paid," he added with a cool amusement, "but a casual glance, even a more curious one wouldn't necessarily shake my name out of it—which cancels out any reluctance Julianna might have about coming for me on my own turf. So to speak. And also gives the advantage of knowing the security bottom to top, and being able to adjust that security to the particular situation."

Though he paused he got no response from Eve, nor had he expected any. "Just to ice the cake, it's just been leaked to the media by my public relations people that not only will I attend the function, but will be making a sizable donation. The donation will be hefty enough to ensure strong media attention for the next little while."

He'd taken over the room, Eve realized. Not just the discussion but the goddamn room. He was in command now, and it infuriated.

"By now, if she wasn't already aware of it, she'll know I'll be attending a public event where there'll be a great deal of people, a great deal of food and drink, and a large staff serving them. She'll know my wife will be attending with me. It's a tailor-made opportunity for her. She'll take it. Odds are, she'd already planned to do so."

"We can't be certain of that," Eve corrected. Though she'd already thought of it, had been planning on finding a way to wiggle out of the event. "If she's just learning of it, it's a narrow window of time for her to confidently blend herself into the staff or guests, and for us," Eve added, "to confidentially assess and adjust security to en-sure the protection of civilians. You won't be the only rich bastard there. This proposal puts others at risk."

He brushed off her concerns, her objections, with an elegant shrug. One he knew would madden her. "The function takes place whether or not I attend. If she's tar-geted someone else ahead of me, they're already at risk. And if she has targeted someone else, the temptation to shift to me while you're there would be very great. It's you she wants to hurt, Lieutenant. I'm just her weapon against you. Do you think I'll be used for that? For any-thing?"

"In your opinion," Whitney said into the thrumming silence, "does the suspect have any reason to believe you're aware of her intention to hit Roarke?"

"I can't know what she's—"

"Lieutenant." Whitney's tone bit. "Your opinion."

Training warred with temper, and won. "No, sir. This subject doesn't fit her pattern, and she specifically informed me of the type she'd targeted. She would have no reason to suspect or believe that I would have concern in this area, that I would look outside the box. She respects me, but is confident I'm running behind her chasing only the trail she's left me."

"Run the play, Dallas." Whitney got to his feet again. "Work the angles, plug the holes, close the box. Whatever equipment and manpower you need, you'll get. We'll discuss this further tomorrow. Tomorrow," he repeated, anticipating her protest. "When tempers aren't so close to the surface. I respect your temper, Lieutenant, as I do your rank and your abilities. Dismissed."

Not trusting herself to speak, Eve gave him a curt nod and walked out.

When Peabody trotted out after her Eve's snarl was enough to hold her off.

"Keep out of the line of fire." Roarke laid a hand on Peabody's shoulder. "It's me she wants to blast into small, bleeding pieces, but you could get caught in the stream and you've had a good day till now."

"From where I'm standing you deserve a blast. Don't you think she took enough of a pounding yesterday?"

To Roarke's considerable surprise, Peabody turned on her heel and marched in the opposite direction. With his temper notching up from slow burn to fast simmer, he strode after his wife. He caught up with her just as she stalked into her office and managed to slap a hand on the door an instant before it slammed in his face.

"Get out. Get the hell out." She grabbed discs, shoved them into a file. "This is still my area."

"We'll discuss this."

"I've got nothing to discuss with you." She slung the file bag over her shoulder, then shoved him when he blocked her path to the door.

"You want to fight then? Well, isn't it handy I'm in just the mood for it. But we'll take this to neutral territory."

"Neutral territory, my ass. There *is* no neutral territory with you. You own the goddamn city."

"We'll take this out of here, Lieutenant, unless you want to have a bloody, shouting fight with your husband for a couple dozen cops to hear. Doesn't matter a damn to me, but you'll be sorry for it when you've come to your senses."

"I've got all my senses." And because she did, she managed to keep her voice low. "Let's take it outside, pal."

"Outside it is."

They didn't speak again, but the volume of their silence had several cops easing back when they pushed into the elevator. She stalked onto the garage level ahead of him, then knocked his hand away when he reached for the driver's side door.

"I'm driving," he told her, "as you've too much blood in your eye to do the job."

Deciding to pick her battles, Eve strode around the car and dropped into the passenger's seat.

He didn't tear out of the garage, though he wanted to. She'd just try to have him arrested for some traffic violation, he thought nastily. He, too, was picking his battles. Still he wove through traffic with a kind of controlled violence that had other vehicles giving way. Another time, she would have admired it, but at the moment his skill simply reinforced her resentment.

He pulled over at the west edge of Central Park, slammed out of the car while she did the same on the opposite side.

"I don't own this."

"I bet that sticks in your craw."

"What I own, don't own, acquire, don't acquire, is irrelevant."

"You don't own my badge."

"I don't want your goddamn badge." He crossed the sidewalk and kept walking across the green summer grass.

"Controlling something's the same as ownership."

"I've no desire to control your badge, or you for that matter."

"That comes off pretty lame from somebody who's just managed to do both."

"For Christ's sake, Eve, that wasn't what that was about. Use your head for a minute. Stop being so prideful, so flaming stubborn that you see everything as a bloody attack. Do you think Whitney would have agreed to consider this angle if he didn't believe it was a viable method of stopping this woman? Isn't that your primary goal?"

"Don't stand there and tell me what my goal is." She jammed a finger into his chest. "Don't you stand there and tell me what my job is. I've been doing this job since you were still running smuggled contraband. I *know* what it is."

She stormed away from him. *Prideful? Stubborn?* Son of a bitch. Then whirled back. "You went over my head, you went behind my back, and you had no right, no *right* to go to my superior and shove your way into this investigation in a way that undermines my authority, that negates that authority in front of my team. And if anyone had pulled that on you, you'd have had their head on a fucking platter and their blood for sauce."

He started to speak, then took a good swallow of his own pride. "That's very annoying."

"Annoying? You call it—"

"It's annoying," he interrupted, "when you're right. When you're completely right, and I'm wrong. I apologize for it. Sincerely."

"Would you like a suggestion as to where you can shove your sincerity?"

"No need." Irritated with himself, with her, he dropped down on a bench. "I'm sorry for the method. That's the truth. I didn't consider the reflection on you carefully enough, and I should have."

"No, you just get a brainstorm and drop in on your good friend Jack."

"And if I'd come to you with it, you'd have given it all the proper consideration? Don't bother to come up with some clever line, Lieutenant, as we both know you'd have pushed it aside. I'd've pushed back, and we'd have had a row about that."

"Until you got your way."

"Until you cleared the bugs out of your head that make you think I'm stupid enough to let some mad tart do for me. I didn't come down in the last shower of rain, Eve."

"What the hell does that mean?"

He sat back, laughed a little. "Jesus, you make me Irish. Why is that, do you suppose? Come sit down. You don't look as well as you should."

"Don't tell me what to do."

He thought about it for about three seconds. "Ah, bollocks to this." And rising, he stepped to her, evaded the leading edge of the elbow jab, and scooped her off her feet. "There, now stay down." He dumped her on the bench. "We both know I'd not have taken you that easily if you were feeling yourself. I need you to listen to me."

He kept her hands gripped under his, felt the anger

and insult vibrating through her. "After you do, if you feel you need to take a punch at me, well, you can have one for free. What I said in Whitney's office was the truth. I'd've done better to come to you so that we could have fought it out between us, but I didn't and I'm sorry. Still, what I said was the truth, Eve."

He squeezed down on her hands until she stopped trying to yank them away. "I'm asking for your help and offering mine to you. She wants to take you apart, little pieces of you sheared off each time she drops a body at your feet. Trying to make you think that you're responsible for putting them there."

"I don't think—"

"No, you know better, in your head. But she made you bleed in that cursed video of hers. In your heart. And she wants to finish you off with me. She doesn't know you. She doesn't understand what's in you, or what it is to love someone. If she managed, through some miracle, to take me out, you wouldn't fall apart. You'd hound her and hunt her. You'd run her to ground. And then, well, darling, you'd eat her alive."

He brought her clenched fists to his lips. "And I'd do exactly the same for you, if you're wondering."

"That's real comforting, Roarke."

"Isn't it?" He said it with such cheer she felt a smile trying to tug at her mouth.

"Let go. I'm not going to hit you. Just let go, and don't talk to me for a minute."

He released her hands, then brushed his fingers over her bruised cheek. Rising, he wandered off to leave her alone.

She sat where she was. The fury had sapped her, left even her bones feeling weak. More than that, she realized, it was the fear that made her weak. The image of seeing Roarke pitch to the floor at her feet, choking, gasping, dying. And Julianna standing there, out of her reach. Just out of her reach. Smiling.

She'd let that happen, Eve admitted. She'd let Julianna plant those weeds of fear, of guilt, of self-doubt. And she'd let them bloom instead of hacking them out by the roots.

That made her ineffective, and it made her slow.

So Roarke had gone for the roots first.

He infuriated her. What else was new? They'd rammed heads countless times in the past, and would ram them countless times in the future. It was part of what they were. There had to be something sick about that, but there it was.

They just weren't peaceful people.

He'd been wrong, but so had she. As a cop, she should have examined and explored the option of using him as bait long before this.

Love messed you up, she thought. No doubt about it.

He came back with two tubes of Pepsi and a greasy scoop of oil fries. And in silence sat beside her again.

"I want to say first that I'm entitled to be prideful when it comes to my work." She dug into the scoop, felt the grit of salt over the grease. And knowing he'd drenched them for her, had to choke back a sentimental sigh. "And second, sometime when you least expect it, I'm going to generate a memo to the top staff of your midtown offices stating that you wear women's underwear under those manly designer suits."

"Why, that's just cold."

"Yeah, then you'll have to strip down at a general meeting to prove it's a filthy lie and my vengeance will be complete." She looked at him then. "She's not just a— what did you call her—a mad tart. She's smart and she's driven. Don't underestimate her."

"I don't. I don't underestimate you, Eve. But I think, for just a bit of time here with one thing and then the other, you've been underestimating yourself."

"Yeah, I have, and I don't like it thrown in my face. Okay. I've got to get home. There's a lot to do in a short amount of time."

She worked with him first, studying all the data on hotel security and on the event itself that he'd already had at the ready. She pitched questions, and he batted back the answers with the skill of a man who knew he owned the plate.

The Regency wasn't an urban castle as his Palace Hotel was. It was bigger, sleeker, and geared more for the upper-end business clientele than the fashionable rich.

It had sixty-eight floors, fifty-six of which were guest room levels. Others held offices, shops, restaurants, clubs, and the conference centers, the ballrooms.

On the seventh floor was a casual bar/restaurant and swimming pool, which was open-air during good weather. The top two levels held eight penthouse suites, and were only accessible by private elevator. The health club, level four, was open to all hotel guests and to registered members. Entry, from inside the hotel or its exterior glide door, required a keycard.

Ballrooms were on floors nine and ten, with exterior and interior entries. The event would take place in the Terrace Room, named after its wide, tiled terrace.

"Lots of ways in, lots of ways out," Eve stated.

"That's a hotel for you. All exits will be secured. There are security cameras throughout the public areas. Full sweep."

"But not the guest rooms."

"Well, people are fussy about their privacy. You'll have views in all elevators, in hallways. We can add monitors if you feel it's necessary. She'd be more likely to blend in as staff or an event attendee than a hotel guest,

I'd say. She'd want to get out of the building after her job's done, not find a bolt-hole inside it."

"Agreed, but we keep a man monitoring all check-ins. I want that set up, along with field offices, ready rooms in a secured area as close to the ballroom as possible."

"You'll have it."

"Hotel security will be fully briefed. I don't want to alert the rest of the staff, or the outside event people. The less chance she gets wind of trouble, the better."

"You don't intend to tell Louise then?"

She'd considered, debated, weighed the pros and cons. "No, I don't. We'll plant cops alongside the attendees, the servers, within your security. You'll arrange with your catering or whatever it is for the extra servers. Nobody will question you about it."

"I should think not," he mused.

"We'll need to go over the other functions in the hotel that evening. You've got two conventions in, and a wedding deal. She may slip in through one of those."

"We'll nail it down. I'm sorry, I have a holo-conference in a few minutes. I have to take it; I've already re-scheduled twice."

"It's all right, I've got plenty to do."

"Eve."

"Yeah, what?"

He bent over her, pressed his lips to the top of her head. "There are a number of things we need to talk about."

"I'm only half-pissed at you now."

His lips curved against her hair. "That's just one of several. For now I'll just say I was half-pissed at you when Mira dropped by my office this afternoon."

She didn't look up, but she went very still. "I didn't ask her to. Exactly."

"But it occurred to me, very shortly, that you'd wanted her to talk to me because you were worried. You knew the trip to Dallas was eating at me, perhaps more than I knew it myself. So thanks."

"No problem."

"And it would be small of me to qualify that gratitude by pointing out that by sending her along without mentioning it to me, you'd gone over my head and behind my back."

Now she looked up, just a shift of the eyes. "Good thing you're too big a man to do that."

"Isn't it?" He bent lower, gave her one hard kiss, then left her alone.

"Managed to get the last word on that one," she commented, then scooped her hair back and shifted focus to the spa and transpo data. She might still win this little battle by snapping Julianna up before she got her chance at Roarke.

An hour later, she was back to being annoyed and frustrated. She'd managed to intimidate and browbeat reservation lists out of two of the resort spas on her list. The others were sticking firm to the protection-of-guests' privacy line. And so were the private transportation companies.

Pushing through an international warrant to free up the data was problematic and time-consuming. The case was a hot enough button that the judge she'd tapped for it was sympathetic rather than annoyed. But it was taking time.

Another advantage for Julianna, Eve thought. She didn't have to jump through the hoops of the law.

She paced, checked her wrist unit, and willed the warrant to spill out of her data slot.

"Problem, Lieutenant?"

She glanced back to where he leaned against the doorjamb separating their offices. He looked very alert, and very pleased with himself.

"I guess somebody's time was well spent."

"It was. The meeting went very well. And yours?"

"Bureaucratic snags." She glared at her computer. "Waiting for paperwork."

"Of what sort?"

"Of the legal sort. Privacy codes. Nobody blabs to a badge anymore, especially a foreign badge. And those fancy spa places are damned tight-lipped about who's coming in to have their hips sheered or their chins lifted."

"Ah, well, if that's all."

"No. I thought about it—thought about it a little too easy and a little too fast. This is just a hunch, and I'm not having you slide under the law to access data on a hunch."

"When you spend this much time and energy on an angle, it's more than a hunch."

"I know this is something she'll do. Maybe not now, but soon. She needs that kind of thing and New York's too risky. She needs to pump herself up, reward herself, before she hits at you. She didn't take the time in Denver, and she could have. She wants something more prestigious, more exclusive. With more . . . what do you call it? Cache. So it's France or Italy or something Old World. She doesn't do off planet. It's too nouveau for her."

"Will you get your warrant?"

"Yeah, yeah, it's coming. Eventually. Protocol, politics, bullshit."

"Then what difference does it make, in the grand scheme, if you begin to accumulate data now, or when a document's in your hand?"

"It's the law."

And in less than three days, Eve thought, it was highly probable that the woman she hunted would try to kill Roarke. Not because she knew him. Not because she hated him. But because she dismissed the law and all it stood for.

Because she wanted payback.

"It's hard for you, being so conflicted over something you want to be black and white. But even the law has shades, Lieutenant, and we both know them all very well."

She gave up, and stepped into the gray. "She'd use her own initials. She doesn't like to give up her identity. The list, in order of probability percentage is already loaded on my machine."

"All right then. Let's find her." He sat down at her desk, rolled up the sleeves of his pristine white shirt. "It's really just a head start on a technicality."

She told herself to think about that later.

"I'm looking for reservations starting from yesterday through the next four weeks. I could be pushing her into relaxation mode too fast. Maybe she's going for it after she's won the war."

"We'll scan for the next month then. L'Indulgence first? Over-priced with a coolly efficient staff. Its ratings have stagnated over the last two years. It's falling out of fashion."

"Which is why you don't own it."

"Darling, if I did, I'd make certain it remained in fashion. This'll just take a minute or two. Wouldn't you like coffee?"

"Yeah, I guess."

"Good. So would I."

She could recognize a cue when she heard one, so trooped off to the kitchen AutoChef to order up a full pot. When she came back with it and two large mugs, he was already scanning a list of names.

"I see a couple on here with the right initials, but they're reserved with companions."

"She'd travel alone. She has no known associates, doesn't make friends. She makes tools."

"All right, we'll move on to the next."

They found two possibles in the next location, allowing Eve to run standard background checks for elimination. She leaned over Roarke's shoulder, reading data on-screen even as the computer voiced it.

"No, these are clear. All their documents check out. Just a couple of rich marks paying too much money to get rubbed and scrubbed. Next?"

He hacked into the guest records at two more facilities before the 'link signaled incoming documents. She snatched out the hard copy of the warrant, rolled her shoulders. "Now we do it my way."

"My way's much more fun."

"Out of my chair, pal. And this time you get the coffee."

Her way offered a different kind of fun by allowing her to irritate reservation managers in several countries. They stalled, complained, cited the insult of invading guests' privacy. And really perked up her mood.

"I don't care if you've got people coming there who get off on turkey baster enemas. Transmit the list, as ordered in the duly authorized warrant or the next sound you hear will be your own ass plopping into the sling of international incident."

"Turkey baster enemas?" Roarke said a few moments later as the transmission hummed through.

"I don't know what they do in those places, but if somebody hadn't thought of that one, they would eventually. She's not here. She's just not here. Goddamn it." She pushed away from the desk to pace. "I'm wasting time when I should be nitpicking the setup at the ballroom."

"You've several more locations on your list."

"They're all low probability. Maybe I'm just projecting what I'd like her to do, to make it easy for myself."

"You wouldn't know how to make it easy for yourself if you took classes on it. My name also comes in low probability, but you've dismissed the computer's brain on that, haven't you? You know her, Eve. Don't second-guess yourself now."

"I'm playing a hunch instead of dealing with estab-lished data."

"Then play it out. Which one appeals to you?"

She went back to the desk, scanned the remaining lo-cations on her list. "This is the one I liked from the get-go, but the computer tossed it. Doesn't fit her usual pat-tern."

"That's nice. Why do you like it?"

"Because it's the most expensive, has the most his-tory—some count guy owned the estate way back when." She looked at him. "Yours?"

"Fifty-one percent of it. Would you like to have the rest?"

"That just lowers the probability. She doesn't want to get that close to you yet. Then again . . ." Eve considered. "She might get a real charge out of it. Pop in, get buffed up, pop out, all the while imagining that in a little while she'll be eliminating the guy who owns the majority share. Yeah, let's run this one."

She slammed into the same reluctance, Italian-style, with the assistant reservations clerk. "Are you having trouble reading the warrant?" Eve demanded. "It comes in a variety of languages, and one of them must be yours."

The clerk was young, gorgeous and more than a little frazzled. "No, signorina."

"Lieutenant. Lieutenant Dallas, New York City Police and Security. I am investigating multiple homicides. You may, at this moment, be harboring a murderer in your facility. How do you figure your other guests are going to feel about that?"

"Villa de Lago has very strict policies regarding guest privacy."

"You know what, I have very strict policies, too." She shot a hand out, caught Roarke in the belly as he stepped forward. She wasn't having him smooth the way. "And so does international law. Would you like me to list what the penalties are for interfering with an international warrant?"

"No, Signorina Lieutenant. I do not feel I am authorized to proceed. I would prefer you speak with the reservations manager."

"Fine. Dandy. Make it snappy."

"It would've been snappier," Roarke pointed out, "if you'd let me speak to her."

"My way, Coffee Boy."

Obliging, he poured the last of the second pot into her cup.

"Lieutenant Dallas." Another woman came on-screen. She was older, and equally gorgeous. "I am Sophia Vincenti, the reservations manager. I apologize for keeping you waiting. I have your warrant here. Please understand my assistant was only following our policy in protecting our guests from any privacy violation."

"I'd think it would be just as important to protect your guests from the possibility of dipping into the hot tub with a murderer."

"Yes. We will, of course, fulfill the demands of the warrant. You have our full cooperation. Perhaps in the interest of sparing innocent guests you could tell me the name of the party you're seeking."

"I can't be sure what name she'd be using. It's likely whatever it is, the initials are J and D."

"Just one moment . . . Lieutenant, we have three guests with reservations in the stated time period with those initials. Justina D'Angelo is expected next week. I know Senora D'Angelo personally. She has been a guest here many times."

"How old is she?"

"Lieutenant, this is a delicate area."

"Come on."

"She admits to fifty, and has so admitted for ten years."

"She's clear. Number two."

"Jann Drew, expected at the end of this month. She is a new guest. Let me pull up her file for you."

"This is more like it," Eve stated and sat back sipping coffee.

"Lieutenant, Ms. Drew lists her address in Copenhagen. She is booked for ten days, and will be joined by a companion for the last three."

"I'm going to have my assistant run her while you give me the data on the third."

"This is a Josephine Dorchester, and is also a new guest. She arrived only last night and is booked through tomorrow."

The back of Eve's neck prickled, and she leaned forward. "Where did she come in from?"

"She lists her U.S. address as Texas. She has our premiere accommodations. I was on duty last night when Ms. Dorchester arrived. She is very charming."

"Thirtyish, athletic build, about five foot, four inches."

"Yes, I—"

"Hold on." Eve snapped the 'link to wait mode. "Josephine Dorchester," she called to Roarke. "Texas. Run her fast, get me her passport ID. It's her. I know it's her."

"On your wall screen," Roarke responded as he came back in from his office. "You've locked her, Lieutenant."

Eve watched as Julianna's image, still blonde, still blue-eyed, flashed on-screen.

"Hello, Julianna." Eve switched the 'link back. "Okay, Signorina Vincenti, listen carefully."

Fifteen minutes later, Eve's teeth were bared as she snarled threats at the Italian police. "I don't care what time it is, I don't care how long it takes you to get there, I don't give a damn if you're short-staffed."

"Lieutenant, I cannot make a move without a proper warrant, and even then, it will take some time. Such matters are very delicate. The woman you seek is a U.S. citizen. We cannot arrest and hold a citizen of the United States simply on the request of an American police officer via a 'link transmission."

"You'll have your paperwork within the hour. You could *be* there within the hour and pick her up as soon as it's in your hand."

"This is not proper procedure. This is not America."

"You're telling me. Stand by. I'll get back to you." She broke transmission, surged to her feet. "How fast can we get there?"

"Knowing the meanderings of red tape, faster than your Italian counterpart will."

"Then let's move. I'll get clearance on the way."

Chapter 20

She was a pleasure to watch, Roarke thought, while he relaxed with a brandy as they raced through the sky above the Atlantic. Raw energy in motion, he decided.

She used a headset, keeping her hands free for a coffee cup or a notebook or a second 'link if she had two transmissions going at once. She paced, up and down, up and down the short, narrow aisle in the cabin of his fastest transport, snapping out orders, chewing out data, vocally flogging anyone who tossed up an obstacle to her goal.

She spoke to Feeney, to her commander, to someone in the United States consulate—whose ears would probably leak blood for the rest of his natural life—to the Italian police captain who continued to hold up his hands, still empty of the proper paperwork. She contacted a lawyer who specialized in international law, waking him without regret or mercy and shoving him into the fray.

"Data port's down?" She raged at the Italian cop on the next transmission. "What the hell do you mean your data ports are down?"

"Such things happen, Lieutenant. We should have them back in an hour or two."

"You'll *waste* an hour or two. You can get oral or e-authorization now."

"I must have the proper documentation, in hard copy, with the authorization stamp and seal. This is the law."

"Let me tell you my law, amigo. You screw up this apprehension and I'm frying your balls for breakfast." She cut him off, kicked the base of the nearest seat.

"We're halfway there," Roarke told her. "You've done all you can do and terrified a number of minor bureaucrats. You should sit down and get some sleep."

"I don't want to sleep."

"Sit down anyway." He managed to snag her hand, tug her into the seat beside him. "Shut down, Lieutenant. Even you can't alter the laws of physics and get us there any faster." He draped an arm around her, drew her head firmly down to his shoulder.

"I need to update the commander."

"When we land. Just rest and imagine Julianna's face when you walk into her suite. And think of all the Italian ass you get to kick."

"Yeah." She yawned. "There's that." On that pleasant thought, she slid into a shallow sleep.

"Jet-copter?" Eve stood staring at the small, sleek, four-person transpo with blurry vision. "You didn't say anything about having to do the last leg in a jet-copter."

"And you slept easier for it." Roarke boosted himself in behind the controls. "Eight minutes from port to port. A great deal less time than ground transpo on Italian roads, in Italian traffic, through the hillsides, around the lake—"

"All right, all right." She sucked in a breath. "Everybody has to die of something."

"I'll try not to take that as an insult to my piloting skills. Strap in, Lieutenant."

"Believe me." She snapped on her safety harness, checked its tension twice. "I hate going up in these things."

"I can't think why." The instant he got clearance, Roarke shot the copter up in a vertical, slicing up two hundred feet in the time it took Eve's stomach to execute the first of a serious of stylish somersaults.

"Cut it out!"

"Sorry, did you say something?" On a rollicking laugh, he punched the jets and arrowed into the pink-streaked sky.

"Why do you think that's funny?" She gripped the sides of her seat with fingers that dug in like steel claws. "You sadistic son of a bitch."

"It's a guy thing. We really can't help ourselves. Christ, look at that sky."

"What's wrong with it?" Images of some horrendous natural disaster layered over a visceral fear of heights.

"Not a bloody thing. It's quite gorgeous, don't you think? It isn't every day you watch the dawn break over the Italian Alps. Next time we have a little time we should spend a few days out here."

"Fine, great. Terrific. As long as it's on the ground. I will not look down, I will not look down, I will not look down."

And of course she did, felt her head spin in the opposite direction of her belly. "Fuck. Fuck. Fuck. Are we there yet?"

"Nearly. You can see the lake, and the first sunlight just sliding over the water."

That only made her think of the horrors of an emergency water landing. "That's the place?"

"That's it."

She saw the pink and white stone of the old estate,

the spread of grass and gardens, the blue gems that were pools and fountains. Instead of seeing beauty, she saw the finish line.

"At least that putz Captain Giamanno's on his way. I'm looking forward to biting out his throat once the formalities are over."

"This is not America," Roarke said in a dead-on mimic.

Eve grinned at him. "You're all right, Roarke."

"Remember you said that." And he sent the copter into a steep drop, chuckled over his wife's thin scream as he touched down onto the helipad. "That got the blood moving."

"I so completely hate you right now."

"I know, but you'll get over it." He shut down the engines. "Smell that air. Lovely. You can still smell the night-blooming jasmine on it."

She managed to jump out, with some semblance of dignity, then gave up, bent from the waist, and waited to get her breath back.

"Lieutenant Dallas?" Eve stayed down as the footsteps approached, then stared at the sharp black shoes as she felt her system settle.

"Yeah? You Signorina Vincenti?"

"Yes, I am. Are you all right, Lieutenant?"

"Yeah." She straightened. "Just getting my wind back. Captain Giamanno?"

"Has not yet arrived. Your instructions were followed. Immediately after we ended our conversation, I contacted security. A man was sent up to guard Signorina Dunne's door. He remains there, as you directed. No one has come out or gone in."

"Good. I'm not going to wait for the local badge. I'll take her as quickly and quietly as I can."

"That would be appreciated. Our guests, well . . ." She spread her hands. "We wouldn't wish to upset anyone.

Signore." She offered a hand to Roarke. "I welcome you back to the villa, despite the circumstances. I hope you and the lieutenant will let me know of any way I can assist you."

"You did very well, signorina. I won't forget it."

"Okay," said Eve. "Tell your security I'm coming in. I want men on that floor, keeping other guests out of the way. No other staff is to go up to that level until I've apprehended the suspect and removed her to a secured location from which Giamanno and I can finalize the paperwork and extradition."

"I have cleared an office on the main level for that purpose. Will I escort you to the suite?"

Eve didn't know if it was guts or courtesy, but she had to give the woman credit. She made the offer as if Eve were a visiting celeb come for a weekend vacation. "No, the elevator's far enough. I'll need a code card for the door."

"I have them." She gestured, explaining as they walked toward the gracious lakeside entrance, "When a guest has retired to his or her room, it is recommended that they activate the night lock and alarm, for their own security. These can only be opened from the inside, or by a second code card in case the staff must enter. An emergency of some nature."

She drew two thin cards from the pocket of her smart jacket. "The white, with the villa's logo, works the standard locks. The red is for the night system."

"Got it." They walked under a kind of portico, smothered with vines that scented the air with vanilla. Double glass doors etched with a portrait of the villa whisked open at their approach.

They moved through a cool sitting area, stylishly plush with color, where the sunlight dribbled in like spilled gold through arched windows. It caught and glinted on the teardrop-shaped crystals on the many tiers of a chandelier. Outside on a stone terrace, a couple in white robes strolled by, arm in arm.

"Some digs you got here," Eve complimented Signorina Vincenti.

"We are very proud. Perhaps one day when you are not on official business, you will come visit us. Life has so much stress, does it not, that one needs the small islands of tranquility. Ah, this is Signore Bartelli, our head of security."

"Lieutenant." He bent slightly from the waist. "Sir," he said with another slight bow to Roarke. "I will accompany you?"

She measured him. He was big, fit, and looked tough. "Sure, that'd be good."

"My man is on post," he began as they moved into a wide area and into the two-level lobby with its rose marble floors and columns. A wide staircase curved up, split, then wound gracefully in opposite directions. "I have also had the corridor on that floor monitored since we received your transmission."

"Anyway she can get out without using the hallway?"

"Only if she leaps from the terrace. It is four floors up, and not recommended."

"Put a man outside, on the ground. Just in case."

"As you wish." He took out a small communicator, relayed the order as they stepped into an elevator.

"I want all civilians kept in their rooms up there. She'll resist if she can, run if she can, take a hostage if she can."

"The safety of our guests is paramount. We will see to their protection."

When the elevator doors opened, Eve laid a hand on the butt of her weapon. She saw the guard outside a set of wide double doors. He sat, blocking them, sipping coffee.

One sharp command in Italian from his superior had

him springing to his feet, rattling back a response.

"She has made no attempt to leave the room by this door,"Bartelli told Eve. "No one has tried to enter. Two guests, one from the next room, one from the end of this hallway, left their rooms. There are morning activities," he explained. "And the health club and pools are open twenty-four hours for the convenience of our guests."

"Handy. All right, move aside and stand by."

She shoved the chair out of the way, slid in the first code. "Which way is the bedroom?"

"It is to the left, through an archway. Perhaps twelve feet from this door."

"And to the right?"

"A smaller sitting room."

She slid in the second code. "Go right," she said to Roarke.

She nudged the door open, soundlessly, and with her weapon out did a first, fast sweep. The living area of the suite was deep in shadow with the privacy drapes snug over the windows. There wasn't a sound.

"On the door," she murmured to Bartelli and slipped inside.

Her boots sank into the soft pile of an ancient carpet, clicked quietly over polished tile. She moved fast and silent through the archway and into the darkened bedroom. She smelled flowers, female. And heard nothing.

"Lights," she ordered. "On full."

Her weapon was trained toward the bed when they flashed on, and she found what her instincts had already told her. It was empty. There was a sheer black evening dress draped over a chair, a pair of carelessly discarded black heels beside it. And on the dresser was a silver-backed brush, a frosted bottle of scent. On the mirror above it, elegantly written in murderous red lip dye were two words.

CIAO, EVE

"She didn't just rabbit because she felt like a brisk pre-dawn run. She knew I was coming." Eve stared at the reservations manager with enough heat to melt stone. "Someone told her she'd been made."

"Lieutenant Dallas, I assure you, I spoke to no one but you, and those you authorized me to speak to." She glanced at the message on the mirror over Eve's shoulder. "I have no explanation for this."

"Obviously the woman had anticipated your movements."

Captain Giamanno, who'd arrived at last with a trio of men, spread his hands. "There was a guard at the door after you requested one. There are security cameras in the hallway. She did not simply poof past these like a ghost."

"No, she didn't *poof* past them like a ghost. She walked." Eve turned back to the bedroom computer, gestured as she ordered it to run the section of the disc she'd already viewed. "Right there."

The screen showed the guard, sitting sleepily in his chair outside the suite's doors. The time stamp read oh-four-fifty-six hours. A door opened from the next room and a woman wearing one of the hotel's white robes, a wide straw hat with trailing scarf, and carrying a large straw purse came out. Her face was shielded by the brim as she mumbled a quiet *buon giorno* to the guard and strolled toward the elevator.

"This is not her room," Giamanno pointed out. "There is no access to that suite from this one, Lieutenant, and as you can see, no adjoining doors."

She stared at him for a full ten seconds. Could he be that dim? she wondered, and riding on fury, stormed into the parlor and flung open the terrace doors.

As the others trailed after her, Eve rose up on her toes,

bent to flex her knees once, twice, then sprinted across the terrace, sprang off the stone banister, and leaped to the neighboring terrace.

Her ankles sang on impact, but she ignored the pain, stepped to the doors. "I wonder if it'll come as a big surprise to you, Giamanno, that these doors are unlocked."

She opened them, peered inside, stepped back. Closed them again. "And that there are two people in bed inside here, still sawing wood."

"Sawing—"

"Sleeping, you—"

"Lieutenant." Roarke interrupted what would no doubt have been a tirade harsh enough to destroy all friendly relationships between Italy and the United States for the next decade. "I believe what Lieutenant Dallas has deduced is that, forewarned in some manner, the suspect fled the premises by the manner just demonstrated, and left the building, in all probability the country, before our arrival."

"You know what's saving your tiny, wrinkled balls, Giamanno?" Eve leaned on the banister. "She'd rabbitted before you could have gotten here to hold her, even if you'd moved your fat ass when requested to do so by a fellow officer. Now we find out how and why. Your office," she said, pointing at Signorina Vincenti. "Now."

And strode into the suite, past the sleeping couple, and out the door.

She refused the offer of coffee, which indicated to Roarke her temper was well beyond flash point. His reservations manager was showing some of her own. The two women butted wills while the Italian cop huffed and puffed and the security head continued to review the discs.

"She goes to the pool." His face was grim as he followed Julianna's movements from suite to elevator, from elevator to the Garden Room off the main lobby, and from there outside toward the swimming pool.

The outside cameras kept her in view as she increased her pace to a light jog, turned away from the pool onto a garden path. And disappeared out of range.

"My apologies, Lieutenant Dallas. I should have anticipated."

"Well, someone anticipated or she wouldn't have bolted, leaving most of her things behind."

"I spoke with you," Vincenti said again. "With Capitano Giamanno, with Signore Bartelli. And no one else."

As she folded her arms, as prepared for battle as Eve, the door opened. A young woman slipped in with a tray of coffee and small breakfast cakes.

"Hold it." Eve gripped her arm and had the tray rattling. "You took my initial transmission."

"This is my assistant, Elena, who referred you to me."

"Yeah, I remember." And one look at her face told Eve most of the story. "Do you know the penalty for obstructing justice, Elena?"

"*Mi scusi?* I don't understand."

"You speak English just fine. Sit."

"Lieutenant, I won't have you browbeating my staff. Elena would hardly have aided a criminal. She is . . ." Vincenti trailed off. She, too, saw the story on her assistant's face.

"*Maledizione!*" From that one oath, she launched into a furious stream of Italian as Elena sank into a chair and began to cry.

The security head joined in, then the Italian cop, until Eve's ears were ringing. Hands were flying, tears were falling. She opened her mouth to shout them down, considered blasting a couple streams at the ceiling, when Roarke shut everyone down.

"*Basta!*" His voice rang with command, and had Eve

gaping at him as he, too, launched into Italian.

"I beg your pardon." With obvious effort, Vincenti composed herself. "Please excuse my outburst, Lieutenant Dallas. Elena, you will tell the lieutenant, in English, what you have done."

"She said, the signora said she needed my help." Tears plopped on her clenched hands. "Her husband, he beat her. He is a terrible, terrible man of great power in the United States. She told me this, in confidence. Signorina Vincenti—"

"Uh!"

Her head dipped lower. "She came here to escape, to find some peace, but she knew he would try to find her and bring her back. He would send, she told me, a police woman from New York City. The police in this place are corrupt and would do whatever he said."

"Is that so?" Eve said, very quietly. Quietly enough Roarke laid a restraining hand on her shoulder.

"She says this, signora." Elena pleaded. "I believe her. I feel great pity for her. She is so kind to me. She says I am like the little sister she loved who died when only a child. And she looks so sad and brave."

Oh yeah, Eve thought in disgust, *she had your number from the first look*.

"She asks only that if this police woman Dallas—if you—contact the villa to inquire, I tell her of this." Elena blinked out more tears. "I give her time to get away before you come to take her back to this very bad man. She does not ask me to lie, only to give her this small chance. So when you speak to Signorina Vincenti, I ring madam's suite and tell her she must run away very fast. I don't believe she is what you tell me until too late. I believe her. Will I be arrested?" Fresh tears spurted. "Will I go to prison?"

"Jesus Christ." Eve had to turn away. The kid was pitiful, and just the sort of gullible mark Julianna used most skillfully. "Get her out, send her home. I'm done with her."

"She can be charged with—"

"What's the point?" Eve interrupted Giamanno, scoured him with a brittle stare. "She's a dupe. Slapping her behind bars doesn't fix any of this."

"Her employment will be terminated." Vincenti poured coffee when Elena ran tearfully from the room.

"That's not my area," Eve responded.

"I believe she's learned a valuable lesson. I would prefer you kept her on, Signorina. In a probationary capacity." Roarke accepted the first cup of coffee. "Employees who learn hard and valuable lessons early often become exceptional at their work."

"As you wish, sir. Lieutenant Dallas, I cannot hope to apologize sufficiently for the . . ."—she seemed to gather all her disgust into one word—". . . *stupidity* of my assistant and what that has cost you. She is young and naive, but this does not excuse her, nor does it excuse me. I take full responsibility for the failure to do all that was necessary to help you in this matter. Elena was under my charge, therefore . . ."

Composed again, she turned to Roarke. "I will tender my resignation immediately. If you wish it, I will stay on to train a replacement."

"Your resignation is neither desired nor warranted, Signorina Vincenti, and will not be accepted. I trust you to handle any disciplinary action regarding your assistant."

"Former assistant," Vincenti said coolly. "She will now be re-assigned to a lesser position where she will have no contact with guests."

"Ah, well. As I said, I leave it in your thoroughly capable hands." He took those hands in his, spoke to her quietly in Italian, and made her smile again.

"You're very kind. Lieutenant, if there is anything that can be done, you have only to ask."

"She didn't walk out of the country, so I'll need to check on transportation services. She's gone, but we'll stick with procedure and do what we can to track her moves. If I can use your office."

"As long as you like."

"I came down hard on you."

"Yes, you did."

"Sorry." She offered a hand. "And that was really good ass-kicking with the assistant. I admire that."

"Thank you." Vincenti accepted the hand. "Believe me, I have not yet finished that particular task."

She'd gone over the Swiss border, using a private car service she'd arranged, probably on her pocket-link. The car had picked her up at the end of the shady lane that led to the villa's gates. She'd been wearing a blue sundress, one she'd probably been wearing under the long, white robe.

From there it became sketchier. Public and private shuttle companies, airports, and ground transportation were being studied for any passengers meeting her description.

"She's probably already back in New York." Harnessed for takeoff, Eve shut her eyes as Roarke's private shuttle began its taxi.

"I imagine so."

"One step behind. After she gets over being pissed at having her little holiday interrupted, she's going to feel really good about it. She took another battle, riding off unscathed while I eat her dust."

"You were right about her, what she would do. What she would need. What she had here, Lieutenant, was sheer luck. Not to discount the value of luck, but I'll wager on the side of brains and grit any day of the week."

"I wouldn't mind a little of that luck to go with them. I'm going to zone out for a while here."

"That's fine." He tapped the release on the table in front of him and brought the data center into position.

"How come I didn't know you could speak Italian?"

"Hmm? I don't, at least not fluently. Enough to handle basic business and employee relations. And, of course, I have a working knowledge of all the more colorful obscenities and sexual come-ons."

She could hear the faint click of him working the computer manually. "Everything in Italian sounds like a sexual come-on or colorful obscenity. Say something."

"Silenzio."

"Nuh-uh, I can figure that one out. Say something in the sexual come-on division."

He glanced over. Her eyes were still closed, but her lips were curved upward. Apparently she'd run out of her mad, he thought, and was ready to recharge. One way or the other.

He shut the computer down, pressed the lever to have the table swing away. Leaning close, he whispered a silky stream of Italian in her ear, while his fingers roamed possessively up her thigh.

"Yeah, that sounds pretty hot." She opened one eye. "What does it mean?"

"I believe it loses something in the translation. Why don't I demonstrate?"

Chapter 21

Julianna stormed into her townhouse, heaved her travel bag aside. The hours on the run hadn't chilled her anger, but instead had bottled it up under the rigid cork of control. Now that she was back, alone, unobserved, that cork popped.

She grabbed the first thing in range, a tall vase of delicate English bone china, threw it and its contents of white roses against the wall. The crash echoed in the empty house and set her on a rampage of temper and destruction. She batted lamps to the floor, pitched a large crystal egg into an antique mirror, stomped the already bruised roses into dust.

She upended chairs, tables, spilling precious crockery onto rug and wood until her foyer and living area resembled a war zone.

Then she threw herself down on the sofa and, pounding her fists onto the pillows, wept like a baby.

She'd wanted those few lovely days at the villa. She'd *needed* it. She was tired, tired, tired of fixing her own hair, of going without the simple necessities of facials and manicures.

And that *bitch* had ruined it all.

She'd had to leave a brand-new gown and shoes behind, as well as several other lovely outfits. And she'd missed her seaweed plunge and mud wrap.

Well, there would be payment made.

Sniffling, she rolled onto her back. If that little Italian twit in reservations hadn't come through, she might have found herself hauled out of bed by the police. Infuriating. Humiliating.

But that hadn't happened. To calm herself, Julianna breathed deeply and quietly as she'd taught herself in prison. It hadn't happened because she was always prepared, always ahead. And it had been Eve Dallas who'd lost this battle, as she'd lost the others in this newly waged war.

That was enough comfort to give Julianna a slight lift. Imagine, racing all the way to Italy only to find an empty suite. And that clever little message. Yes, that had been a stylish touch.

In any case, she'd come back to New York to work specifically to pit herself against Eve Dallas. So it was foolish to become so upset and overwrought when the woman proved herself to be a skilled foe.

So skilled, Julianna mused, that it might be best to back off a bit. At least temporarily. This last skirmish had unnerved her. And yet . . .

It was all so exciting. She'd missed this blood rush, this adrenaline spike when she'd been inside. The only way to bring it all to peak was to finish what she'd planned to do.

Destroy Eve Dallas, once and for all.

What better way to do that than by killing the man she was weak enough to love? With the added bonus of going down in history as the woman who murdered the invulnerable Roarke.

It was really all so perfect. Julianna lifted her hands, turned them, and pouted a bit when she noticed she'd chipped a nail.

Eve ran short, unpainted nails over the heel of a black evening shoe. "The Italian police were persuaded to turn over all personal items from Dunne's suite. This shoe is new. There's barely any marks on the sole. It's Italian, but with American sizing. My shoe authority . . ."—she glanced toward Roarke as she briefed her team—"tells me this means she most likely purchased it here in New York before leaving for Italy."

She tossed the shoe to McNab. "Run it, see if you can find out where she bought it, for what it's worth."

"She's got little feet."

"Yeah, she's a real dainty man killer. As you're aware, we focus now on the upcoming event at the Regency. Feeney, you're in charge of electronics—surveillance, security, and so on. We have the commander's go to put as many men on this as we need. Do. You'll have to keep to background as the subject knows you. She's going to think twice if she shows up and sees a known cop at some snazzy charity deal."

"They usually have good food at those things."

"You'll get fed. Peabody, there's a strong likelihood she'd recognize you. She researches and would have studied my aide. You'll remain in the on-site Control."

"Get your own plate," Feeney told her.

"McNab, we can risk you. You'll dude yourself up appropriately and work the ballroom."

"Hey, frigid."

"If she uses this opportunity to attempt a hit on the target, it's most likely she'll do it as server or staff. Easier to blend, to go unnoticed, to get in close enough to do the job. She'll know the target very well."

"The target has a name."

She met Roarke's eyes. "We know your name. So does she. She'll know you have superior security and superior instincts. She'll know you'll be cautious. But she'll also believe that you are unaware you're a target, that you'll feel reasonably comfortable at this sort of event, at your ease with the small talk and the mingling."

And he would, she thought, while her nerves would be balled up into slippery wires. "She doesn't know, or can't be sure, if I've copped to her moving on you. Her other New York targets have all been similar to her previous choices. You don't fit pattern. She'll consider that one of her advantages. The hit will take form in a drink or possibly some finger food. That means you eat and drink nothing. Nothing whatsoever."

"It promises to be a very long evening. I have a stipulation here, if you don't mind, Lieutenant."

"What?"

"The possibility remains you are her target, or that she hopes to take a two-for-one with us." He inclined his head as he saw this had occurred to her already. "Therefore, you eat or drink nothing right along with me."

"Fine. The media's already picked up the bone about the large contribution Roarke is presenting to Louise Dimatto that evening. This is an open door for her, and she will go through it." Eve had thought long and hard about it. "She will. I nipped at her heels in Italy this morning, put the skids on her nice little holiday. She doesn't care to be crossed. She'll be pissed, but she'll also be determined. So am I. So am I pissed and determined to slam that door shut on her."

She paused, read the faces in the room to see if they understood her meaning. Julianna Dunne was hers. "Feeney, I'll want your input on selecting what remains of the operation team. We'll go over that once we've done a walk-through on-site. We'll meet there, main security office, in thirty. Questions?"

"Not now." Feeney got to his feet. "Imagine there'll be plenty when we start the walk-through."

"Then let's save it. Peabody, you're with Feeney and McNab. I'll transport the civilian."

"And the civilian has a name as well." Mildly irked, Roarke got to his feet. "If you've a moment or two, Lieutenant, the Peabodys would like to say good-bye before they leave."

"Fine. In thirty," she said to her team as she walked out with Roarke.

"You're trying to depersonalize this by referring to me as an object." He paused at the top of the stairs, took her arm. "I don't appreciate it."

"That's too bad. When this is done and she's on ice, I'll say your name five hundred times as punishment." She could see his temper stir. "Give me a break on this, for God's sake. Give me a fucking break. I'm handling this the only way I know how."

"Understood. But you might understand that it's the both of us doing the handling. And I won't be relegated to a thing, Eve, not even for you." He took her hand firmly in his. "You've had a year to learn how it works."

A year? she thought as they walked down. As far as she could tell she wouldn't figure out all the angles of marriage in a hundred years.

The Peabodys were in the front parlor, cozied together on one of the sofas and laughing. Sam got to his feet the minute Eve stepped into the room.

"There you are. We were afraid you wouldn't have time to say good-bye, and give us the chance to say how glad we are we were able to get to know you this way. Both of you."

"It's been a pleasure having you here." Roarke held

out a hand. "And spending time with Delia's family. I hope you'll come back, and know you're welcome here whenever you do."

"We'll look forward to that." Phoebe's gaze rested on Eve, long enough, deep enough to bring on the jitters. "And you, Eve? Will we be welcome?"

"Sure. Um, door's always open."

Phoebe laughed, then swept forward to catch Eve's face in her hands and kiss both her cheeks. "Still don't quite know what to make of us, do you?"

"I don't know much about roots, but I recognize when somebody's got good ones. Peabody does."

Phoebe's humor changed to baffled delight. "Why, thank you. That's a lovely gift to take away with us. Be careful, as careful as you can manage," she added and stepped back. "We'll think of you often."

"That was well done," Roarke said when he and Eve were outside.

"I'm not a complete moron." She yanked open the driver's-side door of her vehicle, then caught herself. Calmed herself and studied him as he was studying her over the roof. "How about if I just call you the Civilian Roarke? You know, like a title."

"Perhaps if you punched it up just a bit. As in the Awesome and All-Powerful Civilian Roarke. Has a ring."

She reached over the roof to take his hand. "I'll think about it."

She ate, drank, slept, she breathed the operation. She could have drawn a detailed blueprint of the Grand Regency Hotel in her sleep. She'd spoken with all of Roarke's key people. Or grilled them like fish, as he'd put it during one of their several heated disagreements on operational procedure.

She had also run thorough and deep background checks on them, and though she'd been mollified and impressed by just how carefully Roarke chose his top security people, she didn't think it wise to mention it to him.

She slept poorly, often waking in the middle of the night with the sick feeling she'd neglected a key detail. The single detail that would lose Julianna.

She was moody, snappish, and continually pumped on caffeine.

She came close to the point where it was difficult for her to spend five minutes in a room with herself, but she kept right on pushing.

The night before the operation, she stood in her office, studying the image of the ballroom on-screen once again while the cat ribboned affectionately between her legs. Calculating the angles she'd already calculated, she arranged, re-arranged the proposed movements of the men who were assigned to the floor.

When the screen went blank, she thought she'd finally blown her eyes.

"That's enough." Roarke stepped up behind her. "You could build a bloody replica of the hotel with your bare hands by now."

"There's always a way to slide through a crack, and she's good at it. I want another pass at it."

"No. No," he repeated as he massaged her shoulders. "It's time we both put it aside until tomorrow. Take a pass at each other." He nuzzled her neck. "Happy anniversary."

"I didn't forget." She said it quickly, guiltily. "I just thought maybe we could . . . I don't know, save it for after tomorrow. Until after everything's clear." She cursed softly. "And when the hell is everything really clear, so that's stupid. But I didn't forget."

"That's good, as neither did I. Ah. Come along then, I've something to show you."

"I'm sort of surprised you're talking to me. I haven't

been a bundle of joy to be around the last couple of days."

"Darling, you're such a master of understatement."

She stepped into the elevator with him. "Yeah, fine, but you haven't been Mr. Smooth yourself, pal."

"Undoubtedly true. I don't care for anyone questioning or countermanding my orders and arrangements any more than you. Let's have a truce, shall we?"

"I guess I could use one. Where are we going here?"

"Back," he said, and when the doors opened led her out.

The holo-room was a large clean space of mirrored black. When the elevator closed behind them, he drew her into its center. "Begin designated program, dual settings."

And the black shimmered, wavered with color and shape. She felt the change in the air—a soft and fragrant warmth that had the faint hint of rain. She heard that rain patter softly against the windows that formed, on the floor of a balcony where the doors were open to welcome it.

And in front of her, the sumptuous beauty spilled around her and took shape.

"It's the place in Paris," she murmured. "Where we spent our wedding night. It was raining." She stepped to the open doors, held her hand out, and felt the wet kiss her palm. "Steamy with summer, but I wanted the doors open. I wanted to hear the rain. I stood here, just here, and I . . . I was so in love with you."

Her voice shook as she turned back, looked at him. "I didn't know I could stand here a year later and love you more." She scrubbed the heels of her hands over her damp cheeks. "You knew this would get me all sloppy."

"You stood there, just there." He walked to her. "And I thought, She's everything I want. Everything there is.

And now, a year later, you're somehow even more than that."

She leaped into his embrace, locking her arms around his neck, making them both laugh as he was forced to take two backward steps to maintain balance.

"Should've been ready," he chuckled against her lips. "I believe you did that a year ago as well."

"Yeah, and I did this." She tore her mouth from his to sink her teeth lightly into his throat. "Then I'm pretty sure we started ripping each other's clothes off on the way to the bedroom."

"Then in the interest of tradition." He got two fistfuls of the back of her shirt, yanked hard in opposite direction and ripped the fabric.

She went after his by the front, tugging until buttons flew, until she had her hands on flesh. "Then we—"

"It's all coming back to me." He pivoted, bracing her back against a wall, ravishing her mouth while he ripped at her trousers.

"Boots." Her breath caught, her hands kept busy. "I wasn't wearing boots."

"We'll ad-lib."

She fought to toe them off as her clothes, pieces of them, hung here and there like rags.

She stopped hearing the rain. The sound was too subtle to compete with the pounding of her blood. His hands were rough, demanding, rushing over her in a kind of feral possession until she could all but feel her skin screaming.

He drove her to peak where they stood, a brutal blinding peak that jellied her knees. His mouth was on hers, swallowing her cries as if he could feed on them.

Washed in the heat, she fell against him. And dragged him to the floor.

They went wild together, rolling over the delicate floral pattern of the rug, whipping all the needs to aching then pushing for more.

There was nothing else. Nothing for him now but her. The way her skin sprang damp as passions ruled her. The way her body lifted, writhed, slithered. The taste of her filled his mouth, pumped into his blood like some violent drug that promised the razor's edge of madness.

He savaged her breasts while her heart galloped under his hungry lips. Mine, he thought now as he had then. *Mine.*

He yanked her to her knees, his breath as ragged as their clothes. His muscles, primed to spring, quivered for her.

She fisted her hands in his hair. "More," she said, and dragged him back against her.

She fell on him, seeking to plunder. Her body was a morass of aches and glory, too battered by sensations to separate pain from pleasure. Clashed together, they equalled greed.

She feasted on him, on the hard, disciplined body, on the poet's mouth, the warrior's shoulders. Her hands streaked over him. Mine, she thought now as she had then. *Mine.*

He rolled, pinning her. He shoved her hips high and drove in, hard. Hard and deep. And held there, buried in her, while she came.

"There's more." His lungs screamed, and the dark pleasure all but blinded him as she fisted around him. "We'll both have more."

She rose to him, wrapped around him, matching him thrust for desperate thrust. When the need lanced through him, through heart, through head, through loins, he gave himself to it, and to her.

He rested his head between her breasts. The most perfect of pillows for a man, in his current opinion. Her heart was still thundering, or perhaps it was his. He felt a raging thirst and hoped he'd find the energy to quench it in the next year or two.

"I remembered something else," she told him.

"Hmm."

"We didn't make it to the bed the first time back then either."

"Eventually we did. But I think I had you on the dinner table first."

"I had you on the dinner table. Then you had me in the tub."

"I believe you're right about that. Then we managed to find the bed, where we proceeded to have each other. We had some dinner and some champagne before the table was so hastily cleared."

"I could eat." She combed her fingers lazily through his hair. "But maybe we can eat right here on the floor so we don't have to move very much. I think my legs are paralyzed."

He chuckled, nuzzled, then lifted his head. "It's been a fine and remarkable year. Come then, I'll help you up."

"Can we get food in here?"

"Absolutely. It's all arranged for." He got to his feet, hauled her to hers. "Give me a minute."

"Roarke? This is a really nice present."

He smiled at her, then went to the wall and keyed in something on a panel. "Night's young yet."

A droid that looked remarkably French wheeled a cart in as the elevator opened. Instinctively Eve tossed an arm over her breasts, the other below her waist. And made Roarke laugh.

"You have the oddest sense of modesty. I'll fetch you a robe."

"I never see droids around here."

"I assumed you'd object to Summerset bringing in the dinner. Here you are."

He handed her a robe. Or she supposed you could call

it a robe—if you didn't define one as actually covering anything. This was long and black and completely transparent. His grin flashed when she frowned at it.

"It's my anniversary, too, you know." He shrugged into a robe of his own, one, she noted, that wasn't so skimpy on the layers.

He poured the champagne the droid had opened, then offered her a glass. "To the first year, and all that follow." He touched his glass to hers.

He dismissed the droid, and she saw he hadn't missed a detail with the meal, either. There was the same succulent lobster, the tender medallions of beef in the delicate sauce, the same glossy hills of caviar they'd shared on their wedding night.

Candlelight shimmered and the music of the rain was joined by something that soared with strings and flutes.

"I really didn't forget."

"I know."

"I'm sorry I tried to push it aside. Roarke." She reached over, closed her hand over his. "I want you to know that I wouldn't change anything, not one thing that's happened since the first time I saw you. No matter how often you've pissed me off."

He shook his head. "You are the most fascinating woman I've ever known."

"Get out."

When she laughed, started to pull back, he tightened his grip on her hand. "Brave, brilliant, irritating, funny, exasperating, driven. Full of complications and compassion. Sexy, surprisingly sweet, mean as a snake. Disarmingly lacking in self-awareness, and stubborn as a mule. I adore every part and parcel of you, Eve. Everything you are is a maddening joy to me."

"You're just saying that because you want to get laid again."

"Hope does spring. I have something for you." He

reached into the pocket of the robe and drew out two silver boxes.

"Two?" Dumb shock covered her face. "There's supposed to be two gifts for this thing? Damn it, marriage should come with an instruction disc."

"Relax." Yes, a maddening joy. "There are two here because I see a kind of connection between them."

She frowned over it. "So, it's really like one? That's okay then."

"I'm relieved to hear it. Have this one first."

She took the box he offered, lifted the lid. The earrings sparkled up at her, deep and rich multicolored hunks of gems in hammered silver.

"I know you're not much on baubles, and you feel I heap them on you." He picked up his wine as she studied them. "But these are a bit different, and I think you'll appreciate why."

"They're great." She lifted one, and because she'd learned enough to know it would please him, began to fumble it into her ear. "Sort of pagan."

"They suit you. I thought they would. Here, let me do that." He rose, came around the table to fasten the earrings himself. "But I think their history will appeal to you more. They once belonged to Grainne Ni Mhaille— that's the proper name for her in Irish. She was a chieftain, head of her tribe in a time when such things were not heard of—or admitted to. She is sometimes called the Sea Queen, as she was a great sailing captain. So . . ."

He sat again, enjoying the way the earrings gleamed on his wife. His voice fell into a storytelling rhythm, so fluid, so Irish, she doubted he heard it. But she did.

"Tribal chief, warrior, queen, what have you. She lived during the sixteenth century. A violent age, in a country that's seen more than its fair share of violence. And known for her courage was Grainne. In her life she had triumph and tragedy, but she never faltered. On the west island where she was fostered, the castle she built still stands on the cliff—strategically. And there, at sea, or at one of the several strongholds she acquired, she held her own against all comers. She stood for her beliefs. She defended her people."

"She kicked ass," Eve said.

"Aye." He grinned at that. "That she did. And so do you, so I think it would please her for you to have them."

"It pleases me."

"And here's the second part."

She took the other silver box. Inside this was a silver medallion, an oval with the figure of a man carved on it.

"Who's this guy?"

"This is St. Jude, and he is the patron saint of police."

"You're kidding? Cops have their own saint?"

"They have Jude, who also happens to be the patron saint of lost causes."

She laughed as she held it up to the light. "Covering all your bases, aren't you?"

"I like to think so, yes."

"So what we've got here are like . . . talismans. Good luck pieces." She draped St. Jude over her head. "I like the idea. Adding luck to those brains and grit you mentioned the other day."

This time she got up, skirted the table. She bent down to kiss him. "Thanks. These are really good baubles."

"You're welcome. And now if you want to clear the table . . ."

"Just hold on, ace. You're not the only one who can give a present. But I have to go get it. Sit tight."

She hurried out in such a way that made him realize she'd forgotten about the sheerness of the robe. Grinning, Roarke poured more champagne and hoped for the sake of everyone's physical health, she didn't run into Summerset along the way.

Since she came back quickly, and with no rantings,

he decided she'd made the round trip without incident. She handed him a package covered with recycled brown paper.

He identified it by shape as some sort of painting or picture. Curious, as Eve was no art critic, he tore the wrappings.

It was a painting, of the two of them as they stood under the blooming arbor where they'd been married. Her hand was in his, their eyes on each other's. He could see the glint of new rings, new vows on her finger and on his.

He remembered the moment, remembered it perfectly. And the one just after when they had leaned into each other and exchanged that first kiss as husband and wife.

"It's wonderful."

"I had it done from the disc of the wedding. I just liked this moment, so I froze, printed and got this artist Mavis knows. He's actually a real artist and not one of the guys she knows who just does body painting. You probably could've got somebody better, but—"

She broke off when he looked up at her, when she saw his raw emotions flash his stunned pleasure. It was tough going to stun the man with anything—including a steel bat. "I guess you like it."

"It's the most precious gift I've ever been given. I liked this moment, too. Very much." He rose, set the painting carefully aside. Then slid his arms around her and drew her in, rubbed his cheek over her with the kind of exquisite tenderness that had her heart spilling out of her chest. "Thank you."

"That's okay." She sighed against him. "Happy anniversary. I need a minute to settle here, maybe one more drink. Then I'll clear that table."

He stroked a hand over her hair. "That's a deal."

Chapter 22

Eve might not have given two credits about fashion, but she'd chosen her outfit carefully for the operation. She was already wired, in more ways than one.

Energy was pumping through her, too fast, too hot. That, she knew, would have to be chilled before she stepped out of the door. Feeney had already fixed the transmitter to her chest, and the receiver in her ear.

Standing naked in her bedroom, she studied herself critically and could barely see the change of skin tones between her breasts were the mike rested.

Not that it would matter. The outfit wasn't designed to show a lot of skin.

Which was a good thing, as some of it was still bruised. Not too bad, she thought as she pushed a finger at the discoloring on her hip. And it only ached a little if she forgot to sit down often enough.

The face? She turned her head, wiggled her jaw. You could hardly notice, and she'd break down and slap on some enhancements to cover what still showed.

That process took her about ten minutes and caused some nominal frustration with the lip dye. Silly stuff never looked right on her, she thought as she went back to the bedroom to dress.

She'd chosen black. The glinting silver threads sparkling through the modified skin suit didn't interest her. The easy give of the fabric was key. Her primary weapon nestled in the small of her back, holstered there by what looked like a decorative silver belt. She'd tagged Leonardo for that little accessory. He'd come through fast and efficiently. And she supposed stylishly but it was tough to prove those things by her.

As she preferred the side to the back draw, she practiced for a few minutes until the movement smoothed out and became more natural.

Satisfied, she shot a clutch piece into an ankle holster, slid a small combat knife into an ankle sheath. Over these she slid soft black boots, then again studied the results. It would do, she decided, then went into a deep crouch and drew both secondaries.

"That's quite a picture you make, Lieutenant." Roarke strolled in, his shirt carelessly unbuttoned. Her vision was sharp enough to see that Feeney had finished wiring him as well. "Sure you have enough hardware there?"

"I'm not finished." She straightened, picked up a pair of restraints from the dresser. She looped them through the belt, secured them behind her left hip.

"Put some heels on those boots, add a whip, and we'd really have something." He walked a measuring circle around her. "As is, you're bound to intimidate the other attendees."

"I got that covered." She picked up a jacket in the same fluid black and silver. It shimmered to her knees.

Angling his head, Roarke circled his finger. Though she was annoyed she did a pair of quick turns. The jacket billowed, giving provocative hints of the body slicked into the skin suit, and draped cleanly over the police gear at her back.

"You'll definitely do," he decided. He feathered his fingers over her cheek, over the fading bruises she'd concealed. "But I wish you weren't quite so worried."

"I'm not worried." She picked up the teardrop diamond he'd once given her, looped the chain over her neck. And added the St. Jude medallion to it. "Got my protection. Anyway, some bitch goes after my man, I'm going to take her down. That's it."

"Darling, that's so sweet."

She met his gaze in the mirror as she fought on the Sea Queen's earrings, made herself grin as he was. "Yeah, that's me. Just a sentimental slob. You gonna suit up, or are you going casual?"

"Oh, I'll find something appropriate, so I don't embarrass my fashionable wife."

She watched him go to the personal department store he called a closet. "Is your transmitter activated yet?"

"No. Tested, then put on hold. Feeney's very strict about EDD eavesdropping in the bedroom."

"Okay. Look I know you're not going in empty. I want you to leave whatever weapon you're planning to take here."

He chose a suit of midnight black. "Is that an order, Lieutenant?"

"Don't get snotty with me, Roarke. You take one of your collection and by any chance have to use it, we've got trouble I don't want to have to deal with."

"I can deal with my own trouble."

"Shut up. Leave your weapon home. I'm giving you one of mine."

He turned, a shirt in his hand. "Are you?"

"I got a temporary carry license for you, one night only. Tibble put it through." She opened a drawer, took out a small stunner. "It's not lethal, but it'll jam up the circuits just fine, and you don't need anymore than that for personal protection."

"This from a woman who currently has more weapons than hands."

"I'm the badge, you're not. Don't make this into some manly ego thing. I know you can handle yourself, and you'd rather play it that way. But this has to go down clean. Any screwups and she'll use them in court to muck up the trial. You take something unauthorized, and you're putting a weapon in her hand."

He opened his mouth and she could see the annoyance, the refusal on his face. She shook her head. "Please, do this for me."

The annoyance came out, one long hiss of breath. But he held out a hand for the stunner. "Fighting dirty. Your way then."

"Thanks."

The please, the thanks, instead of anger and orders, told him she was a lot more worried than she wanted him to know. "You've covered every angle, every contingency, every circumstance," he told her.

"No." She opened the evening bag she'd carried. Her badge, backup communicator, and yet another weapon she didn't feel obliged to mention were already inside. "There's always something else. She'll be there. I know it. My gut knows it. We finish this tonight."

"All clear. No sign of subject. Beginning next sweep. And these little eggroll deals are aces."

Feeney's voice was bell-clear in Eve's ear, and a welcome relief to the party chatter in the ballroom. "Copy that," she replied. Leaving the weight of small talk to Roarke, she did her own sweep.

The badges she'd selected moved through the crowd, mingling, merging. Even McNab, somewhat conservatively dressed in sapphire blue and canary yellow, wouldn't have caused a second glance. No one would make them as cops, unless they knew where to look.

It was always in the eyes. Flat, watchful, ready, even as they laughed at a joke or made one, even as they nibbled on canapés or sipped mineral water.

Out of the twelve hundred and thirty-eight people attending, twenty who roamed the ballroom were armed and wired. Another ten covered other public areas as staff, and six manned equipment in Control.

The predinner mingling portion of the event was nearly at a close. Julianna had yet to make a move.

"We can't have our most illustrious benefactors standing here without a drink." Louise glided up, glowing in silver. She signalled a server, took two flutes of champagne off his tray, and handed them to Eve and Roarke. "You've already received your official thank-you for your donation, but I'd like to add a personal one."

"It's our pleasure." Roarke bent down to kiss her cheek. "You look stunning, as always. Hello, Charles, it's good to see you."

"Roarke. Lieutenant, you look amazing. The sexy soldier." He slid a proprietary arm around Louise's waist. "If I'm ever called to war, I'd want you leading my troops. We were afraid you wouldn't make it tonight. Delia's told me how jammed up you've been with this hunt for Julianna Dunne."

It was a constant puzzle to Eve. Here was a man, a professional companion, with his arm around the elegant blonde he was obviously gone over, talking about the brunette he'd dated for months, and nobody looked weird about it.

Add that the brunette he'd dated, *and* the guy she was currently banging like a hammer on a nail, were both hearing every word through Eve's mike, and you had something very strange on your hands.

Relationships were confusing enough, she thought.

Mix in police work and it arcs clean out of orbit.

"I make time to pay my debts," Eve said with a glance at Louise.

Louise laughed. "I think the million-dollar contribution already wiped that slate clean."

"That's his deal," Eve returned with a jerk of her head toward Roarke. "Anyway, it's a nice do as these dos go."

"Stupendous praise from you, so thanks. We're going to keep the boring speeches over dinner to a minimum, then liven it up again with dancing. But before we herd this mob to the tables, I need to steal your husband."

Eve inched just a little closer to Roarke. "I'd as soon keep him. I've gotten used to him."

"I'll return him, with hardly any wear. The mayor asked specifically to have a word with you," Louise said to Roarke. "I promised I'd deliver."

"Of course." Roarke set his untouched drink aside, skimmed a hand down Eve's back. "Politics must be played."

"You're telling me. Charles, you'll entertain Dallas for a few minutes, won't you?"

Eve had to fight the instinct to snatch Roarke's arm and yank him back. He could handle himself—nobody better. But he'd been no more than a foot from her side since they'd walked into the Regency. She'd wanted to keep it that way.

She watched his back as he moved across the ballroom with Louise.

"I have a message for you, Dallas."

"Huh? What message?"

"From Maria Sanchez. I'm to tell you you're solid, and for a cop, you're a pretty decent bitch." He sipped his champagne. "I assume those are compliments."

"More to you than me, I'd say. Odds are you gave her the best conjugal she's had since they locked her cage, and the best she'll have until it opens again."

"Let's just say that if it should ever be necessary, I'm sure I could use her as a reference. Actually, she was an interesting woman with a very simple outlook on life."

"Which is?"

"The fuckers are all out to get you, so you'd better get them first."

"Somebody ought to sew that on a pillow." When she lost sight of Roarke, her stomach clutched. "Ah, I can't quite see Louise. What was that color she was wearing?"

"I got him, Dallas," Feeney said in her ear. "He's covered on the cam, and Carmichael and Rusk moved in."

"Silver," Charles said with no little surprise. He'd never heard Eve express any interest in clothes. "She looks like she's wearing moonbeams."

"Got it bad, don't you, Charles?"

"A terminal case. I've never been happier in my life. Do you know what it is to find someone who accepts you for what you are, and is willing to love you anyway?"

She searched the crowd for Roarke, settled just a little when she found him. "Yeah, I guess I do."

"It makes you a better person. It makes you . . . whole. And that's enough philosophizing for one night." He shifted, blocking her view of Roarke for a moment. "Those earrings are absolutely fabulous." He reached out to touch one, and had her earpiece registering the click of finger on metal like a dull gong. "Antique?"

"Yeah." She re-angled her body, tried to zero in on Roarke again. "They belonged to a solider."

"They're perfect for you. Anything wrong?" He touched her cheek now, drew her attention back to his. "You seem a little on edge."

"Gigs like this make me itchy. People are starting to drift toward the tables. We'd better snag our dates."

"We're sitting together. We'll catch up with them at the table." He took her arm, was surprised to feel the muscles tense, almost vibrate. "You really are itchy."

Short of knocking him down, she wasn't going to shake Charles. And shoving her way through the milling crowd wasn't the way to keep a low profile. But there was a buzz in her blood that told her to get to Roarke, and get there now.

"There's something I need to tell Roarke, but I've lost his location."

The underlying tone of urgency in her voice had Charles looking over sharply. "All right, Dallas, what's going on?"

"Roarke's at three o'clock," Feeney told her. "Twenty feet from your position. Crowd's closed in, but Carmichael and Rusk still have him in sight."

"Dallas?"

"Not now," she hissed at Charles and pivoted to the right. It was raw instinct that pushed her forward. No logic, no reason, but a primal knowledge that her mate was threatened. She caught a glimpse of him through the spark and color. Of polite amusement on his face as he was cornered by a stick-thin society butterfly. She saw Carmichael get elbowed back by a tuxedoed couple who'd imbibed a bit too freely during cocktail hour. The annoyance on Carmichael's face as she jockeyed back into position.

She heard the orchestra strike up with a bright, jazzy tune. Heard the trills of laughter, the gossipy tones as people dished dirt, the shuffle and click of feet as more went on the move.

She saw Louise turn away to speak to someone, and block Rusk's easy path to Roarke.

And she saw Julianna.

It went fast as a heartbeat, slow as a century.

Julianna wore the trim white jacket and slacks of the servers. Her hair was a soft, honey brown—a short, curly cap that was fashioned like a halo around her face. That face was carefully enhanced, carefully composed to non-descript.

She could have passed for a droid, and was garnering just as much dismissal, as she walked easily through the polished bodies toward Roarke.

In her hand she carried a single flute of champagne.

Her gaze flashed up, met Roarke's. Whatever she saw there must have satisfied her, for she smiled, just the slightest curve of unpainted lips.

"Target sighted." Though Eve spoke clearly, there was too much distance, too much noise between them for Julianna to have heard.

And still she turned her head and looked at Eve.

They moved at the same time, Eve forward, Julianna back. Eve had the small twist of satisfaction of seeing startled temper cross Julianna's face before she swung into the thickest part of the crowd.

"Suspect is dressed as server. Brown and brown, moving west through the ballroom."

She sprinted forward as she spoke, ducking, shoving, flinging herself through startled people. Feeney's relay rang in her ears, had her spinning to the right, knocking hard into a startled waiter. She heard the thunderous crash of his tray behind her.

She caught another glimpse, saw Julianna pass the flute to an oblivious older man before she streaked up the curve of the floating staircase to the second level. People tumbled in her wake like tossed dolls.

"Moving up," Eve shouted. "Close in from positions eight and ten. Now, now, now!"

She ran straight into the man who was just lifting the flute of champagne to his lips. It splattered all over his suit as the glass flew out of his hand and crashed to the floor.

"Well, *really!*"

He was angry enough to make a grab for her arm, and

got a hard stomp on the instep. He'd limp, Eve thought as she leaped up the stairs, but he'd live.

"Inside this area, Lieutenant." One of the two cops who raced forward to flank Eve gestured toward a pair of double doors. "She nicked in. I couldn't get a stream off due to civilian safety. She's flipped the locks and caged herself in. There's no way out unless she decides to jump ten stories."

"She'll have a way." Without hesitation, Eve aimed her weapon at the door and blasted the locks.

The explosion came a second later. The hot gush of air punched like a fist and knocked Eve back a full five feet. She tumbled, head over feet, and her weapon spurted out of her hand like wet soap. Her earpiece went dead.

Smoke belched out of the anteroom, choking and blinding. She heard the nasty crackle of flame, and the shouts around her, below her, as people rushed into a screaming panic.

She slapped her clutch piece out of her ankle holster. "Officer down. Officer down," she repeated, hoping the mike still worked as she saw one of her backup lying unconscious and bleeding from the head. "We need medical assistance, the fire and explosives department. I'm going in after this bitch."

She crouched, sprang, and went through the doors into the smoke in a fast, low roll.

Julianna leaped on her back in a fury of fists, teeth, and nails.

The safety system had water gushing down from the ceiling, fans whirling, alarms screaming. Through it, they grappled like animals over the ruined carpet.

For the second time she lost her weapon—or so the report would read. The satisfaction of feeling her bare fist plow into Julianna's flesh was like a song.

She tasted blood, smelled it. Rode on it.

Her mind was laser sharp as they both gained their feet, circled each other.

"You fucked up, Julianna. Stay back!" she snapped out the order as Roarke burst into the room, steps ahead of McNab. "Stay the hell back. She's mine."

"Sir."

Roarke merely reached over, lowered McNab's weapon hand. "Let her finish it."

"You're the one who fucked up, Dallas. Going soft over a man. I had more respect for you." She spun, kicked out. She missed slamming her foot into Eve's face by a whisper. "He's just like the rest of them. He'll shake you off when he's bored of you. He's already out shoving his dick into other women every chance hc gets. That's what they *do*. That's all they do."

Eve straightened and stripped off the ruined jacket. Julianna did the same with her own.

"I'm taking you down," Eve said. "That's what I do. Come on, let's dance."

"You'll want to hold the troops back, Ian." Roarke reached down to retrieve Eve's discarded clutch piece as fists and feet flew. "Someone could get hurt."

"Man. Some girl fight."

Roarke merely lifted a brow, though his attention stayed riveted to his wife. "And that someone will surely be you if you say that loud enough for the lieutenant to hear. She needs to do this," he stated, and felt the blow in his own chest as Julianna kicked Eve.

She didn't feel it. Her body registered by falling back, pivoting, spinning, feinting. But her mind refused the pain. She felt the dark joy, heard the satisfying crunch of bone when she spun and rammed a fist back into Julianna's face.

"I broke your fucking nose. What're you gonna do about it?"

Blood poured down Julianna's face, ruining beauty.

Her breath was heaving, as Eve's was, but she was far from done. She screamed, came at Eve at a run.

The force of the attack had them both flying through the terrace doors. Glass shattered, wood snapped. Roarke reached the ruined doorway in time to see Eve and Julianna spill over the railing in a tangle of limbs and fury.

"Christ Jesus." His heart in his throat, he raced to the rail, saw them fall, still wrapped like lovers, onto the glide two stories down.

"That's gotta hurt," McNab said beside him. "One of us has to stop this, and I'd rather it wasn't me."

But Roarke was already vaulting over the rail, and leaping.

"Lunatics." McNab hitched his weapon back in its holster and prepared to follow suit. "We're all a bunch of lunatics."

The glide vibrated under the blows of bodies. Civilians who'd been unlucky enough to be on board scrambled down and off like rats off a doomed ship.

The thin silk tank Julianna wore under the uniform jacket was torn, bloody. Lights gleamed over her partially exposed breast as she jump-kicked Eve in the shoulder, followed up with a roundhouse.

Eve ducked the punch, went in low and heard the explosive whoosh of air as she plowed a blow into Julianna's belly.

"Prison fit ain't street fit, bitch." To prove it, Eve rammed her elbow up under Julianna's jaw, snapping her head back. "But let's see how much workout time they give you when you're back in a cage."

"I'm not going back!" She was fighting blindly now, and only more viciously. She got a swipe under Eve's guard and raked her nails down her cheek.

She saw the men storming down the glide over Eve's shoulder. Heard the shouts and rushing feet from behind. In that moment, her body alive with a pain she'd never experienced, she cursed herself for falling into a trap, cursed Eve for outmaneuvering her.

But the war wasn't over. Couldn't be over. Retreat, her mind ordered. And following it she jumped from the glide, springing hard to clear the three feet to the open-air restaurant.

Those who dined were already goggling. Several screamed when the bloody woman, her face blackened with soot, her eyes wild, her teeth bared, landed among the charming glass-topped tables and glowing candles.

Two women and one man fainted when the second woman, equally torn, flew down, feet first, and slammed into the dessert cart.

There were splashes and shouts as a few diners fell into the pool.

Cornered by the cops who burst through the restaurant's doors and the others that ranged on the now-disabled glide, Julianna focused on the only one who mattered. She grabbed a bottle of superior merlot, smashed it against a table. Wine splattered like blood as she turned the jagged edge toward Eve.

"I'm going to kill you." She said it calmly, though tears tracked through the filth on her face.

"Hold your fire," Eve ordered as one of the cops took aim. "Hold your goddamn fire. This is my op. This is my collar." She sensed rather than saw Roarke land behind her. "Mine." She all but growled it.

"Then finish it." He spoke quietly, for her alone. "You've given her enough of your time."

"Let's see if you've got the guts, Julianna, to try to slit my throat with that. You'll have to come in fast. It's going to be messy. Not neat, not delicate like poisoning some poor slob."

She circled as she spoke, gauging her ground, planning her moves. "What's the matter, Julianna? Afraid to try the direct kill?"

On a scream of rage, of insult, of loathing, Julianna charged. Eve felt the rush of facing death stream cool into her body. She sprang off her toes, one leg pistoning out, then the other. The two rapid kicks, both dead in the face, had Julianna flying back, landing without grace on one of the glass-topped tables.

She smashed through it, landed hard in an ugly shower of glass. "Basic rule of combat," Eve said as she reached down, dragged Julianna up by her curls. "Legs are generally longer than arms."

She leaned in, whispered in Julianna's ear. "You shouldn't have gone after what's mine. Big mistake."

Though in a daze Julianna managed to bare her teeth. "I'll be back, and I'll kill both of you."

"I don't think so, Julianna. I think you're done. Now I'm going to give you your civil right to remain silent." So saying Eve punched her full in the face and knocked her cold.

Eve flipped her over, clapped on the restraints, then straightened, stepped back. "Peabody."

"Ah, yes, sir. Right here."

"See that this prisoner is read her rights, transported to the proper holding facility, and given all required medical attention."

"You bet. Lieutenant?"

Eve turned her head, inelegantly spat out blood. "What?"

"I just want to say, you are my god."

With a half-laugh, Eve limped to a chair. Sat. Pain was beginning to leak through and promised to be awesome. "Get her out of here so they can start cleaning up this mess. I'll be in to file the reports and debrief the team after I clean up some."

"She won't be in before morning," Roarke corrected. He lifted a large, unbroken bottle of water, opened it, handed it to Eve.

"Two hours." Eve tipped back her head and drank like a camel.

Wisely Peabody opted to stay out of this particular battle as well.

"Sorry about messing up your pretty hotel."

"You did quite the job on it." He pulled up a chair, sat in front of her. Her face was bruised, bloody, filthy, her knuckles raw and swollen. A gash among the many scratches on her arm would require treatment. But for now he took out a handkerchief, plucked one of the linen napkins from the table, and tied on a quick field dressing. "And you did one on my pretty wife as well."

"I was just lulling her into complacency. You know, playing with her awhile."

"Oh yes, I could see that, particularly when you lulled her by falling off a ten-story terrace with her."

"That was sort of unplanned, but all in all." She happened to glance down at herself and for a moment was paralyzed and speechless. The skin suit was torn at the neck with the material flapping down to play peek-a-boo with her breasts. It gaped down the center of her body almost to her crotch. One leg was ripped open to the hip.

"Well, holy shit." She yanked what she could over her breasts. "You could have told me I'm sitting here mostly naked."

"When a man stands back and watches two women fight, it's with the cherished hope that clothes will be ripped off along the way." But he rose, stripped off his jacket, and offered it.

"Here are your choices. A health center or hospital, the MTs, or a room here where Louise can examine and treat you."

"I don't—"

"Want to argue with me over this. You wanted to take her down with your bare hands—needed to. Otherwise you'd have used your weapon."

"I lost it when I—"

"The knife's still in your boot." He laid a hand lightly over hers. "Say whatever needs to be said in your official report, Eve, but don't pretend with me. You did what you needed to do, and I understand it. I'd have wanted the same if anyone had come at you because of me."

"Okay."

"You did what you needed to do, and I didn't interfere. Do you think that was a simple thing for me?"

She kicked at some of the broken glass with her boot. "No."

"Now you'll let me do what I need to do, and not interfere. Which of those choices suits you best?"

"I'll take Louise," she agreed. "Even though she's going to be royally pissed at me for messing up her fancy charity do."

"Shows what you know about such matters. She couldn't have bought the kind of publicity and attention for her cause that this little adventure will reap. And if she doesn't think of that straight away, you've only to remind her."

"Good thinking." She reached out, brushed his hair back from his face. "I love you. I just sort of felt like saying that right now."

"I always feel like hearing it. Come on now, Lieutenant, let's get you on your feet."

She took his hand, started to lever herself up. He heard her gasp, hiss, and barely strangle a groan.

"Okay, ouch." She had to lower again, catch her breath. "Don't even think about carrying me." Anticipating him, she waved a hand. "Not with all these cops around. Stuff like that undermines your rep."

"I think your rep will stand it, particularly after tonight. Besides." He lifted her, as gently as he could manage. "You can just blame it on the overreaction of the worried civilian."

"Yeah, okay." Pain was stampeding through her now like a herd of buffalo. "I'll pin it on my husband."

"Now that—my husband—is a rare term coming out of your mouth."

"It doesn't stick on my tongue so much anymore. You know, this is a pretty interesting way for us to start year two of this marriage deal."

"It certainly seems to work for us."

He carried his wounded soldier off the battlefield. And considered how annoyed his wife would be when he saw to it she was given a strong enough blocker to knock her out until the morning.

If you enjoyed REUNION IN DEATH,

rn the page for a preview of the next thrilling novel
from Nora Roberts writing as JD Robb . . .

PURITY

IN

DEATH

Chapter 1

Lieutenant Eve Dallas loitered at her desk. She was stalling, and she wasn't proud of it. The idea of changing into a fancy dress, driving uptown to meet her husband and a group of strangers for a business dinner thinly disguised as a social gathering had all the appeal of climbing in the nearest recycler and turning on Shred.

Right now Cop Central was very appealing.

She'd caught and closed a case that afternoon, so there was paperwork. It wasn't *all* stalling. But as the bevy of witnesses had all agreed that the guy who'd taken a header off a six-story people glide had been the one who'd started the pushy-shovey match with the two tourists from Toledo, it wasn't much of a time sucker.

For the past several days, every case she'd caught had been a variation on the same theme. Domestics where spouses had battled to the death, street brawls turned lethal, even a deadly combat at a corner glide-cart over ice cones.

Heat made people stupid and mean, she thought, and the combination spilled blood.

She was feeling a little mean herself at the idea of dressing up and spending several hours in some snooty restaurant making small talk with people she didn't know.

That's what you got, she thought in disgust, when you marry a guy who had enough money to buy a couple of continents.

Roarke actually liked evenings like this. The fact that he did never failed to baffle her. He was every bit at home in a five-star restaurant—one he likely owned any-way—nibbling on caviar as he was sitting at home chow-ing down on a burger.

And she supposed as their marriage was approaching its second year, she'd better stop crabbing about it. Re-signed, she pushed back from the desk.

"You're still here." Her aide, Peabody, stopped in the doorway of her office. "I thought you had some fancy dinner deal uptown."

"I got time." A glance at her wrist unit brought on a little tug of guilt. Okay, she was going to be late. But not very. "I just finished up on the glide diver."

Peabody, whose summer blues defied all natural order and managed to stay crisp in the wilting heat, kept her dark eyes sober. "You wouldn't be stalling, would you, Lieutenant?"

"One of the residents of our city, who I am sworn to serve and protect, ended up squished like a bug on Fifth Avenue. I think he deserves an extra thirty minutes of my time."

"It must be really rough, forced to put on a beautiful dress, stick some diamonds or whatever all over you and choke down champagne and lobster croquettes beside the most beautiful man ever born, on or off planet. I don't know how you get through the day with that weight on your shoulders, Dallas."

"Shut up."

"And here I am, free to squeeze into the local pizza place with McNab where we will split the pie and the check." Peabody shook her head slowly. The dark bowl of hair under her cap swayed in concert. "I can't tell you how guilty I feel knowing that."

"You looking for trouble, Peabody?"

"No, sir." Peabody did her best to look pious. "Just offering my support and sympathy at this difficult time."

"Kiss ass." Torn between annoyance and amusement, Eve started to shove by. Her desk 'link beeped.

"Shall I get that for you, sir, and tell them you've gone for the day?"

"Didn't I tell you to shut up?" Eve turned back to the desk, took the transmission. "Homicide. Dallas."

"Sir. Lieutenant."

She recognized Officer Troy Trueheart's face as it popped on-screen, though she'd never seen its young, All-American features so strained. "Trueheart."

"Lieutenant," he repeated after an audible swallow. "I have an incident. In response to . . . oh gosh, I killed him."

"Officer." She pulled his location on-screen as she spoke. "Are you on duty?"

"No, sir. Yes, sir. I don't know, exactly."

"Pull yourself together, Trueheart." She slapped out the order, watched his head jerk as if he'd felt it physically. "Report."

"Sir. I had just clocked off shift and was on my way home on foot when a female civilian shouted for assistance from a window. I responded. On the fourth floor of the building in question an individual armed with a bat was assaulting the female. Another individual, male, was unconscious or dead in the hallway, bleeding from the head. I entered the apartment where the assault was taking place, and . . . Lieutenant, I tried to stop him. He was killing her. He turned on me, ignored all warnings and orders to desist. I managed to draw my weapon, to stun. I swear I intended to stun, but he's dead."

"Trueheart, look at me. Listen to me. Secure the building, call in the incident through Dispatch and inform them that you've reported to me and I'm on my way. I'll call for medical assistance. You hold the scene, Trueheart. Hold it by the book. Do you understand?"

"Yes, sir. I should've called Dispatch first. I should've—"

"You stand, Trueheart. I'm on the way. Peabody," Eve commanded as she strode out the door.

"Yes, sir. I'm with you."

There were two black-and-whites, nose-to-nose, and a medi-van humped between them at the curb when Eve pulled up. The neighborhood was the type where people scattered rather than gathered when cops showed up, and as a result there was no more than a smattering of gawkers on the sidewalk who had to be told to stay back.

The two uniforms who flanked the entrance eyed her, then exchanged a look. She was brass, and the one who could well put one of their own rank's balls in the blender.

She could feel the chill as she approached.

"Cop shouldn't get hassled by cops for doing the job," one of them muttered.

Eve paused in midstride and stared him down.

He saw rank in the form of a long, leanly built woman with eyes of gilded brown that were as flat and expressionless as a snake's as they met his. Her hair, short and choppy, was nearly the same color and framed a narrow face offset by a wide mouth that was now firmed into one thin line. There was a shallow dent in a chin that looked like it could hold its own against a fist.

Under her stare he felt himself shrink.

"Cop shouldn't slap at a cop for doing hers," she said coldly. "You got a problem with me, Officer, wait until I do that job. Then mouth off."

She moved into the shoe box lobby, punched a finger on the Up button of the single elevator. She was already steaming, but it had little to do with the oppressive heat. "What is it with some uniforms that they want to bite your throat when you're rank?"

"It's just nerves, Dallas," Peabody replied as they stepped onto the elevator. "Most of the uniforms out of Central know Trueheart, and you gotta like him. A uniform terminates on his own like this, Testing's going to be brutal."

"Testing's brutal anyway. The best we can do for him is to keep this clean and ordered. He's already screwed up by tagging me before he called it in."

"Is he going to take heat for that? You're the one who pulled him out of the sidewalk scooper detail and into Central last winter. Internal ought to understand—"

"IAB isn't big on understanding. So let's hope it doesn't go there." She stepped off the elevator. Studied the scene.

He'd been smart enough, cop enough, she noted with some relief, not to disturb the bodies. Two men lay sprawled in the corridor, one of them facedown in a pool of congealing blood.

The other was faceup, staring with some surprise at the ceiling. Through an open doorway beside the bodies she could hear the sounds of weeping and groaning.

The door across was also open. She noted several fresh holes and dents in the hallway walls, splinters of wallboard, splatters of blood. And what had once been a baseball bat was now a broken club, covered with blood and brain matter.

Straight as a soldier, pale as a ghost, Trueheart stood at the doorway. His eyes still held the glassy edge of shock.

"Lieutenant."

"Hold it together, Trueheart. Record on, Peabody." Eve crouched down to examine the two bodies. The bloodied one was big and beefy, the kind of mixed fat and muscle build that could usually plow through walls if annoyed enough. The back of his skull looked like an egg that had been cracked with a brick.

The second body wore only a pair of grayed Jockey shorts. His thin, boney frame showed no wounds, no bruising, no damage. Thin trickles of blood had seeped out of his ears, his nostrils.

"Officer Trueheart, do we have identification on these individuals?"

"Sir. The, um, initial victim has been identified as Ralph Wooster, who resided in apartment 42E. The man I—" He broke off as Eve's head whipped up, as her eyes drilled into his.

"And the second individual?"

Trueheart wet his lips. "The second individual is identified as Louis K. Cogburn of apartment 43F."

"And who is currently wailing inside apartment 42E?"

"Suzanne Cohen, cohabitation partner of Ralph Wooster. She called for aid out the window of said apartment. Louis Cogburn was assaulting her with what appeared to be a club or bat when I arrived on-scene. At that time—"

He broke off again when Eve held up a finger. "Preliminary examination of victims indicates a mixed-race male—mid-thirties, approximately two hundred and thirty pounds, approximately six foot one—has suffered severe trauma to head, face, and body. A bat, apparently wooden, and marked with blood and brain matter would appear to be the assault weapon. The second male, also mid-thirties, Caucasian, approximately one hundred and thirty pounds, approximately five foot eight, is identified as the assailant. Cause of death as yet undetermined. Second vic bled from ears and nose. There is no visual trauma or wound."

She straightened. "Peabody, I don't want these bodies touched. I'll do the field exam after I talk to Cohen. Officer Trueheart, did you discharge your weapon during the course of this incident?"

"Yes, sir. I—"

"I want you to surrender that weapon to my aide, who will bag it at this time."

There were grumblings from the two uniforms at the end of the hall, but she ignored them as she held Trueheart's gaze. "You are not obliged to surrender your weapon without representation present. You may request a representative. I'm asking you to give your weapon to Peabody so there's no question as to the sequence of this investigation."

Through the shock, she saw his absolute trust in her. "Yes, sir." When he reached down for his weapon, she put a hand on his arm.

"Since when are you a southpaw, Trueheart?"

"My right arm's a little sore."

"Were you injured during the course of this incident?"

"He got a couple of swings in before—"

"The individual you were obliged to draw on assaulted you in the due course of your duties?" She wanted to shake him. "Why the hell didn't you say so?"

"It happened awfully fast, Lieutenant. He rushed me, came in swinging, and—"

"Take off your shirt."

"Sir?"

"Lose the shirt, Trueheart. Peabody, record here."

He blushed. *God, what an innocent*, Eve thought, as Trueheart unbuttoned his uniform shirt. She heard Peabody suck in a breath, but whether it was for Trueheart's undeniably pretty chest, or the bruising that exploded over his right shoulder and mottled the arm to the elbow, she couldn't be sure.

"He got in a couple of good swings by the look of it. I want the MTs to take a look at you. Next time you're hurt on the job, Officer, make it known. Standby."

Apartment 42E was in shambles. Though from what was left of the decor, Eve imagined housekeeping wasn't a high priority of its residents. Still, it was doubtful the place was normally a minefield of broken glass, or the walls decorated with surreal paintings of blood splatters.

The woman on the gurney looked like she'd known better days as well. A bandage streaked across her left eye, and above it, below it, the skin was raw.

"She coherent?" Eve asked one of the medical technicians.

"Just. Kept her from going all the way under since we figured you'd want a word with her. Make it snappy though," he told her. "We need to get her in. She's got a detached cornea, shattered cheekbone, broken arm. Guy whaled on her good and proper."

"Five minutes. Miss Cohen." Eve stepped up, leaned down. "I'm Lieutenant Dallas. Can you tell me what happened?"

"He went crazy. I think he killed Ralph. Just went crazy."

"Louis Cogburn?"

"Louie K., yeah." She moaned. "Ralph was pissed. Music up so loud you couldn't think straight. Fucking hot. Just wanted a couple of brews and a little quiet. What the hell? Louie K., he mostly plays the music loud, but this was busting our eardrums. He's had it wailing for days."

"What did Ralph do?" Eve prompted. "Ms. Cohen?"

"Ralph went and banged on the door, told him to cut it back. Next I knew, Louie came busting out, swinging a bat or something. Looked crazy. Blood was flying, he was screaming. I was scared, really scared, so I slammed the door and ran to the window. Called for help. I could hear him screaming out there, and these awful thumping sounds. I couldn't hear Ralph. I kept calling for help, then he came in."

"Who came in?"

"Louie K. Didn't even look like Louie. Had blood all over him, and something was wrong with his eyes. He come at me, with the bat. I ran, tried to run. He was smashing everything and screaming about spikes in his head. He hit me, and I don't remember after that. Hit me in the face and I don't remember until the MTs started working on me."

"Did you see or speak with the officer who responded to your call for help?"

"I didn't see nothing but stars. Ralph's dead, isn't he?" A single tear slid down her cheek. "They won't tell me, but Louie'd never have gotten past him 'less he was dead."

"Yeah, I'm sorry. Did Ralph and Louie have a history of altercations?"

"You mean did they go at it before? Yelled at each other sometimes about the music, but they'd more likely have a couple brews or smoke a little Zoner. Louie's just a little squirt of a guy. He never caused no problems around here."

"Lieutenant." One of the MTs moved in. "We've got to transport her."

"All right. Send somebody in to take a look at my officer. He caught a couple solids in the arm and shoulder." Eve stepped back, then moved to the door behind them. "Trueheart, you're going to give me a report, on record. I want it clear, I want it detailed."

"Yes, sir. I clocked off at eighteen-thirty and proceeded southeast from Central on foot."

"What was your intended destination?"

He flushed a little. Color came and went in his face. "I was, ah, proceeding to the home of a friend where I had arrangements for dinner."

"You had a date."

"Yes, sir. As I approached this building, I heard calls for assistance and looking up saw a woman leaning out of the window. She appeared to be in considerable distress. I entered the building, proceeded to the fourth floor where I could hear the sounds of an altercation. Several individuals came to their doors, but no one attempted to come out. I called requests for someone to call nine-eleven."

"Did you take the stairs or the elevator?" Details, she

thought. She needed to take him through every detail.

"The stairs, sir. I thought it would be faster. When I reached this floor, I saw the male identified as Ralph Wooster lying on the floor of the corridor between apartments 42E and 43F. I did not, at that time, check him for injuries as I could hear screaming and breaking glass emitting from 42E. I responded to this immediately and witnessed the individual identified as Louis K. Cogburn assaulting a woman with what appeared to be a baseball bat. The weapon was . . ."

He paused a moment, swallowed hard. "The weapon was covered with what appeared to be blood and gray matter. The woman was unconscious on the floor, with Cogburn above her. He held the bat over his head as if preparing to strike another blow. I drew my weapon at this time, called for the assailant to cease and desist, identifying myself as Police."

Trueheart had to stop now, and rubbed the back of his hand over his mouth. The look he sent her was both helpless and pleading. "Lieutenant, it all happened fast from there."

"Just tell it."

"He turned away from the woman. He was screaming something about spikes in his head, about blasting out the window. Crazy stuff. Then he lifted the bat again, shifting so it looked like he was going to strike the woman. I moved in to prevent this, and he charged me. I tried to evade, to get the bat. He landed a couple of blows—I believe it broke at that time—and I fell back, knocked something over, hit the wall. I saw him coming at me again. I yelled at him to stop."

Trueheart took a steadying breath, but it didn't stop the quaver in his voice. "He cocked the bat back like he was swinging for home, and I discharged my weapon. It's set on low stun, Lieutenant, the lowest setting. You can see—"

"What happened next?"

"He screamed. He screamed like—I've never heard

anything like it. He screamed and he ran out into the hall. I pursued. But he went down. I thought he was stunned, just stunned. But when I got down to put restraints on him, I saw he was dead. I checked his pulse. He was dead. I got jumbled up. Sir, I got jumbled up. I know it was incorrect procedure to tag you before calling—"

"Never mind that. Officer, were you at the time you deployed your weapon, in fear for your life and/or the lives of civilians?"

"Yes, sir. Yes, sir, I was."

"Did Louis K. Cogburn ignore any and all of your warnings to cease and desist and surrender his weapon?"

"Yes, sir, he did."

"You." Eve pointed to one of the uniforms down the hall. "Escort Officer Trueheart downstairs. Medical attention for his injuries has been called for. Put him in one of the black-and-whites until the MTs can see him. Stay with him until I'm done in here. Trueheart, call your representative."

"But, sir—"

"I'm advising you to call your representative," she said. "I'm stating here, for the record, that in my opinion, after a cursory examination of the evidence, after an interview with Suzanne Cohen, your account of this incident is satisfactory. The deployment of your weapon appears to have been necessary to protect your life and the life of civilians. That's all I can tell you until my onscene investigation into this matter is complete. Now I want you to go, get off your feet, call your rep and let the MTs take care of you."

"Yes, sir. Thank you, sir."

"Come on, Trueheart." The other uniform patted Trueheart on the back.

"Officer? Any of the beat cops know these dead guys?"

The uniform glanced back at Eve. "Proctor has this sector. He might."

"Get him," she said as she sealed up and walked into 43F.

"He's awful shook," Peabody said.

"He'll have to get over it." She scanned the room.

It was a filthy mess, smelling ripely of spoiled food and dirty laundry. The cramped kitchen area consisted of a two-foot counter, a mini-AutoChef and minifridgie. A huge tin sat on the counter. Eve lifted her brows as she read the label.

"You know, I just don't see our Louie K. baking a lot of cakes." She opened one of the two cupboards and perused the neat line of sealed jars. "Looks like Louie was in the illegals line. Funny, everything in here's neat as Aunt Martha's, and the rest of the place is a pigsty."

She turned around. "No dust on the furniture though. That's funny, too. You wouldn't figure a guy who sleeps on sheets that smell like a swamp would bother chasing dust."

She opened the closet. "Tidy in here, too. Clothes show a lack of fashion taste, but they're all clean. Look at that window, Peabody."

"Yes, sir?"

"Glass is clean, inside and out. Somebody washed them within the last couple weeks. Why do you wash your windows and leave—what the hell is this?—un-identified spilled food substance all over the floor?"

"Maid's week off?"

"Yeah, somebody's week off. That's about how long this underwear's been piled here." She glanced at the door when a uniform stepped in.

"You Proctor?"

"Yes, sir."

"You know those two dead guys?"

"I know Louie K." Proctor shook his head. "Shit— sorry, Lieutenant, but shit, this is some mess. That kid Trueheart's down there puking his guts out."

"Tell me about Louie K., and let me worry about Trueheart and his guts."

Proctor pokered up. "Small-time Illegals rat, went after schoolkids. Gave them samples of Zoner and Jazz to lure them in. Waste of air, you ask me. Did some time, but mostly he was pretty slick about it, and the Illegals guys never got much out of the kids."

"He a violent tendency?"

"Anything but. Kept a low profile, never gave you lip. You told him to move his ass along, he moved it. He'd give you a look now and then like he'd like to do more, but he never had the guts for it."

"Had guts enough to open Ralph Wooster's head, bash a woman and assault a uniform."

"Must've been sampling his own product's all I can think. And that's not profile either. He maybe smoked a little Zoner now and then, but he was too cheap to do more. What's out there looks like Zeus," Proctor added with a jerk of the thumb toward the corridor. "Little guy like that going nutso. But he never handled anything that hot I heard about."

"Okay, Proctor. Thanks."

"Guy sells illegals to schoolkids, world's better off without him."

"That's not our call." Eve dismissed him by turning her back. She moved to the desk, frowned at the computer screen.

ABSOLUTE PURITY ACHIEVED

"What the hell does this mean?" she asked aloud. "Peabody, any new shit on the streets going by the name Purity?"

"I haven't heard of it."

"Computer, identify Purity."

INVALID COMMAND.

Frowning, she entered her name, badge number, and authorization. "Identify Purity."

INVALID COMMAND.

"Huh. Peabody do a run on new and known illegals. Computer, save current display. Display last task performed."

The screen wavered, then opened a tidy, organized spreadsheet detailing inventory, profit, loss, and coded customer base.

"So, according to the last task, and time logged, Louie was sitting here, very efficiently doing his books when he got a bug up his ass to bust his neighbor's head open."

"It's hot, Dallas." Peabody looked over Eve's shoulder. "People can just get crazy."

"Yeah." Maybe it was just that simple. "Yeah, they can. Nothing on his inventory named Purity."

"Nothing on the current illegals list by that name either."

"So what the hell is it, and how was it achieved?" She stepped back. "Let's take a look at Louie K., see what he tells us."